D

DRAGON'S BLOOD

Christopher Nicole

THE SHERIDAN
BOOK COMPANY

This edition published in 1994 by
The Sheridan Book Company

First published in Great Britain by Century 1989
Random House, 20 Vauxhall Bridge Road, London SW1V 2SA
Arrow edition 1991

Printed and bound in Great Britain by
Cox & Wyman Ltd, Reading, Berkshire

ISBN 1–85501–663–X

Contents

PART ONE

The Solace of Dreams

1

The Fugitive from Himself

Harrington awoke as the key rasped in the lock. He was always surprised to have been asleep at all; bare boards and manacled wrists were not conducive to repose, any more than the stench rising from the bilges only a few feet beneath him made breathing a pleasure, or the squeaking of the rats that lived down there and occasionally ran across his feet allowed him any peace. Yet man, he had come to realize these past few days, could apparently acclimatize himself to any conditions. Why, were he to be offered a few pints of ale he might even be happy.

But yesterday morning he had listened to the shouted commands from the deck and had recognized the change in the motion of the ship as sail had been shortened. As there had been no question of bad weather, he had discerned that they were approaching the Hugli, the large river which was itself only the westernmost mouth of the Ganges, and sure enough at dusk the anchor line had uncoiled itself only a few feet from where he lay as the ship had come to rest, sails furled, breasting the gentle current. They were into the estuary, and Calcutta was only a few hours away, if the southerly wind held. And then, no doubt, a hanging.

So who would be visiting the prisoner in the middle of the night?

'Are you there?'

Harrington pushed himself up against the bulkhead of the chain locker. 'I've nowhere to go, Captain.'

'You'll try nothing rash,' said the voice in the darkness. 'I'm armed.'

'And I'm chained,' Harrington reminded him.

'As you deserve to be. You'll know we're in the river?'

'I know it.'

'We'll make Calcutta tomorrow.'

'And you'll be rid of me.'

'I've no choice, Michael,' the captain said. 'You were drunk on duty.'

'Aye, well, sometimes a man needs to dream.'

'And when reprimanded, you struck me, in full view of the crew.'

'It's a risky business, interfering with dreams.'

'You'll never learn, more's the pity, Michael Harrington. But you committed mutiny. No doubt you'll hope to laugh when they put the noose round your neck.'

'I would hate to cry,' Harrington agreed.

'It'll be a scandal,' the captain brooded. 'And a waste. How old are you, man? Twenty-five?'

'Twenty-three,' Harrington told him. 'I was born the very minute Bonaparte opened fire at Waterloo. There's an historic occasion.'

The captain had no sense of humour. 'And already a second mate,' he pointed out. 'As good a seaman as I have ever seen. To throw it all away.'

'I'd leave the preaching to the judge,' Harrington suggested.

The captain was silent for a few moments. Then he said, 'I'd prefer you not to see the judge, Michael.'

Harrington peered into the darkness, aware of a slight quickening of his pulse.

'We're in the river,' the captain reminded him. 'You can swim. If you were to slip over the side . . .'

'With manacles on my wrists?'

'I've a key. And the door will be open.'

'And the crocodiles?'

'Better odds than a rope. Listen to me, boy. If I take you to Calcutta, you die. There's no alternative. You committed open mutiny on the high seas. If you make your escape before we drop anchor, well . . . there'll be a to-do, but they can't hang a man they don't have.'

'So I get ashore to be murdered by the coolies. I'll need a weapon. At least a knife.'

10

'No weapons, Michael. And certainly not a knife, for you. Next thing you'd be throwing it like the heathen you are. Where would be the point in escaping the gallows for mutiny only to be hanged for murder? Now, listen to me. Down here are only subsistence farmers. Peaceful men. Honest and charitable. They'll see you don't starve. Lie low for a while, then enter the city, clandestinely. Go to the offices of Teng Tang.'

'A Chinese?'

'A good man. He's brother to Teng Lee. You'll have heard of Teng Lee?'

Harrington supposed everyone who sailed to the Orient had heard of the merchant who operated out of the new British colony of Singapore, in partnership with an Englishman, and whose junks traded from Bombay to Canton.

'The Tengs are practical men,' the captain went on. 'Always on the lookout for good seamen who know these waters. And even more for good seamen who need employment; Teng Lee sails mighty close to the wind on occasion, I've heard. If you've the stomach for it, Teng Tang will give you a berth.'

'Foredeck hand on a Chinese junk?'

'Better than hanging. And if you're half the man I think you are, you won't stay a foredeck hand for the rest of your life. Listen to me. I know Teng Tang. I'll have a word with him when I make port, put him in the picture. He'll give you a berth, if you apply for it. The choice is yours, boy. Hold out your hands.'

Harrington hesitated, then obeyed, and the key was placed between his fingers.

'I'll be visiting you, officially, at daybreak,' the captain said. 'There'll be no chance after that. Good luck, boy. We'll likely not meet again.'

Michael Harrington continued to peer into the gloom, while he listened to the creaking of the timbers, the faint soughing of the wind, the rustle of the water past the hull, only inches from his ear. These were noises he seldom heard, they were so familiar. Suddenly they were important.

Although he had sailed with him for three years, and made two previous voyages to the East with him as well, Michael had never thought of Captain Wright as a friend. Indeed the totally serious, sober, almost gloomy approach to the business of sailing from Portsmouth to Calcutta and back again undertaken by both Wright and First Mate Crockett had been an important factor in driving him to drinking more than was good for him. Which was a lie. He had always drunk more than was good for him, as he had done a good many other things which were positively bad for him, however enjoyable at the time; his own mother had once foretold that he would end on the gallows.

But Wright did not want that to happen. Apparently. It might, of course, be an elaborate trick. If he were to be shot attempting to escape that would accomplish the fact of his death whilst avoiding the expense and publicity of a trial. But however dry a stick Captain Wright might be, Michael did not suppose he was treacherous. There remained, of course, the crocodiles, not to mention the river, which was formidable, no matter how well he swam. But as Wright had pointed out, better odds than the rope. Well, then . . . the coolies? He did not really doubt he could handle any coolie, even unarmed.

Now his heart was pounding with excitement, as he inserted the key into the lock and turned it, with some effort, his hands pressed inwards. It clicked open and the handcuffs fell away. He massaged his wrists as he rose to his knees. Though he was kneeling his curly black hair touched the deck beams above him; Michael Harrington was six feet tall and, a seaman since his teens, had a matching physique. With his wide-set blue eyes and generous mouth, his seafaring background – for all that he had been an Irish Catholic his father had been an officer in Nelson's Navy before he had lost his leg at Trafalgar – he had been born to laugh and to do, but thus far had found only the laughing an easy matter; Great Britain had ceased fighting important wars on the day he had been born, and the Royal Navy had become a dead end. Thus the merchant service. Which for Michael Harrington had become just as much a dead end. Save perhaps through the generosity of a Chinese employer!

He crawled through the door, and up the ladder to the waist. Here was fresh air, so sudden and splendid it hurt his lungs, even if it carried with it the half repulsive, half alluring scent of the Indian jungle, a mixture of rotting vegetation and the perfume of flowers. The night was utterly dark, and the anchor watch was gathered forward. Harrington crawled to the bulkhead and looked over. The river flowed past, as dark as the night, but less quickly than he had feared. And as he stared into the gloom he could make out the trees, perhaps three hundred yards away. A long haul, and then . . . however well he knew the Indian seas, like most Europeans he supposed the jungle to be teeming with snakes and tigers, waiting only the chance to snap up the unwary. But yet not so certain as the rope.

He looked aft, but there was no one on the poop. Above his head the four tall masts pointed at the sky, the sails neatly furled on the yards. He slid his hands along the bulwark to find a belaying pin, and the sheet – one of the ropes used to trim the sails – made fast to it. He released it, allowed it to trail over the side, then slid across the rail on his belly, took the rope in his hands, and lowered himself into the water.

It was like warm soup, seeping over his shoes and torn stockings, his filthy breeches and hardly less filthy shirt. He entered without a sound, used a breast stroke to take him, equally noiselessly, away from the ship, while expecting every moment to hear a shout of discovery from above him. But there was no sound, and when he grew tired and turned on his back, the ship was already fifty yards away, upstream now as the current was carrying him with it, no longer any danger.

It had been replaced by the river. The excitement of leaving his prison had precluded fear of what might be beneath him. Now every stroke of arm or leg seemed to touch a scaly back. But the water itself was more dangerous than any living creature. For the past week he had existed on bread and water with only an occasional scrap of stringy salted meat thrown in, and even his powerful muscles had become wasted. Lack of exercise and his foetid surroundings had left his lungs shallow. His legs were heavy, and he kicked off his shoes and had to fight the temptation to stop swimming and just drift with the current, out into the Bay of Bengal, and death. Yet he swam, moving arms and legs with grim stubbornness, while thoughts kaleidoscoped through his brain. He wondered if he would ever see England again, his mother again; Father, fortunately, was dead, and would never know of the failure which was his youngest son. Brother William, of course, who had opted for the Navy however dismal the prospects of quick promotion, would condemn – he had always condemned his wayward younger brother. As would sister-in-law Henrietta; she had regarded him as a rake and a disgrace to the family ever since he had been caught with his hand beneath the skirt of her younger sister. 'Drink and debauchery, that's all you're good for, Michael Harrington,' she had declared, having boxed poor Florence's ears – their mother was dead and Henrietta had assumed her prerogatives. 'You'll finish in the gutter with a whore for company. As for throwing knives, 'tis a quite heathen pastime. You make me ashamed to bear your name.'

Michael supposed she had been right. The River Hugli could certainly be considered a large gutter. All he lacked was the whore. And what, he thought, would he give for the most disease-ridden Hindu nautch dancer right this minute, especially after three months at sea.

But there were no nautch dancers to be found on the mudflats which clogged the mouth of the Hugli. Only . . . mud. When he first touched it he shuddered and nearly cried out in fear. Then he realized that it was, indeed, mud. He knelt on it and sank into it, forced himself back up and floundered across it, the water only round his waist now. The mud clutched at him and drained the last

14

strength from his exhausted muscles, but he forced himself forward until he reached the mangroves, dragged himself across two of the huge roots, and lay there, head drooping, consciousness draining away.

Malama came upon the ship unexpectedly, and instinctively dropped to her knees. It was her habit to conceal herself whenever she encountered anything unusual, a precaution instilled in her both by her father and her sisters; strangers could menace their very existence. So she sank into the mud, allowing the water to rise over her thighs and submerge the bag of crabs which hung from her waist and to creep up her back to soak the long straight black hair which hung to her buttocks.

She knew what the ship was, of course. She saw many on the river. They came from far away, the other world, her father called it, and they brought men who ruled, in the great city. Malama had never been to the great city. For one thing she was only twelve years old, and for another, her father did not belong there. Her eldest sister, Halya, who had been sold to the merchant Gopinal, had been taken there and had not returned. Malama thought of the city as a huge beast, larger than any tiger, which consumed those who ventured into its always hungry maw. Except for the men on the ships, the so strange men with the white skins and the thick clothing. She had only ever seen them once, when a boat had come to the shore from a ship anchored just like this one, and she had watched the men from behind a tree, but she had never forgotten them. Creatures from another world. But a world which ruled.

The ship was about to continue upriver. As the girl watched, the anchor was raised and the sails unfurled, and the huge craft gathered way, able even to sail against the current. She waited for it to round the bend, could still see the tall masts for a while, then it disappeared. She sighed. It was going to the city. Presumably, when she was sold, she too would go to the city whether she liked it or not. Unless the tax gatherers took her first. She was not sure which fate would be less desirable, although her father always represented the tax gatherers as the worst. She did not know why. She did know, because her sisters had told her, that Siva had made her a woman, and that as such her fate was to belong to a man, all of her life. Right now she and her sisters all belonged to Father, and however often they went hungry, they were happy, with each other and with him. Why should belonging to another man be any different? Panka, who since Halya had been taken away had become the female head of the family, had told her that other men would be different to Father, and even showed her how they would be different – but Malama had found that rather exciting, and had become fond of showing herself, just as she found the embrace of the warm Hugli pleasantly sensuous; she could kneel here for the rest of the day, she thought, the mud gripping her knees and thighs, the water flowing past her naked body – she had left her dhoti hanging on a tree where she had entered the shallows.

But there was the meal to be gathered, and reluctantly she rose to her feet, nostrils twitching as she saw a brilliantly coloured crab scuttling up the branch of the next mangrove tree, just clear of the water. Malama had an exquisitely small brown nose, in keeping with the rest of her features and her liquid black eyes, which in turn matched her slender brown body, hardly less exquisite, but there were muscles rippling in her arms as she brought her stick over without hesitation and with deadly accuracy. The crab seemed to explode, and joined his similarly mangled compatriots in Malama's bag.

Malama continued on her way, then checked in consternation as she saw the man. She knew at once that he was one of the white men who ruled, and equally instinctively that he must have come from the ship which had gone upriver. But she did not know whether he was alive or dead, although she understood that if he had died it must have been very recently; in her morning gleaning expeditions she had come across enough decomposed and crocodile-torn bodies drifting out to the sea.

Cautiously she approached the motionless figure, climbing up the branches across which it lay, studying it for any sign of life. There seemed little, but the man lay on his face, and it was impossible to decide whether or not he was breathing. She sat on the thick branch beside him, her legs dangling in the water only inches beneath, while she peered at him, and then, with great caution, thrust her fingers into his hair and turned his head. And gasped as his eyes opened. She would have slid down the branch into the water but his hand moved too quickly, to close on her thigh with paralysing strength.

They stared at each other, and the man blinked as his gaze moved up and down her. Malama was not embarrassed; she had never regarded clothes as either necessary or important. But she was certainly afraid, and he was hurting her. Yet he did not look fierce, like the tax gatherers, and when he spoke his voice was soft. But she had no idea what he was saying. And she knew she must get away before something terrible happened to her. When, having stopped speaking, the man carefully let her go, she drew a long breath, and in a single convulsive movement slid down the branch and into the water. He gave a shout and reached towards her, but merely overbalanced and fell into the river himself. By the time he had spluttered back to the surface she was several yards away and wading with all her strength for the shore.

Michael painfully regained his branch, and watched the girl disappearing into the trees. If it really had been a girl, and not a spirit or a figment of his overwrought imagination. The last thing he had expected to encounter on the banks of the Hugli had been a naked, brown-skinned and enchantingly lovely child, coated in mud and smelling vaguely of crab meat. The odour of the food made him realize how hungry he was, and how thirsty, too. That at least could be remedied, and he drank some water, hastily spitting it out again as he discovered it to be brackish. This in turn made him realize how exhausted he was, and how his every bone and joint and muscle seemed to be aching. But he could not remain on this branch until a crocodile came along, and the appearance of the girl at least promised humanity, somewhere in the direction she had vanished.

Slowly he left his perch behind and began to make his way through the mud and the steadily shallowing water, clambering over other roots, slipping and sliding, bare feet touching unthinkable objects beneath the surface, but at last gaining the land, although this was a long way from dry, and squelched beneath his feet as he walked. He had no idea where to go. The girl had long disappeared. But although he could not yet see the sun he could feel from its position which direction was east, and that meant away from the river. It seemed the best choice, so he walked towards the glow, making slow progress, belly rumbling with hunger, throat parched, proceeding rather as he had swum during the night, placing one foot in front of the other with an almost somnolent determination to keep moving, unaware of what was happening around him, and thus the more surprised when he found himself surrounded by people.

Who at first sight seemed to consist entirely of young women, as he counted seven, varying in age from the distinctly nubile – for none of them wore more than a single piece of white cloth, carried between their legs and thence round their waists to be tied in a knot over the hip – to the very young, and including the girl who had first discovered him, and who had also dressed herself, if that was the right word. To his great relief, however – he was aware of a distinct fear of being torn to pieces by these so attractive amazons – there was also a man present, wearing no more than the girls, but considerably older, with a drooping moustache. Like his companions he carried a stout stick, and also a long knife tucked into his cloth. The sight of it made Harrington's blood tingle. He had learned about knives from a Spanish seaman, when he had been an apprentice, had been fascinated by the power, the speed, the accuracy which could be obtained by practice . . . and all silent, where a pistol was at once noisy and unreliable.

18

Now he gazed at the Indian, and the Indian gazed back. Then the man said, 'You are English?'

'Well, glory be,' Michael said. 'That's near enough.'

'My daughter says you are from the ship,' the man said.

'Your daughter?' Michael gazed at Malama, who stood on one leg.

'These are all my daughters,' the man said, and came closer. 'I am Rajinder Lall.'

'Michael Harrington.' Michael held out his hand, and after a brief hesitation Rajinder Lall took it.

'You fell from the ship?' he inquired again.

'In a manner of speaking.'

'It is many days to Calcutta.'

'I'm not in a hurry,' Michael told him. 'But I am very hungry and tired.'

'Forgive me,' Rajinder Lall said. 'You will come to my home, and my daughters will care for you.'

Michael looked the girls over. They were quite the most splendid set of females he had ever encountered, although of course he had never actually encountered seven virtually nude young women at the same time before. 'I think I shall enjoy that,' he agreed, and fell into step beside his benefactor. 'Have you no sons?'

'Alas, no,' Rajinder Lall said. 'I am the most cursed of men, doomed to everlasting poverty. I offer them for sale, but it is difficult.'

'Really?' Michael found that hard to believe. 'In Calcutta?'

'I do not live in Calcutta.'

'But you speak very good English.'

'I lived there once. I was boy to a white man, like yourself, Harrington Sahib. But when he died, I left and returned to my people.'

'Here in the delta?'

'That is so, Sahib.' Rajinder Lall parted a leaf curtain and revealed a clearing in the trees. 'My home.'

It was certainly very humble. A single-roomed dwelling, and a paddy field beyond. There was a cow, however, which suggested that Rajinder Lall was not quite as poor as he had claimed, and several goats, carefully tethered. There was also another of the large, well-made knives, resting by the doorway. And within minutes of arriving Michael's nostrils were titillated by the most delightful scent of a brewing masala, into which went the crabs gathered by the younger girls that very morning; their elder sisters were boiling rice to make the sort of meal one went to a restaurant for in Calcutta, while immediately there was coconut water for him to drink.

He had the oddest feeling that somehow he had died and been transported to heaven. A brown and green heaven, to be sure, and very nearly hot enough to be the other place, which was as much as a confirmed sinner like himself could possibly hope for. But if this was hell then he wondered why he had wasted the time going to mass at all. He had never supposed he would be able to sit on the ground with his back against a tree and watch such a parade of rippling limbs, of quivering breasts with their curiously dark nipples, of tight-muscled buttocks and flowing hair, while, now that they were assured their father meant to treat him as a friend, the sisters were all smiles and chattering conversation, especially Malama, who seemed to regard him as especially her own – as well she might, he supposed. If she lacked the voluptuousness of her two older sisters, she already possessed pouting girl breasts, and was far from the least attractive of the seven as she laughed and joked with the rest of them.

The food, when it was ready, was just as tasty as it had smelled, even if there were neither forks nor spoons nor plates, and all nine of them dug into the same pot, their fingers stained yellow with the curry, to roll up fingerfuls of rice and crab meat and convey it to their mouths. The girls all watched him, anxiously at first, but as soon as they realized he was enjoying the meal, the laughter and the chattering resumed.

'Have you no neighbours?' Michael asked their father.

'Indeed, there are many. Farmers like myself.'

'And have they no sons to marry your splendid daughters?'

20

'They are poor men, like myself. They can afford little. My eldest child, I sold to a Calcutta merchant. She was very beautiful.'

'All your daughters are very beautiful,' Michael ventured.

'Halya was the most beautiful of all. She earned me that cow. And not even as a wife. Gopinal would not take her to wife, because we have no caste. But he promised to treat her well.'

'And has he done so?'

'That is not for me to say,' Rajinder Lall pointed out. 'I have not seen her since.'

'Ah.' Michael wondered what little Malama's fate would eventually be. The concubine of another Calcutta merchant?

'I will take you to Calcutta,' Rajinder Lall offered.

'When I have rested.'

Rajinder Lall considered this, obviously also considering the amount of food his unexpected guest might eat while he was resting. 'Your ship will wait for you?'

'I have left the ship,' Michael said, staring at him.

Rajinder Lall looked embarrassed.

'I will find another ship in Calcutta,' Michael told him. 'From the house of the great merchant, Teng Lee. You know of Teng Lee?'

'I have heard of him, Sahib.'

'That is where I shall go, when I have rested. And you will be rewarded.'

Rajinder Lall bowed his head. 'Then, perhaps, you will buy one of my daughters.'

'Perhaps,' Michael said.

'You do not find them worthy of you?' He sighed. 'Alas, they speak no English. But they could learn your language.'

'They look entirely worthy of me,' Michael assured him. 'Whether they can speak English or not. But I must first of all be able to afford them. One of them,' he hastily added.

'They are not expensive,' Rajinder Lall promised. 'And

21

Panka, now my eldest . . .' he touched the knee of the young woman, who was seated beside him, 'is very able. She has the art to make a man happy.'

Michael looked at the girl, and she looked back. She might not speak English but she knew what her father was saying. Michael did not doubt for a moment that she would make any man, including himself, very happy indeed.

'We will talk about it,' he promised in turn. 'When I have rested.'

Definitely paradise, he thought, as after – for him – a lazy day spent sitting in the shade the entire family took to the coconut matting floor of the hut to sleep. As the guest he was placed on the other side of the girls, next to Malama, who giggled shyly as she removed her dhoti and curled herself into a ball, her thigh touching his. He felt he could hardly do less than follow her example as regards undressing, even if he wondered what effect the sight of him might have on her. But she took both his body and his erection as apparently normal masculinity, and was asleep in seconds, as were her sisters and father. They were utterly trusting of him, utterly uninhibited about their sexuality, their lives unaffected by prurient religiosity, for were they not children of Siva, the most uninhibited of goddesses?

He wondered if they would even scream if he were to crawl across them to seek the arms of Panka? But of course, lack of inhibitions was one thing; possession another – the laws of man's ownership remained the same in whatever culture. And however sure he might be that the girl would welcome his advances, to abuse these people's confidence would be vicious, where they had taken him in and shared their limited lives with him. In fact he was so tired he was soon asleep himself, but that did not prevent him from having a succession of erotic dreams as Malama nestled against him during the night.

Next morning he realized that he must move on as soon as possible. He was a man used to indulging his appetites, and here was a continual sensation of animal hunger as the sisters went about their necessaries on awakening, again without being the least disturbed by his presence. He sat beneath his tree and watched the elder girls milking the cow and the goats, while the younger ones set off for their morning's gleaning. Malama indicated that she would be pleased if he would accompany her, but he declined. Were he to find himself alone in the forest with a naked child he feared he would be unable to restrain himself. So no doubt he was as depraved as Sister Henrietta had always claimed; he had never denied it. But at least he could set limits to the chances of his depravity getting out of hand. Malama was very disappointed, and looked from him to her sisters as if trying to establish which one of them he preferred, before leaving.

'I will go tomorrow,' he told Rajinder Lall.

'You are rested?' the Indian asked.

'I am rested sufficiently. Will you show me the way?'

'I will show you the way, Sahib.'

The decision taken, Harrington allowed himself to enjoy the girls where before he had been reluctant to do so. When Panka and her next sister went out to pick coconuts he accompanied them, and stood beneath the tree in amazement as they swarmed up the narrow trunk, naked muscular limbs surging in an erotic ballet. He caught the coconuts as they dropped them, and then caught Panka herself as she slid back down. She gave a shriek of laughter and twisted in his arms, while making no effort to escape them. For a few moments they frolicked together and he allowed himself to cup the heavy breasts, while her sister Shalina giggled, until Michael held the girl away, panting for breath, astounded at the madness which had overtaken him. Panka gazed at him for several seconds, looking down to his tightened trousers while her tongue came out and disappeared again, then she gathered the coconuts and returned towards the farm, leaving him to follow, staring at her back and hair and shoulders, and feeling more of a cad than ever, wondering what might be the outcome of such a game were the girl to tell her father. They were within a hundred yards of the clearing when they heard the low, rippling, guttural sound.

The two girls stopped walking and might have been turned to stone; only the beads of sweat rolling out of their hair revealed their terror. Heart pounding, Michael looked left and right, ascertained that the beast was not actually menacing them, and then stepped past the girls and crept forward, cautiously parting the leaves to look into the clearing, his blood seeming to congeal as he did so.

The tiger faced him, although he did not suppose it was yet aware of him. It was on the other side of the cleared area, having perhaps come through the paddy field, seven feet and several hundred pounds of concentrated yellow and black strength and aggression. It looked at the cow, which was grunting in fear and straining on its halter, and at the goats, also terrified, bleating and jostling against each other. Here was a feast . . . which would also bankrupt Rajinder Lall in a trice, Michael realized. As the Indian undoubtedly knew, but he was equally not prepared to do anything about it. He stood in the doorway of his house, his four younger daughters clustered around him, huddling close in their terror, ready to close and barricade the door should the tiger turn against them.

Panka and Shalina pressed against Michael's back as they stared past him at the huge beast, whispering to each other. But this was a visitation of the gods, an event which perpetually overshadowed their lives, like the monsoon floods and the tax gatherers, about which they could do little.

And could he do anything to help them, Michael wondered? It was certainly none of his business to get himself killed to no purpose. He had never seen a tiger this close before, but he had heard enough about the awesome strength and ferocity of the Bengal variety. And he was unarmed. He must stand here, like the rest of them, and watch his benefactor ruined.

They listened to sound from the forest, and Michael stared at Rajinder Lall and his four daughters. Four daughters! While Panka and Shalina huddled against him. For out of the forest came the cheerfully singing seventh girl, exactly as he remembered her from the previous day, her bag of crabs swinging against her thigh. She was well into the clearing before she saw the tiger, as the huge cat had dropped to his haunches, belly in the dust, thick tail slowly twitching as it watched the approach of yet another mouthful of food.

Malama halted, staring at the animal. Michael watched her entire body tense, her nostrils dilate as she breathed. She knew she was lost, and her brain would be seething with terror and despair . . . but also she would be accepting her fate, because that was the nature of these people forced to live in this cruellest and most uncertain of worlds.

Michael felt a swelling exultation in his veins and chest, a call to action, even as his brain told him not to be a fool. To die, defending a child, when he had fought so hard to live, made no sense. But already he was bursting through the leaf fringe into the clearing. The tiger saw him and rose to its feet, giving an angry roar, huge teeth gleaming in the sunlight, while Malama, startled out of her fatalistic composure, uttered a scream, echoed by the two girls behind him.

'Sahib!' Rajinder Lall shouted.

'Your knives,' Michael snapped. 'Quickly, man.'

The tiger was preparing to charge, tail now swishing violently.

'Quickly!' Michael called, not taking his gaze from his opponent.

The first blade arced through the air and fell to his feet. He picked it up and tested its balance in one movement, drew his arm back and threw in another, as the tiger thundered forward. His aim was as true as ever, and the point entered the cat's head just below the ear as it hurled itself into the air. The beast screamed in pain and outrage as it landed, not six feet away. But Michael was already

25

throwing himself sideways, into Malama, knocking her over and sending her rolling towards the hut, while the second knife fell at his feet.

He seized it and turned, rising as he did so. The tiger was pawing at its ear, roaring continually. Michael regained his breath and drew back his arm. Again the blade flew with all the power and accuracy he commanded, and again it penetrated deeply, this time into the animal's throat. Blood spurted and the tiger screamed, shaking its head. But however distracted, it was a long way from dead, and there were no more knives.

'Help me,' Michael bawled. 'Sticks, Rajinder, sticks!'

Rajinder Lall snapped commands at his daughters and they ran forward, as did the two girls hiding in the bush. They hesitated, and Michael tore the stick from one of their hands and prodded the wounded beast, who roared and turned towards him. Panka had got the idea and now prodded the cat from the other side. Its head turned back, Rajinder Lall was prodding from another direction. The tiger twisted to and fro, panting and bleeding, while Michael cautiously approached from behind. It never noticed him, its attention entirely distracted, until he leapt on to its back, high up, hands groping for the knife in its ear. Then it turned and rolled, snarling, but Michael had withdrawn the knife and jumped clear. The tiger fell on its back, powerful paws sweeping the air. The girls ran forward to poke at it again, and Michael, taking another long breath, ducked under a sweep of the left paw and drove the knife again and again into the creature's breast. He struck three times, his hand and arm and shoulder covered in spouting blood, before he was caught a tremendous blow on the head which sent him soaring into blackness.

Michael awoke to pain, and soothing hands. He lay on the earth in the shade of the trees, but the entire clearing was heaving uneasily above and around him, and the anxious faces of the girls seemed to separate and then come together again. As soon as they discovered his eyes open, his head was pillowed against soft brown breasts while coconut water was held to his mouth.

Rajinder Lall stood above him. 'You are a very brave man, Harrington Sahib,' he remarked. 'And a fortunate one.'

Michael realized his head was bandaged, no doubt in someone's dhoti.

'The beast's claw did no more than tear your flesh,' Rajinder Lall explained. 'When it could have removed your head.'

Michael licked his lips. 'The tiger . . .'

Rajinder Lall pointed and Michael painfully turned his head to look at the dead creature. 'They will speak of this in years to come,' Rajinder Lall told him. 'And ask where you learned to fight with knives so expertly.'

'It's a hobby,' Michael confessed, and closed his eyes again, allowing his head to sink back into soft warmth.

It was another week before he could consider the journey to Calcutta, a week in which he was cared for by the girls more tenderly than he could have expected in any English hospital. He was their hero, and they could not do enough for him. One of them was always at his side, fanning him to keep away the insects which sought his wound, combing his beard, which had grown quite long – he had not had the opportunity to shave since being arrested on board the ship – feeding him water and fruit, or just staring at him.

Rajinder Lall was no less grateful. 'You have saved me from ruin, Harrington Sahib,' he said as they sat together on the evening after the bandage had been finally removed. Michael, having announced his intention of leaving next day, was at last scraping at his chin with one of the famous knives. 'I can never repay you.'

'You repaid me in advance,' Michael reminded him. 'By taking me into your house when I was starving.'

'That was a simple act of charity, as decreed by the gods,' Rajinder Lall pointed out. 'I risked nothing. But you . . . you took your life in your hands. Sahib, I have little to give, yet must I acknowledge your deed. Sahib, I have only my daughters.'

'Eh?'

'You do not like them,' Rajinder Lall said sadly.

'I like them very much,' Michael said. 'But . . .'

'I understand, you are a poor man until you can regain your wealth. Yet would I be a churlish rogue did I leave you bereft in the world. You will take Malama with you.'

'Malama?'

'She is yours.'

Harrington shook his head, so violently it began to hurt again.

'You do not like her? She is young, I know, but she will grow. She will learn to speak English. And she is the one who brought you to me.'

'You don't understand,' Michael said desperately. 'Rajinder Lall . . . I am a bad man. A very bad man.'

'You?'

'Yes,' Michael insisted. 'You have worked with the English. You have seen them when they have drunk too much, and when they are angry, and when they are lusting. They are very wicked people.'

'They are great men, who have conquered the world,' Rajinder Lall argued.

'Some of them. The rest are wretches. And I am one of the most wretched. Rajinder Lall, if you give me your daughter, I will abuse her.'

Rajinder Lall inclined his head. 'That is the way of man, and the fate of woman, Sahib. The girl is yours, and is happy to be so. She has told me this. If you choose to leave her by the wayside to starve, then that was surely the fate chosen for her by the gods.'

Michael looked across the clearing at Malama, who was pretending to pick her crabs, but she faced them as she knelt, and there was no doubt she understood the situation. His mouth was dry, his head light. She was an entrancing creature, but she was only twelve years old. And now she was his. In fact, apart from the tattered clothes in which he sat, she was his only possession. And

28

she was only twelve years old. But, as her father had just said, she would grow. 'I cannot take her into Calcutta wearing only a dhoti,' he said.

'She will wear a sari,' Rajinder Lall promised.

Malama was in seventh heaven, the more so as she could tell her sisters were all put out by their father's decision. Panka felt that she should have been given to the white man. And failing her, the other two who were older than Malama in turn were of the same opinion. But little Malama . . . yet little Malama understood more than they. It was necessary for Father to repay the Englishman for saving their flock, and indeed, saving her life. That was reason enough for giving her instead of one of the others. While the true fact was that while she was the very youngest to be of a marriageable age, she would naturally be a burden on the household longer than the other three, because any prospective husband would by custom have to be offered Panka first. And if Father had been unable so far to sell a beauty like Panka, how would he ever sell Malama? Only the children were less valuable than she, in such a circumstance.

Her awareness of her father's reasoning in no way distressed her. She was too excited and happy at the thought of being sent out into the world with the sahib.

Panka was contemptuous. 'He will beat you until you bleed,' she warned.

Malama could think of nothing better than to be beaten by the sahib.

'And he will thrust his great lingam into your yoni until you scream,' Shalina told her.

'Have you not seen his lingam?' Panka demanded. 'At night it rises nearly to the sky.'

Malama had indeed seen the white man's lingam, without actually relating it to the sexual act as demonstrated by Panka's slender fingers. Now she realized that there might in fact be something better than being beaten by the sahib. 'Then it will carry me with it, to the sky,' she asserted.

They were just jealous, she knew, and even more when Father delved into the old chest which was the only article of furniture in the house and produced a green silk sari. It was several sizes too large, but could be wrapped round her sufficiently to fit. And before she was allowed to wear it, she was taken to the river by Panka and Shalina, and washed cleaner than she had ever been in her life, and then massaged all over with coconut oil – even her hair was washed in the oil – before being led back to the farm and ceremonially dressed, while Father and the sahib looked on. But Father no longer existed for her. She had left his protection and belonged to the sahib. She watched him from beneath lowered lids as he gazed at her in turn. She had no idea what the future would bring, at his side. But she had no doubt at all that, at his side, she would be the happiest woman in the world.

2

The Merchants of Dreams

Teng Tang was a short, grave man, made to look older than he actually was by his long moustaches. He wore blue silk, tunic over breeches, and soft kid boots; a blue silk hat rested on his head. He exuded confident prosperity, as well he might, for even if he was the very youngest of Teng Lee's brothers, as manager of the Calcutta office he was a man of importance. Now he studied Harrington with faintly disguised contempt, for the Irishman was as decrepit in appearance as any beggar in the street. 'Captain Wright has visited me,' he remarked. 'And told me how you went overboard, at the mouth of the river, in the dead of night. Like a thief.'

'I survived,' Michael told him.

'The Captain also told me of your attempted mutiny. I am astonished that he should recommend you to me.'

'He did so because I am a sailor, and a good one.'

'You have the reputation of a troublemaker,' Teng Tang reminded him. 'Why should I offer you employment?'

'Because I am an expert seaman and navigator,' Michael explained. 'More than that I have studied cartography. I will correct your charts for you, and make new ones. More accurate than you have ever seen. And I will serve you and your brother faithfully. And because, as I found it necessary to leave my ship and my position clandestinely, you will understand that I will shirk neither hazard nor . . .' he hesitated, 'irregularity, to re-establish myself.'

Teng Tang considered. 'You are at least an honest man,' he said at last. 'I will send you to my brother, in Singapore. One of our ships is leaving tomorrow. You will sail as third mate, and my captain will report upon your con-

duct and skill when you arrive there. It will be my brother's decision whether you are retained or not.'

'That will be very satisfactory,' Michael agreed.

'You will need some decent clothes to wear, and somewhere to spend the night.'

'I will also need some money to repay the man who
helped me, and brought me here,' Michael said.

Teng Tang regarded him for several seconds. 'An
honest man, but perhaps overbold,' he remarked, perhaps
to himself. He scribbled on a piece of paper. 'My clerk
will give you money. It will be an advance against your
salary, you understand.'

'Of course.' Michael took the paper and stood up. 'I
wish to thank you, for trusting me.'

'I do not trust you, Mr Harrington,' Teng Tang said.
'I am giving you an opportunity to earn my trust. Should
you merely take that money and disappear my people will
find you. Remember that.'

'I will,' Michael promised.

Teng Tang looked past him, through the opened doorway, to where Malama and Rajinder Lall waited, standing
uneasily in the centre of the outer office. 'The man is your
servant?'

'No. He is the friend I spoke of, who helped me when
I got ashore, and has guided me here.'

'And the girl is your wife.'

'Good Lord, no. She is only twelve years old.'

'That is not an exceptionally young age to be married
in India, Mr Harrington.'

'She is my servant,' Michael told him.

Teng Tang made no comment as to her suitability for
such a position, but he said, 'It is good that she is not
your wife. She is untouchable. Are you aware of that?'

'Does that concern the Chinese?'

'Not in the least. But at this moment you are in India.
I would remember that too, if I were you. Good day to
you, Mr Harrington. I will hope you prosper.'

'I couldn't agree with you more,' Michael said, and
closed the door behind him.

'I am pleased that you have reinstated yourself,' Rajinder Lall said gravely. 'I will leave you now. I cannot take your money. You will need it for yourself.'

They stood in the hot, steaming street outside the office of Teng Lee and Company, and Michael pressed the rupees into his hands. 'I will send you more,' he said. 'As soon as I can afford to. This is but a first payment.'

'Why should you do that?' Rajinder Lall asked. 'Malama is a gift.'

'Which I have accepted with gratitude. I owe you money because I owe you my life,' Michael explained.

Rajinder Lall at last took the money. 'You are a good man, Harrington Sahib. My daughter will be fortunate with you.' He touched Malama on the shoulder, addressing her in Hindu. She brought her hands together in front of her face, and bowed over them, and Rajinder Lall stepped into the throng and disappeared.

While Malama straightened again, and gazed at her new master, and yet was unable to prevent herself from glancing from right to left at the people who hurried by, sparing her green sari not a glance. She had, indeed, been in a state of wonderment since leaving her father's farm. She had never ventured north of the delta before, nor had she worn silk before, nor had she belonged to a man before. It had obviously bewildered her that Michael had neither taken possession of her nor beaten her during the week they had spent making their way through the forest from the delta to the city, and she had reflected that he did not wish to touch her in her father's presence. But now her father was gone.

And her bewilderment had grown, as they had reached the metropolis, because she could never have suspected anything quite like Calcutta to exist. The very name, derived from the Hindu word Kalikshetra and Anglicized into Kalikata, which meant Field of the Goddess Kali, was frightening, for was not Kali the goddess of death and destruction? And then the size of the place! And Calcutta was two distinct settlements. Around the fort built by Job Charnock in 1690, and named after the then monarch of England, William, had grown up, even if kept at a distance by a parkland – preserved to give the guns of the fortress an unimpeded field of fire – the teeming native and trading city. Behind that, on higher ground, was the 'city of palaces', so called because of the splendid homes erected there by the British nabobs who had come to rule most of India during the preceding hundred years, and who had indeed made Calcutta into their capital. Up there was light and air and quiet. Here in the streets of the city the heat, the noise, the bustle and the stench were overpowering, just as the contrasts – between the beggars who thronged the streets and the white ladies in their linen and taffeta, driving by in their phaetons and fours-in-hand, beneath ornate umbrellas and in the care of gorgeously clad grooms and attendants, between the hurrying, busy, white-clad English officials and businessmen and their obsequious Indian counterparts, or between the silk-clad Chinese merchant and the ragged Irish fugitive he had carelessly employed – were frightening. Malama could not help but be aware of them, Michael knew, just as she must also be aware that the man to whom she now belonged was near the bottom of this dung heap.

He had never liked Calcutta. Today he positively hated it.

But it was necessary to exist in it before he could hope to better himself, and to exist it was necessary to humiliate her still further. 'She cannot enter,' said the Hindu tailor, to whom Michael was known from his previous visit, and to whom he applied for new clothes. 'She is without caste.' Michael was very inclined to push the fellow's face in and take his business elsewhere, but there was nowhere else in this city which would look upon an untouchable with any more favour, so he motioned her to remain on the street, and she bowed her head in ready acquiescence. He wondered if she understood her situation.

The tailors had no doubt heard the gossip of how he had been lost overboard from his ship, and having seen his money they agreed to have a suit of clothes ready for him by dawn tomorrow. It was then necessary to find

34

lodgings for the night, and for this he had to descend to the very waterfront to find a place which would not insist Malama slept on the street – as did thousands of other unfortunates, every night.

'You will share a bed,' said the bearded innkeeper. 'Is that not what you had in mind?'

'That is what I had in mind,' Michael agreed, marvelling at the manner in which he was keeping his temper. But then, he was marvelling at a good many unsuspected traits in his character, which were revealing themselves minute by minute. Such as how he had not yet found the nearest bar and drowned his sorrows while attempting to alleviate his thirst – it was over a fortnight since he had touched alcohol. Because to do that would be to drown Malama as well, in the misery of his own failure? But his emotions regarding the girl were the strangest of all. After they had found themselves something to eat, they walked by the waterfront and looked at the myriad vessels lying there, amongst them three ships flying the house flag of Teng Lee. Michael had never sailed in a junk before, but he did not suppose it would be very different to a squarerigger. He pointed the ship out to Malama, and when she was uncomprehending, seized her at the waist and lifted her in the air, but that only seemed to excite her, so he set her down again.

They returned to the lodging house. Their bedroom contained twenty beds, and all were to be occupied. Now Michael could thank God for Malama's lack of inhibition, although as she certainly understood Hindu she could not have been unaware of the remarks made by several of the men as she climbed – fully dressed, at his command, as was he – beneath the threadbare blanket with her master, to the accompaniment of a chorus of sighs and, he assumed, salacious comments. And as the bed was extremely narrow it was necessary to hold her in his arms for fear of pitching her on to the floor. But this again was a surprising Harrington, to Michael. He wanted a woman, desperately. He had not had one for too long and his appetite had been whetted by Malama's sisters. Had he been on his own, he knew that he would have spent some of Teng Tang's advance on a whore. And here he was with a willing bundle of femininity lying against him, her feeling arousing him so that he was hard against her, her deep eyes scouring his face as she awaited the inevitable – and he could do nothing more than hold her tightly, and kiss her forehead, as if she were his very sister. 'I have become responsible,' he groaned into her hair. 'By God, Mike Harrington, responsible, for a chit of a girl.' But she did not understand, and there were tears in her eyes as he fell asleep.

Her confusion was compounded next day when, with Michael in his new white duck trousers and blue linen tailcoat, black leather shoes on his feet and a new blue peaked cap on his head, they were ferried out to the junk, which bore the definitely English name of *China Star*. Here they were welcomed by the master, Chow Te, as grave as his employer, who bowed his greeting to his new third mate. 'His Excellency Teng Tang apprised me of your arrival, Mr Harrington,' he said gravely. 'Ho Chu will take you to your cabin.' He allowed his gaze to wander, briefly, over Malama, but made no comment. 'We sail in the hour.'

The sailor, who, Michael gathered, was to be his servant despite the presence of Malama, showed them below, into a spaciousness he had never encountered on board even an East Indiaman out of Portsmouth. Here was six foot head room, and elaborate drapes, carved and polished furniture, and a window rather than a port. 'You have no gear,' Ho Chu accused. He looked at Malama uncertainly.

'I was shipwrecked,' Michael agreed. 'The young lady will see to my needs.'

Ho Chu gazed at the girl again, and then addressed her in Hindustani. She listened, and looked anxiously at Michael. Who nodded. 'You'd best do as he says,' he agreed, and hurried on deck.

As he had suspected, handling a junk was not all that

36

different to an English three master, once allowance was made for the flat bottom and basically shallow draught, which meant that windward work was the more difficult. But the Chinese had allowed for this, and the passage downriver was assisted by the use of huge sweeps, four to a side, worked by the entire crew, with the officers also straining at the great bars of wood, while Captain Chow Te stood above them and exhorted them in a mixture of Chinese and English. It was back-breaking and breath-taking work, and concentration was not assisted by the desire of Malama to help, as she was in no mood to risk damage to her sari and had resumed her dhoti, while she was also in a state of high excitement following her visit to the galley with Ho Chu, where she had certainly been at least fondled by the Chinese sailors. 'The young lady was best below,' Chow Te suggested mildly, after studying her for several minutes.

The captain was mild, and suggestive rather than commanding, in everything he did, and this was the greatest contrast to life on board a British vessel; it was impossible to imagine him ordering the flogging of the most recalcitrant member of his crew. But then, it was difficult to imagine any member of this crew being recalcitrant, as they clearly enjoyed their work. Michael had to consider the week's voyage to Singapore as the most enjoyable of his life. It was not only the pleasure of being at sea in such company. He had not felt so healthy, so confident in his own powers, for a long time; gone were the periods of morose depression which had more than once led him into moods of frightening aggression. Because he had not had a drink in all that time? He refused to credit that, as he refused to accept that it might have something to do with the presence of Malama, his desire always to be the superior white man in her company, which meant all the time.

It was also the most exciting navigating he had done for some time, for now he was exploring waters he had never seen before as the junk found its way down the Straits of Malacca, between the heavily forested Malayan

Peninsula – and the British colony of Penang, at which they stopped briefly – and the mountainous peaks of the huge Dutch-held island of Sumatra to the west. British and Dutch had spent more than a century fighting each other over the right to trade in these waters, but rivalry, at least with guns and swords, had ended with the defeat of Napoleon, and in recent years the contest had been strictly between account ledgers. Yet these were still not peaceful seas. The pirates who had nested on the island of Singapura, and who had twenty years before been dislodged by Stamford Raffles some years before he had descended to an early grave at the age of forty-five, had merely taken themselves to other islands in the straits and in the Java Sea beyond. Chow Te insisted his people keep a sharp lookout, and the junk's six guns were loaded, as they coursed into the narrow waters. Certainly they saw craft in the distance, hugging the shore, and propelled by oars as well as sails to indicate that they were Malay, but perhaps Teng Lee's junks, and his power, were too well known, and none ventured to approach the *China Star*.

Michael's duties done, there was always Malama. He had expected her to be seasick, and certainly afraid of this element she had only ever viewed as a river. But she took her cue from her master, observed that not only was he unafraid but also happy, and was the same. While she was very rapidly getting over her shyness of him, just as she was equally rapidly picking up some words of English. When he indicated that now she should sleep on the other berth in the cabin she shook her head sadly and asked, 'No good?'

She looked so doleful he had to reassure her, by taking her in his arms, whereupon she responded so vigorously he had to hold her at arm's length. When he released her she removed her dhoti, at the same time reaching for his lingam, as she called it. Her fingers were nearly impossible to resist, and when he shook his head, she retired in a pout. She could not understand his reluctance to possess her, except as part of a general dislike. But then, he did not altogether understand it himself. He had slept with

38

Indian girls on his previous visit to Calcutta, and found them more practised in the art of love than any Caucasian could ever be. Nor did he doubt that Malama, if as yet unpractised, would take to the business by instinct. And certainly he wanted a woman, and perhaps this woman most of all. Yet he held back. Partly, he recognized, it was the Judaeo-Christian concept of perversion attached to having sex with a child, even one who was so obviously nubile. But even more he suspected it was the mere fact of possession. His previous relationships with women had either been bought or stolen. Each had involved haste, and uncertainty of the future, and thus anxiety and a certain unfulfilment. This girl was his. He would watch her grow, and become more beautiful, and he would teach her to be his shadow in everything. He could take her at his leisure, when he chose. When he felt she was truly ready, and when she could be enjoyed to the uttermost.

All lies. The truth was he was afraid, of her and for her. He was afraid to interfere with her essential being, by imposing himself upon it, by altering her, as he would the moment he entered her. And he was even more afraid that having discovered the delight of her yoni, he would be good for nothing else but desiring her, twenty-four hours a day. He could not risk that. If he had allowed his weaknesses as a man to wreck his career, he had also been given a chance to recover something from the wreckage. Nothing could be allowed to distract him from that. As he had given up drink, thus had he also given up the flesh – until he was back on top of the world.

So he smiled at her as she lay on the other berth, her hand between her legs, as suggestive as it was possible for a woman to be. 'Very good,' he said. 'I am very pleased with you, Malama. But our time is not yet.'

She sighed, and turned her back on him.

Teng Lee was now growing old. His hair was white as were his moustaches, and his shoulders were bowed. Yet no one could have any doubt that he still dominated the trading empire he had created in the face of so many difficulties and dangers. He studied the report submitted by Chow Te, which had been appended to the letter from Teng Tang, making no sound until he had finished, while Michael sat in front of the desk in the huge office and looked out of the open window at Singapore, and marvelled.

He had of course heard of the place, and its splendour, but he had been unable to imagine it. And that imagination would probably have been a waste of time he had decided from the moment the junk began threading its way through the islands, called the Dragon's Teeth, which surrounded the immense natural harbour. Because beyond was indeed the greatest natural harbour he had ever seen, and one which was being put to good use, for there were more ships anchored here than even in the Hugli off Calcutta, or for that matter in the Solent waiting for the tide to carry them down the English Channel.

Beyond the harbour, the town surrounded an inner basin, into which the junk was warped to a berth alongside the quay, both for complete safety from any change in the weather and for ease of unloading. Here again would imagination have been defeated, for in the strongest possible contrast to Calcutta, or to any other seaport he had visited in the Far East, Singapore had clearly been laid out rather than allowed to grow. The streets were straight and wide, the houses uniformly attractive in their white paint and red roofs, every one raised on stilts to avoid the flood waters of the monsoon season, every one clean and tended by a platoon of servants. The air was fresh, the people prosperous and healthy. There was a native village on the other side of the harbour, but even that seemed immeasurably more salubrious than the Calcutta waterfront.

Behind the town the jungle still gathered on the hilly slopes, and there was little sign of any agriculture, except for the coconut trees which sprouted everywhere. There was plenty of good soil, but as yet no great effort had been made to cultivate it. So Singapore existed perhaps in a vacuum, dependent on the outside world for its livelihood, in every sense, but prospering because of its free port status. And the man who had prospered most of all was sitting in front of Michael, deciding his future.

A future which could be exceedingly rewarding, Michael had no doubt at all – if he pleased this old Chinese gentleman. As to Teng Lee's wealth there could be no question. His warehouses dominated the waterfront, and his offices rose high above the warehouses. The name on the board outside was Hammond and Teng, and Michael understood that there was an English partner, an erstwhile follower of the immortal Raffles, whose inclusion in the enterprise had obviously been a useful social exercise. But Teng was the man who made the decisions. And now he was raising his head.

'My captain praises your ability as a navigator, Mr Harrington,' he observed, his voice soft.

'Thank you,' Michael said.

'And my brother considers you may be useful to our business.'

'I would hope to be.'

'There are, however, some qualifications mentioned.'

'I quarrelled with my captain, and struck him,' Harrington said.

'And thus jumped ship to avoid being hanged.'

'Yes, sir.'

'My brother has remarked on your honesty. You must tell me the cause of your quarrel.'

'I was drunk, Your Excellency.'

Teng Lee raised his eyebrows. 'Are you advancing that as a recommendation?'

'No, sir. I have regretted it. I have not touched alcohol since that day.'

Teng Lee gazed at him for several seconds. 'That is wise,' he remarked at last. 'My brother also tells me that you claim not to be afraid of perhaps taking a risk. Perhaps even with the law.'

'As I am outside the law of my own people, for a moment's madness,' Michael said. 'I have nothing left to lose.'

'Quite so,' Teng Lee agreed. 'You will draw your salary from my chief clerk, and it would be best for you to have some more clothes made. My clerk will also give you the address of some good, and speedy, tailors. I would like you to attend my house in two days' time. There will be ladies present.' His gaze drifted down the by now somewhat soiled uniform.

'I understand,' Michael said. 'Am I to take it you are intending to employ me?'

'That I will tell you in two days' time,' Teng Lee said. 'But until then, you may continue to berth on board the *China Star*.'

The old man certainly intended to employ him. Michael found himself whistling as he descended the hill, Singapore dollars clinking in his pockets, the feeling of having begun a new life swelling in his brain. Who cared if the yellow devil was sailing close to the wind in some direction or other. This was the newest of worlds, where everything was possible, and if he did not take a profit from it his name was not Michael Harrington.

He went to Teng Lee's tailors, was measured and promised his new clothes the next morning. He stood on the street and inhaled the clean air, and the odours coming from the bar across the street. Suddenly his mouth was dry. It was three weeks since he had taken a drink. No one could possibly begrudge him just a sip after so long a time. So tumultuous a time.

It was three hours later when he regained the ship. The road was an uneven one and he stumbled continually as he walked, while the gangplank seemed far narrower than he recalled. When one of the sailors came forward to help him, however, he angrily threw the fellow's hand off, with such force that the Chinese fell to the deck. 'Do you think I'm drunk?' Michael demanded, his voice thick. Then he turned to salute the poop, but the poop was empty. Both Chow Te and his first two mates had gone ashore to be with their families, leaving the Irishman in command. They had no doubt of his competence. Nor should they, he reckoned. He blinked at the sailor, cautiously getting to his feet. 'Mind yourself,' he growled, and headed for the cabins.

Malama had despaired of his returning at all. In the heat of the afternoon she had retired to his bunk, rather than hers, where she could inhale his scent. She even fell asleep, to dream, as always, strange dreams, in which the ship, this so surprising floating house in which she had now spent several days – however often she had watched ships making their way up the river she had never attempted to imagine what they might be like on board – and the jungle, her father and her sisters, were intermingled. Had Father had any concept of what he was sending her to, when he had given her to the white man? She did not think so, because Father could have had no concept of this world himself.

She would have had it no different, save for her master's reluctance to use her as a woman, as Panka and Shalina had promised he would. That shamed her, made her feel that she was unclean in his eyes as in the eyes of so many people. She knew she was not. She washed herself most carefully every day. And he knew that she did that. Yet he would not touch her.

And now he was away from her, pursuing his own life, forgetting about her . . . she heard the so familiar footsteps on the ladder, and sat up. Yet, if the footfall was the one she recognized, it was strangely hesitant, now appearing to stop, then coming on with a rush. And he all but fell through the door.

She gazed at him in consternation. His clothes were untidy, and dirty where he must have fallen down at least once. Perhaps he had been attacked by robbers or tax gatherers! She scrambled from the bunk to help him, put her arm round his waist, but instead of moving to the bunk with her he stared down at her as if he had never seen her before. The look in his eyes was unknown to her, his normally sweet breath so unusually heavy, that she released him and backed away until her thighs touched

43

the bunk. He was speaking to her, half smiling, as he took off his clothes. When he dropped his trousers she inhaled sharply, because he was more ready than she had ever seen him. Thus at last he was going to take her . . . suddenly she was afraid. He will drive his lingam into you until you split, Panka had said. She had not been afraid, then, because Harrington Sahib would never harm her, she knew.

But this was not Harrington Sahib. It was his face, and his body, but possessed by an evil spirit. She knew this instinctively, and knew that he would indeed hurt her. Yet he was her master, and had to be obeyed. She caught her breath as he took her in his arms, held her naked against him, kissed her mouth with a passion that forced it open, to allow his tongue inside. She gasped for breath, and he swept her legs from the deck and laid her on the bunk, then straddled her, kneeling, looking down at her, while he stroked her nipples and drove his fingers into her thick, glossy hair. She continued to pant, uncertain what was going to happen next, but when he parted her legs to kneel between she could not prevent a cry of terror.

His head jerked, and she thought he was going to strike her, and tensed her muscles. Then his expression suddenly changed. The lust and the anger and the strangeness all disappeared, and he was Harrington Sahib again. He continued staring at her for several seconds, while his lingam drooped. Then he got off her and stood above her, speaking for a moment. To her consternation she was sure she could see tears in his eyes. Then he almost threw himself away from her, on to the other bunk, turned his face to the bulkhead, and appeared to sleep.

'No, sweetheart, you may not accompany me,' Michael told Malama as she watched him dress with huge eyes. The Singapore tailors had done him proud, and fitted him out with a navy-blue double-breasted cutaway frock coat worn over tight-fitting grey trousers, which were strapped under his black boots. His shirt was white and his cravat dark blue, and he had bought himself a black silk hat and

44

brass-headed cane. With his curly dark hair washed and brushed and his chin very clean shaven – because of the heat he had even removed his moustache – he thought he looked very good indeed. A veneer of the gentleman, he reckoned, to cover the lust of a blackhearted villain, who would surely fulfil his mother's prophecy and end on the gallows.

He had also bought a new sari for Malama, in deep red. He had owed her at least that. Because she, in her innocence, obviously blamed herself for what had happened. Or rather, for what had not happened. She had been terrified by his drunken approach; he could understand that. Thus she had screamed, and the scream had restored him to his senses, at least partially. But almost instantly she had regretted it, and when he had awakened with a gonging headache and a throat as dry as the desert she had knelt beside him eager to stroke him and offer herself as blatantly as she knew how. But with the evaporation of the rice beer from his mind had come sanity. Once again he had attempted to throw away everything his talent and hard work had earned him; he was only fortunate no superior officer had been on board when he had returned, or he might again be on the street, or in gaol. And he was even more fortunate that Malama had screamed, or he might have committed a crime for which he would never be able to atone. So he had put her hands aside, and smiled at her, and left her as bewildered as she had once been terrified.

But she was a happy soul. When she had seen the new sari she had uttered a scream of pleasure, and immediately wrapped herself in it, posing in front of him and assuming that she was accompanying him wherever he was going. Now she gave one of her devastating pouts and coiled herself on her bunk, her expression clearly indicating that he was beyond her comprehension.

'I go to seek employment,' he got the steward – who spoke Hindu – to explain. 'I will soon be back, and will tell you what we are going to do next.' He stood above her, rested his hand on her glossy head. 'You may cook me a curry for tonight.'

'Ha,' she said, and curled herself even tighter. But he knew that by the time he returned she would be all sunshine again. Only this time he must return sober, as he must return sober on all future occasions. It would be necessary to play the role of the teetotaller in any event, as he was going to the home of his new employer.

He had been directed, and made his way up the slight hill behind the harbour to one of the great houses built on the open ground above the town. It was not quite dusk, and the air was still, and therefore filled with a constant whirr of insects as it gave off the perfume of a myriad of blossoms and flowers from the carefully cultivated gardens. With the ships resting on the calm surface of the harbour, the seabirds wheeling majestically to and fro, the Union Jack flying from several vantage points, the crimson-jacketed officers of the garrison and the black-coated merchants walking the promenade with their parasol-toting wives in their bonnets and flounced petticoats, Michael suddenly realized that this was indeed an outpost of empire, a little portion of the Pax Britannica translated to these distant and hostile shores in a way Calcutta, with its immense heritage of Indian civilization, could never be.

The house he approached was a splendid one. On the high ground there was no necessity for stilts, which were replaced by cellars, so that there was a brief staircase to be mounted to reach the verandahed ground floor. The approach was through a luxurious garden in which orchids and oleander bloomed excessively, as well as jasmine, already giving off its gloriously subtle perfume as the sun sank into the west. The house itself blazed with light on all three storeys, and if Michael had arrived on foot, there were several carriages and equipages waiting before the steps, their drivers, mostly Chinese, sitting together and smoking.

The verandah itself was guarded by a Malay, who asked him his name and then ushered him on to a Chinese major-domo, who took his hat and stick and announced: 'Mr Michael Harrington.'

Michael stepped into a large reception room, where there were some twenty people, all turning to gaze at the new arrival. To his surprise they were not all Chinese. Indeed, most of them were obviously British, or at least European. But Teng Lee was coming forward to greet him. 'Mr Harrington.' He shook hands. 'Why, you are a credit to my tailors. Come in, come in. I would have you meet my wife.'

The woman was at least twenty years younger than her husband. Short, slender, and extremely attractive, with her black hair swept up into a huge chignon on the back of her head to expose her high-cheekboned yellow-brown face, she was dressed in a tunic over her skirt, beneath which there seemed a total absence of petticoats. Nor was she Chinese, Michael was sure.

Teng Lee recognized his uncertainty, and smiled. 'The Princess Jalina is of the house of Rama of Siam,' he said with quiet pride. 'My life has been blessed in that she has chosen to smile upon me.'

'What nonsense,' Jalina countered. 'I am the fortunate one in that my husband carried me off to share *his* life. Now come and meet our guests.'

Michael, his mind whirling as he grasped something of the adventures this strange pair must have shared, found himself being introduced to Teng Lee's partner, Clive Hammond, a large, urbane Englishman in his late fifties, his wife Elizabeth, a somewhat faded blonde, and their children, two young men and a girl, an odd mixture, for while the younger children, a man named Pieter and a woman named Margaret Cooper, both in their middle twenties, did not in the least resemble their mother, the eldest son very obviously took after his father. 'Ali commands one of our ships,' Clive Hammond explained.

'And you would sail with us,' Ali Hammond remarked, looking Michael up and down.

Michael returned the gaze with interest. Ali Hammond – what an odd name for an Englishman – would be about

47

thirty, he estimated, and if he was fair and certainly possessed his father's features, he also wore a somewhat raffish air, as if he was uncomfortable in his fine clothes; his voice, too, was more liquid than the average Englishman's. 'That is my ambition, yes, Captain Hammond,' Michael agreed.

'And so you shall, if you are man enough,' Ali Hammond promised.

'Why, thank you.' Michael glanced at Clive Hammond, still at his shoulder.

'I expect Teng Lee would like to see you, in his office, tomorrow morning,' Hammond smiled. 'This is my younger daughter, Alicia.'

The girl had been hidden behind some taller men when Michael entered the room, or he would have noticed her sooner. Certainly she was the most striking woman present, and not just because of her flaming red hair, which was worn in the fashionable ringlets on to her neck. The hair, and the pale complexion which adorned her quite beautiful if somewhat bold features, were both perfectly set off by her white muslin gown, which exploded over her layers of underskirts, and was worn with a pale blue bodice, cut with a doublet-like vee which exactly matched the décolletage above, into which white flesh swelled every time she breathed. Her pelerine was also white – with a pale blue fringe – as were her gloves and fan, and there were white roses in her hair. To a man who had had no contact with a white woman since leaving England several months before she was breathtaking.

And seemed to find him hardly less interesting, for she gazed at him for several seconds before speaking. He had the same difficulty. 'Miss Hammond,' he said at last, praying he was right in his address.

'Mr Harrington,' she replied. 'I have heard about you, from Papa. Why, you are not at all as I expected.'

Clive Hammond interrupted: 'Now, Mr Harrington, I would have you meet . . .'

There were several other guests, including Margaret

Cooper's husband, all of whom seemed to know something about him, as well as Captain Chow Te – who fortunately did not appear to have heard anything about yesterday's spree – but Michael's mind, and gaze, kept returning to the tall red-headed girl – invariably to find hers seeking him. The elation which had immediately accompanied Clive Hammond's reassuring words regarding his employment seemed to be growing into a huge bubble which surrounded his personality, and when a glass of champagne was thrust into his hand he drank without thinking, and then gazed at it in alarm. How it made his blood tingle, and how he wanted another.

Clive Hammond was still at his side. 'If it is true that you have turned your back on alcohol,' he said, 'I apologize.'

'It is true,' Michael said.

'Then there is some cordial over here.' He rested his hand on Michael's shoulder. 'You should do well with us, Harrington,' he said, and went on to talk to another of the guests. While Michael obtained a glass of cordial and looked across the room at Alicia Hammond. Who was again looking at him, although she was conversing with another young man, whom Michael hated on the instant.

Yet what criminally crazy thoughts was he entertaining? For all these people's charm he was very definitely an employee, on trial, and bound for some shady transaction he did not doubt. While they were equally unaware of the depravity to which he could sink, and, he knew, would probably sink again given the slightest opportunity. And this girl was a daughter of the house. To even look at her too often might be as ruinous as to take another drink. But how he wanted that other drink.

Alicia Hammond opened her eyes when her maid drew the drapes from over the windows and allowed the equatorial sun, strong even in the early morning, to enter. She stretched, hands extended as far as they could reach above her head, body arching beneath the sheet as she sent her toes as far as possible the other way. There were one or two satisfying clicks as her joints awoke, and she subsided, sighing, while Melinda placed the tray on the table beside her bed. 'A good day, Missee,' Melinda observed. She was a Malay, and regarded every day that the sun shone as good.

Alicia sat up, thrust red hair from her face. 'Oh, yes,' she said. 'A good day.'

'I am drawing your bath, Missee,' Melinda said.

'Already?'

'It is ten of the clock,' Melinda said severely, 'and Missee Margaret coming at eleven.'

To go into town. But for a change that was what Alicia wanted to do more than anything else. She rolled on her stomach, face buried in her pillow, legs spreading to the maximum width allowed by her nightgown, and then coming back together again, slowly and sensuously. Because he would be there, somewhere. On one of Father's ships, of course. He should not be difficult to find.

Michael Harrington. He had interested her even before last night as being representative of a dream. Papa had discussed him with Mama at lunch yesterday. 'Some scoundrel,' he had said. 'Recommended by Joe Wright, believe it or not. Seems he and this fellow quarrelled, and the rascal struck him. Joe would have been within his rights to have him flogged. Instead he sent him ashore, and to Teng Tang. Seems he's a brilliant navigator even if he is something of a desperado.'

'Can you use him?' Elizabeth Hammond had asked.

'With things in Canton becoming so fraught, we can always use a man who knows his business and can take care of himself, and others. There's a problem though. Joe says he's fond of a drink.'

'Aren't we all?'

'Some of us control it better than others. He's Irish, there's the trouble.'

'So you won't employ him?'

'I'm inclined to give him a chance. We'll send him to sea with Ali. That'll prove whether he has what it takes.

50

Besides, I think it'll be good for Ali to have another white man on board.'

Elizabeth Hammond's high forehead had creased. 'It is a sad thing, not to trust your own son.'

'I never said that.'

'But you meant it.'

'I . . .' Clive Hammond opened his mouth, then glanced at his youngest daughter and rose from the table. 'I must get back.' He kissed them both on the cheek, left the room.

'Mama,' Alicia had asked. 'Why does Papa not trust Ali?'

Elizabeth patted her hand. 'I'm sure it is nothing for you to worry your pretty head about, my dear.' And she also had left the table.

Alicia had fumed. Her parents had this insufferable habit of treating her as a small child, even when she was eighteen years old. In the context of their lives, of course, she was a small child, born after their adventuring had been completed. She did not even know the truth of those tumultuous years before Singapore had been founded; it was not a subject ever discussed. But Ali was most certainly Papa's and Mama's son, and thus her elder brother – and yet Papa and Mama had only been married for twenty years, while Ali was twenty-nine. Before marrying Elizabeth Blaine Papa had been married to a Dutch woman, and thus Margaret and Pieter were not Mama's children at all, although Mama treated them as her own. It was all so very confusing, and left her so isolated, because she could share no intimacy with any of them, least of all Ali, who often seemed to regard her as a stranger.

The only fact about which Alicia was certain was that *she* had been born in wedlock, and in prosperity as well. Whatever the adventures of his youth, and they must have been considerable as he had followed his friend Stamford Raffles from Penang to Java to Sumatra before founding the colony of Singapore, Papa had arrived at a position of wealth before finally marrying Mama, and Alicia had never known anything less than total luxury and total security.

Yet without position. Because Papa was in business with a Chinese – and more, treated him as a friend. More and more Chinese were coming to Singapore, perhaps lured by the success of their compatriot, who like many of them had begun life as a Canton merchant, expanded to the south, and then cut his links with China altogether as his Manchu overlords had become more demanding.

Teng Lee's life could hardly have been less adventurous than Papa's, and during it he and Clive Hammond had become the very closest of friends, as they were now the most successful of business partners. Yet, to the Resident and the officers of the garrison, and those British merchants who had come here on their own to take advantage of the duty-free port, Chinese were necessarily inferior and heathen. A man like Teng Lee, with his wealth, his contacts and his beautiful Siamese princess wife, could never be ignored, any more than his partner could, but they could never be quite accepted either, and the same went for their children, who were all tainted in some fashion by the events of that wayward, mysterious past.

Which left her, in so limited a society as that of Singapore, absolutely nowhere. Margaret had married an officer in the garrison; she was a product of Papa's period of respectability. Well, no doubt there were several officers of the garrison who would be happy enough to marry Margaret Hammond's young half-sister. But Alicia would have none of that. She had observed how Margaret was always most definitely at the bottom of the military-social pecking order, and might always remain there, even if her husband obtained promotion. The thought of having to spend her life being polite to middle-aged matrons who might know more of her parents' past than she did herself was impossible for Alicia. When she married, it would be to a man who would defy convention and protocol, and carry her off into a wildly romantic world of his own. Thus she dreamed, whenever she heard of a stranger arriving in Singapore, that one day the man she was seeking might appear in this sunbaked outpost of empire.

And last night had discovered that dreams could come true. A desperado, Papa had called him. Was not a desperado what she sought? Of course when listening to her parents discussing him she had assumed that he would also be middle-aged and ugly and unpleasant and not to be thought of twice . . . but instead of that he was young and handsome and dashing and elegant and very much to be dreamed of. As she had dreamed of him all night.

She rolled on her back and frowned at the ceiling. It would not be entirely simple to translate dreams into reality; were Margaret or Mama, who watched over her like a pair of mother hens, to gain the slightest idea that she was interested in Mr Harrington, there would be a disaster. Certainly he would never sail for Hammond and Teng. But Alicia had no doubt that the business could be approached in such a manner that no one would possibly suspect what she had in mind. It was only a matter of being as devious to them as they had always been to her.

'Your bath is ready, Missee,' Melinda said.

Alicia allowed her nightgown to be removed and sank into the tin tub, giving a gentle shiver as the hot water seized her pale flesh. Interested in Mr Harrington. Oh, no, she thought. I am going to *marry* Mr Harrington.

'I believe my partner acquainted you with our decision, Mr Harrington,' Teng Lee said.

'He said I would be acceptable, as mate to Captain Hammond.' Michael glanced at Ali Hammond, who was the third man in the room, today wearing seafaring gear. Could this latterday pirate really be the brother of that gorgeous creature of last night? But Michael did not really wish to think about Alicia Hammond right now. He had thought about her while gazing at the naked Malama on his return to the junk, and had felt intensely guilty. If Alicia were even to suspect Malama's existence, much less what had so very nearly happened between them, she would never look at him again.

'Captain Hammond trades with South China,' Teng Lee said. 'It is a voyage of about a month.'

'Have you ever been to Canton, Harrington?' Ali Hammond asked.

'No,' Michael replied.

'It is a sometimes dangerous voyage,' Teng Lee remarked quietly. 'The South China Sea is infested with pirates. Does this disturb you?'

'No, sir,' Michael said.

Teng Lee looked at Ali.

'Nor should it,' Ali said. 'We go well armed. However, there is also some risk attended to trading with China itself.'

'More pirates?'

'There are certainly pirates on the China coast,' Ali agreed. 'But we are more concerned with the attitudes of the Manchu government.'

'There is friction between the Ch'ing – or the Manchu as they are popularly called – and the British at this time,' Teng Lee explained. 'We would have you understand these things, Mr Harrington.'

'Thank you. Does this friction involve the house of Hammond and Teng?'

'It involves all ships trading with China,' Teng Lee said. 'No man can say when there may be an embargo placed upon all foreigners. And should that happen, and one of my ships be in the port, it would go hard with her crew.' He gave a slight smile. 'I speak as a native of Canton myself.'

'So, do you still wish to sail with us?' Ali asked.

'I require employment, and I am a sailor,' Michael told them. 'And you have a berth. Yes, I wish to sail with you.'

'Then you shall.' Ali Hammond held out his hand, and Michael took it. 'But the South China seas are no place for females. Even Indian servants. Besides, women are unlucky at sea.' He glanced at Teng Lee. 'Would you not agree, Uncle Teng?'

'Sometimes,' Teng Lee remarked. 'But Captain Ham-

54

mond is right, Mr Harrington. You will leave your servant in Singapore.'

'She has no one, except me, Your Excellency.'

'She will be employed in my household,' Teng promised. He gave another slight smile. 'She will be there when you return, Mr Harrington. You may be certain of that.'

'I wish you to explain that I am going to sea tomorrow,' Michael told Ho Chu. The monsoon of 1838–9 was over, and the ship was ready to sail. 'But that she is to remain here. Tell her she will live in the house of our employer, Teng Lee. Tell her how wealthy he is, and how comfortable she will be.'

Ho Chu spoke in Hindustani, while Michael, seated on the bunk opposite, watched Malama's changing expressions, from excitement at the mention of the voyage, to alarm and disappointment as Ho Chu continued speaking. Then she looked at Michael.

'Tell her I will come back in a few weeks,' he said. 'Tell her she will still belong to me.'

Ho Chu did some more translating, but Malama hardly seemed to be listening. Tears welled out of her eyes and rolled down her cheeks.

'Oh, hell,' Michael said. 'All right, Ho Chu. You have done your best.'

The Chinese bowed. 'She wishes to be your woman, Mr Harrington,' he remarked. 'Why do you not make her so? She is ripe, now.' He left the cabin.

Why do I not make her so, Michael wondered. And make her happy. And then utterly lost if I do not return? Both Teng Lee and Ali Hammond had been conveying something to him, in a most roundabout manner. They wanted him to know he was undertaking a dangerous voyage . . . and the danger had nothing to do with either pirates or typhoons in the South China Sea. They were clearly trading against the wishes of the Chinese government. He could only wait to find out why. Not that it mattered. If he did not sail with Ali Hammond he would starve. But Malama, as a servant for Teng Lee in the security of Singapore, might well prosper.

As if that was the least important. If he took her now, he would never be able to dream of Alicia Hammond; because if he took Malama as his woman, he knew that he would irrevocably have committed himself to her for life. To sink into the passionate servitude that was Malama's personality would leave no avenues for escape. But if he did not so commit himself . . . the memory of Alicia had grown over the day, her perfume, the way she arched her eyebrows, her slight smile – and that glorious décolletage. The boss's daughter. The pathway to all things, and what a splendid pathway. As he was admitting villainy to himself, he could think thoughts like that.

He sat beside Malama and put his arm round her shoulders. 'I will be back,' he said. 'Then . . .' he touched her nipples, small and dark and boyish, and as she gave a ripple of pleasure, slid his finger down her chest and belly to the first curl of her pubic hair, while feeling an utter pervert. And a lying wretch.

She reached for him, and he stood up. 'When I come back,' he said. He knew she understood him, because she pouted. 'Now you must go ashore,' he said. 'I will take you to the house of Teng Lee. Come on deck as soon as you are ready.'

He left the cabin, because if he had stayed a moment longer he would indeed have made her his woman. But to do that, while thinking of Alicia Hammond . . . he reached the deck, and paused in consternation, because there she was.

Alicia Hammond rode in a phaeton driven by a Malay groom, which had stopped on the quay beside the *China Star*. She wore pale blue, obviously her favourite colour, and sheltered her complexion beneath an enormous straw hat. Now she stepped down in a swirl of petticoats while the maidservant who was accompanying her held out her parasol.

Michael glanced forward, but the deck was deserted.

The cargo had been discharged and the ship would not load until tomorrow, while the crew, no doubt warned by the unfortunate watchman of two nights before that Mr Harrington was a man of violent moods, preferred to avoid him.

'Well, Mr Harrington?' Alicia asked. 'Aren't you going to invite me aboard?'

Had she really come to see him? He could think of no other explanation at the moment, even if her action seemed incomprehensible. Yet she had gazed at him time and again last night. 'It will be my pleasure, Miss Hammond,' he said. 'Although I had hardly supposed it necessary, as your father owns the vessel.'

She was at the gangplank, and he hurried forward to give her his hand. 'And you are now to work for him,' she remarked.

'That is my good fortune,' he agreed. 'I am to sail with your brother Ali.'

'Then I am sure you will do very well.' She walked to the taffrail, open parasol propped against her shoulder, taffeta underskirt rustling, and looked down into the somewhat dirty waters of the inner basin.

'He has a strange name,' Michael ventured, following her.

'He has had a strange life,' she pointed out, which actually told him very little. 'But you will not find a better seaman.'

'I did not doubt that, Miss Hammond.'

'And when you return from China, will you make your home here in Singapore, Mr Harrington?'

She was definitely interested. It might be, and probably was, only the reaction of a natural flirt to a new face, but he saw no reason not to take what advantage he could of her mood. '*If* I return from China, Miss Hammond, I may well do so.'

She raised her eyebrows. 'If?'

'I am constantly being told that it could be a dangerous voyage. Do you never fear for your brother?'

'Rather I envy him the experience of that danger, Mr

Harrington. As I shall envy you. I have known nothing of that. I was born in Singapore and no doubt I shall die here.'

She was challenging him. 'Do you, then, consider death already, Miss Hammond?'

'Should I not, as it is the one certain thing in life?'

'You are a philosopher.'

'And you do not approve of philosophy, in a woman.'

He gave a little bow. 'I approve of philosophy, in anyone, Miss Hammond. Do you suppose I would be welcome, were I to settle here? And make my career in your father's company?'

She gazed at him. 'I am sure you would be most welcome, Mr Harrington. Now I must return. My sister is shopping, and I left her for only a breath of air.' Her mouth widened into a little smile. 'It was a happy chance we met.'

'A very happy chance.' She had extended her hand, and he took it to kiss her gloved fingers, then had them suddenly withdrawn.

'Who is this person?'

Michael straightened, glanced at Malama, who stood beside him in her green sari, her small bundle of clothes in her arms. 'Ah.' He wondered if she had chosen her moment. But there was nothing he could do save face it out. 'This is my servant.'

'But . . .' Alicia's brows drew together. 'She is a female.'

'Why, yes, Miss Hammond. So she is.'

'And she sails with you?'

'She has done so, up to now. But I am leaving her in the care of Teng Lee for this voyage.'

'She . . .' Alicia gazed at Malama, who returned her look with utter composure. Then Alicia glanced at Michael. 'You, sir, are a . . . a pervert,' she snapped. She stamped across the deck and down the gangplank. Her groom assisted her into the seat beside her maid, and the equipage moved off.

'She no like you,' Malama ventured happily. She was slowly learning English.

'Not now, she doesn't,' Michael agreed sadly.

A disaster? Or was Alicia's reaction actually an indication of her interest? He was tempted to go up to her house and try to explain, but his instincts warned him against showing any great interest of his own in Clive Harmond's daughter, when he was still very much on probation. Time enough for that when he returned from China, having, hopefully, established himself. Nor was it really reasonable to be angry with Malama, although he was now in a hurry to be rid of her so-dangerous presence. He took her to Teng Lee's house, as instructed, where he was greeted warmly by the Princess Jalina. 'What a lovely child,' she remarked, holding Malama's shoulders. 'How did you come by her?'

'She was given to me by her father,' Michael explained. 'I did him a service.'

'A service,' Jalina observed. 'You must be a man of many parts, Mr Harrington. She is very young.'

It was a question more than a remark. 'Yes,' Michael agreed. 'She is twelve years old.'

Jalina raised her head to gaze at him.

'And remains as she was the day she was given to me,' Michael told her.

Jalina smiled. 'I am glad of that, Mr Harrington. Be sure that I will take good care of her, and return her to you even better than that.'

Malama was by now reconciled to her fate, and obviously reassured by the greeting she had received from the princess, yet she wept more than ever as Michael kissed the top of her head before making his way back down to the harbour and the *Golden Dragon*, as Ali Hammond's ship was named. He felt indeed a great sense of relief, to be freed from so much temptation, and to be able to concentrate on making his way in this strange company into whose midst he had stumbled.

And also be able to think of Alicia, when he needed to

think of a woman? Now there was someone he could very easily love, he knew. A woman he would be proud to marry, and have on his arm for the rest of his life. A woman who had called him a pervert. But in ignorance. Perhaps the Princess Jalina might be of assistance there, as she had certainly believed him.

'Mr Harrington.' Ali Hammond shook hands. 'You will be second mate. Mr Wong Sung is my first officer.'

Michael shook hands with the young Chinese, not much older than himself, he estimated.

'Mr Wong will acquaint you with the ship,' Ali went on. 'And her weapons. And yours. You can use a sword and pistol?'

'Some,' Michael said.

'Well, you will have to practise. You'll not forget where we are bound.'

He turned away and Wong Sung escorted Michael below, into one of the luxurious after cabins he had come to expect on board these amazing ships. The *Golden Dragon* was in fact considerably larger than the *China Star*, and even more splendidly appointed; her very bulwarks were lined with gilt. While the entire ship was pervaded with a strange scent, almost sickly sweet. 'What are her timbers?' Michael asked Wong.

'They are iron wood, what is called teak, from the forests of Burma,' Wong explained. 'There is none better in all the world.'

'And does it always smell so sweet?'

'Smell? It does not smell at all, unless it is oiled. No, no, Mr Harrington.' Wong took him to the main cargo hatch, which stood open. 'The smell is our cargo.' He pointed into the depths, which were entirely filled with bulging sacks. 'Opium.'

3

The Wrath of Lin

'Opium?' Michael was astounded. 'The Chinese wish to import opium?'

'There is a great demand for the drug in China.' Wong gave a brief smile. 'The people there have many sorrows to forget.'

'But . . .' Michael scratched his head. 'The British government permits this?'

'The British government encourages it. Opium is one of the main crops exported from India. Our master, Teng Lee, brings it here for trans-shipment to Canton.'

'And the Chinese government would stop it entering,' Michael said, suddenly understanding much of what had been mystifying him before.

'They have prohibited its entry officially.' Another quick smile.

'You mean our purpose is to smuggle.'

'Only in a manner of speaking. The Chinese authorities have no desire to provoke a dispute with Great Britain. They are merely concerned about the drain of silver from their country to pay for the opium.'

'I have heard that opium depresses the brain.'

Wong shrugged. 'It is doubtful the Manchu care that much about what happens to any Chinese. Now come forward and I will introduce you to the crew.'

Michael actually knew very little about the properties of opium, except that it was used as a painkiller in medicine, and had the power to induce hallucinations. If he still found it odd that an entire cargo should be composed of something with such limited value, he was not prepared to concern himself with it at this moment. Rather was he excited at the prospect of again venturing into unknown seas, as far as he was concerned, even as he felt his heart-beat quicken as he was given a very serviceable sword and two pistols; he would have felt more comfortable with a pair of well-balanced knives, but saw no reason to acquaint his new employers with all of his talents at this moment. He was not required to carry weapons about his normal duties, but they had to be primed and readily available at all times, Ali Hammond warned him. He discovered, indeed, that the *Golden Dragon* was almost a floating arsenal, for although she was armed with only six cannon, she carried an enormous number of muskets and powder and ball, enough for twice the number of men actually in her crew.

Then they were away. The Hammond family came down to bid their son and brother farewell, and Alicia was naturally with them, but she chose to ignore Michael completely, pointedly turning her back on him when he would have addressed her. The rest of the family were however apparently unaware of anything odd in her behaviour, and both Clive and Elizabeth Hammond shook his hand most warmly, while Ali looked on with a faintly mocking smile. Then the ship was cast off, the boats towed her out into the harbour, her sails were set, and before a light northerly breeze she made her way through the Dragon's Teeth, where a course was laid to the east, north of the island of Bintan, and thence into the South China Sea.

With the wind still northerly, and their course north-easterly, progress was slow for a day or two, and Michael's sun sights told him that they were actually being driven south of their intended track, but this did not seem to disturb Ali, once they were clear of the several groups of small islands which lay north of Borneo. 'The wind will change soon enough,' he asserted confidently.

'I would have supposed we would wish to stand well clear of the Philippine Islands,' Michael said. 'Are they not one huge nest of pirates?'

'In the main,' Ali agreed. 'It is a fact that the Spanish

authorities are quite incapable of suppressing them. But they will not trouble us.'

'I suppose we are a little large,' Michael said.

Ali grinned. 'There is a better reason than that. You'll come below, Mr Harrington. Mr Wong?'

He glanced at the Chinese officer, who nodded and remained on the poop. Michael followed the captain into the great cabin. 'Sit down,' Ali said. 'Drink? Oh, I forgot, you do not.' He poured himself a goblet of wine, sat opposite. 'Teng Lee, my honorary uncle,' he said without preamble, 'has been so unfortunate as to lose all of his children. And now of course he is unlikely after all these years to impregnate his Thai princess. It is therefore almost certain that I shall inherit the main part of the company. Do you find that interesting, Michael?'

'It must be a pleasant prospect.'

'Indeed it is. But for my friends as well as myself. My trusted friends.'

Michael waited, gazing at him.

'It may happen that you will witness certain events on this voyage,' Ali went on, 'which may seem to you somewhat strange. Events which perhaps might be misinterpreted by many people. It is therefore necessary for me to ask you never to repeat to anyone anything that you may see or hear while sailing on my ship. Understood?'

'I assume we are not talking about smuggling opium into China?'

'That is hardly a secret matter.'

'Then am I permitted to inquire into the possible nature of these events?'

'You will be breaking no more laws than in smuggling opium, if that is what is bothering you.'

'Well, then . . .'

'Nonetheless, I must demand absolute secrecy. Especially from my family, or Teng Lee.'

Michael considered. 'Do I have a choice?'

Ali grinned. 'Not really, if you wish to return to Singapore. But I accepted you as my mate because I could recognize in you a man who is determined to make his way. I can tell you there will be a considerable profit in it for you. This also must be kept secret, of course, but it will be real enough. Added to which will be my trust, and my patronage. I estimated that you were a man who would understand the way of the world.'

Michael nodded. 'And you had a vacancy. May I ask what happened to your previous second mate?'

Ali Hammond shrugged. 'He met with an unfortunate accident.'

'For betraying your trust?'

'I would prefer to say that he was careless. A fatal weakness at sea. You do not look like a careless man to me, Michael.'

'I will endeavour not to be, to be sure. Are all of your crew equally trustworthy?'

'They are all good men. I am glad to welcome you amongst them.' Ali leaned across the table and held out his hand, and after a moment's hesitation Michael took it. Clearly Ali Hammond was indulging in some private business, unknown to his father or Teng Lee, the profits from which were divided up amongst his crew. And to protect which he might be willing to kill? That was a chilling thought. But Michael supposed, having been forced to step into these murky waters, that he had to expect to find a few predators floating around. And it really was no concern of his whether Ali was cheating his own company. While as the man had said, he really had no choice. Presumably Ali was certain that, once Michael had accepted his share of the illegal profit, he would be in no position to betray him, even if there were no physical risk involved – and from what he had seen of Ali Hammond, Michael had no doubt he would murder anyone who attempted to betray him.

Besides, it was an added spice to feel that he was tying himself even more closely to this family – and thus to the fascinating Alicia. He wondered what Ali's reaction would be were his latest accomplice to ask for his sister's hand in marriage?

Meanwhile, the junk continued to make more east than

north, even though the wind did indeed shift to the south two days later; Ali still recorded it as northerly in the log. They sailed between Swallow Reef and Amboyna Cay into the midst of the large archipelago of tiny atolls known as the Spratly Islands, now within two hundred miles of the Philippines, when sail was shortened, and the junk hardly seemed to move through the water, while lookouts were doubled. Before nightfall a ship was sighted from the masthead, and then full sail was resumed and a course laid towards the stranger which, to Michael's consternation, could soon be seen to be a large proa, an open boat which was propelled by both oars and a single sail, and which was the preferred vessel of the pirates who abounded in these waters, for its speed even when heavily laden. And this boat was certainly heavily laden, with armed men.

'You'll prepare yourselves, gentlemen,' Ali Hammond commanded, and muskets were served out to the crew, while the guns were loaded and run out. Michael asked no questions, although it seemed incomprehensible that Ali should actually be seeking a fight when he could have sailed away from the stranger; he remained on the poop to watch the approaching vessel, aware of sweat-wet hands and parched throat – he had never actually been in a fight at sea before – or on land, for that matter.

Darkness fell, but soon a tropical moon was swathing across the calm sea to turn the night into day. The two ships steadily came nearer to each other, until they were only two cables – four hundred yards – apart. Then both were hove to, and a small boat put out from the side of the proa. It was manned by six of the grimmest-looking Malays Michael had ever seen, every man armed with a kris, the fearsome, curved, Malayan short sword, and pistol. Their commander, in the stern, also Malay, wore a richly decorated tunic over his sarong, and carried a Western-style sword.

The boat came into the side of the junk and the pirate captain came on board, to be greeted with much warmth by Ali. Michael did not understand Malay, and had no idea what was being said, but that the two men were old friends could not be doubted – and more than that, old partners, for now several small bags which clinked most interestingly were passed up from the dinghy. Soon it was the turn of Wong and himself to be presented, and then the pirate and Ali went below, leaving the Chinese seamen looking down at the men in the boat, and the pirates looking up.

Michael wondered what on earth the pirates could wish to buy, from a ship which carried only opium, and then realized he had forgotten that the *Golden Dragon* did not only carry opium, as Ali and his friend returned on deck and orders were given to bring up several stands of arms and a chest of powder. This was lowered into the waiting boat, the pirate captain embraced Ali, took his place, and was rowed back to his ship.

'Twelve pounds of silver,' Ali said. 'A good night's work. You'll make sail, Mr Wong.'

'You sell arms to the pirates,' Michael said. 'Doesn't it concern you that those bullets may be one day used against a British ship?'

'I owe no allegiance to the British,' Ali declared. 'My allegiance is to myself and my friends. Bodaw Wing and I grew up together, in Singapore, before the British ever came there and drove the pirates out. Now I arm him, and he in return never attacks a vessel flying the flag of Teng. I think that is an admirable arrangement, Mr Harrington.'

'But Teng Lee would not agree with you. Or your father.'

'No, they would not. They have old-fashioned ideas. As perhaps you do too. But you are one of my people now, Michael. Remember that. And enjoy your share of the silver.'

Over dinner Ali told him some more of his remarkable past – and that of his mother. For Elizabeth Blaine, as she had then been, had been carried off by the Singapura pirates while pregnant. She had been ransomed, but forced to leave her son behind in captivity. Save that he had never been a captive. He had been treated as one of the sons of the famous pirate Bodaw Minh, who had then ruled Singapura. Ali had grown almost to manhood with them, and had then been 'rescued' by his real father, Clive Hammond. But he had never forgotten his childhood friends, just as he had never truly become reconciled to his birthright as an English gentleman.

It was a fascinating story, and explained many things which had previously puzzled Michael, not least the name Ali. But it did not alter the fact that the man was a blackguard, and a traitor to both his race and his family. Nor did it alter the fact that he was Alicia's brother. Or that Michael was now his accomplice. How simple life had been before he had struck Joe Wright in a drunken fit.

Now the junk made north with a purpose. Whatever his faults, Ali Hammond was a consummate seaman, who drove his ship hard when he wanted to. The Philippines were left far behind them, and only a couple of days later they sighted the Portuguese trading post of Macao, at the mouth of the Pearl River. East of Macao was a cluster of islands, and into the midst of these the junk cautiously felt her way, Michael gazing in astonishment at yet another magnificent natural harbour unfolding itself before him.

'It is called Hong Kong,' Ali explained. 'And is ideal for our purpose, as it is concealed from prying eyes.'

The main island of the natural breakwater was apparently inhabited only by fishermen, with whom Ali was well acquainted. Having visited the junk, one of these sailed over to the mainland, only a few miles distant, and within a week the junk was visited by several merchants, all anxious to bid for her precious cargo. The transactions were left to Wong Sung, who spoke the language more fluently than did Ali. Ali himself took Michael aft to greet a middle-aged man who wore the distinctive hat and robes of a mandarin, and the crystal button with the silver pheasant badge to denote that he was of the fifth rank, and whose servant was taking part in the bidding for the opium. 'Teng Hu is a cousin of Teng Lee,' Ali explained. 'My new second officer, Michael Harrington.'

Teng Hu bowed and took Michael's hand. 'You will prosper with the house of Teng,' he said in surprisingly good English. 'My cousin is well?'

'Oh, indeed,' Ali said. 'He sends his felicitations. And he would like to know what is the situation here.'

Teng Hu glanced at the opium being brought up from the hold, and then at the group of merchants standing around the hatch. 'It is best we talk in private,' he said. 'When you come to my house. There are those I would have you meet.' He bowed towards Michael. 'Bring this gentleman with you, that he may understand our situation.'

Ali Hammond was apparently in the habit of visiting Teng Hu whenever he was in China, and a sampan was provided for their trip from Hong Kong into the mouth of the Pearl River and thence up to Canton, this being reckoned a safer way of travel than the somewhat quicker journey across country, which might involve an encounter with a band of Manchu bannermen, the descendants of the warriors who had followed the great Nurhachi out of Mongolia to conquer China from the Ming Dynasty in the seventeenth Christian century, and who, riding beneath their clan banners, composed the Ch'ing – the Manchu royal clan – standing army. Even after nearly two hundred years, Michael was told, the Mongolian Manchus ruled China as a conquered land, keeping themselves aloof from the Chinese population, as symbolized by the pigtail, which every Chinese, even one as well to-do as Teng Hu, was forced to wear to demonstrate his inferiority.

This was a startling state of affairs, but Michael was delighted at the opportunity to explore something of the country, even if Ali impressed upon him that they should keep a very low profile, as foreigners were forbidden to enter Canton itself. Fortunately, Teng Hu's estate was apparently outside the walls.

Michael was fascinated by the way the native boat was

worked, by means of huge sweeps rather than oars, for it was a considerable size. With these the craft was driven across the small area of open sea into the mouth of the river, where they passed beneath the guns of two fortresses, called the Bogue, before beginning their ascent, when he learned that Canton was actually ninety miles away, and would not be reached for two days. Yet the interest provided by the journey never flagged: apart from the teeming traffic on the river, ocean-going junks, smaller vessels, and of course hundreds of sampans like their own, all laden, as was theirs, with produce on its way to the Canton market, the cartographer in him could not help noting the deep-water passages between the many sandbanks which littered the delta. Beyond the ships were the riverbanks, often reinforced with a levee to prevent flooding, behind which were numerous small farms and villages, while occasionally he caught glimpses of a many-roofed pagoda, rising in stately splendour above the squalor. There were mountains in the distance, but the river valley was wide and deep, and on the third morning after leaving Hong Kong they saw the pagodas and walls of the city.

It looked larger than even Calcutta, for it had spilled beyond its walls into a multitude of small streets and rickety houses. It was hardly less crowded than Calcutta either, and on going ashore he discovered there were a surprising number of Europeans to be seen, all men, but he gathered that although the East India Company had lost its monopoly of English trade with China some years before it was still very active, and in addition other English companies and several French concerns as well as the firm of Hammond and Teng all traded with this greatest city of South China. The houses outside the walls were mostly small and mean, and the shops had overflowed into street traders, who kept up a noisy babble, surrounded by barking dogs and screaming children, while there appeared a total lack of sanitation, or indeed desire for any, as men and animals urinated in the roadway, but every so often he and Ali came across a pagoda of some beauty, while it was reassuring to observe the friendly greetings which were bestowed on them from almost everyone they encountered. Only the occasional patrol of Manchu soldiers looked the least hostile – but then, they also looked hostile to the Chinese. Ali, however, continued past them with a jaunty air, and Michael followed his example.

After a considerable walk they left the city behind and entered an attractive parkland, which contained several houses of some size, and it was to one of these that Ali led him. They were greeted by servants who obviously knew the English sea captain, and given iced sherbets for refreshment before being shown into a large, high-ceilinged reception room hung with expensive drapes, where Teng Hu and several other guests awaited them. Michael immediately gained an impression of considerable wealth, and even perhaps some power, and yet Teng Hu was a member of the conquered race, and was well aware of it.

He was introduced to the other guests, all Chinese, coming lastly face to face with a young man not greatly older than himself who, instead of bowing a greeting like the others, took his hand and gazed into his eyes for several moments. Somewhat taken aback, Michael experienced a very strange sensation indeed. For if the young man's features were unremarkable save for a stubborn set to his jaw, his eyes, deep and black, and intelligent, were almost magnetic, and seemed able to see right into his soul. 'You are an honest man,' the strange fellow said at last.

'I am not sure everyone would agree with you,' Michael replied in some embarrassment.

'Do not belittle yourself,' the young man said. 'My father approves of you, I can feel, and therefore so do I. It pleases me to make your acquaintance.'

'This is Hung Hsiu-ch'uan,' Teng Hu explained. 'He is one of our bright young men.'

'My pleasure,' Michael said, at last getting his hand free, and wondering which of the older men could be

Hung Hsiu-ch'uan's father, who had managed to convey approval without actually saying anything.

He and Ali were invited to sit down and drink jasmine tea while Teng Hu told them of affairs in Canton.

'The situation is not good,' he said. 'The trouble is that there is no direction from Peking. The Emperor does nothing but dally with his concubines instead of attending to affairs of state.'

'They will die the death,' Hung Hsiu-ch'uan announced in sepulchral tones. 'They are the guilty, and they oppose the will of my father.'

Teng Hu waited patiently for him to finish before continuing, while Michael again looked from face to face in another attempt to discover who this so-positive father was, but the other men's faces all wore expressions of respect whenever the young man made a pronouncement. 'This means that here in the provinces we are very much at the mercy of our local commissioners and army commanders, and they act as they choose. We have recently been sent a new commissioner, Lin Tse-hsu. A bold and prejudiced rascal, who hates all trade with the West, and has openly denounced the importation of opium, saying that it is destroying our people.'

'Is it?' Michael asked.

'Who can say? There are people who become addicted to it, but then, there are people who become addicted to alcohol. We must hope that Commissioner Lin does not let his prejudices interfere with his good sense.'

'Because it would cost your brother and yourself some profit?'

'Because it would provoke war with the British,' Teng Hu corrected. 'They are determined to maintain the opium trade, and have said so. Teng Lee is but one of their agents in this matter. As are you, Mr Harrington.'

Michael made no reply; as he was here as mate on one of Teng Lee's ships the rebuke was irrefutable.

In any event there came another declaration from Hung Hsiu-ch'uan. 'Lin Tse-hsu is an enemy of my father,' he

71

growled. 'He will die the death. When the time comes, he will die the death, like all the Manchu.'

Once again his elders listened to him with respectful silence, and indeed he held forth several times during dinner with the reported opinions of his father on various subjects, nearly all of which involved a sanguinary end to those who might differ. 'His father must be a mighty powerful man,' Michael remarked to Ali as they retired for the night after a satisfying meal.

Ali laughed. 'The most powerful of all. His father is God.'

'Eh?'

'Fact. Hung Hsiu-ch'uan believes he's Jesus Christ's brother. His elder brother, mind.'

'Good God! You mean he's mad.'

'Well, who's to say? I suspect a lot of people thought Jesus was mad. You'll have observed that Teng Hu and his friends all listened to him.'

'I had no idea there was that much Christianity in China,' Michael confessed.

'There isn't. It is an unpopular religion, at once with the government, which sees it as a possible rival to Buddhism, and with the people, who find it too mealy-mouthed. Hung has just got hold of some of the more dramatic tenets expounded in the Bible and grafted them on to his own ideas. He is especially taken by the concept of a god able to perform miracles.'

'You are saying he is at least a total fraud.'

'Now as to that, again I keep an open mind. If he is a fraud, then he is an unconscious one. I tell you, he genuinely believes he is the son of God.'

'Then what will become of him?'

Ali shrugged. 'His head will probably be whipped off for blasphemy before he is too much older. Now come, shall we not enjoy these handmaidens? They were certainly intended for enjoyment.' For their chamber had been invaded by two yellow-skinned girls who were bowing, and now began to help them to undress. Ali had clearly enjoyed their ministrations on previous visits. He

72

allowed the girl to remove all his clothes, then did the same for her before sitting on the bed and drawing her on to his lap, while she giggled happily.

Michael looked down at the girl who had been undressing him. 'Michael,' he said, pointing at himself.

'Wu Yei,' she replied softly.

He touched her head, and then her chin, and then her shoulder. She released the one tie that held her garment together, and allowed it to slide to the floor. She was undoubtedly older than Malama, but yet had a less mature body. Although attractive enough for him, at this moment. And as she had been provided by the house, she could be taken without guilt. He lifted her on to the bed, and she murmured happily as she aroused him to erection, while he played with her little button breasts and twisting bottom, and then sat on him to introduce him into her. It had been so long since he had last had a woman that he enjoyed her, time and again – and as he did so, thought of Alicia.

Teng Hu took them on a tour of his estate the next morning, and also introduced them to his wife and daughters, who were, somewhat ceremonially, carried into their presence by their servants and placed in their chairs. Michael assumed this was indeed a ceremony, and was horrified to observe discreetly as the conversation proceeded – translated by Teng, as the ladies spoke no English – that each of the three had terribly deformed feet, in which heel, toe and instep appeared as a straight line.

'What a terrible misfortune for poor Teng,' he remarked to Ali afterwards. 'In that all three of his womenfolk should have been afflicted in the same way.'

Ali gave one of his sardonic grins. 'They are not afflicted, my dear fellow. Their condition is deliberate. As children they, and any female children the girls may bear, have their feet bound in that shape until the bones take up the position permanently. It is called the lily foot.'

'But why, in the name of God? Those girls last night were not deformed.'

'But they were servants,' Ali explained. 'The lily foot is a sign that a lady is a gentlewoman, born of wealthy parents. Thus she will never have to lift a hand to help herself, and certainly never have to walk.' His grin widened. 'These are strange people, Michael my boy. But they are a large part of our bread and butter. Just remember never to propose marriage to a Chinese lady.'

Like all his family, Teng Hu had made his money in trade, even if unlike his cousins he had accepted Manchu rule and indeed had become a local dignitary. Yet he had been one of the principal purchasers of the illegal opium, and certainly secretly opposed the government and longed for its downfall without having any idea how that might be accomplished.

When they returned to the house after touring the estate they found Hung Hsiu-ch'uan waiting for them. 'I would speak with Mr Harrington,' Hung said. 'I would invite him to accompany me, on a visit.'

Michael looked at Teng Hu in surprise, and his host bowed. 'I am sure it will be informative, Mr Harrington.'

Then he looked at Ali, who grinned and shrugged. 'Go ahead. He's never invited me to go visiting with him. Just don't let him exhaust you. We leave tomorrow.'

'I have horses,' Hung explained, and Michael mounted beside him, wondering if he was being taken to some religious meeting. They rode alone, save for a solitary attendant, and Hung did not speak for some time. Then he said, unexpectedly, 'Why do you work for Teng Lee?'

'A man must work, or starve,' Michael reminded him. 'I have no estate of my own.'

'Yet are he and all his people evil,' Hung said.

Michael frowned. 'You dined with his cousin. Is he not a friend of yours?'

'Indeed. Does that mean I must see him with blinded eyes?'

'I suppose not.'

'And that Captain Hammond is a rogue. Yet you sail with him.'

'Well, right now I don't have much choice. In what way is he a rogue?'

'He brings opium to my people.'

'I thought it was the government who opposed that? Your merchants all seemed eager enough to buy it. Including Teng Hu.'

'Because they too are evil, destroyers of men. But when my father gives the signal, they too will perish in the fiery furnace.'

Michael considered this as they approached the city, and wondered if Teng Hu was aware of Hung's feelings. 'But your father doesn't quite see me that way.'

'He sees your honesty, and has allowed me to do the same.'

'You don't suppose he ever makes mistakes? There are a large number of people would disagree with his judgement.' Michael spoke flippantly.

'Because they are fools, who cannot see the truth,' Hung reproved him gravely.

'Yet, as you say, I sail with Captain Hammond, and sell opium to your people.'

'That is because you do not understand its properties. I will show you those properties, Mr Harrington. And perhaps you will be able to convince your compatriots that they should abandon such evil practices. Come.'

They had reached the houses, with the walls of the inner city looming in front of them. Michael wondered if he was going to be taken inside the forbidden sanctuary, but Hung turned the horses aside and led him up to a somewhat larger than usual house, the door of which was guarded by an armed man. Here they dismounted, leaving the horses in the care of the groom, and Hung addressed the man in Chinese. Immediately they were admitted into a small antechamber, where there were two other men and a woman, and a kind of bar counter; Michael's nostrils were immediately assailed by the same sickly sweet smell he had first noticed on board the *Golden Dragon*, and he realized where they were, and that the woman was filling two long-stemmed pipes, while Hung was paying over some money to the men.

'I'm not sure I want to try it,' Michael said.

'Then do not,' Hung agreed. 'Only pretend. It is necessary to take a pipe, or we will not gain admittance.'

Cautiously Michael held the piece of clay between thumb and two fingers of his right hand, as Hung was doing. The girl bowed to them, and opened an inner door, ushering them through and quickly closing it behind them, so that it banged against Michael's shoulders as he stepped backwards in consternation. For it seemed all his senses had been assailed at once. The room was large, but low ceilinged and gloomy, as it was illuminated by only a few oil lamps, and there were no windows. It was thus filled with choking smoke. It was also filled with people, of both sexes he realized with growing disgust. Some were quite well dressed and sat and chatted in low voices while they smoked. Others might have been well dressed once, but their clothes were sadly soiled and gave off the most fearful stench as they lolled or lay on the floor, occasionally reaching for their pipes; clearly they had been here for several days without moving. Others were in various stages of undress, some quite naked, and several playing with each other's genitals – it seemed regardless of the sex of their neighbour. Occasionally one of these would take offence and scream or strike at their molester, but the noise would soon subside, and be submerged beneath the wheezing breaths which filled the room.

'There are more than a hundred opium dens like this in Canton,' Hung told him. 'There are thousands in this province alone.'

'It is perfectly disgusting,' Michael said.

'It is worse than that. Many of these people were well to do before the coming of opium. Now they have sold all they possess just to be able to afford to lose themselves in their dreams. They neither eat nor drink nor work. They smoke and they die. Can you support the men who inflict this upon my people, Mr Harrington?'

'By God, not now,' Michael declared.

'As I knew when I looked into your eyes, you are an honest man and a compassionate one. You must stop this horror.'

Michael hesitated. 'I am of very little importance, Hung.'

'You will grow to importance. I see it in your eyes. You must stop this horror. Then my father will honour you, and you will be my friend. When the day comes, and I ride in triumph into Peking itself, to do my father's work, you will be at my side. I promise you these things, Mr Harrington, when you have put a stop to the trade. Let us leave this place.'

Michael had a great deal to think about as he and Ali began their return journey down the river. More and more he was becoming astounded at the way his life had been turned upside down from the fateful moment when he had struck Joe Wright. But there was something more than the mere fact of having had to seek employment from the shady side of seafaring. He had always been a man who had sought pleasure and nothing else; he had gone to sea in the first place because he found pleasure in being afloat, in handling great ships, in triumphing over storm and tide, in deciphering the riddles of sandbanks and reefs, tides and currents. He had never cared a damn for any other human being. And now, in the space of less than six months he had risked his life to save a coolie family, found himself become almost a husband to a beautiful little girl, just about fallen in love with a young woman far above himself in station, and now learned that she was actually part – even if, surely, an unaware part – of a vast criminal conspiracy. Which he had more or less promised now to oppose to the best of his ability. Easy to promise a fanatical madman like Hung. Because Hung was undoubtedly deranged. And yet he alone, of all the Chinese Michael had met, seemed to care about his people. There was the rub. Easy to promise, and then forget; he would never see Hung again. But . . . he *wanted* to do something about it. Certain it was that with the sickening memory of what Hung had shown him he could not again sail for Hammond and Teng, if their cargo was going to be opium.

Which left him where, vis-à-vis Ali, who was smoking a cheroot as they went downriver considerably faster than they had ascended it?

'So where did Hung take you?' Ali asked.

Michael decided to seize the bull by the horns. 'To an opium den.'

Ali's head turned sharply: 'Did he now? I have often wondered what addled that fellow's brain. It's not something you want to make a habit of, Michael.'

'We went to look.'

Ali raised his eyebrows. 'Why?'

'He wanted to show me just how much damage opium is doing. It was quite horrifying.'

'I imagine it is,' Ali agreed. 'I have seen some of its effects.'

'Yet you sell it to these people.'

'I am a merchant, not a philosopher. For God's sake, I have traded in arms and ammunition. They kill more quickly than any drug. And people do not buy such things not to use them.'

'Only a profit matters, in your opinion.'

'Why, that is absolutely right. You'd do well to remember it.'

'I shall endeavour to,' Michael agreed, and fell silent. Clearly he was not going to change Ali Hammond's point of view. He rather felt his best bet would be to approach Clive Hammond himself, even if Clive must know the consequences of his trade. And perhaps the Princess Jalina; it was hard to conceive that so splendid a woman would knowingly be a part of so horrible a concern. And if he met with the same bland indifference? He preferred not to consider that, until it happened.

Meanwhile he was in a hurry to regain the ship, and be away, and look forward to seeing Malama again, and watching her smile, and perhaps forget some of the misery he had witnessed. And Alicia? Well, any pursuit of her

78

would have to await the outcome of his protests to Clive and Jalina.

They tied up at a small village for the night, alongside several other sampans, were fed by the crew, and turned in to sleep heavily. Next morning, Michael thought, they would gain the junk and be on their way. But just before dawn they were awakened by the clink of harnesses and the stamping of hooves. He sat up just as the sampan's captain knelt beside Ali, to mutter urgently in Chinese.

Ali replied, then turned to Michael. 'There are soldiers in the village, searching all the craft. We are going to get under way immediately.'

'Who are they looking for?'

'Ting Lo suspects it may be us. He says there have been rumours of some move against foreigners for some time. I wish to God someone had told us about it sooner.' He dragged on his boots, checked the priming of his pistols. Michael did the same and they crouched in the bottom of the boat while the crew prepared to cast off, a difficult business as there were now three other boats moored outside them. 'He should let them all go,' Ali growled savagely.

'But he has to make his way up and down this river all the time,' Michael reminded him. 'He can hardly antagonize his fellows.'

'What do I care about his fellows?' Ali snapped. 'Oh, Jesus Christ.'

The raft of sampans was swaying and heaving as the soldiers stamped across them, and the preparations were suspended. Ting Lo and his men might have been prepared to slip away if they could do so unnoticed; they were not prepared openly to defy the mighty Manchu bannermen. Voices sounded very loud above them, and Ali cursed again. 'The rat is betraying us. We must make a run for it, Michael.'

'Would it not be best to surrender?'

'To these scoundrels? We'd be better off dead. Come on, now.' He leapt to his feet and Michael followed his example, heart wildly pounding, sleepy brain still not quite comprehending the catastrophe which was overtaking them. Ali reached the narrow deck which ran round the well of the sampan, levelled his first pistol and fired. There was a cry and a splash as someone went overboard, and Michael, cautiously pushing his head out of the well, saw that several dark figures were on the sampan moored between them and the bank; even in the darkness their swords gleamed.

Ali meanwhile had leapt on to a boat which had moored outside them. One of the crew tried to grapple him, and he struck down with his empty pistol to send the fellow tumbling into the hold. Michael gained the deck in his turn, heard shouts as he stepped on to the next boat. 'Shoot the bastards!' Ali bellowed, discharging his second pistol. Michael turned to face their assailants, levelled his pistol, and was hit between the shoulder blades by the Chinese sailor, emerging from the well. He fell to his knees, the pistol exploding harmlessly. Panting for breath, he looked to Ali for aid. Ali hesitated for a moment, stared at the advancing Manchus, back at Michael again, then turned and dived over the side into the swift-flowing river. Michael gasped in disgust, but before he could regain his feet the soldiers were upon him, seizing his arms and legs, his hair and his clothing, driving the breath from his body with the fury of their assault. He tried to fight them and throw himself overboard as Ali had done, but there were too many of them, and he was dragged, being bumped unceremoniously, across the various boats to the shore, into an immense hubbub of noise and excitement. Thrown to the ground, he was surrounded by eager people, all anxious to show their enmity for the 'foreign devil' by kicking or stamping at him. He tried to protect himself but had his arms seized and twisted behind his back and there secured, so that he was unable to stop the blows raining upon him. The kicks, accompanied by the swirling dust, had him choking and he felt very close to death when the commander of the bannermen returned with his men from his apparently fruitless search for Ali, and drove the people away.

Michael was dragged to his feet and pushed and prodded towards the waiting horses. He supposed he was going to be given a mount, but instead his hands were brought forward again, secured at the wrists, and then tied with a length of line to one of the bannermen's saddles. The cavalcade set off, while Michael ran behind, or fell to be dragged over the uneven ground.

The nightmare intensified as they made their way back to Canton, a journey which took three days. He lost all feeling in his arms, while his legs and thighs and belly were a constant torment of exhausted muscles and lacerated flesh – he had no idea whether or not he was still a whole man. He was fed only once a day, when the soldiers stopped for the night; then a bowl of water was held to his lips and a few handfuls of rice were thrust down his throat. When his escort slept, he remained with his wrists tied to the saddle and one foot attached to a stake in the ground, so that he was utterly helpless. He was given no opportunity to relieve himself and grew steadily more filthy, although as his clothes were in any event ripped to shreds and soaked in mud and horse dung it hardly mattered.

Even worse than his personal misery was the humiliation of passing through the various villages which lay along the riverbank, when men and women, children and dogs turned out to jeer and laugh at him, and poke at him with sticks; they might hate and fear the Manchu, but they were eager to show their loyalty when the occasion arose. Michael could not imagine any human being wishing to treat another quite so barbarously, realized why Ali had been prepared to sacrifice him and risk drowning rather than submit, and indeed prayed for death or the relief of a prolonged faint himself – but he was not the fainting kind, and his constitution was too strong to be defeated even by such an ordeal.

Nor could his mind accept defeat. He had friends in Canton, he knew. Teng Hu, and Hung Hsiu-ch'uan . . . but would they lift a finger to help him? Would they be able to? Or were they not themselves perhaps arrested for having shown him hospitality? And what indeed was the reason for his arrest? It could only be connected with the opium they had smuggled into the country. Then he tried to take refuge in the memory of everyone saying how the British were determined that the trade would continue. He was British. He could claim the protection of that mighty symbol of power, the Union Jack, and indeed there were sufficient British merchants living outside Canton to effect his rescue, surely.

That hope ended when he was dragged through the streets of Canton itself, taken inside the walls before a jeering crowd, and thrust into a cell beneath the Commissioner's palace – because already there were a dozen Englishmen.

They had apparently all been arrested on the orders of Commissioner Lin on the same night, which meant that the others had already spent three nights in confinement. They had been beaten and humiliated, but to a lesser extent than Michael, and did their best to care for him when he was thrown into their midst. They were all terribly afraid, although the older men attempted to maintain some confidence. Lin had undoubtedly committed an act of war, they asserted, and with their arrest he had seized and burned some twenty thousand chests of opium from warehouses outside the city. 'Mark my words,' said William Parker, the senior merchant, 'he will pay for this with his head. Undoubtedly he has acted without the authority of the Emperor. And when our people make remonstrances, oh, indeed, he will lose his head.'

'Supposing we are alive to see it happen,' sighed the Reverend Small. 'We must pray.'

They did so, regularly, to no great avail, while with every day their misery grew. The cell was small, and they occupied every inch of it. It was below the ground, all but the last twelve inches, which was composed of a grating looking out on to a central courtyard. This was their only glimpse of the outside world, as well as their only source of fresh air, but it was also a permanent reminder of the horrors which might yet lie ahead of them. For it was where the punishments and executions were carried out, with a terrifying nonchalance on the part of both gaolers and sufferers. Michael lost track of the number of men, and women, who were dragged across the beaten earth courtyard from one of the other cells which surrounded it, and made to kneel at the stone block which occupied the centre, while the executioner held their pigtails with one hand and struck off their heads with a single blow of the huge sword he held in the other. They seldom protested, or made any sign that they were even afraid, but accepted their fates with silent resignation; Michael did not suppose he would do as well.

Then there were the wretches sentenced to the bastinado, and held naked on the ground by four men while two more belaboured their buttocks with long canes; no great power was put into the blows, but they were continuous, one after the other, for sometimes more than an hour, and it was not long before the victims were screaming and shrieking their pain and despair as their flesh was rhythmically destroyed. More than once the victim died; invariably they were unconscious when the punishment ceased.

The most terrible moment came, about a week after Michael's return to Canton, on the morning when he gazed at Teng Hu himself, together with his wife and daughters, being dragged across the compound to the block. Their hair dishevelled, their bodies half naked, bruised and cut, the young girls could not restrain their tears as the Manchu guardsmen jeered at their deformed feet. One died in the act of screaming for mercy, her mouth gaping open as the executioner threw her head aside. Teng and his wife died with all the dignity they could muster, yet Michael was left with a retching stomach as he waited for Hung Hsiu-ch'uan to be dragged out in turn.

But he was not, and neither were any of the English. Commissioner Lin had apparently not yet made up his mind what to do with his foreign prisoners . . . or he might equally have forgotten their existence. They were fed twice a day, water and rice, and left to themselves. Lack of exercise, bad food, filth and lice, fleas and untreated sores, soon turned them into living skeletons, and the arrival of the monsoon rains – the first real indication that they had been imprisoned for several months – compounded their misery as the water poured from the courtyard through the bars to inundate the cells to a depth of several feet, so that they were forced to remain standing until the flood subsided. In his more rational moments Michael understood that they were probably experiencing approximately the same conditions as obtained in the opium den Hung had shown him – without the benefits of being in a poppy-induced dream. And, as they had all been concerned in bringing the dreadful substance into the country, did they not deserve their fates?

He could find little in common with his fellow sufferers. He was in any event the stranger, as they had all known each other before being imprisoned. But he was also the outsider, mentally as well as physically. For he was not only Roman Catholic and Irish with it, he made the mistake of expressing his half-formed opinion – that they might be receiving their just deserts – on his first day in the cell, and received cold stares followed by total ostracism. To the others the Chinese were scoundrels, who had dared to lay hands upon Englishmen, and who would thus surely suffer as soon as those at 'home' learned of the outrage.

Michael was content to be left to himself, to endure the misery in introspective reflection. No doubt the others also had things to dream about, but he suspected his were the most real as he remembered the sweetly soft body of Wu Yei nestling against his, and before her the even more passionate adoration of Malama, and translated them both into the glowing white body which was surely Alicia Hammond's possession. He wondered if Wong Sung would have had the sense to sail away when his captain did not return. Either way, news of what had happened in Canton would filter down to Singapore, and the women would weep, Alicia for her brother, Malama for himself. But at least she was safe in the household of the Princess Jalina; he did not doubt she would be well cared for.

And he would never see her again. That became more and more certain as week followed week and there was no sign of release or even of their being put on trial. Spirits, reasonably buoyant at first, began to dwindle, and the coming of the monsoon proved too much for them; they began to die. The first corpse, that of a young lad who had been a bookkeeper with Mr Parker's firm, was viewed with indifference by the guards, although they did drag him away. When however the following week two more men just stopped breathing, the prisoners were visited by a senior official, who wore heavy silk and held a handkerchief to his nose while gazing in distaste at the huddled filth in front of him. That day their food ration was increased and for the first time in months they were given meat to eat, although their teeth and gums were so reduced they could hardly chew. Then they were taken outside and made to walk; only Michael succeeded in doing this without repeatedly falling down. The following week they were again led outside, their hands manacled, and informed, through the Reverend Small, whose Chinese was fluent, that they were being taken away to another prison. Their removal was obviously to be secret, for it occurred in the middle of the night. They were placed in a closed wagon, as walking was clearly impossible, and driven through the sleeping city and out on to a road which bumped away from the houses.

It was impossible to tell where they were going, but just to be away from the foetid atmosphere of the cell and the courtyard was a tremendous relief. Michael was at the very rear of the cart, and for all the bouncing and jolting he lay back and inhaled the fresh air and could almost feel the strength returning to his limbs. As to the rest of him he did not dare consider the true state of his health any more than he dared consider the fate which they might soon be facing. But he did not suppose they were intended to die, as when the cart stopped, at dawn, they were again given meat with their rice and water, and then allowed to sleep for a couple of hours before their escort got moving again.

'Mark my words,' Reverend Small said. 'There have been representations.'

'Well, I hope we are not being sent all the way to Peking in this contraption,' Mr Parker muttered.

'We are probably being taken down to the coast,' Small said.

Michael did not enter into the conversation, because he would have had to dampen their hopes; he could tell from the sun that they were travelling north, not east.

That night they stopped on the road itself rather than at a village, and it seemed to him that their escort, a squad of twelve bannerman and a captain, were uneasy. Extra guards were posted, and the captain spent a lot of time gazing at the trees which clustered to either side. With justification, for Michael was awakened by a sudden flurry of sound in the middle of the night, a hiss of arrows followed almost immediately by a clash of steel.

'We are attacked,' Reverend Small said, excitedly and unnecessarily.

'Robbers, do you suppose?' Parker whispered.

'Robbers would never attack an imperial caravan,' objected another man.

'Then who?' Small asked, almost plaintively. Because by now it was obvious that they were about to change gaolers. The noise outside the wagon had risen to a crescendo of shouting and cries of pain, but was now dwindling, and triumphant voices were accumulating around the wagon. Then the flap at the rear was thrown up and Michael found himself gazing into the face of Hung Hsiu-ch'uan.

4

The Vengeance of the Lion

'Hung!' Michael shouted. 'By God, it is good to see you.'

'It is my father's will,' Hung replied. 'Come, let us be away from here.'

The escort had all been killed, some clearly after surrendering, and Hung was accompanied by a large band of mounted men. The rescued men were placed behind various of the horsemen, and carried away into the hills. They travelled indeed for several days to reach what Hung considered safety, in the mountainous region west of Canton. It was an exhausting journey for men in such a debilitated state, but with every day, as they were fed proper food and given goat's milk to drink by the villagers with whom they encamped at night, they felt themselves becoming stronger, while their sores were carefully washed and treated.

'Your appearance was certainly like a miracle,' Michael confessed. From being the outsider of the group he was now the most important member, as he was Hung's friend, and indeed the young man made it perfectly plain that he had only been rescuing the Irishman, and that the rest just happened to be there. 'But I must admit I do not understand how it came about.'

'I have spies in Canton,' Hung told him. 'I know everything Commissioner Lin plans. I could not help you while you were inside the fortress, but as soon as I learned that he planned to move you from the city while he negotiates with the British, I recognized my opportunity.'

'The British are here?'

'There is a squadron of men-of-war in Hong Kong harbour,' Hung explained.

'Negotiating?'

'I do not know their real purpose. Because perhaps they do not know what really happened.'

'I must go to them,' Michael said.

'When you are strong enough for such a journey. I do not think they will go away.'

Michael knew he was right. But there was so much else to be understood. 'Your part in this confounds me,' he said.

'Why? I am but carrying out my father's wishes.'

Leading a band of outlaws? Michael wondered. Perhaps Jesus would have had more of an immediate impact had he been similarly aggressive from the start. 'But . . . you have given up your home?'

'My home is the heaven above. Oh, I have an earthly home, in Kwangsi, just as I have an earthly mother and father, and brothers and sisters. They are safe there. But my friends were all arrested – such as Teng Hu.'

'I saw Teng die,' Michael told him.

'Indeed has he gone to heaven,' Hung agreed, seemingly forgetting that he had once condemned him as evil. 'But I escaped, and realized that Lin's action was a sign from my father, that it was time to act. And that indeed he sent you to assist me.'

'Me?'

'You have survived Lin's executioners. And I have saved your life.'

'Believe me, Hung, I shall never forget that.'

'Then you will tell the British of this, when you go to them. Teng Hu has told me they are very strong men, whose numbers cover the earth. Is this true?'

'Well, not exactly. But they are very strong men.'

'Who will help me to drive out the Manchu, and restore China to the rule of the men of Han.' Which, as Michael knew, was how a true Chinese referred to his own people.

'Well . . .' Michael scratched his head. Hung had earlier indicated hatred for the British; clearly he was the most utter pragmatist. 'They are also the men who import the opium into China.'

'It is not for me always to understand the means my

father uses to achieve his ends,' Hung told him. 'It is sufficient that I know I must have outside help to overthrow the Ch'ing Dynasty and their followers. This help will come from the British, when you go to them and tell them that I and my people are ready to assist them to achieve this.'

'Your people?' Michael could not help but look around at the three score ragged horsemen who composed the outlaw band. They could hardly be described as even the nucleus of an army.

'There will be others,' Hung declared. 'Many others. My followers will be thicker than the leaves on the ground after an autumn gale. It is my destiny, my father's will, to restore China to the men of Han, and to rule it in his name. It will become the Kingdom of Celestial Peace, and be the envy of the world. That is my destiny. As it is your destiny to assist that to happen, Michael Harrington. I read that in your eyes, when first I saw you.'

It was difficult to argue with such certainty, and Michael discovered that Hung's followers appeared to share the conviction. Michael spoke with Hung's second-in-command, Feng Yun-shan, who, in contrast to his ethereal leader, was a practical, down-to-earth man with a gift of leadership; it was he, Michael discovered, who had organized the ambush of the caravan. He also had sufficient English, and Michael soon learned sufficient Chinese, for them to converse freely. Feng said, 'These are simple men, who have suffered much from the Manchu, and from those Chinese landlords who rob and beat them. They will follow any man who promises them respect and freedom from oppression.'

'But can so small a group ever hope to oppose the Manchu bannermen?'

'The group will grow,' Feng said. 'And these fearsome bannermen, they are not the same men who followed Nurhachi out of Manchuria two hundred years ago to destroy the Ming. They have grown soft with easy living, with unopposed conquest. The Emperor himself is a lecherous weakling. All we need is the help of an outside power, and we will push this rotten edifice to the ground.' He gazed at Michael. 'My master sees in you an extension of that power. You will not fail him.'

'By God I will not,' Michael agreed.

He was in a desperate hurry to get down to the coast, but Hung insisted that he should be fully restored to health and strength before he undertook such a journey. His friend's patience was as remarkable as his sublime faith that he was carrying out his father's will, and even when news came that the English squadron had sailed away, heading north, Hung prophesied that they would be back. Certainly it was heavenly to relax in the outlaw village, and be tended to by their women, amongst whom Michael was delighted to find little Wu Yei. She had escaped the general arrest of Teng Hu and his household and like all the other survivors fled to the comparative safety of Hung's camp, and was now eager to resume her ministrations to Michael.

'Enjoy her, she is yours,' Hung said carelessly.

Definitely, Michael concluded, if he had indeed studied the Bible, it had not been the New Testament.

Yet he could not help but be impressed with the loyalty shown to Hung by his followers, or the way in which he preached at them, again in Old Testament terms. His father was a god of wrath, of fire and brimstone, who would destroy all evil. That included not only the Manchu, who were evil by definition, but adulterers, murderers, robbers and opium smokers. Fortunately, not fornicators, Michael thought, as Wu Yei huddled close against him in terror as they listened to Hung making one of his speeches, her eager body entirely reassuring him that he had not after all been emasculated by his ill treatment at the hands of the Manchu.

'You have the oddest friend,' Reverend Small confessed. 'He quite frightens me. And yet, what a fruitful ground for the spread of the Word.'

'I would think carefully about that, if I were you,' Michael suggested, but Small merely gave him an old-fashioned look. And apparently determined to ignore his advice, for the next day Hung was angry:

'You will take that man with you when you leave here, Michael. He knows nothing of my father's intentions, and would pretend to do so. He is a fool.'

Winter came, and they huddled together in their huts as the snow clouded down. The world seemed to have receded from them, and although Hung continued to gain news from both Canton and the coast, there was none of the British. For the fugitives from Lin's wrath it was a trying time, which stretched on interminably, for apart from the real primitiveness of their life and surroundings, the discomforts of being always cold and never having quite sufficient to eat – while much of the food was of a variety strange to them – they were separated from all news of their loved ones or, it seemed, any prospect of regaining them. Michael could at least reflect that Malama would be well cared for, but it seemed an age since he had seen her laughing or pouting face, and he knew she would be distraught to learn of his death, for so it would certainly have been reported by Wong Sung – supposing he had managed to take the *Golden Dragon* to safety. As for Alicia, Michael could scarce remember what she looked like.

His own creature comforts were well looked after by Wu Yei, whom he almost came to regard as his wife: indeed, when in the spring it was clear that she was pregnant, he approached Hung and suggested that marriage might be a good thing. Hung however dismissed the idea. 'She is but a whore,' he pointed out. 'Enjoy her, and the child, if it pleases you. There is no need to undertake responsibility for them.' A decidedly unchristian point of view, Michael considered, when he had had more pleasure from this girl than from any other female in his life. But she also did not seem to expect anything more of him than the act of love. He had little use for Reverend Small, but yet felt called upon to discuss the situation with him, and was concerned to discover that the reverend gentleman held roughly the same view as did Hung.

'These people are heathen savages,' he pointed out. 'One could hardly consider a Christian marriage with them, Harrington. I mean, we . . . I mean, my colleagues, are all being cared for in a proper fashion by these itinerant females . . .'

'And is that not a Christian sentiment?' Michael asked.

'It is a human sentiment, on which Christianity has built a magnificent edifice,' Small said severely. 'And in this case, I very much fear, is encouraged by a very primitive lust on the part of these hoydens.'

'I do not see how you can call the Chinese primitive,' Michael argued. 'They were civilized when our ancestors were painting themselves blue.'

'But without the benefits of true religion,' Small declared triumphantly. 'We have long overtaken them.'

For all the horrors of the cell in Canton, Michael, who had heard of how unpleasant it could be in an English gaol, was not convinced. But there seemed nothing he could do about it, save smile at Wu Yei, which was all she wanted from him as her belly swelled, and then enjoy the laughing baby boy who was born in the summer.

For by now the return of the English squadron seemed a fantasy, and his colleagues were fast becoming as Chinese as possible, as their own clothes rotted away and they were forced into the loose blouse and trousers of their rescuers, while they all spoke Chinese, or at least, Cantonese, with some facility; Michael, his brain always active, had indeed progressed into Mandarin with the aid of Hung himself. Only the Reverend Small preserved the essential niceties of the English way of life, convening them to worship every Sunday. Michael attended, for all that he felt amongst devilish heathens, and even Hung sometimes appeared, although always with expressions of contempt.

Because Hung was in a perfectly happy frame of mind. Michael suspected that he had long wanted some event to force him into taking action, something he could assume was a sign from his 'father'. That it involved the British, to whom he looked for help in his fight against the Manchu, was all he could possibly have asked. This did not mean that he had to accept British sentiments regarding the religion he had adopted as his own, indeed he found their religious views wholly unacceptable. His was more than ever the Jehovah of the Old Testament, under whose auspices he intended to smite the Manchu hip and thigh; the preachings of Jesus he regarded as absurd.

With the coming of good weather Hung led his men down from the hills, accompanied by Michael, now entirely restored to health and strength, and carried out a series of raids on Manchu caravans, and 'reprisals' on those Chinese considered guilty of supporting the regime. The raids had a practical purpose, for although the village in which they had spent the winter had loyally supported him and his people, they had eaten the unhappy farmers almost to starvation by the time the snow melted, and it was very necessary to find food, and replacement arms, in a hurry. But it was also an excuse to extend the fame and terror of Hung's name. Again following the precepts of the Old Testament rather than the New Testament, he and his followers slaughtered without mercy. Michael had no reason to feel sympathetic towards any Manchu bannerman, and indeed, towards any Chinese landlord if the stories of their extortion were true – but his stomach turned as he saw men, once dignified and prosperous, being dragged to execution like so many cattle, while their women were raped and often executed as well, together with their children. Not that anything he could say had the slightest effect upon Hung's bloodthirsty vision of himself as the right arm of God.

And his tenets, or at least his revolutionary stand, began to attract adherents; his few score followers had swelled to several times that by the following winter. As if less than a thousand men could ever hope to oppose the Manchu bannermen in all their arrogance and power. But soon after Mr Small's celebration of their second Christmas since being rescued from Canton, word came from

93

the coast that the British squadron was back, in Hong Kong harbour.

Michael immediately made preparations to depart, but Small was the only other of the Englishmen to be allowed to accompany him. Hung was reassuring. 'They will be here when you return, with your soldiers,' he promised. 'And with arms and ammunition for my people. And with guns. Tell your people to give us cannon, and I will blow down the great gate in Peking itself.'

'One cannot help but wonder if he intends them as hostages,' Small muttered.

'I am quite sure he means them no harm,' Michael told him. He was more concerned with bidding farewell to Wu Yei and his son. But she too would be here when he returned. With the soldiers.

Then, accompanied by Feng and three others, their faces and arms stained yellow and wearing Chinese clothes, Michael and Reverend Small descended from the hills. The quickest way to Hong Kong was by the river, and to find a sampan it was necessary to return to Canton. Michael was aware of a distinct nervousness as he once again saw those high walls of such dreadful memory, but Hung had told the truth when he had claimed that the city was filled with his agents, and Feng safely guided them to the waterfront where a sampan was already waiting. Michael observed, however, that there were a great many more soldiers around than before, and that additional guns had been mounted in the embrasures on the walls, while to add to his fighting strength Commissioner Lin had summoned out his irregular forces, or Green Flags. Was the Commissioner preparing to defend himself against Hung, or the British?

The journey down the Pearl was also a simple matter, under Feng's expert guidance. There were several Chinese war junks on the river, but these paid no attention to the heavily laden sampan, one of many to be using the waterway. However, Feng was informed that no local craft were being allowed to pass the Bogue forts; the river was entirely closed to all traffic save the Manchu navy. This was reassuring, as it had to mean the British squadron was still in the vicinity. But it necessitated abandoning the sampan above the forts and making their way across country to the beaches to the east. This had to be done at night, because the coast was filled with Manchu bannermen and Green Flags. It was a matter of skulking from point to point, at times even crawling, and remaining hidden all day before resuming their journey in the dark.

At dawn on the second day they reached the secluded cove for which Feng had been searching, and again concealed themselves while a patrol of bannermen trotted up and down the beach. From their position they could look across at the islands, so close it seemed possible to swim the channel, and Michael was sure he could make out the mastheads of the warships. Feng meanwhile was negotiating with the local fishermen, and by nightfall had found one who was willing to ferry the two Britishers across after dark.

'Aren't you coming with us?' Michael demanded.

Feng shook his head. 'I have been away too long as it is. I must get back to Hung.' He gave a smile. 'Sometimes his enthusiasm outweighs his judgement. But we will be ready to cooperate with you when you take Canton.'

'Take Canton?' Michael scratched his head. 'It is a long way in from the sea.'

'The river can be ascended. You will show them how, Mr Harrington. And it is only by taking Canton itself, where the insult to your flag took place, that the power of the Manchu will be seen to be defeated. All else is but nothing.' He clasped Michael's hands. 'You will not fail us. I believe Hung is right when he says that you were sent by God to assist us.'

'Whose god, Feng?'

The Chinese smiled again. 'There is but one God, Mr Harrington. And he fights for us.'

'Strange people,' Reverend Small commented as they set out in their small boat under cover of darkness. 'I doubt

95

any admiral will wish to take his squadron ninety miles from the sea into the midst of a hostile land.'

'Then I must persuade him,' Michael said. 'As Feng points out, bombardment of a few coastal towns is not going to have any effect at all.'

'And you wish to assist this madman in bringing down the Manchu?' Small asked.

'Don't you?'

Small considered for a while, and then said, 'Let us hope *this* madman knows his business.'

For they were amongst the rocks and shoals that guarded the island harbour; and less than an hour later were being challenged by one of the guard frigates. The squadron consisted of no less than sixteen ships, of which six were of the line, and there were transports with some four thousand soldiers also on board. Late as it was, Michael and Small were taken to the flagship, the *Royal Oak*, and there met Captain Smallpiece, as well as Rear Admiral George Elliott, and General Sir Hugh Gough, commanding the soldiers. These dignitaries listened in silence as Small listed the outrages and horrors suffered by the prisoners, of which they had not previously been aware; the British presence had been established simply because it had been learned that all imports of opium had been stopped – the *Golden Dragon* had apparently regained Singapore with that news, and captained, remarkably, by Ali Hammond, who had indeed described Michael as dead.

'So it's right glad we are to see you alive, Mr Harrington,' Elliott remarked. 'And none the worse for your experience, eh? Now we must decide what's to be done. We've occupied Chusan island, and made a couple of other demonstrations, but these people don't seem to take much heed of such things.'

'With respect, sir,' Michael said. 'They would take heed were you to capture Canton itself.'

Elliott raised his eyebrows. 'I doubt that is practical, Harrington. That's a long, shallow river.'

'You can take your ships up, sir. I will pilot you.'

Elliott looked at Gough, who looked at Small. 'Can he, Mr Small?'

'I am no sailor, sir. Harrington is. But I would certainly like to teach those rascals a lesson.'

'I can also promise you the support of a considerable body of anti-Manchu Chinese, when you attack Canton,' Michael said eagerly.

'Can you now,' Elliott remarked with interest. 'I think we should take first things first. There are forts at the mouth of the river.'

'Yes, sir. The Bogue.'

'The fishermen I have interviewed have told me the estuary is encumbered with sandbanks.'

'There are passages through.'

'Which you know?'

'I have been through them.'

Elliott regarded him for several seconds, then he nodded. 'Very good, Mr Harrington. We shall assault those forts, under your pilotage. We will investigate them tomorrow. And when they are taken, we will consider our next move.'

Michael was elated, Small, for all his desire to be avenged on Lin, less sanguine. 'I hope you know what you do,' he remarked. 'You could be the cause of a great disaster.'

'I know what I do,' Michael told him. And it was what he wanted to, more than anything else in the world, more even than returning to Singapore. So Ali had escaped! There was a remarkable fellow. An utter scoundrel, but with talent. And now Malama, and Alicia, definitely thought him dead. But hadn't he recognized that probability over a year ago? Besides, now that Wu Yei was to all intents and purposes his wife . . . Alicia had been only a dream, and a brief one at that. And Malama? He would find her a good husband. Because his eventual return would be the greater triumph after having guided the British fleet to the sack of Canton. And launched Hung upon his ambitious dream. Certainly he felt no fear of the

97

morrow. He had survived too much to suppose he was going to fail now.

The next day Elliot took Michael with him on board a frigate for a reconnaissance of the river mouth. They approached close to the forts and were fired upon, but the shots were wide and the British ship made no response. Elliott studied both the fortifications and the river through his glass, then remarked, very much as Small had done. 'I hope you know your business, Mr Harrington. However, we shall approach this matter with caution. They do not appear to have fortified the beaches.'

'They are regularly patrolled.'

'Patrols we can deal with,' Gough declared. 'Just set us ashore, George.'

It was to be an amphibious assault. Next morning at dawn the fleet was under way, the frigates guarding the transports in close to the shore while the army was ferried across. The ships of the line took up their positions opposite the forts and began a bombardment. It was a majestic and compelling experience, as the broadsides were fired with total precision, all thirty-odd guns in each discharging at the same instant, to wreath the ships in smoke. When that cleared the clouds of dust and rubble rising from the forts could be seen, so that Captain Smallpiece slapped himself on the thigh with glee. 'I doubt a land assault will be necessary, sir.'

'Don't you believe it,' Elliott said. 'Those men are well sheltered.' And even as he spoke the batteries on the land replied, although their shot was invariably wide or short. 'Poor powder,' the admiral remarked.

Michael was thrilled, just to be standing on the snow-white decks of the huge eighty-gun ship, surrounded by the blue-jacketed tars and in the company of the red-coated marines drawn up in the waist waiting to play their part, to be looking up at the billowing sails and listen to the orders, as having passed the forts the squadron put about to resume the bombardment on the other tack. If he still wore his Chinese blouse and loose trousers, he could readily imagine himself in the smart blue tail coat and white breeches of an English officer. This was the life to which he had been born; he had been foolish to let himself be sidetracked.

His elation grew half an hour later as, after the squadron had made its second pass at the forts, there was a cry of 'sail ho' from the masthead, and they saw, emerging from the river mouth, four war junks.

'Fools,' Elliott growled. 'It will be a massacre.'

And so it proved. The British three-deckers turned their guns on the approaching Chinese, hardly smaller in size but much less well armed or manoeuvrable. In a few broadsides the Chinese squadron was destroyed, three of their ships shot to pieces and sinking, the fourth, dismasted, desperately regaining the apparent safety of the river, towed by sampans.

The sea between the British squadron and the forts was littered with wreckage and struggling bodies, and Elliott magnanimously ceased firing and stood off while the Chinese rescued their sailors. While Michael's heart swelled again to be a part, if even a supernumerary part, of such power and majesty.

But he was out to prove his worth. By nightfall the army was ashore and prepared to attack, having apparently encountered very little opposition from the bannermen. 'Now we must prepare to force the river,' Admiral Elliott declared. 'Mr Harrington, while I have every confidence in your good faith and indeed your ability, I still am not prepared to risk one of Her Majesty's ships to a failure of memory. You will sound the way and chart it, if you please.'

Which was actually somewhat more than Michael had expected, considering that it would have to be done under the guns of the forts. But there was nothing for it. Two boats were lowered, twelve seamen took their places in each with a midshipman on the tiller, and Michael knelt in the bow of the lead boat with a petty officer beside him to cast the line. The sun was rising rapidly but the day was still cool as they pulled away from the side of the flagship and into the estuary. For a while they proceeded in silence save for the dipping of the oars and the cries of the seabirds; the Chinese were obviously unsure what they were about. Then the first gun fired, followed immediately by others, and the water became dotted with plumes of white. It was the first time Michael had ever actually been under fire, and he was relieved when the fleet began to reply, causing the Chinese shooting to slacken. Even so it was hot work, although taken with the utmost calm by the seamen. Michael directed the petty officer, who cast the lead and reported the depths to the midshipman, who took the necessary bearing with his sextant and compass and jotted it down on his pad, while at his signal the boat behind dropped marker buoys attached to small anchors to delineate the channel. This way they actually proceeded past the forts and into the river itself, where they saw a sampan bearing down on them, filled with armed and gesticulating men.

'That will do for today,' Midshipman Crane announced, and put the tiller over. 'Pull lads, pull!'

The seamen were still fresh, as their previous progress had been slow. Now they gave way with all their strength and raced back out into the estuary. The sampan followed, but in turn withdrew when the fleet, which had already begun to venture into the marked channel, observed what was happening and sent a couple of shots close to it. Remarkably, having survived for several hours while moving slowly through the water, now that they were hurrying the first boat was itself all but hit. A shot plunged into the sea right beside them, snapping off four oar blades and tumbling them all about like ninepins, while water cascaded over the side. But Crane, who was only eighteen, immediately had them in hand, commanding the broken oars to be discarded, sufficient brought over from the starboard side to balance the boat, and the four men left oarless to commence bailing until they regained the flagship.

Elliott was impressed by the passage found, and the assault was ordered immediately. The signal guns – small-bore cannon whose light report was unlike any heavy guns

– were fired, and the army moved forward, their red jackets clearly visible amidst the green of the trees and bushes behind the beach as the ships approached the shore. Soon it was necessary to cease firing for fear of hitting their own people, but as the squadron entered the channel they found other targets both in the sampans clustered in the river and the squadrons of bannermen who could be seen galloping their horses towards the scene of conflict. Presumably not all the sampans were being used by the military but they all suffered beneath the bombardment, while the unfortunate bannermen, and their horses, were scattered by the flailing shot; Michael watched in a mixture of horror and awe the destruction of men and animals being wrought. Once inside the river Elliott signalled his ships to anchor, and the boats were put down to ferry the marines ashore for a frontal assault on the left-hand fortress. The entire afternoon was an explosion of sound and violence as the cannon boomed, the muskets cracked, the marines and sailors and soldiers cheered, the Chinese shrieked defiance, the clouds of smoke rolled skywards, the ships trembled to their broadsides, and men died. While Admiral Elliott and his officers walked slowly to and fro on the quarterdeck, observing and remarking.

'Great stuff,' Small declared. 'Oh, great stuff. Smite the heathen hip and thigh.'

Michael presumed that even Hung Hsiu-ch'uan would have appreciated him at that moment.

In any event, the battle was quickly won. The redcoats on the right, the marines on the left, forced their way into the now sorely battered forts, and the even more battered defenders either surrendered or fled into the surrounding countryside. The bannermen, met by rolling volleys of musketry after having survived the flying cannon balls, accompanied their flight, and the Union Jack flew to left and right by dusk while the victors cheered themselves hoarse.

The forts captured, Michael had assumed the fleet would

immediately continue its way up the river, but that was not the Navy's way. The dead – there were only a dozen or so of these – were buried, the wounded tended to, dispatches were sent, and Michael was put back to work charting the river. When Elliott did decide to take his ships upstream it was very slowly and carefully, anchoring every couple of hours to reconnoitre and allow Michael to proceed with his chart work. Not that they encountered any opposition before they approached Canton itself, which was not until mid-May, nearly three months after the taking of the forts. Then the lookouts again shouted their warning, and they beheld, bearing down on them on the current, several blazing rafts.

'Fire ships, by God,' remarked Captain Smallpiece.

'In these narrow waters, they could be dangerous,' Reverend Small muttered at Michael.

But the Navy were unconcerned. Boats were immediately put down to pull up to the drifting infernos, grapples were thrown, and the rafts dragged on to the mudflats to burn themselves out, while a couple of broadsides sufficed to clear the banks of the bannermen who had gathered there in the hopes of at last gaining a victory.

Immediately below Canton they were visited by Feng Yun-shan who wished to be informed of their plans. Michael explained who Feng was, but Elliott had become sceptical. 'Mr Small has told me that these fellows are mere bandits, and are not real Christians at all,' he complained. 'Ask this chap how many men he will bring to the assault.'

Michael put the question, and to his dismay Feng replied, 'My master will employ the forces of his father in this matter.'

Clearly he had been told what to say by Hung, but Elliott was even less impressed, especially when he discovered who Hung's 'father' was. 'I think we can do without any heavenly assistance, Mr Harrington,' he decided. 'Tell your friend that I will interview his master after I have taken Canton.'

Feng was obviously offended, and left without further

comment, but Elliott's confidence was not misplaced. Once again an amphibious assault was launched on the outer forts with total success, and when they had fallen the commander of the garrison sent out a flag of truce and asked for surrender terms. In fact the Manchu's efforts to defend themselves would have been hampered by the crowds of terrified Cantonese who thronged the streets, while an English assault would undoubtedly have caused a massacre. 'These people appear to be reasonably sensible after all,' Elliott commented, and smiled at his officers. 'Well, gentlemen, I think we have proved our point, eh? Now, Mr Harrington, will you send to your religious friend and regain those of our people he still holds, and we can be away from this benighted spot.'

Michael did not understand. 'Do you mean, having come up here and seized the city, that you just mean to sail away again, sir?'

'I certainly do not mean to remain here,' Elliott told him. 'I was sent to punish these people for their insult to the flag and to reinstate the opium trade. This I have done. I do not think that after today's work they will dare prevent our merchantmen from ascending this river with whatever goods they please. Oh, there will have to be an indemnity.' He gave a cold smile. 'We will make them ransom their city or we will lay it in ashes. I should think something in the nature of a million pounds will make them understand they cannot insult British citizens with impunity.'

'With respect, sir, they will merely pay the ransom, hate you more than ever, and wait for their opportunity to avenge themselves.'

'You mistake the situation, my dear fellow. Our quarrel is with the Emperor, in Peking. What we have done here will show him that we mean business. It is my intention now to take this fleet north to the Gulf of Pechli. When he learns what has occurred here, Emperor Hsuan Tsung will soon come to heel, and make sure nothing like this happens again.'

Michael wanted to tear his hair. 'Believe me, sir,' he

said, 'the Emperor is as much interested in what happens here as on the moon. Nor would it matter if he did care. The Manchu empire is falling apart. Each provincial viceroy regards himself as an independent monarch, and acts the part. Your only hope of a lasting peace with China is to overthrow the Manchu completely.'

'Now you are raving,' Elliott replied bluntly. 'With a few thousand men?'

'It can be done,' Michael insisted. 'This man, my friend Hung Hsiu-ch'uan, is determined to do it, to destroy the Ch'ing. All he needs is our help. British support, British arms and ammunition, British artillery, and he will raise the entire south. That will be the mainspring of your victory, and the certainty that you will have a ruler in China who will be your friend, the friend of Great Britain.'

Elliott gazed at him. 'You have a great deal of confidence in this Hung fellow,' he remarked at last.

'He saved my life.'

'That does not mean he is anything more than a bandit. I can tell you that it is not the purpose of Her Majesty's Government either to arm foreign bandits or to provoke a civil war in a foreign country. We are in dispute with the Emperor of China. We are well on the way to settling that dispute in our favour. That is what we are about and that is what we shall accomplish.' He pointed. 'And don't start any talk about this fellow being the right hand of God. That is utter blasphemy and you should be ashamed of yourself for even saying it.' His tone softened. 'Believe me, Harrington, I am exceedingly appreciative of your efforts and your skill as a navigator. I both intend to make more use of them and to see that you are rewarded. But it would be best if you left the conduct of your country's affairs to those best qualified to handle them. Now go and get your fellow prisoners back.'

Hung and his people, together with Feng, were assembled only a few miles beyond the surrendered city, awaiting the order to ride to the attack. There were some seven hundred of them, primitively armed, to be sure, but desperate to play their part, and not the least pleased to learn that they had no part to play.

'As I told you, my people are strong men,' Michael said to Hung. 'They are used to fighting, and conquest.'

'They are agents of the Devil,' Hung remarked. 'But they are our allies, and they have gained the victory. I salute them, Michael. Now take me to their commander, that we may lay plans for the conquest of the Manchu.'

Michael sighed and explained the situation.

'He will not fight with us?' Hung was aghast.

'You must understand, Hung, that to my people China is a remote and perhaps unimportant land. This admiral was sent to redress a wrong, nothing more than that. He intends to force a further surrender from the Emperor, but once that is done he will sail away.'

'China is the centre of the universe,' Hung declared.

'I may agree with you. My admiral does not.'

'And can he not see that his defeat of the Ch'ing will be more readily achieved with my help?'

'He does not see how seven hundred men can assist him, several thousand miles from Peking.'

'Your admiral is a fool,' Hung declared angrily. 'Had I those cannon, those muskets and bayonets that I asked for, thousands would flock to my banners. Will he not give me those, at least?'

Michael sighed again, and shook his head.

'Truly, those who say the foreign devils are not to be trusted are right,' Feng growled.

'I did my best,' Michael assured him.

Hung embraced him. 'I am sure you did, Michael. I did not include you in my condemnation. But your people are now my enemies. And you say they will insist on the trade in opium being resumed? You will not permit this, surely.'

'I will not take part in it,' Michael promised. 'But I alone cannot stop it.'

'Nonetheless, you will remain true to me. This I knew from the moment I saw you. And you may tell your admiral that with or without his aid I will still conquer this land, and turn it into my Kingdom of Heavenly Peace. And when I do that, he and his people, and his tradesmen and his opium, will no longer be welcome in China. Only you will be welcome here, Michael. I would be a happy man were you to agree to remain, now.'

Michael was embarrassed. 'I have things to do, Hung.'

'Of course. You must oppose this trade in opium. But you will return to me. This I know. Now, take your fellows and go.'

'And my woman and her son.'

Hung frowned. 'It were best she remain with me.'

Michael stared at him. 'Is she not my woman? You gave her to me. And she is the mother of my son.'

'She is my woman, of whom I gave you the use. She will await your return. As will your son. But she, all of these people, are mine, to lead to their destiny, Michael. Which is my destiny also. And yours.'

Michael could not believe his ears. 'You will make me leave my son behind?'

'I will care for him as my own. But you will leave him, Michael.' He smiled. 'That way I know you will come back.'

Hung had absolutely no doubts that whatever he did was the right thing, the only correct action. Even when he was manipulating people's lives. Michael was very tempted to call on Elliott for help, but reflected that it would hardly be forthcoming on his behalf; the admiral had made it perfectly plain that he had accomplished what he had set out to do. Besides, almost immediately an insidious reaction set in. Michael did have a great deal to do with his life, a prospect of some advancement with the support of the admiral's report on his efficiency and skill as a pilot, a war yet to be fought even though none had been declared, and indeed the Chinese were quite unaware that this was the British intention – at least in Peking. Michael could not possibly reach for the heights he saw ahead with a native mistress and a half-caste little boy in tow. Nor could he ever take them back to Singapore and hope to woo Alicia Hammond, which, as a returned hero from the war, he might now be able to accomplish – supposing she was not already married. Even while opposing her father's trading plans? But he still regarded Clive Hammond as a potential ally.

Thus he was, after all, a wretch, he reflected as he said farewell to Wu Yei and little Hung Cho – for Hung Hsiu-ch'uan had insisted the boy take his own name – and promised them he would soon return, while feeling as much of a wretch as when he had made a similar promise to Malama. He might be going to be able to keep that promise at last – but not in the manner she had anticipated. As for Wu Yei, he doubted he would ever see her again, after having shared his life with her for close on two years. Yet she was less tearful than he had feared. No doubt she had always known – perhaps she had always been told – that he would one day abandon her and return to his own people, and she was not the least concerned that the upbringing of their son would be her responsibility alone; she was a fervent admirer of Hung and had no doubt she would be well cared for. So Michael held her in his arms, and kissed the boy on the forehead – it was impossible to see the slightest resemblance to himself in the tight little yellow features – and then clasped Hung's hand, and Feng's as well.

'Until we meet again,' Hung said. 'There are great things in store for us.'

The Englishmen were waiting for him, delighted to be at last released. 'A strange fellow,' Parker remarked. 'There were times when he was almost convincing. I suspect, like most prophets, he will end upon the gallows. Whether what he preaches survives him, why, that will have to await the judgement of history.'

The citizens of Canton duly paid their ransom, although with every expression of hatred, both Chinese and Manchu, that Michael had anticipated, and the fleet took its leave. But if Michael thought that he was immediately to be returned to Singapore he was mistaken. When Elliott had said he intended to make further use of his talents he had meant it. He had been impressed by the size and safety of Hong Kong harbour. 'I have been considering your opinions, Harrington,' he remarked. 'It seems to me that it may indeed be necessary for us to maintain a perpetual presence in these waters to remind these villains to treat our people with respect. To do that we need a snug haven for our ships. Singapore is too far away for immediate response to any act of aggression. But here . . .' He looked around at the islands. 'Some forts on those hills, and a couple on the mainland, and our ships would be as secure as at Spithead.'

'In a foreign land, sir?'

'Oh, we shall make the cession of this place, and a suitable mainland area, part of the indemnity we shall require at the peace table. Now what I wish you to do is carry out an extensive survey of the harbour.'

Like Hung he seemed to have no doubts as to the outcome of the war. Michael was given a temporary rank of lieutenant and command of a sloop with a crew of forty men to carry out his work; he even received a uniform and pay. While the fleet awaited replenishments of ammunition from India. This did not arrive until just before the onset of the monsoon season, which meant that further movement was delayed for several months. And longer than that, as the winter set in with unusual violence. It was a grim time for both soldiers and seamen, who suffered from lack of activity and the inevitable epidemics which swept large numbers of men cooped up together for long periods.

For Michael it was a particularly frustrating time. He had completed his survey of the harbour by the summer, and had looked forward to accompanying the fleet north. Now, as he kicked his heels in Hong Kong, he first of all tried to get in touch with Hung, and through him with Wu Yei and the boy, but it was impossible. The bannermen had resumed their control of the countryside with the departure of the British fleet – although they never attempted an assault upon Hong Kong or the British battery erected on the mainland – and the peasants with whom Michael spoke told him that the bandit Hung Hsiu-ch'uan and his men had fled into the mountains. No doubt to disappear for ever, Michael thought.

So instead he wrote letters to his mother to reassure her that he was still alive, and to Brother William to inform him that he had, after all, found a place in the Navy, even if temporarily – he had already decided that as regards pay and conditions he was better off in the merchant service. With this in mind he also wrote to Singapore. He sent letters to Clive Hammond, Ali, and Teng Lee, informing them of his situation, and Teng of his cousin's death, and that he hoped to return to their employment at the conclusion of the war. In his letter to Teng was a note to the Princess Jalina, for her to read to Malama, in which he expressed his hopes that she was being a good girl and progressing well. Finally, daringly, he wrote to Alicia, a formally polite letter, regretting that she had condemned him without reason, hoping that the princess had by now restored his reputation in her eyes, and begging her permission to call upon her when next he was in Singapore.

It was the following spring before any replies were received, and to his delight they were distinctly positive. William wrote to congratulate him, and said how pleased their old mother was that he was at last leading a regular life. So, needless to say, was Henrietta, and Florence sent her very kindest regards. More important, Clive Hammond wrote to say that he was delighted to learn of his survival, and the work he was doing for the Navy, and to assure him that a berth, and probably a command, awaited him when he returned. Teng Lee did not write himself, having apparently been gravely shocked by the news of the destruction of the last remaining members of his Chinese family, but the princess did so, telling him that Malama was grown into a fine lady, who anxiously awaited her 'father's' return; to Michael's amazement there was a shy note written by the girl herself, Jalina having also attended to her schooling, in which she expressed her everlasting devotion to him. His heart swelled, as he thought of that slender little creature who had so strangely become a part of his life.

There was also a formal note from Alicia Hammond: 'Miss Hammond wishes to assure Mr Harrington that she is now in full possession of the facts surrounding his relationship with the Indian maiden and therefore withdraws her condemnation of him. Should Mr Harrington at any future date find himself in Singapore and wish to call, then she would be pleased to receive him.'

She was not, at any rate, married, he thought triumphantly. And all his life lay ahead of him. So he had fathered a son, and lived for a while an existence he had never supposed possible. That needed to be forgotten, as he sought his future. If only the war would end.

In fact it did, with surprising suddenness, in that same spring of 1842. Admiral Elliott, who was ailing like so many of his men, was replaced as commander-in-chief and plenipotentiary by Sir Henry Pottinger. Immediately the fleet and the army felt the impulse of his vigour, Hong Kong was abandoned save for a garrison, and the fleet sailed north, bombarding several coastal towns and eventually arriving off the mouth of the great Yangste Kiang, and the teeming city of Shanghai which made Canton look like a village. This fell to an assault, and after Michael had charted the river, the fleet actually ascended to the old imperial capital of Nanking, which also fell to a bombardment. After this the Chinese surrendered, and plenipotentiaries were sent down from Peking to conclude a treaty. Michael was one of the principal interpreters at the various meetings which went on for weeks, becoming impressed with the stoic indifference to their defeat shown by the Manchu negotiators. For the British obtained all they wanted, an indemnity of some five million pounds, the opening of several ports – known as 'treaty ports' – for their trade, the right to establish themselves in such ports, the right to enter the walled cities of Canton and Peking, the right to maintain an ambassador in Peking, the right to import as much opium as they wished, the rights to extraterritoriality, which meant that British subjects could only be arrested by British authorities, and tried and sentenced by them, and, the biggest prize of all, the perpetual lease of the island of Hong Kong, and the strip of land facing it on the mainland. 'Truly it has been a veritable triumph,' Michael wrote his brother. 'One I had never expected to be accomplished so easily. It is remarkable that our tiny nation can so dictate terms to the rulers of many millions of people.'

For his visit to Nanking and his observation of the surrounding country left him in no doubt that here in Central China, and therefore no doubt even more in the north, the Manchu still ruled with all their erstwhile majesty, or that they intended to restore their old authority in the south as well. Equally he realized that Elliott had been quite right in considering that to overthrow such a well-entrenched power would be a task beyond the resources of Great Britain, and certainly of an itinerant bandit chieftain. He wished there was some way he could let Hung know what he was up against, but there wasn't, and now he had his own life to attend to. With the official ending of the war his engagement with the Royal Navy was terminated, and although he was offered a commission as a cartographer he declined and was given a passage back to Singapore.

Again it was necessary to await the end of the 1842 monsoon before he could make the journey, and it was thus October when he once more sailed through the Dragon's Teeth, on board a sloop-of-war on passage to Calcutta. He had last been here in February 1839. Three of the longest and most important years of his life had elapsed. And yet, nothing in Singapore need have changed. No one recognized him as he went ashore wearing his naval uniform, and now, with his back pay in his pocket, he could hire a phaeton for the ride up the hill. But first of all he called at the warehouse of Hammond and Teng, where he was shown into the office of Clive Hammond himself.

'Michael Harrington!' Hammond came round the desk to shake his hand. 'But it is good to see you back. We have been reading about your exploits in the newspapers. Teng,' he called. 'Teng. You remember Harrington.'

The door to the adjoining office opened and in came, not Teng Lee as Michael expected, but Teng Tang, who gravely shook his hand. 'My brother has been called to his ancestors,' he explained. 'The shock of what happened to Teng Hu was too great for him, and he was an old man.'

'I am sorry to hear that,' Michael said, suddenly very anxious. 'The Princess Jalina?'

'The princess experiences honourable widowhood,' Teng Tang explained.

'Ah,' Michael said.

'Of course, you are concerned about the Indian girl,' Clive Hammond said, and slapped Michael on the back. 'She has become quite a young lady. You must set about finding a husband for her, Harrington. As we must discuss a berth for you. Ali is away at sea right this minute, and we have placed him in charge of seagoing appointments, but I know there is a vacancy in the command roster. The old *China Star*. Chow Te wishes to retire. So why should you not take her?'

'I would be honoured, sir.'

'Splendid. As I understand that you now speak fluent Chinese, and that we are now permitted to trade along the entire coastline, you will be invaluable to us.'

'Thank you, sir.' Michael had already decided against making any representations about the opium trade until he was fully re-established. And he had an idea how that could be accomplished, quicker even than commanding one of the company ships. 'In that regard, I have a recommendation to make.'

'Indeed? You must tell us.'

Michael told them about Hong Kong. 'It is the place of the future, sir. It could even equal Singapore, given time. And we have the opportunity to be in at the start.

Were you to erect warehouses and offices there, all China would be at your feet.'

'Hm,' Hammond said. 'Hm.' He glanced at Teng Tang. 'This is something we must discuss, and with Ali when he returns. But it does indeed sound a promising idea. My congratulations, Harrington. Now, you'll come to dinner tonight. I know my wife and daughter would be delighted to meet you again.'

Michael kept his features still with an effort. So she was still unmarried. And he still carried her note in his breast pocket. He bowed, gravely. 'It will be my great pleasure, Mr Hammond.'

But first, Malama. He paid a visit to his tailors, ordered some very necessary new clothes, found himself a lodging with a Malay landlady on a weekly basis, until he was confirmed in command of his ship, and then rode up the hill in his hired phaeton. He seemed to be travelling in a balloon of exuberant confidence, and achievement too, which made the horrors of the cell in Canton, or the rigours of his life with Hung's 'army' seem no more than a bad dream. And Wu Yei and the boy? But they too had now to be dreams.

Bowing maidservants showed him into the reception room, and there he was greeted by Jalina, dressed all in white, as she was still in mourning, and indeed, would be for the rest of her life; he did not suppose a princess who had also been the wife of Teng Lee, however well she had retained her looks, would ever consider marrying again.

'Mr Harrington,' she said, taking his hand and allowing him to kiss hers. 'How good to see you.'

'As it is to see you again, Your Highness. But I am sad to learn of your bereavement.'

She motioned him to a chair. 'My husband and I lived, and adventured, for thirty years together, Mr Harrington. I knew it must end, some day. Now I have sufficient memories to keep me warm for the rest of my life. But you have come to see Malama.'

'Well . . .' he was embarrassed. 'I can only apologize

for having forced her on you for so long. I had no idea I would be away for this much time.'

'How could you? And she has been no burden to me. Rather has she been the daughter I no longer have. Have you plans for her?'

'Well, I don't really know.'

Jalina gave a sad smile. 'You will wish to see her first, no doubt.' She rang a little golden bell on the table beside her, and then rose. 'I will leave you alone with her.'

'But . . . I . . .' he was more embarrassed than ever.

Jalina's smile widened. 'She is yours, Mr Harrington, and therefore her future is yours to decide. Should you wish her to remain in my household until that future is determined, however, I should be more than happy to have her. I beg you to remember that.' She went to the door as it opened. 'Mr Harrington is here,' she said, and stepped outside.

Malama closed the door behind her, while Michael stared at her in consternation. Panka was only a distant memory now, but here was Panka with her beauty redoubled. The small, delicate features were unchanged, the straight black hair still fell down her back, but the legs had lengthened as the breasts had grown to sheer perfection; this was easy to tell because she wore only a sari. Now she brought her hands together and bowed.

'Malama,' he said, and held out his arms. She raised her head, and was in them, hugging herself against him, moving her body on his in an ecstasy of welcome. 'Oh, Malama,' he said, holding her away from him, to kiss her forehead and then the tears from her cheeks.

'I thought you had forgotten me,' she said, her English flawless but delivered with a lilting quality which was quite enchanting.

'Forgotten you? Did you not get my letter?'

'It was a long time ago, Master.'

He held her hands and led her to a settee, made her sit and took his place beside her. 'I am not your master. I would have you call me . . .' He really did not like to

114

consider himself a father to a sixteen-year-old girl. 'Your uncle.'

'But you are my master.'

'I am your friend. And I am very pleased with the way you have developed. Now . . . we must find you a husband.'

Malama stiffened. 'I do not wish a husband.'

'Every woman needs a husband, Malama. Every woman should have a husband.'

Her face took on the stubborn pout he remembered so well. 'No man will marry me, I have no caste.'

'Here in Singapore they will be interested only in your beauty and the size of your dowry.'

'I would rather stay with you . . . Uncle Michael.'

He squeezed her hands. 'That is impossible.'

'But why? I am yours. I was given to you by my father. That you have never possessed me is a cause of great shame to me.'

'Another man will possess you, and make you happy, Malama. I cannot do so.'

'But why?' she wailed. 'Am I not beautiful enough for you?'

'You are beautiful enough for any man,' Michael assured her. 'But . . .' he sighed. 'My heart is lost to another. The woman I am going to wed.'

With everything running in his favour, he had no doubt at all that he was right.

5

The Colony of Victory

Three years a prisoner of the Chinese, Alicia Hammond thought, as she watched in her dressing mirror Melinda setting her hair. Well, perhaps not three years as a prisoner, but the rest of the time he had spent either living with them or fighting against them. He would have changed. And she had only actually seen him twice in her life. Yet he was the man she had determined almost at first sight that she would marry.

Three years ago. And there had been that confusion over the girl. She had reacted hastily, and conventionally. Aunt Jalina had convinced her of that. Aunt Jalina had become her confidante, indeed her mentor. The princess, who had run away from the power and splendour of her royal apartments in Bangkok, in the company of a humble trading captain, in order to escape an undesired marriage, was a woman who understood the true values of life; that she had found happiness and prosperity with her sea captain had made her the more confident of that. But . . . three years!

Alicia knew that she had not consciously waited for him to return. Indeed, when Ali had come back he had been adamant that Michael Harrington had been killed by the Chinese, or at least taken to be executed. She had not shed a tear, because she had recognized that he had, after all, been nothing more than a dream. Yet his appearance had been a watershed in her life. Because if a man like Michael Harrington could appear, here in Singapore, then might not another man like Michael Harrington one day appear – and not go off to be killed by the Chinese? Thus she had looked with even less favour on the various second-raters who had called and left their cards and endeavoured to court her burgeoning beauty. Mama had not been amused, and even Aunt Jalina had been concerned. 'I was but seventeen when I fled to Teng,' she said gently. 'And you are nineteen and unwed. You are wasting your life.'

Margaret agreed with her, and kept trotting out promising young army officers, but Alicia had treated them too with contempt. She was happy, with her books and her horse and her dogs – or at least contented – and if she could appreciate her own beauty, that made her only the more concerned that the man on whom she decided to bestow so much should be in every way worthy of it. Her family's disapproval of her course only made her the more determined to sustain it, until she triumphed.

As she had. Just before Christmas last year had come that amazing letter, an epistle from the grave. He was alive, and well, and he was coming back. She recalled that Ali had been utterly astonished, and a look of almost fear had passed over his face. But her own emotions had been entirely joyful. She had been proved right. Even Mama and Papa had had to accept that, although they had muttered that after his experiences Michael Harrington would hardly be the man they remembered. But Aunt Jalina had been entirely encouraging. 'You must not let him escape you again, my dear,' she said. 'If you do mean to make him your husband.'

'I do,' Alicia had replied. 'He is the only man I have ever considered for that position.' But she had frowned as she had watched the princess's ward, the Indian girl Malama, walking in the garden – an attractive child grown into a remarkably lovely young woman. Who belonged to Michael. Aunt Jalina had explained the circumstances, because Malama had explained them to her, and to think of Michael taking on a tiger virtually singlehanded made Alicia's heart swell with pride – there were still tigers roaming the jungle behind Singapore, so many, and so fierce, that a bounty was paid for every carcass brought in . . . but there was no man of her acquaintance who would face one alone and armed only with a knife.

117

But Malama, however innocently she might have found herself in her position, and however Michael may have decided to respect that innocence when she had been a child, was yet a threat, and growing more so every day. Her position would have to be resolved, and immediately. Nor did Alicia doubt she could force this. Malama might be a lovely girl, but she was an Indian, and still a girl. Alicia looked in the mirror at the pale, bold features of a beautiful English woman, twenty-two years old, at a flawlessly full figure in her cream taffeta gown, and at a head of the most magnificent auburn hair, clustering on her shoulders with a single ringlet, longer than the rest, down her back. As she knew she was the only woman *she* could ever love, she had no doubt that she was equally the only woman Michael Harrington could ever love – especially as he seemed to have carried her memory with him on his travels.

She listened, to wheels crunching on the gravel drive outside the house. 'Enough,' she said. 'See who that is.'

Melinda stood at the window, looking down. 'Is the man,' she said.

'Ah.' Alicia picked up her fan as she rose, flicked it open, gave a quick flutter. Sound travelled upwards through the wooden house, and she heard the front door open and close, the animated sounds of greeting, although she could not make out the words. It was time.

Her skirts in her left hand, her fan in her right, she moved to the top of the stairs, and looked down. She did not know what to expect, what she dared expect. But he was more handsome than she remembered him.

The next day they went driving together, Melinda ensconced in the seat behind. But to consider Melinda a chaperon was merely amusing; she would do exactly as she was told. As perhaps Mama understood. Mama's attitude had changed since Mr Harrington had become something of a hero, wore good clothes and exuded confidence, had returned to work for the company and was, so Papa had said, a man of ideas, who would go far.

118

Michael drove away from the house and the town, although remaining by the shore; Papa had warned him about the tigers and today he did not even have a knife. It was reasonably cool, as there was some cloud cover, suggesting the possibility of rain, so they did not venture very far, halting where a sizeable stream came rushing down from the hills to lose itself in the sand as it tried to force its way into the sea. Here there was a beach, and after Michael had tethered the horse he escorted her to the sand and spread a rug for her. Melinda remained with the phaeton, from where she could see them but not hear what was said.

Carefully arranging the skirt of her grey habit, and then releasing the ribbon which secured her bonnet beneath her chin, Alicia wondered what would be said that the maid should not overhear. It had all seemed so natural, so pre-arranged, as indeed it had been, at least in her mind. But no doubt in Mr Harrington's as well. Margaret and Jeremy Cooper had joined them for dinner – Pieter was now managing the Calcutta office – and the talk had been general, yet it seemed that everyone had understood just why Mr Harrington was there, and why he had been placed next to her. He had told them something of his adventures, and they had listened with rapt interest. Even if they had known that he was avoiding relating anything of a sensitive or indecent nature, they had yet been receiving a glimpse into a world of ugly violence none of them, save perhaps Mama and Papa, had ever experienced, and Mama and Papa had forgotten what it was like to starve or be dirty or be aware that each moment might be their last.

Then Papa had wanted to hear about this strangely named place, Hong Kong, and Mr Harrington had become enthusiastic about its future. His voice had grown animated and his eyes had sparkled, and every so often he had looked at her, his expression extending an invitation for her to see for herself. Well, she had resolved, she would. When, the meal over, he had been making his farewells, and Papa had said, 'We must talk about this some more, Harrington. Come to the office tomorrow,' she had added, 'I too would like to know more about Hong Kong, Mr Harrington. It sounds entrancing.'

'And I would like to tell you more, Miss Hammond.' He had looked at Papa. 'Would it be permissible for me to take Miss Hammond for a drive tomorrow, sir?'

'You had best ask her,' Papa had replied, being by now privy to the unspoken conspiracy.

'I think that would be very pleasant, Mr Harrington,' she had agreed.

So here they were, and he was sitting beside her on the beach, looking at the sparkling waters of the Java Sea; it was just three o'clock, too early for the sand flies to make life a misery in the open air, but with the October sun already sinking towards the horizon.

'How did your conference with Papa go?' she asked.

'Very well. Indeed, I am enormously flattered. He agrees with me that the company should establish a warehouse on Hong Kong island just as rapidly as possible . . . and he has done me the honour of requesting that I manage the business.'

'How exciting for you,' she said. 'Then you will be leaving Singapore again.'

'Not for a few weeks. He wishes to discuss the matter with your brother, when he returns.'

'Of course,' she said. 'Papa is giving Ali more and more responsibility. Tell me of him.'

'Ali? Your brother?'

She glanced at him. 'I am sure you know him better than I do, Mr Harrington. I see him when he is in Singapore. When he is acting a role, perhaps. You have sailed with him. Fought beside him, indeed.'

'Yes,' Michael said thoughtfully.

'Did he fail you?'

His head turned. 'You are very direct.'

'It is my nature.'

'Well, no man can tell how he will react to a given circumstance.'

'Then he did fail you.'

'I do not think he could have saved me. Only shared my captivity.'

'You are very generous. Tell me of your captivity.'

'I did, last night.'

'You told us nothing of importance, Mr Harrington. Thirteen men, cooped in a cell for several months, at the mercy of heathen guards? The thought makes my blood run cold.'

He smiled. 'Ours, on occasion, ran very hot. It was an unpleasant experience, Miss Hammond.'

'How unpleasant?'

'Too unpleasant for your pretty ears.'

Now she looked him full in the face. 'I could never achieve true regard for a man who would treat me as just a pretty face, with an empty head behind, or would not be utterly frank with me, at all times.'

Their gazes locked, for some seconds, and to her annoyance she could feel the heat gathering in her cheeks; there would be red spots on the pale flesh. Then he said, 'Do you really want to know what it is like never to change your clothes, to feel lice crawling over you, to have to relieve yourself where you stood or sat, in the midst of a dozen others, doing the same, to be ashamed of your body – and to have to watch men and women being beaten and executed almost every day?'

Her nostrils dilated. 'If I am to know you at all well, Mr Harrington,' she said, 'I must know the horrors over which you have triumphed.'

'And do you wish to know me at all well, Miss Hammond?'

'I think I should like that.' She did not lower her gaze, but her heart was now pounding quite fiercely. No man could have been given a more open invitation, and she sensed that he was about to take advantage of it, restrained only by the presence of the maid. Still gazing at him, she raised her voice. 'Melinda, why do you not gather some seagrapes?'

'Yes, Miss Alicia.'

The phaeton creaked, and the horses stirred, as Melinda climbed down.

'You are a very unusual young woman,' Michael remarked.

'Because I know my own mind?'

He smiled. 'That *is* unusual in a young woman, if I may dare say so.'

She had broken the spell. But it could be mended, and Melinda was by now certainly out of sight. Alicia gave a little sigh and lay on her back, gazing up at the coconut trees. 'Then as you say, I am unusual.'

He propped himself on his elbow beside her. 'And perhaps unwise. You know very little about me.'

'And you know nothing whatsoever about me,' she retorted, looking up at him.

'Save that you are very beautiful.'

'Am I, Mr Harrington?'

'The most beautiful woman I have ever met,' he said, but thoughtfully, as if not absolutely sure.

'That is a very great compliment,' she remarked. Heavens, would he never kiss her? 'But one I think I can reciprocate.'

Still he gazed at her. Perhaps she had been too forward. She made to sit up, and his hand touched her shoulder. She lay back again, the sudden movements leaving her a little breathless. She saw his face coming down to her, and desperately inhaled. His lips rested on hers, lightly for a moment, very like the kisses the various officers from the garrison who from time to time had escorted her had attempted to steal. But she wanted more, and put her arm round his back to hold him closer. Then she was taken by surprise, as his tongue drove against hers, his leg was thrown across her thighs, his left hand rested, lightly, on her bodice, his fingers making gentle patterns on the material and the soft flesh beneath. Now she did hold him close. His sudden passion was as compelling as it was startling. Their bodies rolled against each other and it was only when his hand slipped from her breast and down her tunic to her skirt that she recalled herself, released him, and sat up, gasping.

Now he lay on his back in turn, watching her. 'I said, you did not know me very well.'

Slowly she got her breathing under control. How she wanted to turn and throw herself on him, feel him against her again, feel his tongue inside her mouth, feel his hand on her body, wherever it chose to roam. But that would be madness. She meant to be his wife, not his mistress. And to be his wife on her own terms.

'That would seem to be my misfortune,' she said softly.

He sat up, his arm round her shoulders. 'Alicia . . .'

'I think we should return,' she said, and stood up.

He got up also. 'Now you are angry.'

She turned to face him. 'No, Mr Harrington. I am not angry. But I cannot permit any man to treat me as a wife, until I am one.'

Once again the invitation was so plain it took him by surprise. But he was becoming used to her. 'Then be my wife,' he said.

'Just so you can make love to me?'

'That, certainly. I wish to love you more than anything else in the world, Alicia.'

'Make love.'

'Love,' he corrected. 'I wish you at my side, always. I wish to take you to Hong Kong with me, as my wife.'

'Hong Kong,' she said thoughtfully. 'I would love to see it.'

'You shall live there, and be the queen of the colony.'

She smiled. 'As you will be the king?'

'I shall be your consort.'

She saw his hand move, and remained still. He took her hand and drew her against him, then let his fingers run up her sleeve and over her shoulder to her back. She put her arms round him in turn, and they kissed, even more deeply and longingly than before, their bodies pressed against each other, while his fingers moved up and down her back, drifting down to her waist before returning, somewhat to her disappointment.

'Oh, Alicia,' he whispered in her ear. 'I have dreamed of you so. It was all that sustained me.'

'As I have dreamed of you.'

'Will you marry me?'

'Oh, yes,' she said. 'And come to Hong Kong with you.'

'Your maid . . .'

'Will not return until I call her.' She moved her head back to gaze at him. 'But I would like to go home now.'

'Oh.'

She smiled, and kissed him again. 'I am yours, dearest Michael. I will be yours. You know this. But I will be yours as your wife. I am sure you would not have it any different.'

'No,' he agreed. 'I suppose I would not.'

'And there are Mama and Papa to be told. I suppose you should first speak with Papa, before we can consider ourselves betrothed.'

'My God, yes,' he agreed. 'You will think me a total boor.'

She kissed him again. 'I think you are preoccupied. With me. The wedding will be as soon as propriety allows, I promise you. A month, no more.'

'A month,' he said. 'I am the happiest man alive.'

'As I am the happiest woman, my dearest.' She held his hand as they walked back to the phaeton. Melinda, who had not been all that far away, came hurrying back. Alicia waited until they were all settled, and Michael had taken the reins. Then she said, 'And now, my darling, do you think we could discuss Malama?'

'Mr Potts is here, my child,' said the Princess Jalina.

Malama looked at her anxiously, then at Michael.

'I think you should stand to greet him,' Michael suggested, himself rising. 'It would be courteous.'

Malama stood, drawing a deep breath which seemed to inflate her slender body. Presumably what was about to happen had been decided by her Karma many centuries before. It had been foolish of her to hope that Uncle

Michael might indeed take her for his own. He was a man on his way to great prosperity; that was *his* Karma. She was without caste, and was fortunate she was not being given to some itinerant tradesman. According to both Uncle Michael and the princess, Paul Potts was a young man of charm and some promise, a clerk at a rival trading house, who had expressed the most lively interest in the beautiful Indian maiden. That he had been told he could only have her through marriage was undoubtedly Uncle Michael's doing. But that, having reflected, he was now coming to call, was, she supposed, a suggestion that he was indeed interested – and a gentleman.

Michael opened the door of the princess's drawing room himself, to admit the suitor. Mr Potts was something of a disappointment, to a girl whose hopes had centred on Michael himself. He was not very tall, and inclined to plumpness, although he was only in his early twenties. His face was too red and his hands too white. But his suit was well cut and his shirt clean, and he was clearly much in awe of both the princess and Uncle Michael.

And of her? He had seen her on several occasions. But this was the first time he had been able to look on her with the eye of a future husband. His greeting was laboured; he had a slight stammer.

'You'll take some tea,' the princess invited.

'That would be very kind of you, Highness.'

Michael gestured him to a chair and he sat, anxiously, knees together and back straight, gazing, Malama observed with annoyance, not at her but at Michael.

Jalina had rung her golden bell, and the tea was quickly brought in. Mr Potts sipped his cautiously.

'Well,' Michael said. 'I have spoken with Malama, and she has indicated that she will be pleased to be your wife.'

'Ah,' Mr Potts said, and looked at her for the first time. 'How splendid.'

'Yes,' Michael agreed. 'So if it suits you, we will have the banns pronounced commencing on Sunday.'

'Ah,' Mr Potts said again. 'About the other matter . . .'

'I have drawn up the necessary papers,' Michael promised him. 'You have but to come down to the office tomorrow, and they can be signed before witnesses.'

'Ah,' said Mr Potts a third time, greatly relieved. 'Well, then, I am a very happy man.' He looked at Malama again, and she arranged her features into a smile. 'Oh, very happy,' he assured her. He felt in his pocket and produced a little box. 'I have bought the ring.'

He gave it to Malama, who looked at Jalina, received a nod, and opened it. It was a rather small diamond mounted on a plain gold band.

'How lovely,' Jalina said, and kissed Malama on the forehead. 'I am sure you would like to speak with your fiancée alone, Mr Potts. Mr Harrington?'

Michael rose and Malama made as though she would rise also, then recalled herself and subsided. Michael held the door for the princess and followed her into the library. 'I feel like a murderer,' he said.

Jalina sighed. 'There are few of us fortunate enough to marry the person of our choice, Mr Harrington.'

'Or brave enough to refuse a person not of our choice?'

Jalina made a moue. 'I was very young. Hardly older than Malama. And very arrogant. I had been brought up to be arrogant. I could not conceive that life could ever harm me. And very fortunate, in the man I eloped with. Had I been older, and wiser, I would undoubtedly have accepted my fate.' She touched his hand as he did not seem reassured. 'Malama has not been brought up in a royal palace,' she said quietly. 'She has been taught from birth to accept what fate inflicts upon her. No doubt it is fortunate that none of us can foresee that,' she added.

Michael gazed at her, suddenly aware of how lonely she must be, with Teng Lee dead, for all the brave front she put on her situation. She was past fifty, he knew, and yet had the figure and complexion still of a young girl. But she was a royal princess, even if disowned by the nephew who now sat on the throne of Siam. She could seek no solace without demeaning herself.

Jalina held his gaze for a moment, and then smiled. 'She will make Potts a good wife, and become a mother for him, and have a satisfying life. Far more satisfying that scraping an existence in the delta of the Hugli. You have nothing to reproach yourself with, Michael.'

Presumably she was right. He had not asked for the girl. That they had shared one or two moments of passion had been in the nature of things, but not because of any irrevocable feeling between them. If only he could get over the feeling that he had sold her. And not even sold her. Mr Potts had been easy to introduce as a prospective suitor; Jalina had kept a careful list of all the young white men who had shown an interest in her lovely ward during the past year or so; she had anticipated having to find a husband for Malama, and in Singapore, under British rule, she had understood that only a white man would be truly acceptable – like all Orientals, she had a totally pragmatic approach to life. To invite the young man to dinner, allow him to drink in the beauty of the girl and the opulence of the surroundings in which she lived, had been a simple matter, while Michael had now played his part in leaving him in no doubt he would approve of the match. When Potts, while plainly enamoured, had hesitated at the thought of marrying a Hindu, even one as comely and as well connected as Malama, the offer of the dowry had been made, and that had clinched the business. And it was not even his money, Michael reflected bitterly; he had none. But Clive Hammond, who seemed to understand his daughter, had wanted a man-to-man talk when asked for Alicia's hand, and out of it had come the offer to make Malama a really worthwhile bride. When Michael had protested, Hammond had waved his hand. 'Think nothing of it, my dear boy. You are joining the firm, not only as one of our best young men, but as my son-in-law. I want my daughter to be happy, as I want you to be happy. And I know the Hindu is much on your conscience. Let it be my charge to make her happy too.'

So, Michael wondered, at the end of it who exactly had been bought and who sold?

Jalina watched his changing expressions with some anxiety, and then touched his hand again, more positively

127

than before. 'When you first came to us, Michael, my husband told me that you were a promising rogue, who by your circumstances could be of use to the company. I did not agree with him, when first we met. Now I know that I was right, and Teng wrong. You are a good man, Michael. You have nothing with which to reproach yourself. I count your friendship one of my dearest possessions.' Still clasping his hand, she stood on tiptoe and kissed him on the cheek.

Michael was taken entirely by surprise, and then reflected that it had clearly been a maternal gesture: the princess was at least twenty years his senior. And she could tell he was deeply upset at the thought of Malaina marrying a man she as yet did not know, much less love. He had to remind himself that it was all to enable himself to marry Alicia, who was everything he had ever dreamed of in a woman. If her straightforwardness was sometimes breathtaking, it was nonetheless a trait he would have wanted in a wife, had he ever supposed he could find it. Having found it, it was surely absurd to be embarrassed or disillusioned by it. She wanted him as much as he wanted her, and she had the wealth at her call to flick any impediments aside. He certainly intended to justify his position as her husband, both by loving her with all his soul and by fulfilling his responsibilities to the company with all his strength.

Then what of the man who had promised Hung Hsiu-ch'uan that he would do everything in his power to put a stop to the opium trade? Where did his acceptance of his situation leave Jalina's flattering judgement of him? Well, he reflected, he had warned Hung that there was very little a penniless sailor could do about the opium trade. But he had also promised himself that he would not again work for any company that took part in the ghastly business. That too had gone out of the window, with so many other good resolutions. Yet here again he could tell himself that while he could do nothing about it now, as Clive Hammond's son-in-law – and it was very obvious that

128

since Teng Lee's death the English half of the partnership had taken control, as Ali had foreseen it would – as he rose to a position of authority and power, then indeed he would be able to have a hand in deciding company policy.

Supposing Ali let him. Ali returned the week after the betrothal of Alicia Hammond and Michael Harrington was officially announced in the *Singapore Free Press*, and made a point of immediately seeking out his prospective brother-in-law. Michael was supervising the unloading of a junk just in from Calcutta when he saw the tall, lean figure approaching him. He handed over his pad and pencil to his assistant, and went to greet him.

It was a meeting he had anticipated, without quite resolving his attitude. But Ali looked friendly enough, held out his hand. 'Welcome . . . brother,' he said.

Michael squeezed the proffered fingers. 'Thank you. I trust you have no objections?'

'My dear fellow, I can think of no one I would rather have as a brother-in-law. I think we should have a drink to celebrate.'

Michael hesitated. But he had had several glasses of champagne with Clive Hammond when the engagement had been announced, without ill effects, just as his Navy rum ration had never provoked the fighting Irishman that he knew lay buried beneath the genteel veneer he had so carefully cultivated. 'Why not?'

They drank saké in the nearest bar. 'I hope you bear no grudge for what happened on the Pearl,' Ali said, studying him.

'If I did, it lasted no more than a moment,' Michael said. 'If you had tried to help me, we would both have been taken.'

'Indeed. And I had the ship much in mind. But you remained on my conscience. To see you looking so well is a great relief.'

'Thank you,' Michael said, not the least disturbed by the certainty that Ali was lying.

'And now we are to be in harness together. That, too, is most satisfying. By the way, I have something for you.'

129

Michael raised his eyebrows, and Ali felt in his pocket and produced a small, clinking bag.

'Silver,' he explained.

'For me?'

'Your share of the money we got from Bodaw Wing.'

Michael looked at the bag, then up at the smiling face. 'Keep it.'

Ali's smile slowly faded. 'I see.'

'I will not betray you, Ali,' Michael said. 'Because I gave you my word that I would not, and because, as I am becoming a member of your family, I have no wish to cause dissension between you and your father.'

'Thank you,' Ali said sarcastically.

'But I will warn you now that if you persist in dealing with those pirates, and I learn of it, I *will* denounce you, both to your father and the naval commander here.'

Ali stared at him. 'You feel you are now achieving a position of prominence.'

Michael shrugged. 'Let us say that you no longer have me at quite such a disadvantage as four years ago.'

'And you're determined to be a law-abiding citizen. It doesn't go all that well with your past.'

'I'm interested in my future, not my past.'

'And what do you think my sister is interested in?'

Michael would not lower his eyes. 'Why do you not ask her, and find out?'

Ali continued to stare at him for a few moments more, than he laughed. 'It ill becomes future brothers-in-law to quarrel. Landlord, we'll have another bottle of this stuff, and for Christ's sake make sure it is properly heated this time.'

Michael stood up. 'I'll take my leave.'

Ali leaned back in his chair. 'Determined not to be my friend?'

'I am sure I shall be your friend, if you wish it,' Michael told him. 'I have simply had enough saké.'

'Weak head, is it?'

'Why, yes, I suppose you could say. After two bottles

of saké I am inclined to start breaking things.' He smiled at Ali. 'Like heads.'

The Hammond house, no higher up the hill than that built by Teng Lee, was nonetheless suddenly a cooler place as the men dismounted, away from the noise and the heat and the forced jocularity of Malama's wedding. Elizabeth and Alicia had also been invited, but had declined. Margaret had attended, with her husband; they were still there, so far as Michael knew. But he had been unable to stay longer, as Clive Hammond had understood. Ali had left with them.

The Malay butler was waiting at the head of the steps to present them with a glass of iced champagne each. 'I'm not sure I shall make it back down to the town,' Michael groaned. 'I have had more than enough.'

'Then sleep here,' Clive suggested. 'There are several empty guest rooms.'

'And we can always lock you in,' Ali said, with one of his sly grins.

Obviously they were never going to be friends, Michael reflected. The sooner he was in Hong Kong the better. And tonight the mixture of guilt and too much to drink was making him angry with the lout. 'I am sure someone would be found to let me out,' he retorted.

'Why . . .'

His sister interrupted. 'I should do so myself.' She linked her arm through Michael's, drew him along the verandah to the swinging settee. 'You should learn to ignore what Ali considers humour.'

He finished his champagne, sat down with a sigh. 'Believe me, sweetheart, I endeavour to. But there are occasions . . .'

She sat beside him, kissed his cheek. 'Was it very terrible?'

'It was magnificent. I owe Jalina more than I can ever repay. She spared nothing.'

'What did Malama wear?'

'A white sari.'

131

'White? Good heavens. As transparent as ever, and with as few underclothes?'

'She looked quite marvellous. If Potts did not fall in love with her immediately, then I am sure there were a lot of other men present who did.'

'So you grieve for your little bint.' She leaned her head on his shoulder, and his arm instinctively went round her.

'Is that so very wrong?'

'Indeed it is not, my dearest. I have felt the same way over having a sick puppy put down. When Brutus died, why, I cried my eyes out.'

'Yes,' he agreed drily.

She sat straight. 'Now you are angry with me as well as Ali.'

'Malama is not a puppy, Alicia. She is a sensitive and sensible girl, who is devoted to me.'

'Of course she is,' Alicia said soothingly. 'But now she is a woman, and it is time for her to be devoted to someone else, just as I am now devoted to you instead of to Mama and Papa. Why, I am abandoning them to follow you to the ends of the earth, all but. You will not pretend that Hong Kong will have any of the refinements of Singapore.'

He gazed at her. She was triumphant, because her only possible rival for his love was now bound to another. Bound, he thought bitterly. She had looked so lovely in her white sari, with her dark limbs clearly delineated as she moved, the swell of her breast as she breathed; but she had looked so bewildered at the Christian ceremony which had flowed around her glossy black head; and she had looked so miserable as Mr Potts had planted a possessive kiss on her mouth while his friends cheered, and lined up for a similar privilege. And within the hour Potts would have the privilege of kissing other places than her mouth, if he chose, as his hand would choose other resting places than her arm. He shuddered, and Alicia frowned in concern. 'You have caught a chill.'

He shook his head and stood up, a trifle uncertainly. 'I have had too much to drink. I must get back to town.'

132

'You mean you must stay here. Why, you are in no fit state to ride.'

'If I stay here, I will seek your bed, and if Ali tries to stop me, I will break his head.'

She gazed at him, mouth open. 'You wanted her for yourself.'

'Why, yes, so I did. And never yielded to temptation, and have often regretted it. Now I must forget her, as quickly as possible.'

'In the arms of a whore.'

'As direct as ever.' He smiled at her. 'Not necessarily, my love. Perhaps in the arms of several more bottles. After that, who can say.'

Alicia's eyes gleamed in the darkness. 'As are you as honest as ever. I would prefer you to stay here.'

He peered at her. 'I meant what I said.'

'I know you did. That is why I have asked you to stay. I would not have you forget Malama in any arms but mine.'

She was breathless at her own audacity. But his mood had frightened her. She had perhaps underestimated his feeling for the Hindu. Even if he had never taken Malama to bed, and Alicia believed him when he claimed that, the girl had yet occupied a niche in his mind, in his personality. If it were not to become a permanent niche, then it needed to be exorcized, now. Besides, it was a temptation which had been growing on her for weeks. It had indeed nearly overwhelmed her that first day on the beach. He clearly knew so much, she so little, about the art of love. If he had ever loved an Indian, and that she did not doubt, then he would know things white men only whispered of, and white women hardly suspected. Ali of course had been to Calcutta, on many occasions, and had teased her with his knowledge. 'Did you know, my dear girl,' he had laughed, 'that the Hindu uses thirty-five separate positions for the act of love?' Ali had long since ceased to be able to make her blush. But the thought had occupied her mind for some time, to no possible conclusion. Mama, who had been a prisoner of a Malay pirate in her youth, had no doubt experienced a great deal, but in her lessons to her daughters had admitted of only one 'Christian' way – which was not to say she had not enjoyed the others. While Margaret, who had only ever known the arms of her soldier husband, yet hinted on occasion, during the sisterly chats they shared, that she had hovered on the brink of ecstasy even with him – without ever quite toppling over.

Thus temptation. If Alicia had not previously succumbed it had been because she had been unsure of Michael himself, and of the girl, and of a great many things. But now the girl was teetering on the edge of oblivion. She, or her memory, needed but a gentle push, to fall into the pit of things forgotten. And her own marriage was hardly a week away. There was no longer a risk involved, not even that of a premature pregnancy. And there was all the reason in the world, apart from desire, or she would risk having Michael standing beside her at the altar and thinking of his dark-skinned ward – who would still be honeymooning.

Supposing it would happen. He was decidedly drunk, and she had warned him to wait at least an hour after the last of the family had retired to bed before making his way along the corridor to her room. No doubt he would fall fast asleep and forget all about it. It was, indeed, only after the meal was completed that she had her first doubts, as the initial excitement of having dared so much, so much more than she had ever intended, began to wear off. Supposing he was too drunk to remember? Or to perform? Margaret had told her that when Jeremy got drunk, for all his amorous intentions, he could accomplish nothing. But then, suppose he was just drunk enough to hurt her? And he was going to hurt her, in any event, according to Mama and Margaret.

But she could not change her mind, if he came. That would be to make him angry, and that would be a disaster. If he came, she would have to surpass anything he might have imagined Malama might have been capable of. Oh my God, she thought: anything he might *know* Malama to be capable of.

'What you brooding on?' Melinda demanded as she finished sponging Alicia's neck and shoulders, and applied soothing powder. 'You ain't well?'

'I am very well, thank you,' Alicia said. 'I think it must have been that other glass of champagne at dinner. Just let me sleep.'

Melinda raised the mosquito netting for her, then tucked it in. 'You sleep,' she agreed, and blew out the candle.

Alicia listened to the door close, then sat up, aware that she had been holding her breath. Melinda was a dear child, but she did prattle so – and she had a very perceptive eye. My God, she thought again, the blood! According to Margaret there would certainly be blood, and there was no chance of that escaping Melinda's eagle eye.

Alicia chewed her lip. She could lock her door, and pretend that Ali had done it. She could . . . she drew a long breath. She was behaving like a fool. She, who had always ordered her own life as she thought best. So they found blood on her sheet tomorrow. What would they do about it? Insist that she married Michael?

She listened to the clock chiming one. He was not going to come. Still unsure whether to be glad or sorry, or even angry, about that, she got out of bed, stood at her window looking down at the moonlit garden, and heard her door open.

She turned, hips against the window sill, gazing into the darkness. 'Is it you?' she whispered.

For reply he came across the room – he could see her silhouetted against the light – and took her in his arms. To her relief he was wearing, if not a nightshirt, one of the sarongs which were always kept in the guest rooms. And when he kissed her it was the kiss of a man who certainly knew what he was doing; the kiss she remembered from the beach. So all she had to do was surrender. She had never willingly surrendered, to anything. But

135

surely she could do so with her future husband – sexually, at the least.

His hands moved up and down her back as his mouth left hers to allow them to breathe. Instead he kissed her ear, as she felt little shivers of anticipation following his fingers down her spine. She could not stop herself speaking, banally. 'I thought you had forgotten me,' she whispered.

His head moved back, and as the moonlight lit his face she thought she saw a frown. But then he was kissing her again, almost savagely, and his hands were back, now moving lower than before to grasp her buttocks and lift her from the ground; she had already been standing on tiptoe.

She discovered he was turning her round, to look at the bed, and his grip was slackening. She stepped out of his arms and moved towards the bed, and he held her arm. She turned back to him, and he came against her again, and she realized that he had released the sarong, which had slid from his waist to the floor. She could not stop herself gasping; if she had, willy-nilly and from a distance as she had driven by a beach, from time to time observed the Malay men bathing, she had never been this close to a naked man before. She kept her eyes fixed on his face as he touched her nightdress, and knew what he wanted. What she had to allow. But she could not do it herself. She drew a long breath and raised her arms above her head. His hands gathered the muslin on her thighs and lifted it. For a moment she was enveloped in it, then it too fell to the floor. Slowly she lowered her arms again, gazing at him, and he touched her breasts, lightly, no more than one finger circling each nipple, before his hands gently cupped them. Her body became one immense reservoir of feeling, and she gasped. When he stepped back she was unable to move.

He raised the mosquito netting, and she went to it, hesitated. To climb into bed, before a man, naked, with the moonlight filling the room . . . but once again it had to be done. She ducked her head, put one knee on the

136

mattress, made to raise the other, and felt him against her. She wanted to scream. To have him touch her buttocks, perhaps by accident, and through her clothes, had been thrilling. To feel both hands and penis against her naked flesh was paralysing. She hurled herself forward, on to her face on the pillows, and before she could set up any kind of a barrier he was in bed with her, and kneeling astride her thighs.

She lay still. Whatever he would do, he would do. His hands stroked her shoulders, his fingers kneading the muscles there, and some of the tension began to evaporate. They moved lower, tracing the serrations of her backbone, sliding away to caress her sides. By the time they reached her buttocks she had her legs pressed tightly together, but could not resist him when he parted them, burying her face in the pillow as the hands slipped between, again to caress and stroke. She had to breathe and raised her head again, and he rolled her on to her back, his hands now sliding over the front of her groin and again between. 'You know I must hurt you,' he said.

'Yes,' she gasped. 'Yes.'

He came down on her, and kissed her. 'There are many things I wish to do, to you, and with you, and for you,' he said. 'But I cannot, while you are a virgin. I must . . .' he kissed her mouth, and she felt him between her legs now, questing, but gently. 'Treat you softly.'

Now she wanted it, more than anything in her life before. She spread her legs, and when the gentle probing continued, brought them up. Then suddenly the probing became a thrust, and another, and another. The first produced a sharp pain and she gasped again, and almost tensed. But she made herself relax, and the second and third were easier, while by then she found her legs had come round on to his back, her ankles locked. However painful, he was inside her, and she did not want him ever to go out again. Thrust now followed thrust, but then she could feel him flooding her, and the thrusts became easier with the lubrication. Now she found his mouth and kissed it herself, again and again and again, as the thrusts slowly dwindled, and she lost the feel of him.

'You said there was more,' she whispered as he lay in the crook of her arm.

'Much more,' he promised. 'When we are married.'

Much more, Alicia reflected. Her bed had become a shrine, in which she had for the first time understood the true meaning of life. Even without Michael, it remained a shrine, because of the memory, because of the things he had taught her to do to herself. The necessity of waiting for the wedding, of undertaking another subterfuge so that he could spend another night in the house, had been merely a nuisance.

By then, she was fairly certain, at least all the females in the household knew what had happened. Melinda, of course, and the laundrymaid. And therefore the other maids. And therefore Mama? If so, Mama did not learn of it until after Michael had returned to his lodgings, but at her session with the dressmaker that morning, when for the tenth time the wedding gown had been fitted on her, and pins removed and pins put in, and underskirts added or subtracted for the best effect, Mama had gazed at the yards of white silk and taffeta somewhat pensively, and when the seamstress had left, had seemed about to say something, and then thought better of it. Alicia was afraid Mama might confide her suspicions to Papa, but if she did he gave no sign of it, nor did either parent object when Michael spent that other night in the house. Certainly it was clear that Ali had no suspicion of it.

The wedding, a great affair, was itself nothing more than a nuisance. Alicia begrudged every moment that kept her from Michael's arms. If she had selected him as her husband it had been for utterly romantic reasons, in the beginning. Now the urge was purely sexual. He had released within her some long-pent-up tropical explosion of desire and feeling. The thought that he might ever have done as much for some other woman was horrifying. As for if he might have done so for the Hindu . . . but he swore he had not, and the Hindu was gone. And from his mind, she was sure, if only because, however lacking in experience, she herself was so willing a pupil.

Margaret, who acted as her matron of honour, was the closest observer of her feverish mood as the great day dawned. 'Pray God he loves you as much as you love him,' she said, when they were alone together for the last few minutes before setting off for the church, with everyone else save Papa departed – and he was downstairs awaiting them.

'Should I not love my husband?' Alicia retorted.

'Indeed you should. But I think he is getting the better of the bargain. Has got,' she added, perhaps without thinking.

Alicia looked at her. 'He is the most wonderful lover in the world.'

'That I can believe,' Margaret agreed. 'As he has made you so very happy. Alas, my dear, wonderful lovers, like great musicians, too often find it necessary to practise. And there may be times when the chosen instrument is not to hand, or not in tune. If you would be happy with your wild Irishman, I beg you to remember my words, and understand them.'

As if she would not always be in tune with Michael, Alicia thought contemptuously. And to be with him, always! Every minute of the day and night. The voyage from Singapore north had been the most memorable of her life, especially as Michael had been supernumerary, with nothing to do except be with her, and yet so knowledgeable that he could explain everything about the ship, the weather, and even the land they occasionally saw, and so obviously respected by Captain Wong Sung – with whom he had apparently sailed before – that the captain often asked his advice.

And with a cabin to themselves, in which they could do whatever they wished, as they were now man and wife. As he explored her body, so she explored his. He taught her to make love in many different positions, to use her lips as much as her fingers. If he had found a wonderland of swelling breast, eager buttock and anxious vagina, she was no less satisfied with her possessions, loved nothing more than to sit astride him and feel him in her and in her, until she could imagine he had himself entered her womb.

And together they were going to create a new empire, although it would be nothing more than an extension of the old. She was on deck at dawn when the masthead shouted 'Land ho!' Standing between Michael and Melinda – who was no less anxious to discover where they were about to be marooned – she gazed at a myriad of islands, clustered in every direction, through which Wong Sung seemed able to find his way with total confidence.

As they approached, Alicia discovered that some of the islands were of a good size, and very hilly compared with Singapore; several of the peaks were clearly over a thousand feet high. Now they saw other craft, trading junks, coastal sampans, and one relatively large vessel, anchored. 'An imperial warship,' Michael remarked, and pointed, to where the islands seemed to recede to the west. 'That is the mouth of the Pearl River, the road to Canton. And that land over there is China.'

She glanced at him, because his voice had changed slightly as he spoke, and she wondered if he was recalling his horrifying experience there. But then he smiled again, and this time pointed to the east. 'Hong Kong.'

They were now in a fairly wide channel leading to what appeared to be the mainland. Close at hand there was a promontory, a mass of high hills and secret valleys. It was only when they rounded an eastern outcrop of this cape that she discovered that it was, actually, an island, and that in the sheltered stretch of water separating it from the mainland there were half a dozen ships of the line flying the White Ensign, as well as a good dozen trading junks and European-style ships, all at anchor. To the left as they turned into the harbour, on the mainland, there were barracks and a line of fortifications. To the right, on the island . . . 'There's nothing there,' she said.

'Well, there are some things, my love.' Michael put his

arm round her shoulders as he pointed. 'There are the military headquarters, by the flag, and there are some go-downs, by the beach . . . they don't belong to your papa, unfortunately. But we will soon build the biggest and best go-downs in the colony. As we shall build the biggest and best house.'

'We?'

'There is nobody else, my dear.'

Alicia swallowed. Although she had understood they were to undertake an adventure, she had supposed their house, for instance, would be a matter of summoning an architect and telling him what they wanted. 'I find it hard to understand why the British wanted this desolate place,' she remarked. 'When they could have had anywhere in China, presumably.'

'Nowhere as useful as this,' Michael told her. 'For a maritime power. Or for a nation of tradesmen. This is the real gain of our victory in the war.' He squeezed her against him. 'And you will be the first white woman to set foot on it.'

PART TWO

The Inspiration of Action

6

The Love of a Good Woman

Michael's energy and enthusiasm were contagious, and rapidly overcame Alicia's first sense of rejection of her situation. Wong Sung was under orders to remain in Hong Kong for as long as Mr and Mrs Harrington required him, and of course he had his usual cargo of opium to discharge and sell to the Chinese merchants, who had quite recovered from the sudden onslaught of Commissioner Lin, now exiled in disgrace, and which had caused the death of several of their number apart from Teng Hu. This meant that Alicia and Michael could remain living in their comfortable cabin, free of the discomfort ashore, while the latest extension of the firm of Hammond and Teng took shape.

Alicia was again a little taken aback when Michael built the first warehouse before their own dwelling, but was then entranced when he took her for a ride up into the hills on horses purchased from the Chinese, and showed her where the foundations of their home had already been laid: labour was plentiful, and again came from the mainland, where the Chinese regarded the arrival of a British colony on their doorstep, offering high wages and unceasing employment – Michael was not the only entrepreneur building as fast as he could – as a gift from the gods. Alicia stood on the ledge of rock which extended from the little plateau and looked down at the busy harbour – named Victoria after the Queen – the numerous building works, the shipping in the strait, and across at the huge mist-shrouded land mass beyond. 'It is heavenly,' she agreed. 'It is going to be heavenly.'

He stood beside her. 'Just so long as you are happy, my dearest.'

She turned, against him, oblivious of the Chinese work-men only a few yards away. 'I am happy where you are. Michael . . . no regrets?'

It was the first time she had asked him that. He looked down into her eyes for some seconds before replying. 'No regrets.' He kissed her.

But she knew he had, if only for a moment, thought of how Malama might be doing. Her possession, she realized, was not yet complete. But it would be, once she was a mother.

The house was completed in four months. Built to Michael's own design, it comprised a wide front porch looking down at the harbour, then a conventional entry hall, to the left of which was the dining room, off which opened the pantry and thence the kitchens and the ser-vants' quarters. On the right was a huge drawing room, like the dining room enjoying the view down the hill, and behind it the study, large enough to be called a library, the books for which he had already ordered. Behind the library was a private half-open parlour, where they could take breakfast and afternoon tea by themselves, shaded from the sun and sheltered from the rain, but yet able to look out at the interior garden, which was reached by a door at the rear of the entry hall as well as from their patio. The pantry and kitchen side was high walled, and although there was also a door from the kitchen into the garden, so that a servant could attend them when needed, it would normally be kept shut so as to leave the master and mistress to themselves.

The upper storey was similarly shaped like a thick inverted U. Three guest bedrooms ranged the left-hand side of the house. The entire right wing, and thus again that portion of the house which overlooked the private patio, was the master suite, with a dressing room for Michael and a luxurious boudoir for Alicia. Nearly all the furniture was made on the island or on the mainland, although it was necessary to send to Singapore for things like mattresses and pillows.

But by the onset of the next monsoon season they were installed, much to the relief of Captain Wong, who was anxious to get back to Singapore lest he be trapped in the north for several months. And in fact this was a severe season, with the rain teeming down without cessation and the wind howling out of the mountains. The garrison, as usual, encamped down by the harbour, suffered severely: it amazed Michael that any government could be so wanton with the lives of its soldiers as to leave them to die of fever in distant outposts when the least care as to commissariat and medical supplies could have prevented such misery.

Up on the hill he and Alicia were secure, for the house was strongly built, above the risk of flood water, and the mountain itself provided an unequalled windbreak. By the following spring, with the arrival of the first ships from Singapore, their furnishing was completed, and by the following spring too, to their mutual delight, Alicia was pregnant.

The cargo brought by the ships was entirely, from a trading point of view, opium. There was nothing Michael was able to do about this for the time being, especially as one of the ships was commanded by Ali himself. 'I've come to see how my baby sister is getting on,' he announced.

'Your baby sister is on her way to presenting you with a nephew, dear brother,' Alicia told him.

'Why, Mama and Papa will be delighted,' Ali said. 'And,' he added, going on to the front verandah to look around him, at both the house and the outer garden which was now beginning to take shape, 'I will be able to tell them that you have done yourselves proud. I must say, there were some eyebrows raised in the accounts department by the size of the bills you kept sending in, Michael my boy, but it seems to have been well spent.'

'It will be paid for,' Michael told him.

'Oh, indeed it will. No doubt by Alicia's inheritance when Father passes on. Can't be too much longer.'

'If you weren't my brother-in-law I'd punch you on the nose,' Michael told him.

'Won't you two ever see each other without wanting to fight?' Alicia demanded. 'Your trouble is you do not have a wife, Ali. One would do you so much good.'

'I have a hundred wives,' Ali told her. 'I should be bored to confine myself to just one.' He had, as usual, readily recovered his affability, and yet his malice was never far beneath the surface. And he had a great deal of material with which to work, even if some of it was supposition. When he and Michael went down the hill to inspect the warehouse he remarked, with apparent carelessness, 'How are our relations with the Chinks?'

'With the Chinese on the mainland here, very good.'

'But not with the Manchu, eh?'

'We see nothing of the Manchu. I think they have chosen to ignore our existence. I was thinking of the people of the interior, of Canton itself.'

'Our customers.'

'A few money-hungry merchants may be our customers,' Michael said. 'And sufficient fools may wish to dream themselves to death to satisfy them, but for the most part the Cantonese hate us. And that is a shame, because you may remember that when you and I visited there in 1839 they were very friendly.'

'We were selling them opium then.'

'Oh, quite. In the main they hate us not because of the opium, but because we are British, and because the British Navy inflicted such a heavy indemnity on them after the war. It was an indemnity *they* had to pay, not the Manchu against whom the war was fought.'

'You are starting to sound like a radical politician,' Ali remarked. 'One should never complain about the goose which keeps laying golden eggs for all of us, which in our case is the Royal Navy which reopened the trade in opium, and the opium itself. But I can appreciate your fellow feeling for the Chinks, seeing that you lived amongst them for so long. Tell me, have you ever heard again of that lunatic who rescued you? Hung Hsiu-ch'uan?'

148

'No,' Michael said shortly. In fact he hadn't, but then he had made no effort to find out if Hung was still alive – or any of his people. It lay heavily on his conscience, and for far more than the opium he still marketed. But he could not dare risk Alicia finding out that he was already a father; if she was the most loving of women she was also very prone to upsets, when her coldness could be biting – and thus far in their brief married life she had never had anything important to be upset about.

A relationship Ali no doubt suspected. 'That must be sad for you,' he remarked. 'Did you not form any attachments while you were with them?'

Michael shrugged. 'I was a friend of Hung's, I suppose. He certainly saved my life. But he was a difficult man to know well.'

'And what did you do for sex, during all of that time?'

Michael turned to look at him. 'The same as any man, in such circumstances.'

'A different yellow-skinned beauty a night for a year? And people think you suffered.' Ali smiled. 'I envy your ability to love and leave, as it were. I find it strange that you have not even asked after your dusky charmer.'

'She was never my charmer,' Michael said evenly. 'Although she was certainly my responsibility. I had assumed you would tell me, if there were anything worth telling.'

'Oh, indeed. I believe Potts flogs her with great regularity.'

'Your humour quite escapes me,' Michael told him coldly.

Ali grinned. 'But it is quite true, my dear fellow. It is said they can hear her shrieks throughout Singapore.'

The temptation to throttle the bastard – and he was that – was all but unbearable. But then, so was what he had said: Michael knew an even greater temptation to take ship back to Singapore. But that would be suicidal, as regards Alicia – and especially when he could not be sure whether or not Ali was merely having a joke at his

149

expense. Instead he retired to his study when he returned home, and wrote to Jalina. The letter had to be given to Ali to deliver, and Michael could not doubt that it would be steamed open and read, yet there was nothing else he could do, save phrase his inquiries in such a way that Alicia, were she ever to see a transcript, would be unable to take offence.

During that summer the colony really began to take shape. Several other factors had built their own houses in advantageous positions, and one or two had brought out their wives, providing Alicia with some much-needed company. And, being Englishmen accumulated far from home, their thoughts immediately turned in two directions for recreation; a race course was laid out beneath the Harrington home, and a jockey club founded, with Michael the first secretary, and a cricket pitch was also laid and a cricket club undertaken. The horse racing was a success from the start but the cricket club suffered not only from a shortage of members – even Michael, who had never held a bat in his life, had to be roped in to play – but also from a total lack of opponents except when a warship was in harbour. Efforts to teach the Chinese to play the ancient game were quite ineffectual.

The growing social and business life of the community was gratifying, and did much to solace Alicia's irritation at having to give up sex as her belly became swollen. Michael went out of his way to be as solicitous as possible, and this seemed to reassure her, but she spent a lot of time bemoaning her fate and swearing that childbearing had to be more trouble than it was worth, only to be entirely reassured when in October she was delivered of a lovely baby girl. But by then, Michael had had a reply from Jalina:

It grieves me to write in this vein, but unfortunately what Ali told you was nothing less than the truth. I was unaware of what was happening for some time. Malama used to call regularly, and we would take tea together. I knew from the start that she had not enjoyed her honeymoon, but reflected this is not so very unusual, and, if pensive on occasion, she gave every indication of settling in as a housewife and hopefully a mother. But then I began to discern that relations between her husband and herself were less happy than I had hoped, and the afternoon came when she burst into tears, told me of Potts' mistreatment, and even showed me some of the marks on her body. These were the result, I was given to understand, of alcoholic excesses. I was appalled, but unable to advise her. To come between husband and wife is a terrible responsibility, nor had I his side of the story. I did, however, invite her to bring him with her when next she called, in the hopes of getting to the truth of the matter and possibly reconciling them if that were proved necessary.

Alas, my dear Michael, I have not seen her since, except once in the street, and then she hastily turned and walked the other way. But it is said that Potts mistreats her most shamefully, and there seems little doubt that when she conveyed my invitation to him, he not only refused to accept it, but forbade her to visit me again. On the other hand, things may not be as bad as rumour would have it, because I have also, only yesterday, been told by one of my servants that Mrs Potts is said to be pregnant. I am sure you will understand that in such circumstances it is even more important that Malama make the best of her life with Potts, and indeed, her condition, and the happy event which should result from it, may effect an improvement in her situation far more certainly than any outside interference. It may distress you, and myself, to suppose that we made an error of judgement in our choice of a husband for the sweet girl, but alas these things happen in too many marriages, even where actual blood relatives are involved. You have your own life to live, Michael, your own beautiful wife to love and, I have learned, your own child soon to be cherished. I am afraid that you must make up your mind to leave

Malama to live her own life as well, for better or for worse.

Yours with great affection,
Jalina

Michael sat staring at the words for some minutes, while his fingers slowly curled into fists, carrying the letter with them. Malama, all of that anxious desire to love and be loved, to be possessed, with love, at the mercy of an alcoholic boor. But then, was not her main memory of him also acting the alcoholic boor?

And now, Malama, pregnant. That perfect body swollen and heavy, as Alicia had been all these months. But perhaps delivered by now. In any event, as Jalina had reminded him, she was no longer his to care for, just as she had ceased to be Rajinder Lall's the moment she had been given to Michael. He could do nothing for her, or about her, and, again as Jalina had written so wisely, to brood on her fate would be to endanger his own marriage.

The letter lay crumpled in his hand. Now he threw it into the trash basket beneath his desk, and went upstairs to be with Alicia and baby Joanna.

'God,' remarked Paul Potts, looking down at the babe in his wife's arms. 'God Almighty! A total nigger.'

Malama held the child the more tightly. She was sitting up, and had, on instruction from the midwife, given the little boy her nipple to chew although her milk had not yet come in. With her hair spread like a shawl on the pillow behind her, and her breast exposed, she made an entrancing picture, but not to her husband. And the child was certainly dark; he took after her exactly. 'He will change, Mr Potts,' she said hopefully.

'Christ, I shall be blackballed from the club,' he said.

'They did not when you married me,' Malama ventured.

He stared at her for several seconds, then left the room. A moment later she heard the front door bang. He was

152

sober, and when he was sober he was generally ineffectual, even if she could feel the waves of hostility beating on her mind. But he was going out, and when he returned he would be drunk, and vicious.

She wondered if all men were so. Certainly on the one occasion when Michael Sahib, as she thought of him now, had got drunk, he had all but raped her. Save that that would not have been rape, and he had never been vicious. Aggressive, yes. No man to cross, certainly. But not vicious.

She had never attempted to cross her husband. However much she regretted the turn of events which had caused her to be given to him, as it had been done, she had been prepared to make the most of it. Even when he had lain, so heavily, on her during their honeymoon, she had rejected the temptation to fantasize that he was Michael in favour of seeking enjoyment from her husband. It had been impossible. She did not like his odour, his grunts, his attempts at humour, and most of all, his weight, which all but crushed her. Thus she had made her first mistake. After enduring him for several nights she had allowed herself the smallest hint that there might be other, more enjoyable ways of performing the sexual act, and when he had stared at her uncomprehendingly, had shyly endeavoured to guide him. He had called her a black-faced slut, and slapped her face, forbidding her to attempt such filth in the future. Malama, who had been educated by Panka and Shalina to believe that sexual relations should always be conducted in a mood of total enjoyment, had been astounded and frightened by his reaction. That night for the first time he had got drunk and beaten her, before lying on her more heavily than ever before, while the tears had still been streaming down her face.

After that the beatings had become more frequent. And they were an aspect of those very relations she had sought to improve. He whipped her with his belt, making her kneel or lie in front of him, clearly dreaming of acts he dared not perform, and then massaging the tortured flesh with heavy fingers before rolling her on her back. He never attempted to stimulate her in any way, and when he had once discovered her attempting to stimulate herself he had called her a whore and beaten her again.

In her bewilderment she had gone to the only friend she possessed in Singapore, the Princess Jalina, but had been unable to explain the truth of the matter, for fear the princess might herself not understand.

Jalina had been concerned at Potts' brutality, however, and had even tried to help. That had been Malama's third and biggest mistake. Potts had been enraged at the thought of her taking her domestic problems to an outsider, and had beaten her more severely than ever while forbidding her to speak with the princess again. But his own behaviour had improved once he had learned that others might know of it, and to that extent had she benefited, while within a few weeks she had become pregnant. Since then her life had been almost pleasant, even if she knew it was not her Karma ever to be happy.

Until the babe had been born. Then she had indeed been happy, for a few hours. Until Potts had seen its colour.

She did not know what he had expected. But his anger was again frightening. Because now he did not have just her to beat. And he was going to be drunk when he came in. Malama chewed her lip as the babe chewed her teat. The feeling from her breast was heavenly; the feelings consuming her mind were unbearable.

She got out of bed, still holding the babe, stood at the jalousie, looking through the slats at the street, able to see without being seen. It was a mean street, because this was a mean house in a mean quarter of the town; Potts was no more than a clerk, and had very little prospect of ever being much more than that. The street was also, however, almost empty, because it was raining, as the monsoon had begun a week before. The drumming of the water on the roof seemed to isolate her inside the wooden prison which was her home, awaiting the return of her gaoler. But if he hurt the child . . .

154

Yet he would. Her instincts told her that he would regard the baby as an entirely suitable receptacle for his sadistic anger. And she, in her weakness after her pregnancy and delivery, would be helpless.

If she was here. It had never before occurred to her to leave him. He was her husband, and there was an end to it. But just to protect the child, for a few precious days, until he was stronger . . . until she was stronger, and more able to resist him.

She laid the babe on the bed, dressed herself in a sari and added a cloak, then wrapped him up as well, and tucked him inside her own clothes. She had no servants, as Potts refused to allow her that much money, so the house was empty. She did not even lock the door behind herself, but hurried into the rain and began the walk up the hill.

It was long, and wet. The rain splashed on her head and soon the cloak was soaked through, and so were she and the child. Clear of the town there was a wind as well, strong enough to make her stagger as she bent over, still hugging that precious bundle to her breast, climbing towards the brilliant lights of the houses of the wealthy. By the time she stumbled up the steps she sought, she was dripping water, and the child was uttering a thin wail.

There were some carriages outside, and the drivers, huddled beneath the overhang for shelter, peered at her in amazement. She ignored them and rang the bell, to be greeted superciliously by the major-domo. 'Her Highness is entertaining.'

'Please let me in,' Malama begged. 'I am so cold and wet. My babe is so wet. He will die if you do not let me in. Please, just while you tell the princess I am here.'

The man hesitated, but he remembered her of course, always being treated as a friend rather than a servant by his employer. So he stepped aside and she entered the warmth of the house, to drip water on his polished wooden floor. 'Wait there,' he commanded. 'Do not move.'

Malama waited, shivering, water gathering in a pool around her feet, her child shuddering in her arms.

155

'Malama? Oh, my dear, dear child!' Jalina wore her Thai tunic and skirt, and her cap was bright with jewels. Her period of mourning over, she had begun to sparkle again, and with Teng Lee dead she had even sought a reconciliation with her nephew, Phra Neng Klao, who ruled Siam as Rama III. This had been successful, as Rama was in favour of good relations with the British, and had recently signed a treaty with them. As a result of this Jalina had recently returned from visiting Bangkok for the first time in more than thirty years. Singapore gossip indeed had it that she had been looking for a new husband – but if she had there was no evidence of it. Now her warm, confident, powerful personality flowed over the miserable girl. 'My Lord Buddha, your condition!' The princess clapped her hands and they were surrounded by servants. 'Quickly! Take her upstairs and dry her. And the babe. Oh, what a lovely child he is. Tell me his name.'

'He has no name, as yet,' Malama said.

'No name? Heavens. Then we must find him one. But first, dry clothes. Quickly,' she told her women. 'And prepare food for them both.'

Malama sighed, and allowed herself to be taken upstairs and put to bed. The last time she had been happy had been in this house, when she had still supposed she would one day belong to Michael Sahib. Now, at least for an hour or two, she could be happy again.

'I have come for my wife,' Paul Potts said, only grudgingly adding, 'Your Highness.'

The Princess Jalina regarded him for several seconds. 'She is not well,' she said at last.

'Indeed? Surely I am entitled to know why?'

'She has caught a cold. Her babe also is unwell.'

'She inflicted this upon herself, by walking here through the rain,' Potts said. 'With the babe. She is totally irresponsible.'

'She was very afraid, Mr Potts. Of you. Won't you sit down?' Jalina seated herself.

156

Potts remained standing. 'I wish to see my wife and son.'

'Of course. You shall. But you must not frighten or alarm her. She has confided to me many of her misfortunes. Of which you are the author. I am disgusted. And you should show a proper love for your son. Why should a child not take after his mother? The next one will probably look just like you.'

Potts opened his mouth and then closed it again. He did not work for Hammond and Teng, but he knew the financial power of these people; the widow of Teng Lee was no one with whom to quarrel. 'I was hasty,' he acknowledged.

'You terrified your wife out of her senses,' Jalina said severely. 'She was, she is, convinced that you meant to harm the boy.'

'What nonsense.'

'Then you must convince her that it was nonsense, Mr Potts. She wishes to love you and be your wife, in all things. You must respond to her. Or she will leave you, for good.'

Potts snorted. 'How may a wife leave her husband? Especially a Hindu bint like Malama?'

Jalina stared at him. 'A wife may do whatever she pleases, Mr Potts, so long as she has support. Malama does not lack support. From myself, certainly. But I think you should know that Michael Harrington is still greatly interested in Malama's well-being. He and I are in constant communication, and thus far I have endeavoured to make him believe that all is well between your wife and yourself. Were I to acquaint him with the true state of affairs, you might find him in Singapore before you could draw breath: it is only a week's sail from Hong Kong.'

Potts endeavoured to meet her gaze, but his face had paled. 'Harrington has nothing to do with Malama any more,' he protested. 'She is my wife.'

'Yet is she still his responsibility, in his eyes. I think this is something you should remember. Now you may visit your wife.' Jalina rang her golden bell, and a servant

157

immediately appeared. 'Escort Mr Potts to Mrs Potts' bedchamber, please, Achmed. Oh, and Mr Potts, Malama is aware of Mr Harrington's continuing interest in her. I have told her of it.'

Potts gazed at her for a moment, then followed the footman out of the room. The door was closed, and Jalina took a long breath. Then she got up and stood before the ashes in the golden urn on the mantelpiece. 'What else could I do?' she asked. 'Save invoke his name? Where I would never dare invoke the man himself?'

The news that Michael was still inquiring after her was like the most soothing of drinks to a parched throat, for Malama. He had not forgotten her, whatever the glories of his red-haired Englishwoman, the responsibilities of his new position. He still cared for her. And in his caring, even at a distance of several hundred miles, was she protected. And with her, the babe. Nearer at hand, she knew she could now rely on the princess. Jalina indeed, having heard the sad tale from beginning to end, had insisted on giving her an allowance of her very own. This was nothing to do with Potts, and indeed he knew nothing of it; Malama would collect the money in cash from the princess's bank when she went to market. It gave her independence and an increased sense of security; it had never occurred to her to refuse the generous offer – that would have been to insult the princess.

As Potts showed no interest in the child, she named him Janus, after the Roman god of whom she had read in the princess's library. That Janus had been the god of the doorway had no particular significance to her; she merely liked the name and she felt it would have been impolitic to use the name Michael. Potts attended the christening with a bad grace, although he was all smiles when he discovered that Jalina had brought with her both the senior Hammonds and Margaret and Jeremy Cooper. But when they returned from the ceremony he immediately left the house, and did not return until after midnight. This had become his regular pattern, as it had been his pattern before her confinement, but nowadays there was a difference: he never sought her body, either to love or to abuse, and slept in the other room. Their marriage had in fact ended, even if they remained man and wife.

Malama was perfectly happy about this. She had Janus to love, she had Jalina to visit, and she had Michael to dream about. Through Jalina she was able to learn of him, and devour every bit of news that came her way. Thus she learned how he had become the father of a girl and then a boy, how the business was prospering as Hong Kong was developing into the goldmine he had always known it would, and how he was in the best of health. As was his wife. Jalina claimed they were very happy, and Malama had no doubt they were, nor was she put out by this. She wanted Michael to be happy more than anything else in the world. Her only concern was the news that there was again friction between the Chinese and the British, and especially in the south, where the Cantonese had objected to the foreign devils freely entering their walled city, and where there had been several incidents. But Jalina assured her that Canton was a long way from Hong Kong, and that in any event the Chinese would never dare attack a British colony.

Learning about Michael, knowing how he was prospering, enabled her to go about her own life with purpose, the purpose of having Janus grow up and perhaps go to work for Hammond and Teng. She was sure Michael would give him a position, and with Clive Hammond visibly ailing she was also sure that Michael would soon be in a position of even greater authority than he now held. He might even return to Singapore. But that was to make her dreams almost painful.

But meanwhile, Janus. He was a strong child, and indeed recovered more quickly than did she from their soaking on the day after his birth. By the time he was four years old he was a sturdy, lusty little boy. Unfortunately he remained as dark-complexioned as herself. Not that she supposed his father would have cared much for him even if he had miraculously turned white; Potts con-

tinued to do his best to ignore both of them. Which led
to a very peaceful household. When Janus was four
Malama had reached the age of twenty-one, and was in
the fullest bloom of her beauty, her breasts heavy but not
yet begun to sag, her hips slender, her legs long and
straight. Left to herself, she invariably wore a sari, and
she equally indulged the weakness of her race and loaded
herself with gold jewellery, from bangles on her arms to
anklets and earrings; thanks to Jalina's allowance she was
a reasonably wealthy woman. When she went to the
market or walked her son she attracted a host of glances,
to which she returned one of her gentle smiles, and the
people of Singapore came to understand that if her marriage had begun badly she now seemed to have reached a
very good relationship with her husband.

When she reflected that she had to have done better
than any of her sisters, in view of her lack of caste, she
felt very pleased with herself, and in her mood of totally
relaxed contentment was the more taken entirely by surprise to be awakened on the morning of the first of January, 1849, by her bedroom door being nearly torn from
its hinges as it crashed open.

She sat up in amazement more than alarm, while Janus,
who nowadays shared her bed, began to cry, and stared
at her husband. Malama was well aware that the last day
of their year was one of great importance to the British,
important in the sense that everyone went out and danced
and got very drunk and used the opportunity to kiss and
fondle every possible woman except their own wives. She
had never been invited to accompany Potts on one of these
occasions, nor would she have gone even if asked; that
sort of entertainment had no appeal for her. But that Potts
would hardly return before dawn, and then very much
the worse for wear, was inevitable. Now it was certainly
not yet dawn, but that he was the worse for wear was
obvious; his cravat was undone, his coat and waistcoat
both open, and he leaned drunkenly against the door.

'The little bint,' he said. 'Come and look at the bint.
She's a sight to warm the heart of any man.'

160

The doorway was suddenly filled with other men, and Malama gasped and pulled the sheet to her throat; she had learnt a great deal about modesty since coming to live in the white man's world. 'Get them out,' she said.

Potts grinned at her. 'See how she orders me about. Friends in high places, she has. But not tonight, you black-skinned bastard. Not tonight. See how she hugs the child? What, do you suppose she uses him as her dildo?'

'Get out of my room,' Malama said, speaking quietly but loading her voice with all the venom she could manage. She looked past him at the other three men. 'Can't you see he's drunk?'

But they were drunk as well, and grinning at her.

'They're my friends,' Potts told her. 'I invited them back here. I told them my wife would entertain them. My wife!' His voice suddenly became a snarl, and he seized the sheet. She clung on to it, then let it go as she was almost jerked from the bed. She panted, and drew up her legs to hide her nakedness, and found the bed surrounded by the men.

'Let's take her into the other room,' one of them said. 'Give her a little drink.'

Malama looked from face to face, seeking the slightest sign of humanity, of pity, even of uncertainty, but there was none. When one reached for her, she struck at him, but he laughed and caught her wrist.

'Don't mark her, now,' Potts warned. 'Nothing she can show that yellow bitch.'

'Nothing but love bites,' said another of the men, seizing one of her ankles as she attempted to kick.

'As for you,' Potts said, as Janus began to scream, 'I'll shut your miserable trap.' His hand slashed sideways, and Janus gave a wail and fell out of bed.

'My baby,' Malama cried. She tried to throw herself away from them, and had her other ankle seized. Potts then caught her last free wrist. 'If you scream,' he told her, as her lips drew back from her teeth, 'We'll take it out on the boy.'

Janus was quiet now, but at least she knew he was alive,

161

because she could hear him whimpering. She closed her mouth again, attempting to think, to compose herself against the coming ordeal. She knew she could not fight them, and she knew they were drunk enough to carry out their threat. All that mattered was that Janus should not be harmed. So she did not attempt to resist them as they carried her through the doorway and into the living room, where she was thrown on the settee.

'A little drink,' one of the men said. 'To warm her up.'

A bottle was produced. She attempted to refuse, and had her hair seized to pull her head back. Fingers squeezed her cheeks to make her open her mouth, and the liquid was poured down her throat. She gasped and choked, for it was not wine and burned her mouth and throat, but before she could spit it out someone had dug her in the ribs and she swallowed.

'There,' said another of the men. 'Have another.' He sat beside her and played with her breasts while he made her drink; his friend was still holding her hair, and now the third man sat on her other side, and pulled her legs apart to put his hand between. She had to fight back the urge to scream as loudly as she could, to fight until she made them knock her unconscious, instead stared at her husband, standing facing her, grinning at her.

'If you give her too much,' he said, 'she'll pass out.'

'I'll take her first,' said the man holding her hair. He released her and came round the front, dropping his breeches. 'You owe me most.'

'Yes, Jimmy first,' said another of the men.

'Christ, she's something,' the man called Jimmy said, standing above her, naked and eager.

Malama closed her eyes, and had her arm nearly torn off by a jerk. 'You look at him,' Potts snarled. 'And you move. You like to move, don't you, sweetheart? Well, you move.'

Jimmy was kneeling between her legs, and a moment later was inside her. She was dry with revulsion and fear, and he hurt so that she did indeed move, jerking with pain, but the alcohol swirling around her brain made her less aware of what was happening. Hands fondled her breasts, and she realized Potts had released her wrist. But she was too afraid to risk striking at her tormentors.

Jimmy was quick, and then it was the turn of the second man. From their chatter she gathered Potts had lost her to them in a card game. All of them. And the second man, whose name was Bob, was seeking something new.

'They like it best on their knees,' he slobbered.

'On your knees, bitch,' Potts commanded.

She was dragged off the settee and made to kneel against it, while Bob mounted her from behind. Then the third man took her, while the pain faded into a general misery, and the hate balloon began to fill in her mind. Malama had never hated before. Hatred did not come into the philosophy into which she had been born. One's life was ruled by Karma, and to rail against the dictates of fate was senseless. Michael Sahib had taught her differently, and her life amidst his people had completed her education; the white men moulded fate to their own ends, whenever they could. Thus she had sought to do the same, in her own small way, by means of her friend the princess. And had thought she had succeeded. But hatred was an emotion she had found it hard to develop. She had never even hated her husband, until tonight, because, whatever he had done to her, he was her husband. But to kneel, and feel strange men inside her, and have their fingers scouring her body, pushing into her, fingering her breasts, driving into her hair, while he, her natural protector, stood by and grinned, suddenly filled her mind with only anger. Perhaps, she felt, the emotion which had inspired Michael Sahib to attack and destroy the tiger.

Her body sagged against the settee as she only slowly realized that no one was actually raping her, or even touching her. Dimly she heard their chatter, realized the men were tearing up the IOUs given them by Potts. 'We must play again,' the man called Jimmy was saying. 'Soon, Potts. I could stand some more of that.'

Malama remained still until she heard the door close. Then she pushed herself to her feet. Her eyes were dry, where earlier she had wept in shame and misery. She was exhausted, and she was hurting, everywhere. Her head was still spinning from the brandy they had made her drink. She wanted only to lie down, but she knew she could not do that. Not in this house. Not any more.

She stumbled towards the bedroom door, and heard movement behind her. She stopped, every muscle tensed. 'My turn now,' Potts said. 'Christ, but you looked good, kneeling there. You kneel now, against the bed. That's how I want you, kneeling there.'

She turned and struck at him. He was taken by surprise, and her nail opened a gash on his cheek. He staggered, and she stepped past him, to lift Janus from the floor where he still lay. There would be no time to dress herself, but that didn't matter.

'Bitch!' Hands grasped her shoulders and she dropped the child, who gave another wail of alarm. 'Bitch!' Potts snarled again, spinning her round and driving her towards the bed.

Malama struck backwards with her elbows and heels, and connected, because he gave another grunt of pain and his hands slipped on her sweat-wet flesh. Freed, she scrambled over the bed, reached the far side, and turned to face him. They stared at each other in the gloom, then he reached for the boy. 'I'll show you,' he said.

'No,' Malama cried, speaking for the first time in an hour; it was almost painful so tightly had her jaws been clamped together. 'No. Please.'

Potts checked, and turned back to her. 'You'll be good,' he said.

'Yes,' Malama promised. 'Please, do not hurt him.'

'Ha,' he said, and took off his belt. 'Come here.'

She shuddered, and knelt, and the leather strap slashed into her buttocks, time and again. She wept, and her brain seethed, until he was finished. But he would not let her rise, as he knelt behind her in turn, and drove himself into her, while horror welled into her chest. She was tied to this man for the rest of her life. And so was the child. If he did not harm Janus now, he would certainly do so at some time in the future. He was a devil sent by hell to drive them both to destruction. The hate had now gained control of her entire mind, her entire body as well; she could feel it throbbing through her system, even when he let her go and fell across the bed. 'That was good,' he said. 'That was good. We'll do that again, when I wake up.' His eyes opened. 'When I wake up,' he said. 'Or I'll beat the skin from that little bastard's behind. Remember that. A man can beat his own son, eh? Not even your yellow bitch friend can stop me doing that. I should've thought of that before.' He grinned as he fell asleep, chest heaving.

Malama dragged herself to her feet and stood looking down at him for some seconds. The only sound in the room was herself breathing, great rasps of air sucking out of her very belly and through her nostrils. Her teeth were clamped again, her muscles tight. If she had been taught to accept the whims of fate, she had also been taught to avenge the ills of her family, where they were wrought by other men. Now only vengeance mattered. Vengeance which would end the danger to Janus for ever.

Malama went into the kitchen, moving quietly. She picked up the large knife she used to chop meat, and returned to the bedroom. But, convulsed with outrage as she was, her brain was as cool as it had ever been. She knew what she must do, now, and after. But after could only happen if the now was done properly. So she picked up the blanket and draped it across her husband's chest. He moved, and snored. Malama knelt beside him and arranged the blanket from his neck to his waist. Then she picked up the knife, and drove it through the blanket into his chest. Blood soaked the blanket and Potts opened his eyes in a gasp of horror, but nothing stained even Malama's fingers as she drove the knife into his chest again.

7

The Anger of One Wronged

The Christmas and New Year celebrations of 1848–49 were the best yet enjoyed by Hong Kong, certainly in the eyes of Alicia Harrington. The colony had been growing rapidly, and there were some twelve couples who shared the festivities. In whose midst she was the queen. Almost certainly these people knew she was a daughter of Clive Hammond of Hammond and Teng, but here in Hong Kong there were no Chinese associates to be seen, only servants, and with her husband not only factor for the wealthiest trading company on the coast, but also well known and highly respected by the naval authorities – who were still very important as mainland China, only a few hundred yards away, seethed with revolt and xenophobia – she was the most sought-after guest, the most valued hostess, on the island..

Which was what, she reflected, she had always been intended by nature to be. At twenty eight years old, and twice a mother, she was by some way the most beautiful woman in the colony. Her clothes, sent to her from Singapore, were the richest, as was her jewellery. Her horses were the best, her phaeton the most equipped with gilt and polish; she employed Chinese grooms and had them dressed in a sky-blue livery, often to match the colour of her gowns or habits. Her table was unequalled, both in its splendour and its variety, for she had two chefs, one Chinese and one Malay, to ensure no two dinner parties were ever the same. She was in superb physical health, and found the somewhat cooler temperature of Hong Kong such a relief after the heat and humidity of Singapore that she abounded with energy. And more than any of the other women on the island, she was loved.

The public proof of this were her children. Joanna at four already possessed her mother's auburn hair and traces, too, of her individual approach to life; little Ralph at three was a sturdy and healthy youngster. Their births had caused her little more than discomfort; she had satisfied at once convention and her mothering instinct by feeding them for four months before handing them over to a Chinese wet nurse, and vanity by thus preserving her figure.

Because the private proof of her totally happy existence lay in her bed, where daily she used her magnificent white body – no sunbeam was ever allowed to come near an inch of her flesh – to rouse Michael to peaks of performance she doubted he had supposed he was capable of achieving, which left her exhausted and utterly sated, a tumultuous red and white mound of seething flesh.

That she was utterly happy, and possessed everything her heart could desire, she well understood, but as with her life even before she had met Michael, she counted it nothing more than her birthright. And she was careful to maintain herself, not only by being always healthy and laughing and loving to ensure that Michael himself was totally happy, but by refusing to return to Singapore or to allow him to do so. Indeed, he had too much to do in Hong Kong, as he worked to establish the business, nor could she have travelled very much during the preceding few years because of her confinements. But she had no intention of returning, even briefly, to being a second-class citizen; even less did she have any intention of ever allowing Michael to lay eyes on his dark-skinned ward again. Out of sight, out of mind, at least until Malama Potts would be fat and ugly – Alicia had been informed by self-pronounced experts that this invariably happened to Indian women, and at an early age.

That was worth waiting for. Nor did she suffer any great feeling of separation from her family. Mama arrived for each confinement, and Margaret came for a visit. The other ladies of Hong Kong were amazed at the temerity of the Hammond family, in view of the severe piracy

167

problem in the South China Sea. Almost every month news arrived of some atrocity or other committed by the Filipino freebooters, whom the Royal Navy seemed quite unable to bring to justice – the pirates could identify a warship a long way off, and would then disappear into their creeks and lagoons, inside Spanish territorial waters – but remarkably, no ship flying the house flag of Hammond and Teng was ever attacked. That obviously well-known power was something else to be proud of.

Not everything in Alicia's life was unadulterated pleasure, of course. She was often concerned about her husband's moods, for Michael, if in the main an utter charmer, could be almost frighteningly sombre on occasion. At first she supposed it might still be a memory of Malama, but she soon concluded it was merely a result of his tendency to worry – an unusual trait in an Irishman. But he certainly looked very grim when the piratical horrors were being discussed, as if he doubted his ships' immunity could last much longer; nor was he very happy whenever a shipment of opium arrived from the south, and positively glowered at the eager Chinese merchants who crossed from the mainland to bid for the precious drug. This she related to the increasing rumbles coming out of China, and in particular to the activities of a bandit called Hung Hsiu-ch'uan, who was some kind of latterday prophet, so far as Alicia could gather, and who had suddenly emerged in the mountains beyond Canton as an outlaw leader, stirring up the people of the south against the Manchu. Michael had told her that he knew this fellow Hung, and indeed that Hung had once saved his life, but that then he had disappeared so completely that Michael had supposed him dead. Now Hung had reappeared and was causing as much trouble as ever, and this obviously bothered Michael, much as the growing Manchu hostility to European encroachment – and the terms secured by the British at Nanking had hastily been required by the French and the Germans and the Russians, while even the Americans were obviously much interested in what was happening in China – was also unsettling. Alicia could not understand why. Whatever happened on the mainland, she had no doubt at all that the memory of their total defeat only a few years ago would inhibit the Chinese from ever attempting to retake Hong Kong. Michael's tendency to worry was the only real cloud on her sunlit horizon.

Michael Harrington stood on his office verandah and swung his telescope slowly to and fro over Stonecutters Island and then down to the West Lamma Channel. At any moment now the *China Star* should appear there, bringing Wong Sung and a cargo of opium. Another cargo of opium, another huge profit for the company, another substantial bonus for himself. It was now all but ten years since Hung had shown him the opium den and illustrated the horrible end product of the trade from which he was now taking his livelihood. Thus, it was ten years since he had sworn to have nothing more to do with it.

The channel was empty; Michael sat down with a sigh. Easy to find excuses. He had felt he could do nothing about the trade until he was established in the firm. But was he not established now? Was he not in a position to go to Singapore and say to Clive Hammond, 'You obviously do not understand the evil you are perpetrating. Now I say that it has got to stop. There are many other goods from India and from England which the Chinese will be happy to purchase from us. None with quite the financial return of opium, perhaps, but which will yet show a profit.' The old man might well be taken aback, but Michael did not suppose he would dismiss his son-in-law, especially where the well-being of his youngest daughter was concerned – Michael tried to convince himself that Alicia loved him so much that she could be persuaded to follow him in whatever he chose to do. He could entirely understand her reluctance to return to Singapore at this time, her fear of allowing him to go on his own. But if he explained the circumstances, assured her it was a business and moral undertaking and nothing more . . . yet he had not done so. Because he feared

169

rejection? Or the woman herself? That was not an admission he would make to anyone save himself. But Alicia moved through life with such assured conviction – rather like Hung Hsiu-ch'uan he would think with a smile – and could express her anger so forcibly, that to confront her with a situation she might find unacceptable required a great deal of determination to see it through to the end of her displeasure.

Thus neither had he made any attempt to stop the Chinese from buying the stuff out of his warehouses, when he could easily have forced the issue by jettisoning the lot in the harbour. Because he was, after all, a scoundrel? Well, he had never really denied that, to anyone. If he drank sparingly nowadays, that was because he had a beautiful and ardent wife to satisfy daily; if his attentions never strayed to another woman, it was for the same reason – he did not doubt that Alicia was as well aware of those things as himself. If they differed in any approach to life, it was simply because she did not understand the properties of opium, and he had never told her – for which he had to take all the blame.

Because the truth was, he did not want to interfere, in any way, with the life, the happiness, which was now his. That was why he had never denounced Ali's dealings with the pirates, although all the evidence indicated that his brother-in-law was still doing so. He had fallen on his feet, and he was too much enjoying the feel of the firm ground beneath him.

He had even, with the passage of time, ceased to think about it, until quite recently; he had convinced himself that if the Chinese did not drug themselves to death they would surely find some other way of accomplishing that end. Having watched them killing each other, and starving, and hating, with the same indifference, he had even been able to persuade himself that those with the wherewithal to withdraw into the dreams of poppyland were the most fortunate. Until news had come of a raid launched on a town some distance from Canton by the bandit Hung Hsiu-ch'uan. He had been so sure that Hung had disappeared for ever, a dreamer who had lacked the support for substance. But he had survived, and if the tales of him riding at the head of several thousand men were true, then far from being a fugitive he had been consolidating his strength in the mountains.

And did he return to his encampment to pat a comely young mother on the head, and perhaps raise a seven-year-old boy on to his knee? What right did Michael Harrington have to be happy when his eldest son was living in conditions of squalor and danger, every day of his life?

But was Michael Harrington going to do anything about that, either?

'The ship, Master,' Ho Chu said, emerging from the back of the house.

Michael sat up, levelled the glass once more. The junk was running up the channel before the fresh southerly breeze. He nodded. 'The ship, Ho Chu. Perhaps you will ride down to the harbour this afternoon and ask Captain Wong to dine.'

'Of course, Master,' Ho Chu said.

Michael leaned back again. The *China Star* would not dock before dusk, and there could be no inspection of the cargo until tomorrow, when unloading would begin. It was time to stop brooding and start again being the Michael Harrington that Hong Kong knew and loved.

There was a meeting of the Jockey Club to be attended, which did not end until just after six. Michael swung into the saddle for the ride up the hill, looking forward to seeing Wong Sung again and hearing all the Singapore gossip. There would also be letters, certainly for Alicia, which would please her greatly. There might even be one for him, he thought. Perhaps from Jalina. She had not written for some time. Although that had to be a good thing, as it meant all was well with Malama.

'Master!'

He turned his head, saw Ho Chu astride his mule on the other side of the street. The big Chinese sailor looked extremely unhappy.

Michael rode towards him. 'Is the ship not in?'

'The ship is in, Master.'

Michael frowned at him. 'Is Wong Sung not in command?'

'Captain Wong is in command, Master. But he asks to see you.'

'He'll see me at dinner, Ho Chu.'

'He wishes to see you now, on board the ship, Master. It is a most urgent matter.'

Michael's frown deepened. An epidemic, perhaps? Well, he thought grimly, that would prevent at least this cargo being landed. He rode beside his servant towards the docks. 'You know of this matter?'

'It is Captain Wong who knows of it, Master,' Ho Chu said enigmatically.

The *China Star* was alongside, which did not suggest that the harbour authority had been concerned she might need quarantining. Her crew were on deck to greet the factor, bowing respectfully as he jumped down from the gangway. Wong Sung was also on deck, looking as far removed from his usual jaunty self as possible.

'What the devil has happened?' Michael asked.

'If you will come below,' Wong said, and opened the cabin door.

Michael stepped inside, and the door closed. He blinked to accustom his eyes to the light, and gazed at Malama.

For a moment Michael was too bemused to speak. Or even think. 'Malama?' he asked stupidly.

'I brought her on the instructions of the Princess Jalina,' Wong explained. 'There is a letter.'

Michael continued to stare at Malama, who had already bowed, and now raised her head to meet his eyes. 'I did not know what to do, Michael Sahib,' she said.

He took in her beauty, the gold bangles which clasped her arms, but also the sadness in her expression and the fact that she no longer wore her wedding ring, tried to restrain the feeling of the most utter joy to be seeing her

172

again flooding his brain. But she was so clearly unhappy. 'You spoke of a letter.'

She held it out, and he sat down to slit the envelope. 'Michael,' Jalina had written.

It seems that some lives are steeped in catastrophe. Your Malama may be one such unfortunate, unless you are able to help her. I can think of no one else. Michael, the poor child has slain her husband.

Michael raised his head in horror, to stare at the girl, who this time did not lower her eyes. He looked down again.

If what she has told me is true of the way he has misused her, and I have every reason to believe that it is, then no man deserved more richly to die. Yet will the world, his world – your world, Michael, the world of the white conqueror – call it murder. Having struck him, she has fled with her babe to her only friend in Singapore, myself. I was aghast at what she has had to say. She wishes to destroy herself, and for the child to be sent to you. I cannot permit this, any more than could you. Thus, as I know Wong Sung, who is a faithful friend of yours, is due to depart for Hong Kong tomorrow morning, I have devised at least a holding operation: today is a public holiday, and there is little chance of Potts being discovered before tomorrow.

Malama now understands that in her circumstances her son is best with me. I have thus taken him into my care until events turn again in our favour. As to when they will do this I am quite unable to say. Michael, this girl, whom I know you love as dearly as do I, will be hanged should the authorities here arrest her. Presumably they will be able to send behind her to Hong Kong, should they discover that is where she has gone, but this may well take them some time. For my part, I will tell the truth, that she brought her child to me, and then left again. Wong Sung and his people are faithful

173

and will volunteer no adverse information, although I would not ask them to lie should they be asked a straight question; in taking her to Hong Kong they are of course in ignorance of what she has done even if they may suppose a crisis has arisen. Her fate is therefore in your hands. Even if my husband's relatives are now all dead, I know you have friends on the mainland of China, which is beyond the reach of any British authorities. If you could convey Malama to these friends, and establish her there, we will surely find a way of reuniting her with her son, and enable her yet to find a modicum of happiness.

Your affectionate accomplice,
Jalina

Michael continued staring at the sheets of paper for some seconds, while his brain tumbled. He dared not allow himself even to consider what Malama must have suffered to cause her to murder her husband. Nor was it any use considering Jalina's naïveté, in supposing first of all that the Singapore authorities would not immediately know what had become of Mrs Potts, or in assuming that finding her a haven in China was a mere matter of snapping his fingers. Or in failing to recognize that the girl's appearance in Hong Kong, if discovered, would utterly disrupt his life. But neither did he want to consider any of those things. She was here, where she had always belonged, and he would save her, no matter what it cost.

Although he recognized that it was not going to be easy; Alicia's reaction to the situation equally did not bear consideration – even if he was right in assuming that his wife adored him, he knew too well that it was a jealous adoration. At last he looked at Malama, then at Wong Sung. The captain and himself had indeed become good friends, and Wong had confessed to him that he had as little taste for dealing with the pirates as Michael – but like him, having accepted money from Ali to do so, felt unable to denounce his employer. But he could certainly be trusted to aid Malama to escape the consequences of her crime.

'She will remain on board,' Michael said.

'Of course,' Wong agreed. 'But I cannot take her back to Singapore.' He gave a little shrug. 'She has confessed to me.'

'But you will not betray her.'

'No, Michael, I will not betray her.'

Michael clasped his hand. 'The princess recommends that she be found a home on mainland China, at least until we see how the situation develops.'

'China?' Malama asked fearfully.

'Yes. I have friends who will help you.' Did he know that? Did he know they would still be his friends, after so long? He had no alternative but to find out. 'When Wang An arrives tomorrow, I will speak with him. In the meantime, no one in Hong Kong is to know of Mrs Potts' presence. Understood?'

'Of course,' Wong agreed again.

'No one at all,' Michael repeated. 'You will come to dinner as invited, Wong. We will ride up together.' He turned to Malama, took her hands. 'It will be all right, I promise you. It will be all right.'

Her fingers were tight on his. 'He prostituted me, Michael Sahib. And beat me. Perhaps I could have stood all that, but then he threatened my babe. Michael Sahib, I had to do it.'

'I know, Malama, I know. And I will see that no harm comes to you.'

'Will you accompany me to these friends of yours?'

Michael sighed. 'Yes,' he said. He had no choice.

'Wong was strangely silent tonight,' Alicia commented as Melinda brushed out her curls.

'Yes,' Michael agreed. 'The situation in China is becoming as difficult as ever it was in thirty-nine.'

'Oh? Mama mentions nothing of that in her letter. Nor Margaret.'

'Well, I suppose your father does not care to keep them

as informed about affairs as I do you, my love.' He sat on the bed to watch her, as he usually did, and smiled at her face in the mirror, while preparing to lie to her like the blackest villain in all the world. 'In fact . . .' he sighed.

'Tell me?' She was frowning.

'I'm afraid I am going to have to go up to Canton.'

'Canton?' Her voice rose an octave and she turned on her stool, to the discomfort of Melinda, who hovered, brush in hand.

'I shouldn't be away more than a month.'

'But why? Oh, Melinda, get out, do.'

Melinda hesitated, then put down the brush with a flourish and left the room.

'It is a political matter, really. I must see some people there, urgently.'

'I shall come with you,' Alicia announced.

'Now, darling, I simply cannot permit that.'

'Why not? I would adore to see China. It is stupid, to have lived here for six years and never set foot on the mainland.'

'You cannot,' he said firmly. 'You will not. It is far too dangerous. It is a highly secret mission, and I shall have to travel rough.'

'But it will not be dangerous for you?'

'It is something I have done before, therefore I know what to expect. It will be distinctly uncomfortable, I assure you.'

'Michael,' Alicia said, 'I would like to come with you. I am not the least concerned with danger or discomfort. I wish to be with you.'

'And I have said you cannot, my darling. What, leave the children for a month? You know you cannot do that.'

She glared at him for several seconds, then crossed the room and threw herself on the bed, her back to him. When he touched her shoulder she did not respond.

Well, he thought, she would just have to sulk. He could at least tell his conscience that he would not have taken her with him even if Malama had not been there: it was far too dangerous and uncomfortable for a woman like

Alicia. And for Malama? But Malama's life had reached such a state nothing could involve any greater risk than her present situation.

'It will be very difficult,' Wang An pointed out, burying his folded arms in the huge sleeves of his blue silk blouse. 'And very dangerous. I do not know if it can be accomplished at all, Mr Harrington.'

'It can be accomplished, Wang An, if we are both determined that it should be,' Michael told him.

They sat in the cabin of the *China Star*, and Malama, who of course spoke no Chinese, looked from one to the other with intense anxiety. So far as Michael knew, her presence in Hong Kong was still a secret from anyone other than the crew, Ho Chu and himself. Although the ship had been in port five days, she had only ventured on deck after dark for a breath of fresh air. He had seen her every day, and gradually some of her fear and despair had dwindled under the influence of his confident personality. Yet she was still afraid, and close to despair, as she gazed at the pessimistic Chinese merchant. And every day made it more important to get her out of the reach of British justice just as rapidly as possible.

Fortunately, Michael knew that Wang An was always pessimistic, about everything. They had first met in Teng Hu's house all but ten years before. Wang had been one of the very few of that circle to have escaped the wrath of Commissioner Lin – how, no one knew, and Michael had thought better than to ask. But Wang had kept himself and his wealth intact, and remained one of the biggest of the opium dealers – and he had certainly been acquainted with Hung Hsiu-ch'uan, while as he was one of the few wealthy landlords whose estate had not been attacked by Hung's bandits, he had to be at least acquainted with Hung still. Michael indeed had little doubt he was one of those supplying Hung with both arms and information.

Now he said, 'I cannot promise that Hung Hsiu ch'uan will even wish to meet with you.'

'He will wish to meet with me,' Michael assured him. 'You will not fail me in this, Wang An, or I will sell you no more opium. I wish to ascend the river, secretly, the day after tomorrow. And I wish to make contact with Hung Hsiu-ch'uan when I reach Canton. You will arrange these things.'

Wang An bowed. 'I will do my humble best, Mr Harrington.'

'You will arrange it, Wang.'

Wang An bowed again, looked at Malama, and left the cabin.

'You are going to so much trouble for me, Michael Sahib,' Malama said.

'I will go to a lot more, Malama,' he told her. 'Are you not my responsibility?'

'I would be your woman, Michael Sahib. If I could have been that . . .'

'You are, and always will be, my responsibility,' he said. 'But you cannot be my woman, Malama. Tomorrow night.' He squeezed her hand, and left the cabin. When he inhaled her beauty, her desire to be his, when he knew his own certainty that she would be the most marvellous experience of his life, he felt like a juggler, who had three balls in the air, and saw one of them rising so high as to be uncatchable without taking his eyes from the other two. Which one? He was returning to Hung . . . and to Wu Yei and his son. With Malama. While his wife waited in ignorance. But which of them did he truly love?

Why, Alicia, of course. There could be no question about that.

'I will leave tomorrow night,' he told Alicia, 'and cross to the river in one of Wang An's sampans. Then the ascent will be easy.'

Her pique had become submerged in her anxiety at his departure. 'At night?' she asked.

'It is best that way. By dawn I will be on the river and we will be just another sampan.'

'I thought English traders had the right openly to use the Pearl,' she said.

'They do, officially. I have the right to command Wong Sung to take the *China Star* up to Canton. But I do not think that would help me to accomplish my purpose.'

She reached across the dining table to squeeze his hand. 'Oh, Michael, I am so afraid. If only you'd tell me what is so important that you have to do this?'

He had already devised an elaborate lie to cover his journey. 'Well,' he said, 'the fact is that I am going to meet with Hung Hsiu-ch'uan.'

'The outlaw?' Her eyes were wide.

'He regards himself as a patriot, rebelling against Manchu overlordship. Now I have learned from Wang An that as part of his campaign against the Manchu, he is threatening destruction to all the merchants who buy our opium. The merchants are terrified, as you can imagine, as the bannermen are quite incapable of protecting them. I'm sure you can also understand that the loss of our opium exports to China would be a disaster for the company.'

'Yes,' she said thoughtfully. 'I have always felt that you were against the opium trade.'

'Morally it is indefensible. But as your brother would say, it is a mistake to let morals and business mix. Hung and I are old friends, as you know. If I can meet with him, I can perhaps head off a crisis.'

'Yes,' she said, more thoughtfully yet. 'But perhaps this time morals and business *should* mix, Michael. If the trade is as disgusting as you say, perhaps we should just cut our losses and get out.'

He stared at her in a mixture of delight and consternation. He had never expected to hear Alicia say something like that. But if she would support him . . . against Ali? But if she *would* support him, then he had something to offer Hung in return for Malama's safety. 'Oh, my dearest girl,' he said. 'It would mean a quarrel, perhaps, with your father.'

'I doubt Papa has anything to do with business decisions any more. It is all left to Teng Tang and Ali.'

'Well, then, with them.'

179

'Perhaps that would be no bad thing. To have it sorted out before Papa dies.'

They gazed at each other, and he knew that he did love this woman, more than any of the others. Yet he had to go on deceiving her, for at least a while. 'We'll talk about it, when I return from seeing Hung Hsiu-ch'uan.'

Her fingers were tight on his. 'But you will return?'

'Oh yes,' he said. 'Oh, yes.'

To leave her bed was almost agony, of mind as well as body. And yet he was eager to be away, while the memory of her clouded his senses. If only he could be sure of keeping his senses clouded for the next month. The appearance of Malama, the understanding that he was returning to the woman who mentally was perhaps more his wife than even Alicia, and even more, that he would have to face Hung again with not a promise fulfilled, had forced him to realize what a moral sham he had been living these six years. That he had, indeed, been almost stifled by the awareness of his own guilt, the desire to shake off the shackles of prosperous conformity to do what he knew was right tempered always by his fears of the consequences. But he would fear no longer, he was determined. Alicia's help, so unexpectedly offered, was like a suit of armour. Thus he would have to be completely straightforward with her – once Malama was in safety. The sooner his mission was completed the sooner could he try to become an honest man.

The *China Star* was due to depart the following morning, but Wang An's sampan rested alongside, and in the darkness, without any delay, Michael bade farewell to Wong Sung, and then climbed down the ladder into the boat. He reached up to assist Malama, and she slid against him, a long rustle of silk sari. He guided her into the well, where they sat in the midst of bags of opium, while more were piled around them by the crew. Wang An had already left; he would ride back to his home outside Canton, and hopefully dispatch messengers to find Hung, and arrange a meeting, long before the sampan reached the city.

Malama was trembling with a mixture of excitement and anxiety as the sampan cast off, the sweeps dipped into the calm water, and the huge rowboat crossed the harbour, threading in and out of the ships anchored there. There was no challenge; Chinese sampans were always arriving or leaving Victoria. 'When will we reach Canton?' she whispered.

'Three days,' Michael told her.

'Three days?' she echoed.

'There is nothing to be afraid of.'

'I am not afraid, Michael Sahib. Three days alone with you is more of a blessing than I had ever hoped to achieve.'

He looked down at her eyes, gleaming in the darkness. That she was a widow, and he still a married man, would not, he knew, be concerning her. She was his. She had always been his because she had been given to him by her father. That he had given her to Potts in turn had been merely an interruption in her belonging, as it were. That she had had to destroy Potts to preserve her child was to her no more criminal than the way he had destroyed the tiger to preserve her, even if she understood that in a world ruled by thousands of other Pottses she would hang for it. Now she was where she felt she had always belonged, however briefly. Nothing else mattered.

And now he had turned his back on the wife he loved, if only for a while. But during that while, did anything else matter, for him, either? As he was, after all, a rogue? But it had to matter. However much Malama might wish to be taken into his arms, however much he might be unable to keep his eyes from feasting on that quite magnificent body beneath the sari, his destiny lay elsewhere. As well as his love. He kissed her forehead. 'I will teach you to speak Chinese,' he promised.

Alicia sat on her verandah and sipped a cooling drink as she watched the shipping in the harbour far beneath her. Michael had been gone four days. He would have reached

Canton by now. His meeting with Hung Hsiu-ch'uan should take place within another week. And he would be back a week after that. Surely. He had told her he might be away a month, but she knew that had been a cautionary pessimism. So, just another fortnight, really.

It was the first time they had been separated for more than a few hours since their marriage. She had felt quite devastated when he had ridden down the hill. She had wanted to go with him at least as far as the dock, but he had refused to let her even do that; he wanted his departure to be utterly secret, and in fact had told none of their friends that he was leaving. Well, they had found out now as he had not asked her to lie about it – although no one knew where he had gone, and she was under strict instructions to keep *that* secret. He had simply left Hong Kong for a while.

She could not really understand why the secrecy had had to start at home. The British had secured full trading rights on the Pearl River and in Canton. So he was undertaking a secret meeting with a wanted outlaw. But surely it would have been simpler, and safer, to visit Canton as the representative of Hammond and Teng and then undertake the secrecy.

Of course Michael knew a great deal more about handling the Chinese than she, and she had to assume he knew exactly what he was doing on this occasion. She was only concerned with his absence. The mornings were bad; if he was always out all morning in any event, she had at least always been sure he was coming back. The evenings were flat, without him, even if she had accepted one or two invitations. The nights were hell, because she kept waking and stretching an arm or leg across the huge tester bed, to touch him, only to discover that he was not there. But the afternoons were unbearable. She had deliberately cultivated her passions since her marriage; lovemaking had become as important a part of the daily cycle as eating or drinking, playing with the children or managing the house – perhaps the most important, because it was the crowning reward of the day's activities. To retire upstairs

182

in the heat of the afternoon, although often a sea breeze would come swirling through the opened windows to rustle the drapes and flick the coverlets, and lie naked and sweat-wet in his arms, was the apex of human existence. It was actually even better in the monsoon season, when the windows would be closed against the pounding rain, which in turn enveloped them in a cocoon of sound, so that they could have been the only two people in the world, alone to tease and tickle, play and fondle, kiss and couple, until they fell into the deepest and most perfect of sleeps.

Well, Michael would be back long before the monsoon came, at any rate. But now for four days she had been alone in the heat and the breeze. And today would be the fifth; it was nearly time for lunch.

She frowned down the hill at the horseman approaching on the road. There was something familiar about him, and a moment later she recognized her brother. Ali could only have come on a company ship, and yet Wong Sung had left just four days ago. Something else that made no sense. But it was at least company.

Alicia stood up, rang her bell. Ho Chu, no less lonely in the absence of his master, appeared immediately.

'There will be another cover for lunch, Ho Chu,' Alicia said.

Ho Chu bowed, while Alicia went to the head of the steps to watch Ali dismount and hand his reins to the waiting groom. 'Welcome,' she called. 'An unexpected visit.'

He took off his hat as he came up the steps, kissed her on each cheek. 'Where's Michael?'

Alicia raised her eyebrows; the greeting had been a little brusque. 'He's away, right now.'

'Away?'

'In China, on business.'

'God, I need a drink.' He sat down, fanning himself, and Alicia rang the bell again. 'Well,' he said. 'I suppose that means I was wrong.'

She sat beside him. 'Wrong about what?'

'There's all hell to pay in Singapore. Do you remember that Hindu bint your husband had accumulated in his travels?'

'Yes,' Alicia said watchfully.

'She was married off to a clerk named Potts.'

'Yes,' Alicia said.

'Well, she's stuck a knife through his chest. Twice.'

'She did *what?*' Alicia was aghast.

'Well, there have been rumours for years of how he's mistreated her. But still, who'd have thought it of such a subservient creature?'

'Has she been arrested?'

'Not yet. She's disappeared.'

'But she *is* guilty?' Alicia was anxious.

'Oh, no doubt about it at all. She virtually confessed as much to Jalina.'

'Jalina?'

'She was always her friend, you may remember. It seems that on the morning of New Year's Day she appeared at Jalina's house, carrying that brat of hers, told Jalina that she had done something terrible, asked the princess to care for her babe, and went off into the night. Jalina assumed she had just run away from her husband; it wasn't until the next day that his body was found.'

'Good lord! Then where is she? Malama?'

'Nobody knows. The authorities are actually inclined to think she might have thrown herself into the harbour. That saves them having to look for her, you see. But I couldn't help wondering . . . the *China Star* left Singapore for Hong Kong on January second. Did she get here?'

'Of course. She discharged her cargo and left four days ago. You must have passed her coming up.'

'We didn't sight. But you say Michael was away?'

Alicia was frowning, as several very unpleasant thoughts crossed her mind; the *China Star* had taken far longer than usual to unload, almost as if Captain Wong Sung had been waiting for something. Or someone. And then she had left on the same night as Michael. 'No,' she said. 'He wasn't away then.'

'Ah. But nothing odd occurred after Wong Sung docked?'

Alicia stared at him. The thoughts were beginning to crystallize.

As Ali could see. 'By God,' he said. 'I was right all the time. Where is he hiding her?'

Alicia continued to stare at him. Michael had sworn her to secrecy. The only man she had ever loved, or would ever love, she knew. But did he love *her*? Perhaps he had never loved her. He had sworn his innocence of any relations with Malama, and had been supported by Jalina. But Jalina had always been his friend rather than hers. Indeed, their friendship had been quite unusual. No doubt he had bedded the princess, who even in her mid-fifties was still a most handsome woman, as well. Perhaps the two women had shared him at the same time. She could feel her cheeks burning. The wretch! The horror! To whom she had given so much. All she had to give, in fact. And the moment Malama had appeared, begging for his help, he had abandoned his wife and gone off into China, to find a refuge for his dark-skinned mistress, beyond the reach of British law.

The humiliation of it!

'You will have to tell me, little sister,' Ali said gently.

Alicia burst into tears.

'Michael!' Hung Hsiu-ch'uan dismounted and held out his arms, and Michael, who had been waiting on the ground in front of his horse, embraced him. 'It has been a very long time.'

'Too long,' Michael agreed, gazing at him. The years of campaigning had removed the slightly effete air which had previously characterized his friend; his face had grown harder as had his muscles, while he had developed a pair of straggly moustaches. But the eyes still burned with a compelling fanaticism – and he had cut off his pigtail, indicating that his break with the Manchus was irrevocable.

His followers had also allowed their hair to hang free.

185

Feng Yun-shan was at his shoulder, as ever, and there were some fifty obviously battle-hardened veterans forming an escort, sitting their horses motionless beneath the trees of the wood some seventy miles west of Canton into which Wang An had led Malama and Michael. They had been three days on the journey, riding only at night, and had entered the wood in the pre-dawn darkness which was only now fading. Wang An and the woman had remained at a discreet distance behind; the merchant had been distinctly afraid while they had waited for Hung to appear, and his mood had communicated itself to Malama.

'And now you have come back to us,' Hung said. 'To ride with us to Peking.'

'I have come back to visit you,' Michael corrected him. 'And to beg of you a great favour.'

Hung stared at him for some moments. Then he said, 'How can there be favours between friends? There are only duties. Have you no thoughts for your son?'

'Many.'

'He is here.'

Michael's head jerked, and he looked at the horsemen, through whose ranks there now came Wu Yei, also mounted, and carrying on the saddle in front of her an eight-year-old boy.

His throat felt as dry as his eyes were moist. Wu Yei was as pretty as a picture, and looked in the best of health. As did her son, who had Chinese features but the oddest curls in his black hair. Now Wu Yei slipped from the saddle, carrying the boy with her, holding him in front of her. 'I am pleased to have you back, my husband,' she said.

Michael licked his lips, and looked at Hung, who smiled. 'Every mother should have a husband,' he said. 'And who may Wu Yei call hers save the father of her son? Will you not embrace the boy?'

Hung Cho stared at Michael with huge black eyes as he was swept from the ground and held close. Clearly the boy did not remember his father. But this was his eldest son. It was as if all the hidden doubts about his life had been brought together to confront him, at a single time.

'Now,' Hung said, motioning Wu Yei to take her son back, although Michael had done nothing more than touch her hand in greeting. 'Tell me of this favour.'

Michael hesitated, then turned, and beckoned Malama forward. 'This young woman is my ward. She is in trouble, and needs a home beyond the reach of the British law. If you would give her one, until her affairs improve, I would be for ever grateful.'

Hung inspected Malama, with more interest than Michael would have thought likely in a man who had acted the celibate when last he had known him. 'She is from south of the mountains,' Hung remarked at last. 'I have seen people of her race in Canton, years ago.'

'That is correct,' Michael said.

'And she is your ward?'

'She is like a daughter to me.'

Hung stared at Malama again, while Malama looked from one to the other anxiously. 'You will dine with me,' Hung said. 'And we will discuss this matter.'

It was a ride of another forty miles to reach the current encampment of the outlaws, and it was not until dusk that they were able wearily to dismount; by then Malama, unused to riding at all much less for long periods, was exhausted and Michael insisted she be allowed to retire immediately. Hung agreed, and gave orders that she should be put to bed.

For this was hardly a camp. It was a fair-sized town, inhabited by several thousand people, all of whom, while certainly neither rich nor militarily inclined, seemed eager to obey Hung's every command. 'They are my people,' he said proudly. 'We have formed ourselves into the Society of God Worshippers: the Pai Shang-ti Hui. We are the elite of the new China, placed upon earth to make the Manchu tremble, and eventually, soon, bring them to their knees and drive them back into the northern fastnesses from whence they emerged. Do not suppose these are all of my followers. There are many more such, beyond those hills, in Kwangsi, my home. The Hakkas, my kinsmen, are entirely mine. My brothers train a huge army. Soon it will be ready, and then we will openly declare war on the Ch'ing. It will be the greatest day in the history of the world. But there will be a greater to come, the day I hang the Emperor in front of his own altar in Peking.'

Once again Michael was reminded of some Old Testament patriarch, summoning up the forces of fire and brimstone to smite the heathen. But, no doubt like those patriarchs if totally unlike the Jesus he claimed as a brother, Hung was very aware of his prerogatives. He and his principal captains, and on this occasion Michael and Wang An, as well as Malama, were housed in the mayor's dwelling, and the meal they were sitting down to was hardly less than a feast, with several kinds of meat, succulent pancakes, sweet and sour sauces, and an abundance of rice, served by bowing young women.

And no one uttered a sound, while the master was speaking. There was undoubtedly a touch of megalomania, Michael thought, amongst the other irrationalities in Hung's personality. But then, had there not always been, even before he had commanded any power at all?

'Why is it that you cannot find it in your heart to join us?' Hung asked him.

'Believe me, it is much in my heart to do so,' Michael replied. 'Were I not encumbered with other responsibilities. Yet it does my spirits good to see you thriving. I am amazed, indeed, with your reputation so widespread, that the Manchus have not launched a campaign against you.'

'Bah,' Hung declared. 'The Manchu are nothing, here in the south, while we are like the leaves on the trees. They know this, and leave us alone, praying only that we will leave them alone.' He smiled. 'We do not, of course. We take from them what we wish. What they have, and we require.' His smile died. 'But they have too little, and we require too much.'

'Yes,' Michael agreed, bracing himself.

'I ask myself,' Hung went on, 'where are my friends?

My true friends. Ten years ago, Michael, you swore to put a stop to the trade in opium.'

'And I have failed you,' Michael acknowledged. 'I have been making my way, as you told me I should. I now think I can promise you some results, at least from the house of Hammond and Teng.'

'That would be good news,' Hung agreed. 'And yet, the ending of the opium trade is no longer of great importance. When I take power, I shall end it with a sweep of my sword. That day would come closer had I some English cannon. Eight years ago I asked you to assist me there also, my old friend.'

'And I failed you there also,' Michael said. 'I could not persuade the admiral of our navy to do so.'

'But now you are a man of importance, do you any longer care for the words of your admiral?'

'Well . . .'

'Have you no cannon on board your junks? How do you resist the pirates on the coast?'

'There are cannon on board my junks,' Michael said.

'Weapons I could use.'

'We are more than two hundred miles from the sea, Hung.'

'There is the river.'

'Guarded by Manchu warships.'

Hung gazed at him. Then he nodded. 'That is so. But yet can we achieve our objective. There is a deep bay on the coast, some fifty miles north of your people at Hong Kong. Do you know of this bay?'

'I have sailed by it.'

'At the head of the bay there is a community of fisherfolk. They are God Worshippers like myself, and faithful to my cause. There are many such communities. I tell you, when I wave my fiery cross, my people will arise in their millions to march behind me. If you were to take your ship into that bay, and unload cannon, and ball, and powder, my fishermen would help you, and send word to me, and conceal the guns until I could come for them. Will you bring me the guns, and powder, and shot?'

Michael hesitated. 'I will discuss the matter with my associates, and see if it can be done.'

'Anything can be done, Michael, if a man determines on it.' Hung expertly conveyed a ball of rice to his mouth with his food sticks. 'As you have come here, with difficulty no doubt, to place your woman in my care. It will be equally difficult, I know, for me to care for her, and protect one of such beauty, both from her own passionate nature and those of others. Yet shall I do so, because we are friends. Nor do I ask payment for my efforts. I ask only that you be my friend, the friend of my father, as I know you are in your heart, and assist me in this great enterprise on which I have been dispatched.'

Michael sighed and bowed his head. 'It may take a little time,' he said.

But it could be done, with Alicia's help. That was the nub of the whole affair. Undoubtedly he had been stupid not to take her into his confidence from the beginning. Could any woman, who had loved as totally as she had loved him for six years, doubt that he loved her with an equal fervour? That he had never, and would never, betray her for another woman? He had now spent more than a week in Malama's company, in conditions of the most utter intimacy. He had admired her beauty and savoured her little habits. He had often enough slept with her head on his arm. But she remained like a daughter to him.

Then what of Wu Yei, who brought the boy to him to say goodnight, and then returned. 'You have been away too long, my husband,' she said, releasing her girdle.

'And now, alas, I have not yet returned to you,' he said. 'I am committed to another, Wu Yei. It would be best were you to find yourself another man.'

'I am your woman,' she said.

'It cannot be so,' he insisted, feeling as usual an utter heel. But she returned to sleep with her son. If it was not something he could ever boast of to Alicia, it at least

190

enhanced his own opinion that he had nothing to be guilty of in their marriage.

Alicia was perfectly sensible. She would understand that he had had to save Malama from the gallows, that had he permitted her to be executed he would never have slept again. She had already pledged her support to an ending of the opium traffic. The transference of some guns and ammunition to Hung's army could be considered an investment, for if the Society of God Worshippers did nothing more than seize control of South China, it would still, if the house of Hammond and Teng were regarded as his benefactors by Hung, be of enormous value to them.

Malama wept when he said farewell. 'I shall return for you,' he promised. 'As soon as is possible.'

'These people are so strange,' she sobbed. 'They are not like the Chinese in Singapore. Or in Hong Kong,' she added.

'If you mean they are not naturally subservient to a white face, that is because they are the true Chinese,' he pointed out. 'One day they will rule this land, and we will have to learn how to deal with them as equals. That will be no bad thing.'

'But that woman . . . and the child. He is your son, Michael Sahib.'

'I lived with these people, with Wu Yei, for more than a year, Malama. I had no choice. And the woman was given to me.'

'I was given to you twelve years ago,' she said.

He kissed her nose. 'I was not married, when I lived with Wu Yei. I did not then know if I would ever return to my own people. You must understand these things, Malama. Now Wu Yei will be like a sister to you, and care for you.'

'She went to your bed last night,' Malama said. 'While I was spurned.'

'She did not share my bed, Malama. I sent her away.'

'Then you *do* love me, Michael Sahib!' For the first

191

time since her arrival in Hong Kong she looked almost happy. And thus redoubled her beauty.

Michael sighed. Why was it, he wondered, that even to think of Malama as a woman made him feel guilty? Because she was so like a daughter to him? Or because he knew that to yield to her love but once would be to forget that any other woman could exist? Then why not do so, and stay here, and ride at Hung's side, as his instincts kept telling him to do, because here were men, and women, pursuing an ideal rather than merely a profit . . . and abandon everything that he had fought for ten years to achieve, the woman to whom he had given his love, his two children . . . he doubted that any man had been so tormented by the devil as he. But he had now plotted a new course, and he would sail it until he reached his destination – even if he had no idea what that destination might be.

'If I spurn your body, Malama, it is because I love you too well,' he said, happy to be able to tell at least her the truth, even if his words left her more confused than ever. But he was all finished with lying, to anyone. On that he was determined. 'I will soon be back. And I will bring you great happiness.'

Feng Yun-shan sat his horse beside Hung Hsiu-ch'uan and watched Michael and Wang An ride out of sight. 'Why do you trust the Englishman so?' Feng asked.

'Because he is an honest man, and my friend,' Hung replied. 'And the friend of my father.'

Feng snorted. But if he did not entirely believe that Hung was the son of God, he yet understood that his friend's power lay in that mystical supposition. It was best to stick to mundane matters. 'He has failed you before. I do not doubt he will fail you again.'

'He will bring us arms,' Hung said, as he turned his horse.

'And then you will cease being a bandit and become a general.' It was more a statement than a question.

'Then I will lead my people to victory over the Manchu,' Hung told him.

'It will be time,' Feng observed. 'They grow weary of preparations.'

'They are my people,' Hung said angrily. 'They will follow me wherever I lead.'

'So long as you lead,' Feng insisted. 'And what of this woman the Englishman has foisted upon you? Upon us?'

'She is his woman.'

'That is not so,' Feng told him. 'They did not sleep together. Nor did he sleep with Wu Yei. He is an unnatural man, Hung. And this girl is not one of us. It would be best were she to die, before Harrington returns.'

'Die? I have sworn to keep her safe.'

'As he has sworn to bring you guns and powder. Very well, keep your word until he has broken his. But why not take the woman as your own? You too are unnatural in your dislike for women.'

'I do not dislike women,' Hung said with dignity. 'But I am the son of God.'

'Who is wearing the body of a man, and therefore must be expected to have a man's appetites.'

'I cannot take a Chinese woman,' Hung said. 'It would cause dissension amongst the others.'

'That is very possibly true,' Feng agreed. 'That is why I say, take the dark woman, and then cast her aside when you have satisfied yourself.'

They rode back into the village together, and Hung dismounted before the mayor's house, stamped inside. Feng was too used to giving him advice; on occasion it even sounded like a lecture. He was the Son of God, who must pursue his father's will in his own way. Feng did not seem to understand this.

He stood at the window and stared at the street, at the people going about their daily tasks; he could hear his men drilling beyond the houses. Were they discontented? He had brought them little for ten years now except a limited revenge upon their oppressors. It had not been intended to be that long. He waited for a sign from his father, had assumed that the sign would be the coming of the British, to aid him in his appointed task. But the British had proved to be selfish, broken reeds.

Then he had almost despaired. He had all but despaired before, when as a young man he had failed for the third time the examination to join the Civil Service, and work as had his ancestors before him. The shock of that third failure had been too much for his then weak body and mind; he had become ill and all but died. But it had been while he was writhing in delirium that he had first seen the old man with the golden beard. The old man had told him how evil the world was, and how Hung had been chosen to rid mankind of the demons that tormented him. And when the old man had disappeared, Hung had been visited by a younger man, who had identified the demons for him, and told him how they must be destroyed.

He had not known what to make of these visitations, so clearly remembered when he had regained his senses. He had failed the Civil Service examination a fourth and last sitting, and yet accepted his fate with equanimity this time, and had gone to work as a schoolmaster. It was not until his meeting with the American missionary, the Reverend Roberts, who had taught him to speak English and about the God of the Christians, that he had suddenly realized that the old man with the golden beard had been God himself, and the younger man Jesus Christ. From that moment he had understood his relationship with the Deity, realized that he had been sent to earth upon a heavenly mission.

All things had seemed readily possible, then. True, his claim had brought him a whipping from his earthly father, and tears from his mother, as well as much contempt from his fellows. But as his certainty had never wavered, he had earned respect, even if he knew that most of his mandarin friends thought him mad. He had never doubted then. Whenever he closed his eyes to sleep he had seen his father standing before him, and he had known that one day the sign would come. But if not the British, then who?

Harrington himself? He had felt a most peculiar sense of comradeship with the big white man from the moment of their first meeting. He could not explain why. But then, there were so many things he could not explain, about himself and his feelings. He had come to recognize that they were the whims of his father, and he could do nothing more than obey them. And there had been as yet no feeling, no instinct, that he should declare himself and his followers, and then perhaps truly bring down the wrath of the Manchus on his head. Once that was done, his course would be irrevocable: victory or death. He wanted to be sure it would not be death, until after the victory, at the least.

Perhaps, if Michael were to return, with the guns . . . to reclaim his woman? Hung went up the stairs and looked in at the room she had been given to share with Wu Yei. The Chinese girl had taken her son out, but Malama sat on the bed, the picture of misery. At the departure of her lover, Hung thought contemptuously. But she was the picture of beauty too. And despite what he had said to Feng, Hung was only too aware of the pressures of his masculine desires, when he looked at all the girls and women who followed him, any one of whom would give her all to spend a night, or even an hour, in his embrace. Of course he could never risk taking one as his own, as he had explained to Fang. That would be to cause feuds and dissensions which could strike at the very basis of his power. Besides, he did not know enough about the art of love, or the making of it; he had never had the time to practise – to be shamed by a Chinese girl would be an irrevocable disaster for the son of God.

But with a girl who knew no one and spoke no Chinese, and who was so beautiful . . . Hung Hsiu-chuan stepped into the room, and smiled at Malama as she raised her head.

Alicia watched the hills of Hong Kong sinking into the distance as the *Golden Dragon* slipped down the Lamma Channel to the open sea. Melinda watched the hills too, clutching the children against her. They, no less than their nurse, were confounded by the sudden upheaval in their lives. Their father, and Melinda's master, had gone away, on business it had been said, and suddenly their mother, and her mistress, was going away too. Without a word of explanation. Alicia had simply packed her bags and had them sent down to the dock. She had not said farewell to a single one of her friends. She had known only a compulsion to flee from the shame of Michael's desertion of her, for a woman with brown skin, had left Ho Chu and the other servants standing on the verandah in dumb amazement.

While Ali had stood at her elbow, and attended to everything. Now he stood at her elbow again. 'It would be senseless to regret him, or Hong Kong,' he said.

'I loved him. I loved my house.'

'The house is still yours. Without you Michael Harrington is nothing.'

She glanced at him. 'And can I ever be anything, without Michael Harrington?'

'You are Alicia Hammond. I will see to it that you will be Alicia Hammond again. You will obtain a divorce. You will marry again. And be happy again. And live in Hong Kong again, if you wish.'

'And when Michael comes looking for me?' Oh, pray to God he comes looking for me, she thought. Even if she felt she could have done nothing else but leave him, she wanted him to come looking for her.

'If he does, he'll go to gaol as an accessory after the fact of a murder.'

Alicia's head swung. 'No,' she snapped. 'Never. You have no proof.'

'You will testify against him.'

'No,' she said again. 'Never. Whatever he has done, I will never send him to another prison.'

Ali frowned, and then smiled. 'Very well. I can see you still have a weakness for the scoundrel. You must put him out of your mind, at the least. You will never see him again.' I will make sure of that, he thought.

But never is a very long time, Alicia thought. And if Michael did want to see her again, she did not see Ali stopping him. And if he did want to see her again, it would have to be because he loved her, no matter what his relations with the Hindu.

Then why had she run away? Because Ali had told her to, because her senses had been outraged. So why did she not command Ali to stop the junk, turn it round, and carry her back to Hong Kong? Because that would be to surrender. She had never surrendered, to anyone. Michael would have to come to her. Besides, suddenly she was anxious to regain Singapore. She had in fact missed her childhood home more than she had admitted to herself, and the children had never even seen it. As Papa had never seen them – he had never visited Hong Kong – there would be a great family reunion. And there, in a month or so, Michael would appear, looking for her. She no longer had any doubts about that.

But they were taking a ridiculously long time to get there. She stood on the high poop of the junk and stared at the distant land, like nothing she had ever seen before. 'Where are we?' she called down to Ali, who was standing beside Lee Tung, his sailing master.

'That is the coast of Palawan.'

'Palawan?'

'It is an island, which is generally included as one of the Philippines,' Ali explained, climbing the ladder to stand beside her. 'Although it really is independent of any Spanish authority.'

'Then it is the home of pirates,' Alicia suggested.

'It is certainly the home of independent spirits,' Ali agreed.

'And we have business there?'

'Briefly,' Ali assured her. 'Ah.'

The shout of 'Sail ho' had come from the masthead, and now Alicia saw, emerging from the shadow of the land, a fast sailing proa, filled with armed men.

'My God,' she said. 'We are going to be attacked.'

Ali shook his head. 'These people are my friends,' he

197

told her. 'I have a charge to give them, that is all.' He went to the break of the poop, looked down. 'Heave her to, Lee Tung, and lower a boat. I wish to pay Bodaw Wing a visit.' He squeezed Alicia's hand. 'I shall not be long, and when I return, we will make sail for home.' He kissed her nose. 'With all our troubles behind us.'

8

The Settlement of Grudges

Michael returned to Hong Kong as clandestinely as he had left, Wang An's sampan creeping into Victoria Harbour in the dead of night. Even in the darkness, however, he identified a Hammond and Teng junk alongside, her cargo already discharged. As he had been gone just on a month, this was entirely normal. He was, indeed, tempted to board her and find out from Wong Sung the latest news from Singapore. But that could wait until morning, until he had established himself as being once again in residence; presumably, if the Singapore authorities had succeeded in tracing Malama this far, he could be held as an accessory after the fact of Potts' murder. If that were so, it was more than ever necessary to regain both the arms and the confidence of Alicia. Once that were done he could snap his fingers at the world of authority.

So he bade farewell to the captain and crew of the sampan, who had been his faithful followers for the past week, and then awoke the night watchman and saddled one of the horses stabled at the Hammond and Teng godown. 'Now go back to sleep,' he told the Chinese coolie, and walked his mount up the hill.

It wanted only a couple of hours to dawn, and as the moon had long set it was very dark. But the February air was crisp and cool, and because of the time of year there were few insects about. And he was happy, however tired. Happy of course because he was approaching Alicia and the children again. But also happy because he had no doubt that Malama was safe with Hung, and that Wu Yei, who had no spark of jealousy in her character, would indeed treat her as a sister. And happier yet that he had made his decision, and was determined to implement it:

199

to assist Hung with all his power to achieve his goal of regaining China for the men of Han, the Chinese themselves. He had never been intended to be a factor at all, much less remain one all his life. He was a sailor, and an adventurer; Alicia, in her moments of tender passion, would call him her desperado. He had been born to do, not sit. And now he was going to live again, and devote himself to a worthy cause – with Alicia at his side, which was the happiest thought of all.

The horse's hooves sounded dully in the breeze, being wafted down the hill. Michael was upon the house watchman before the sleepy fellow was aware of it, then he started to his feet with great energy.

'It is your master,' Michael said.

'I but closed my eyes, Master,' the man gabbled. 'I heard you, a long way off.'

'I'm sure you did. Well, now you can close your eyes again.' Michael rode up to the front steps, dismounted, and tethered the reins. The front door was open; doors were seldom locked on Hong Kong. And the house was silent. He tiptoed across the darkened hall to the foot of the stairs, waited there for a moment, then ascended. A board creaked beneath his weight, but there was no other sound.

He reached the landing, turned to his left, and opened the door of Alicia's sitting room. Here he hesitated, his nostrils twitching to an unfamiliar scent – yet one he had inhaled before, he was sure. Perhaps Alicia had changed her perfume. He undressed in the boudoir to avoid waking her, then opened the bedroom door and stepped inside. The windows were open and the wind was causing the drapes to fly, the mosquito netting to rustle and balloon – even in February Alicia slept beneath the netting to prevent the slightest risk of any insect causing a blemish upon that lily-white skin.

He raised the net and crawled into the bed, and frowned. The woman who lay there, fast asleep, had black hair and a dark complexion, and was hardly more than half Alicia's size. For a moment his flesh almost crawled

200

as he imagined it could be Malama, become a ghost to haunt him at every turn, then he rolled out of the bed again, almost carrying the net with him, reached his feet and found the candle on the mantelpiece at the same time. In his alarm it took him several scrapes of the tinder to produce a spark, and by the time he had done that the woman was also awake, and sitting up.

The candle flared and he held it above his head. And stared at the Princess Jalina.

'Michael,' she said. 'Forgive me. I had no idea when you would return.'

Michael crossed the room and placed the candleholder on the dressing table, out of the direct draught from the window. And watched the princess getting out of bed, with a total lack of self-consciousness. She picked up her sarong to wrap herself in it, then saw that he was as naked as herself, and let it fall again, while he stared at her; she did, indeed, still have the body of a young girl, and her hair, which he had only ever seen in its heavy chignon, was loosed and longer even than Malama's – and as black as the night surrounding it. 'I have embarrassed you,' she remarked.

'Confused me, at the least,' Michael said. 'Where is Alicia? Is she ill?'

'Alicia is in Singapore,' Jalina said. She went into the boudoir and he followed her, inhaling her scent, forgetting his own nudity.

'I don't understand.'

'It is simple.' She sat on the settee, half turned, knees together. 'Although the police were willing to assume that Malama had committed suicide, your brother-in-law refused to allow them to do so. He therefore came here and acquainted Alicia with the situation, which she was able to relate to your sudden departure for mainland China.'

He sat beside her. 'And left. Just like that.'

'Did not your William Shakespeare have a phrase for it?'

'Heaven has no rage, like love to hatred turned, nor Hell a fury, like a woman scorned,' Michael quoted absently. 'It was actually written by Congreve, not Shakespeare. Do you mean that Alicia now hates me?'

'She gives a very good impression of it.'

'For saving Malama? Could you not explain the truth of it?'

'She will not speak to me.'

'Hm. Well, thank God Wong Sung is in the harbour. We'll sail tomorrow.'

'It is not Wong Sung, Michael.'

He frowned at her.

'It is Lee Tung. Ali's creature.'

'Is there then a warrant for my arrest?'

'Yes. As an accessory after the fact of a murder. Whether they have the proof with which to convict you is another matter, because they can never prove that you knew of Malama's crime when you helped her. The only certain fact is that you ran off with another woman. But still, I would have supposed you had spent sufficient time in prison cells not to wish to repeat the experience.'

'I do not propose to let my wife and children walk away from me, whatever the risk. We sail tomorrow, as I have said.'

'As I am sure Ali at the least was always sure you would do. Thus Lee Tung instead of Wong Sung.'

Michael stared at her. 'You think Ali plots my murder?'

'In the circumstances, it would be simpler than having you arrested. He has never liked you. He may have put a good face on it, but he was against your marriage to his sister. Teng Tang, my brother-in-law, has told me this.'

'Yes,' Michael said thoughtfully. Ali actually had more reason for wanting him dead than disapproval of him as a brother-in-law. And if Alicia's love had been withdrawn . . . that involved thoughts almost too painful to bear. But which yet had to be expressed. 'Do you think Alicia is a party to this?'

'I do not know,' Jalina said.

'But you came to warn me.'

'I could not write; Lee Tung would merely have thrown the letter overboard.'

'You are exceedingly generous to me, Princess.'

'On the contrary, Michael; I am too aware that I involved you in this catastrophe in the first place.'

'And now you have compromised yourself.'

Jalina smiled. 'I compromised myself forty years ago, Michael, when I fled my brother's palace. That I used your bed is simply because I found it more comfortable than those in the spare rooms. I am afraid I have grown used to comfort.'

Michael gazed at her in the faint light of the guttering candle, and remembered that kiss on the cheek, six years ago. She alone of any woman he had ever known, save Malama herself, had stood by him without any ulterior motive. He did not believe she had an ulterior motive now, save that she was weary of acting the unhappy widow. And Alicia had left him, with the children, on the say-so of her brother. Common sense was trying to whisper in his brain that the fault was entirely his, for not having confided in Alicia before. But angry masculinity was proclaiming that she might have acted just like this *had* he confided in her, or worse, tried to bring Malama to the gallows. And now . . . a party to his assassination? He could hardly doubt that, as she had to have known who had come to fetch him.

And for a month he had dreamed only of taking her in his arms, had rejected Malama time and again out of loyalty, left the poor child utterly miserable, amidst strangers.

'I will move out now,' Jalina said, watching his expressions.

'I would rather you stayed, as you find it comfortable, Jalina,' he said.

Her head moved, very slightly, as if she were attempting to see him more clearly. 'And you?'

'I think I would like to stay with you, if it would not inconvenience you.'

Jalina continued to gaze at him for some seconds, then

203

stood up. 'I think I have waited for you to invite me to your bed since first we met, Michael,' she said.

Presumably, if she had been past twenty when he was born, she was old enough in this world of child brides to have been his mother. And yet in her health, her energy, her capacity to stimulate and to enjoy, she had not aged. Michael considered he had taught Alicia the art of love, and she had proved an eager and delightful pupil. But yet had she been taught. Jalina flowed in a peculiarly oriental manner, in a way a westerner found hard to imitate. She sensed, from her hair to her toes, and passed her sensations to her partner. How happy a man Teng Lee must have been, Michael thought, to have experienced this nightly for more than a quarter of a century.

Yet was she still a woman, with the anxious curiosity of her sex. 'What will you do?' she asked, as the first fingers of dawn fluttered at the window.

Her head was on his shoulder, his cheek resting on her hair. Her leg, thrown across him, was hardly more substantial than his wrist; her toes barely reached his knee. He had hardly felt her weight on him – but she had borne his on her without a murmur. Here was strength, as well as generosity, and sensuality.

But she was not his wife. Did that matter, as he had now, at last, betrayed that wife? It mattered to him. His physical faithfulness, or lack of it, he suddenly realized to be irrelevant. Alicia was his wife, and the mother of his children, and he had loved her, and them, and still did so. Even if she had plotted his death? He would have to hear her say that to his face. And besides, now that his brain was uncluttered with desire, he could think more clearly, and realize that all was not as it seemed.

'We will sail today.'

'For Singapore? With Lee Tung?' She raised her head and rolled on to his stomach.

'Yes. I think perhaps you have mistaken their intention. Did they make any attempt to prevent you sailing with Lee?'

'Of course not. I took passage to Bangkok, as I have done regularly over the past five years. We were at sea before I informed Lee that I wished to accompany him to Hong Kong instead.'

'Did he demur?'

'No.' Jalina was frowning.

'So he knew you would warn me he was in command instead of Wong Sung, and also of everything that has taken place since I left for China. Had his orders been to murder me on the voyage he would have endeavoured to prevent you coming at all, because after listening to you I might decide against returning.'

Jalina considered. 'Perhaps what you say is true. I still think you are taking a great risk.'

'I've taken risks before. You will remain here.'

'Of course I will not. I will accompany you.'

'Jalina, if there is some kind of plot . . .'

'There is no one going to plot against the Princess Jalina,' she assured him. 'I am Teng Lee's widow. Do you not realize I hold a fifty-two per cent share in the company?'

'Good God! You mean you control the company?'

'I have never sought to exercise my control. But I could do so, whenever I wish. Would *you* like to control the company, Michael?'

He drove his fingers into her hair to scratch her scalp. 'Indeed I would, my wonderful princess. But . . .'

She smiled, and kissed him. 'I am not asking you to divorce your Alicia and marry me. I know you still love her, and I will do all in my power to see that you are reconciled. That you have made a lonely widow very happy is my private joy. Perhaps you may see your way to doing so again before we regain Singapore. But you will permit me to extend you my protection until you have attained your goal. With my backing they will not even dare arrest you. And I also give you my word, that my share of the company, which is lodged with a Calcutta lawyer and thus is beyond the reach of Ali Hammond, or anyone else, will be thrown behind whatever action you think best, for yourself and for Hammond and Teng.'

'Can you trust me that far?'

'You are an infinitely more trustworthy man than Ali. As long as Clive lives, I have confidence that all will be well. But Clive is an old man. And Teng Tang is a cipher. I have no son of my own. It must be you, Michael, or it will be Ali. Indeed, the Hammonds have long assumed that to be inevitable. But nothing in this life is inevitable, save death.'

Michael gained an insight that perhaps she had not after all made the journey to Singapore merely to warn him about Alicia. Or to satisfy her personal desire. But if she meant what she said . . . 'And you wish it to be me,' he said. 'Even if I am determined to end the opium trade?'

'That would make me more confident in you than ever,' Jalina told him. 'It is the one aspect of our business that Teng Lee and I differed on. Now love me again, Michael, and then let us go and seek your destiny.'

Ho Chu was overjoyed to have his master back, safe and sound, even if he was embarrassed to learn that Michael had already discovered the presence of the princess, a piece of news the servant had been anxious to impart himself, with due importance. However, he happily packed the necessary gear for their departure, while Michael rode down to the harbour to acquaint Lee Tung with his determination to return to Singapore with him. Lee bowed gravely. 'I had felt that might be your wish, Mr Harrington,' he said. 'Thus I waited a day longer than usual for your return.'

Michael smiled; Jalina had already told him that the junk had been waiting more than a week, and would have remained in Hong Kong as long as was necessary. 'I am grateful for your patience, Lee Tung,' he said.

They boarded that afternoon and left before dusk, with a westerly breeze to take them down the channel and into the open sea. Jalina stood at the taffrail to watch Hong Kong receding. 'Do you know, that is the closest I have ever been to China, although I was married to a Cantonese? Teng Lee would not take me on his voyages when we were first married; indeed, I would not go – I used to be most terribly seasick when I was a girl. And in addition there was a war on, and pirates abounded. It was all really rather dangerous. So he left me in the care of Clive. Thus I thought I would never venture into the China Sea at all. I would like to return, to visit Alicia and you, when you are again settled.' She gave a little tinkle of laughter. 'Do not fear, I shall sleep at the other end of the house.' Then grew serious again. 'Unless you decide to make Singapore your home.'

'Would you like me to do that?'

'The decision must be yours, Michael. I will never interfere with that.'

She was the most enchanting woman he had ever met, not only in her sexuality, but in her awareness and total acceptance of the different spheres which belonged to the different sexes. She knew her power, and she had every intention of using it, in so far as it should be used by a woman. But the living of his life, and the organization of the company when it should be his to rule, was his province, and she would never interfere. Save withdraw that vital support should she feel he was failing her? But he would never fail Jalina.

And to rule Hammond and Teng! There was a heady thought for a thirty-four-year-old Irish itinerant. What would brother William and sister-in-law Henrietta say to that? How splendid it would have been could Mother have lived just long enough to have heard about her ne'er-do-well's success.

And what would Alicia say to that? And Ali! The thought made him want to burst out laughing.

The breeze took them rapidly south, too far south, and when it eased back to the north, Michael was disturbed to discover that Lee Tung still held his southerly course. 'We are too far south already to avoid the Spratlys, Mr Harrington,' he explained. 'Besides, I have a letter to deliver to Mr Brooke in Kuching. It is best we stand on for Palawan and turn along the coast, which is unencumbered.'

That was not altogether true, but Michael reflected that Lee, as he usually sailed with Ali, probably knew the inshore passage better than the open sea, assuming that Ali was still carrying on his illicit support of the Palawan pirates. Besides, he thought he would enjoy visiting Sarawak, and meeting the now famous Englishman, James Brooke, who landed in the Malay kingdom in his own schooner some eight years before, earned the friendship of the rajah – by helping him put down a revolt – and had been rewarded with a province of his own. Now *there* was a success story. Nor was he unduly concerned at the prospect of encountering one of Bodaw Wing's proas, as the ships of Teng were inviolate, although the next afternoon he espied one of the pirate craft even closer inshore, apparently keeping pace with them.

'Have you nothing to say to him, Lee?' he could not help asking.

'It is Captain Hammond who deals with those fellows, not I,' Lee declared unctuously.

'He seems to have identified us,' Michael remarked to Jalina, who had just come on deck.

'They used to respect the flag of Teng Lee,' Jalina said.

'They still do. Because Ali Hammond sells them powder and shot.'

Jalina frowned. 'Is this true?'

'Yes. That is something else I mean to put a stop to.'

'The fellow is an absolute scoundrel,' Jalina observed. 'Do you suppose they think we are carrying something for them now?' For the proa had moved closer.

'No. They're just observing, I reckon.'

'Then what about those?' The princess pointed ahead, and Michael snatched his telescope. Directly in front of them, having emerged from round a headland, were two more proas, waiting for them.

Michael went to the captain. 'Has your master fallen out with Bodaw Wing?' he asked.

'I do not know, Mr Harrington. I do not like what I see.'

'Well, load the guns and alter course back out to sea. We'll smash through them.'

Lee Tung hesitated, then gave the necessary orders. Powder and shot were passed up, and Michael equipped himself with sword and pistols, because that they were going to have a fight was now very obvious; all three of the proas were steering for them, and with the breeze light could not be outsailed. He could not imagine what had gone wrong with Ali's arrangements, but was still not particularly alarmed; he was confident that the junk was powerful enough to repel any piratical assault. 'You had best go below,' he told the princess. 'There is going to be a fight.'

She sighed. 'And I will be in the way. Be sure you blast them, Michael.'

He nodded. 'I intend to do that.'

She disappeared, and he could concentrate on the coming encounter. His heart pounded and the blood flowed through his arteries. He realized that, having determined to confront Ali, he was actually anxious for a fight.

The proas were now quite close, and travelling at some speed. 'It is time to give them a broadside,' Michael told Lee.

'Open fire!' Lee shouted in Chinese.

The guns boomed, but the shots were wide, and the proas were now very close.

'Prepare to repel boarders,' Michael called, drawing his sword. With the junk surging forward the Malays would not find it easy to get on board, and would be at their most vulnerable as they attempted to do so – at least if faced with determined resistance.

To his dismay, however, the crew looked to their captain rather than obeying him, and to his absolute consternation Lee Tung seized the wheel from the helmsman, and swung the junk up into the wind to heave it to.

'Are you mad?' Michael shouted.

'There are too many,' Lee said. 'We must surrender.'

209

'Surrender?' Michael swung to face the bulwarks, levelled his pistol, and sent the first Malay tumbling back over the side. But he was replaced by several others, and then an avalanche of men poured on to the decks of the junk. The crew made no attempt whatsoever to resist them, and Michael observed that none of them were cut down in the first rush. Only Ho Chu ran to his side, as the pirates' objective was clearly himself. He fired his second pistol and dropped another, pinked a third man with his sword, and then was thrown to the deck and his weapons wrenched from his hands, while his arms were secured. Ho Chu had also felled one of their assailants, then he was in turn struck down, and to Michael's horror the servant was not secured, but was immediately despatched by a kris.

'I am sorry, Mr Harrington,' Lee Tung said as Michael was pulled back to his feet. 'They wish you for ransom.'

'I will see you hang for that surrender,' Michael spat at him. 'You have caused the murder of my servant.' And then a dreadful realization dawned as he observed that the pirates were making no effort to secure the captain or any of the members of his crew: they wanted him, and nothing else. 'Your master's doing, by God!'

'How can you say such a thing, Mr Harrington?' Lee asked.

Michael faced Bodaw Wing. 'You,' the pirate said in Chinese. 'We will have sport with you.' He spoke to his men, and Michael was forced to the rail.

Lee Tung was speaking in Malay. Michael could not tell what he was saying, but he caught the name Jalina. He tried to turn and was pushed on, through the now open gangway into one of the proas, which immediately cast off. Hurled into the bottom of the boat he lost his breath, but yet struggled back to his knees to look at the ship, and see Jalina also being pushed over the side into another of the proas. They had been outwitted, simply because it had never occurred to them that Ali would employ his Malay friends to destroy them. By God,

Michael thought, when I get hold of him . . . but was he ever going to get hold of him?

The junk had resumed its course, undamaged. And the shore was now very close. Within minutes the proa had rounded the headland, which was a high, curving promontory rising some three hundred feet, and entered a creek, invisible from the sea behind the high land, on the bank of which, again sheltered by the headland, was a good-sized village, from which women and children were running down to the water's edge to congratulate their menfolk. Michael was unceremoniously thrown on to the sand. His wrists tied behind his back, he was as helpless as when in the hands of the Manchus, and could only tense his muscles against the blows which were showered on him, while the other boats came in to the creek, and to his horror he saw the princess being similarly ill treated, her hair loosed and her clothes torn.

Bodaw Wing stood above him. 'She is an unexpected pleasure,' he said. 'Her husband helped to destroy my father, Bodaw Minh. We will make her scream before we send her to join him.'

'You will hang,' Michael told him. 'I will attend to that, myself.'

'Ha ha,' Bodaw Wing laughed. 'You will watch her die, then you will die yourself, Harrington. Me . . . I shall live for my allotted span.' He spoke to his men, and Michael was forced up the beach and into the village, a scattered collection of huts raised on stilts, built around a mosque of some size and grandeur, faced by a much larger building, with a verandah and wings, clearly the palace of the pirate chieftain.

Between the mosque and the palace there were several stakes set in the earth, and to one of these Michael was taken, and there secured, by ropes round his neck and wrists. He was then handed over to the village children, who stripped him of his clothing while poking and prodding at him, thrusting their sticks and fingers into his genitals and scampering away as he kicked at them, all the while laughing in high-pitched cackles. Endeavouring

211

not to give way to the despair which was gnawing at his mind, he looked for Jalina, and saw her also being forced up the beach, while men pulled at her clothing and her body to render her as naked as himself. The princess's face had settled into an expression of determined stoicism, and she did not look at him. Clearly she knew she was about to be raped, and was composing herself to withstand whatever was done to her.

Michael watched the slight figure being thrown to the ground in the midst of the laughing, shouting men, and strained against his bonds, with some success, he thought. While the children, having grown tired of tormenting him, joined the throng to watch what was happening to the princess, who still refused to utter a sound as man after man rolled her to and fro to enter whatever orifice he chose. Michael sweated and panted as he recalled his own moments of utter joy in Jalina's arms, and strained again and again. He felt sure he could work himself free, given time, and at whatever damage to his wrists, but was he going to be given the time? For Bodaw Wing, having been the first to take the princess, now left the throng and sauntered towards him, grinning. He had discarded his jacket and wore only a sarong – and that hastily donned, with just a kris thrust into the sash round his waist. 'She is no sport,' he remarked. 'She does not fight, or beg. She is like a sack of coconuts.'

Michael inhaled. 'Lee Tung spoke of ransom,' he said. 'Do you not know that the princess is one of the wealthiest women in Asia?'

Bodaw Wing shrugged. 'That is a pity.'

'But you mean to murder us both?'

'It is her misfortune to be in your company.'

'And Ali wants me dead.'

'He regards you as an enemy,' Bodaw Wing explained. 'And has told me you are an enemy of mine, also.'

'And you would murder me like the treacherous assassin you are,' Michael said.

Bodaw Wing struck him across the mouth, so hard his head jerked, while blood dribbled down his chin. 'I do not

212

betray my friends,' he said. 'I will execute you. Slowly. It will be sport.'

Another strain, and Michael was sure his wrists were all but free; once he could achieve that, he knew he could rip the cord from round his neck. 'The sport of a coward,' he sneered at Bodaw Wing; he had to keep the pirate chieftain fully occupied.

'Ha,' Bodaw Wing remarked. 'We shall see who is the coward, at the end.' He turned as the crowd ceased its seething over Jalina, frowned, asked a question, then gave a command. Michael's heart sagged with horror and grief; he had no more than a few words of Malay, but knew what the men had been saying. And now he watched the princess being dragged towards him. A man held a wrist each, and Jalina's naked body bumped and jarred lifelessly behind them, her hair trailing in the dust.

Michael wanted to scream his rage and indignation that so lovely, so gracious a lady should have been so driven into her grave. He stared at her as she was thrown at his feet, a crumpled vision of beauty, who had been his for a brief moment, and who had been going to lead him to power and prosperity. Oh, Jalina, he thought. Had you not sought me out you would yet live, and smile, and create happiness wherever you went.

Bodaw Wing grinned at him. 'You will soon join her in the shades. She will wait for you, her legs spread wide.'

'You are filth,' Michael told him, speaking loudly, while continuing to work his wrists; the pain was severe and he could feel blood dribbling down his fingers, but he wanted nothing less than pain. 'Lower than the scorpion upon which decent men stamp. Your sport is tormenting helpless women. Your father was a *man*, Bodaw Wing. But you are no more than the shit that dribbles from a man's ass.'

Bodaw Wing stared at him and made to strike him again, then checked himself and glanced at his people. Clearly some of them understood Chinese.

'Are there no men amongst you?' Michael shouted. 'No one who will dare face me in combat?'

He did not care now whether he lived or died, so long as he could perhaps take Bodaw Wing with him.

Bodaw Wing kicked Jalina's body. 'She was your mistress,' he said contemptuously. 'So you grieve for her. But she had no spirit.'

'Try mine,' Michael begged.

The men had clustered around now, with their women, and several were speaking to their leader. Bodaw Wing scowled as he listened to them, then he grinned. 'They wish you to prove your words,' he said. 'Very well, Harrington. We will let you fight. But you will not die. When you have lost your fight, then will I give you to my women, that they may cut you up, slowly, before your eyes. That will be sport.'

'When I have lost,' Michael said. 'What if I do not lose?'

Bodaw Wing stared at him. 'You will lose,' he said.

Michael was released from his stake, led out of the village and on to the hillside. It was necessary to take stock of his surroundings. He could do nothing for the princess now, save avenge her. To accomplish that he had to escape. Somehow. Only by appearing to commit suicide.

A kris was thrown at his feet, and he picked it up. If he had hoped to face Bodaw Wing himself, he discovered he was mistaken; his opponent was to be one of the biggest of the Malays, a man almost as tall as himself, who now swaggered away from the watching throng, also armed with a kris. It was a weapon Michael had never used before, but as he tested its weight he realized that it was, actually, nothing more than a very large knife, and beautifully balanced.

He spun it through his fingers, while the Malays laughed and jeered at him, and his opponent took his stance, feet apart, shoulders hunched. Michael faced him, standing straight, while he sized up the situation. The pirates obviously did not consider that he could possibly

214

escape, and were clustered on the village side. To his right there was only the cliff, perhaps two hundred yards away. It would be a long sprint . . . and he had no idea what lay beyond. If there were rocks or beach he would have no hope. But it would still be a better death than being castrated by the Malay women. And if there was deep water . . . the afternoon was far advanced, and in these latitudes there was no twilight; the darkness would be sudden and entire.

He took a long breath, tensed his muscles, thrust his left leg forward as he seized the knife blade, and hurled it with all his force. The Malay was taken utterly by surprise as the razor-sharp weapon slashed into his chest with such power that it all but protruded out the back. His fellows were also astounded by the sudden end to the anticipated contest, and before they could recover Michael was racing across the rising ground to the cliff, legs pounding, muscles surging, breaths coming in great pants. Behind him there came a shot, and then another. Muskets were fired, but wildly, and he was at the edge, pausing only to take another long breath before launching himself into space.

He seemed to hang in the air for an interminable time, looking down now, to anticipate his fate. But before him was rolling green sea. He entered feet first, so fast that he sank some twenty feet and actually touched the sand before a powerful kick sent him back to the surface. The waves were big enough to roll him over and over, and his first thought had to be how to avoid being yet dashed to pieces on the rocks he had so narrowly avoided. At the same time the surging sea offered him some protection, for looking up, he could see the Malays looking down, trying to ascertain what had happened to him.

Then he heard more shouts, and knew they would be fetching their proas. But also that it would be dark before they could reach his position. It was just a matter of keeping his nerve. He swam right in against the cliff, in the bobble of water which splashed there, found a rock, and clung to it. In half an hour one of the proas was out, and the men were using lanterns to search the water, but Michael sank beneath the surface whenever they came too close, and after a while they gave up and returned into the creek. By then it was utterly dark, and it was Jalina's memory that drove him on, to reach the beach. As if the beach promised much succour, come dawn; Palawan was a nest of pirates, from end to end. But he would survive, and avenge. He wanted nothing more than that.

From the window of her bedroom Alicia could see the Dragon's Teeth, and thus, having got out of bed with the first light, could watch the junk entering the harbour. She recognized it immediately, and felt her heart pounding most painfully. Although the *China Star* had been put into dry dock for repainting by Ali, she had insisted that a ship be sent to Hong Kong as usual, and to her surprise Ali had raised no objection. No doubt he thought that Michael either would not return at all, or if he did and discovered that she had left with the children, would be too angry to follow her. She had known better.

The only ship available had been the *Golden Dragon*, apparently, and although she had been required to take the princess on one of her now regular visits to Bangkok, Ali had given orders to Captain Lee that he was to continue to Victoria as usual and discover what was happening there. And now the ship was back. With Michael on board? Certainly she had to find out.

She summoned Melinda and hurriedly dressed. The children were already being fed their breakfasts by Soo An, and she had no desire to encounter her mother or father. They had been appalled at what had happened, and had wanted her to institute proceedings for a separation immediately. She had of course declined to do so, but that had not prevented them from returning to the subject time and again until she had more than once all but lost her temper. But yet she was glad she had returned to see them – even if she would have preferred it to be in happier circumstances – because Papa was now sixty-nine and suffering from pains in his chest. He would not live much longer, she knew – which made it all the more important to be reconciled with Michael as soon as possible, before Ali finally took over the running of the firm.

But this was surrender. She checked on the verandah even as Mansur the groom brought the phaeton to the steps. She had been going to remain coldly at home and make him come up the hill to her, at least metaphorically on his knees. If she went to the ship . . . but she knew she was going to the ship. More than a month was too long to be out of his arms, no matter what he had done.

'The harbour,' she said as she seated herself.

The phaeton rumbled down the hill and through the just-awakening city. She was at the waterfront long before the *Golden Dragon* was actually warped alongside, pulling off her gloves to snap her fingers with impatience. And wondering where Ali was. He maintained his own establishment now, although he had still not married, situated in the city itself. But he nearly always greeted his returning ships. No doubt, she reflected, he does not want to be present at the great reconciliation.

But as the ship came nearer she realized that there was no one on the poop except Lee Tung. Her whole being seemed to sag with disappointment. He had not come. Ali had been right after all – or something had happened to him in China. 'Captain Lee!' she shouted. 'Captain Lee. What news?'

Lee Tung's face was a picture of misery. 'Oh, Mistress Harrington,' he cried. 'But it is bad. Too bad.'

Alicia's heart, already sagging, seemed to constrict. 'Bad?' she snapped. 'What do you mean?' As soon as the gangway had been put out she ran up to it, looking from left to right.

'Mr Harrington,' Lee Tung wailed. 'He is gone.'

'Gone?' Alicia almost shook him in her anxiety. 'Gone where?'

'He was taken by the pirates, Mistress,' Lee said. 'He and the princess. Taken by the pirates.'

Alicia could only goggle at him in horror, unable to

217

assimilate what he was saying, only half hearing the thunder of hooves on the quayside. A moment later Ali was on board.

'Lee!' he snapped. 'What news?' He glanced at his sister. 'Alicia? Are you all right?'

'Pirates,' she moaned. 'Michael. And the princess. I don't understand, Ali. I don't understand.'

'What happened?' Ali asked Lee.

'We were attacked,' Lee said, gazing at his employer. 'There was nothing we could do. There were three proas, maybe a hundred and fifty men. We were surrounded. There was nothing I could do.'

'And they took Mr Harrington?'

'Yes, Mr Hammond. And the princess.'

Ali stared at him in consternation. '*What* did you say?' he whispered.

'The princess.'

'You took her to Bangkok.'

'No, sir. When we were at sea she informed me that she did not wish to go to Bangkok, but to Victoria instead.'

'And you took her?' Now Ali was shouting.

'What could I do, Mr Hammond? She is the Princess Jalina. She is the widow of Teng Lee.'

Ali gazed at him with an expression so venomous that Lee stepped backwards. 'What could I do?' he asked again.

'Ali,' Alicia said, holding his arm.

'Bodaw Wing must have lost his senses. Or made a mistake. Anyway, at worst they will be held for ransom. I will get them back,' he told her.

'But . . .' Alicia at last began to come to *her* senses. 'How was Jalina on board? Why did she go to Hong Kong?'

'That is something we shall have to ask her, when she is returned here. Unload your cargo, Lee, and prepare to put to sea by tonight.'

Alicia looked at the ship, the impassive faces of the crew, the brightwork and the sails, the polished cannon . . . her brain was still swinging, and she only wanted to lie down and cry, and yet . . .

'You fought the pirates?' she asked the captain.

'Oh, indeed, Mistress. But there were too many.'

'And there is not a scratch on your bulwarks? A tear in your sails?'

'We were surrounded. One of my men was killed.' He pointed to the still visible bloodstain on the deck.

'One man! You just surrendered,' Alicia shouted. 'You did not fight at all. You just surrendered and let them take my husband and the princess.'

Lee Tung looked at Ali, who put his arm round his sister's shoulder. 'It must be a captain's decision, when he can fight for his ship and when the fight must be abandoned, Alicia. No one who wasn't there can criticize such a decision.'

She shrugged herself free and left the ship. Mansur drove her up the hill and she threw herself on her bed, the tears at last flooding from her eyes. Her mother and father, awake now, attempted to ask her what was wrong and she locked her door. Michael had after all been coming to regain her. And now he was dead. Or at least being most terribly mistreated. Poor Michael! He had suffered so much ten years ago at the hands of the Chinese, and now . . . with Jalina. It simply made no sense for Jalina to have been on board, to have gone to Hong Kong . . . she sat up, clawing hair from her eyes. She had gone to see Michael. But what about? Nothing made any sense. Nothing!

Not even the catastrophe. No Teng junk had been attacked in her lifetime, or even before it. Teng Lee and the old pirate Bodaw Minh had been friends as young men. By the time they had fallen out Teng had had the backing of the British, and Bodaw Minh's days had been numbered. When he had been killed, his eldest son, Bodaw Shan, had willingly acknowledged British supremacy. His younger brother, Bodaw Wing, had preferred to take his people and leave for the Philippines, and resume their old trade, but he had been a childhood friend of Ali's and had continued to grant Teng ships safe conduct in the South China Sea. Until now.

Because it had happened. Even if she could understand none of it, it had happened. Michael was lost.

There was a knock on her door. 'Come on, Sis, open up,' Ali said.

Alicia blew her nose and let him in. 'I'm sailing tonight,' he said. 'With extra men. I shall take the crew of the *China Star* with me; Wong Sung is already recruiting them. I told you, we'll get them back. If it can possibly be done.'

'If,' she said. 'If not, you will avenge them.'

'I shall certainly endeavour to do so,' he promised, and took her in his arms to kiss her. 'Trust me.'

There was no one else. She wanted to go with him, but knew he would refuse. In any event, she could not possibly sail away and leave the children. Even if she did not know how she would survive until his return.

Papa and Mama were now sympathetic, went out of their way to relieve her misery – but they clearly already considered her a widow. A widow! Oh, why had she ever listened to Ali and fled her safe and comfortable home? Did it matter if Michael had gone off into China with his Indian whore? He had come back. Oh, if only she had stayed.

She watched the harbour almost from dawn until dusk, scarcely ate for the next ten days until Ali returned. And knew long before the junk docked, for its topsides were draped with white cloth; they were mourning the princess.

He sat beside her, and held her hands. 'They were renegades,' he said. 'Bodaw Wing has explained it to me. He was as shocked by what had happened as I was myself. Renegades, who surrounded my ship, and then took Michael and Jalina ashore. Bodaw Wing had heard of it from men who saw what happened. They both died almost immediately.'

'Died?' Alicia whispered. 'Oh, my God! But why?'

Ali shrugged. 'No one can say. I can only suppose they

were men against whom perhaps Michael had already fought.'

'Michael has had nothing to do with any Malay pirates since going to Hong Kong,' she sobbed.

'Well, before that, perhaps.'

'Oh . . .' she did not know. 'And the princess. I can't understand about the princess.'

Ali sighed. 'You need to rest.'

She raised her head, looked at him. 'Tell me the truth, Ali. Tell me the truth.'

He sighed again. 'I don't know how to say it. Lee Tung has told me. Michael and Jalina were lovers.'

'Were what?' she screamed.

'They shared the same cabin on the voyage from Hong Kong. She obviously determined to go there to be with him from the moment you returned here and she learned what had happened.'

'Oh, my God!' Alicia wailed.

'He seems to have been somewhat omniverous in his tastes, your husband,' Ali said.

Alicia stared at him.

'I would say they were lovers before he married you,' Ali said. 'He used to spend a lot of time at Teng Lee's house, remember? We thought he was seeing his Indian bint. Now it seems he was seeing both of them. Don't forget she took the murderess's son into her home. He's still there.'

Alicia remembered wondering about Michael's relationship with the princess, once before. And she remembered too how Margaret had warned her about the probability that Michael would be unfaithful. But with Jalina! Then perhaps he had not been coming back to her after all. Perhaps he had been coming back to be with the princess.

Ali studied her changing expressions, the way her tears had dried. 'Anyway, it seems she refused to let them take Michael without her. You have to hand it to her for courage. And she died hard. She was literally raped to death, Bodaw Wing reports. Michael was drowned trying to escape.' He held her hands. 'So there we are, Sis. At

221

least you have discovered what he was really like. Now you must put him behind you, and try to start living again.'

Alicia drew a deep breath. But he was right, of course. Michael had betrayed her, and would have continued doing so. If she grieved for his death, it was because he was the father of her children – and because he had made her so very happy. From constant practice, Margaret had suggested in one of her letters. 'Who will be our factor in Hong Kong?' she asked.

'I shall have to advertise. In the short term, I suppose Teng Tang can do it. He is going to be upset by the news of his sister-in-law. It will distract him. There are also a good many business matters to be cleared up as well,' he added thoughtfully.

Margaret returned from Calcutta to be with her sister in her bereavement. She avoided saying I told you so, but clearly thought that. 'He was a desperado,' she said. 'I suppose something like this was inevitable. And the princess . . . never trust an Oriental, Jeremy always says. And I am sure he is right. Now, after a decent period, of course, we must set about finding you a husband.'

Alicia didn't want a husband; she thought she had had all the husband she could stand. She just wanted to care for her children, and ride her horse, and stare at the sea. The community as a whole was shocked by this latest piratical catastrophe, and by the death of the princess – the Hammonds kept the personal details of the tragedy to themselves. Clive and Ali, as well as Teng Tang, were concerned to discover the whereabouts of Teng Lee's shares in the company, which had been bequeathed to his widow. Teng Tang naturally felt they should go to him, as the last living relative of Teng Lee, and recalled that the shares had been lodged, by Jalina, with a Calcutta lawyer. Ali immediately left for India to inform the advocate of what had happened, discover if Jalina had made a will, and seek a ruling; it was clear that there was going to be some considerable dispute before he would give over control of the company to Teng. He returned in a few weeks, more thoughtful than ever.

It all seemed so irrelevant to Alicia. Her beautiful house overlooking Victoria would belong to another. And she would never again writhe on her bed in the ecstasy of physical love. She was only just thirty years of age, and her life had come to a full stop.

Wong Sung was nearly as distraught as she, and came to see her. 'If only it had been my ship, Mistress Harrington,' he said. 'Oh, we would have fought off those pirates. Lee Tung is a coward. Mistress, Captain Harrington was my friend. This is something I would have you know. He was my friend. And the Princess Jalina was my honoured employer. One day I will avenge her death. This I swear.'

And being a man, Alicia thought, Wong would have no criticisms for Jalina's and Michael's peccadilloes. Well, did she? Would she not condone any peccadillo in the world just to have him walk through the door? She sat on the verandah and rocked herself, while the children crawled about her feet, and felt her heart constrict as she gazed at the man coming up the drive.

Alicia stood up. She might have been looking at a scarecrow, whose clothes were in tatters, whose beard was at least a month old, and whose body was burned by the wind and the sun. She was also looking at a ghost.

'Soo An,' she said, and discovered she was whispering. 'Soo An!' she called.

The nurse hurried out from the interior of the house, casting the ragged man not a glance.

'Take the children, Soo An,' Alicia said.

'Yes, Mistress.' Soo An picked up a child in each arm and went inside.

From the steps themselves there came a deep growl, and Caesar the mastiff rose, his hair standing, his teeth bared. But the man came steadily onwards, and the dog did not attack him. Instead, as Michael reached him, he dropped to his haunches and wagged his tail.

Michael stepped past him, while Alicia took a step

forward, and then checked. Her throat was dry, her mind spinning almost as fast as when she had heard he was dead.

'Where is your brother?' Michael asked.

Alicia opened her mouth, licked her lips, and found she could just speak. 'He is . . . in the office, I suppose,' she said.

'Then I know where to find him.' He climbed the steps, and looked at her.

'Michael . . .'

He stepped past her, went into the house. Gopal the butler hurried from the pantry. 'What you doing in here, you ruffian?' he demanded. 'Out. Out, I say, or I will set the dog on you.'

Michael stretched out his hand, seized Gopal's white jacket, and pulled the astonished man against him. 'Have your people draw me a bath,' he said. 'I will take it in Miss Alicia's room. Now do it.'

Released, Gopal staggered back in dismay, looked past him at Alicia, framed in the doorway.

'Yes,' she said.

Gopal ran for the pantry. Michael went up the stairs. Alicia followed. At the top, he looked through the opened door at the two children in the nursery. Joanna immediately began to cry, and Soo An hugged the little girl to her breast. Michael went on into Alicia's bedroom.

She stood in the doorway, watched him undress. He was thinner than she recalled, and had suffered some severe bruising. 'They told me you were dead,' she said.

'Who told you I was dead?'

'Ali. And . . . Lee Tung. And . . .' she bit her lip.

Gopal and Mansur were bringing in the tin tub, the maids were following with jugs of the hot water which were always kept simmering on the range. Melinda brought up the rear, staring at the naked figure of her erstwhile master in horror.

Michael watched the tub filled. 'Now get out,' he said. 'You too,' he told Melinda, 'and close the door.'

'Would like me to leave as well?' Alicia asked, uncertain whether to be outraged or outrageously happy.

'It is your room,' he told her, and sank into the water. 'I need a razor.'

'I will fetch one.' She left the room, took her father's. It gave her time to think. But to no purpose. He was alive! And he was angry. Angrier than she had ever seen him. She left Clive Hammond's dressing room, and faced her mother.

'Is it true?' Elizabeth asked. 'What Gopal has said.'

'Yes,' Alicia told her. 'Yes. It's true. He's alive, Mama. He's alive.'

'My God!' Elizabeth said. 'I must send for your father. And Ali,' she added as she went to the stairs.

'He's alive,' Alicia said, more quietly.

'To bring more catastrophe upon us, no doubt,' Elizabeth said grimly. 'Your father will know what to do.'

Alicia watched her descend, then went back into her room. Michael still soaked, soaping himself with great care. 'Would you like me to shave you?' she asked.

'I would prefer to cut my own throat,' he said.

She sat on the bed; his anger was directed at her. When she should be angry at him, for giving her such a scare, and for Jalina . . . but there were so many things to be understood. 'They told me you drowned,' she said.

'I can swim.'

'You swam back here?'

His head turned, as if he was unsure whether or not she had intended the joke. 'I swam far enough,' he said. 'And existed on an islet hardly bigger than this room until I managed to hail a passing vessel. I lived on crabs and coconuts. I will appreciate a good meal.'

'You will have one. Did they not feed you on this ship you hailed?' Now she was definitely angry. To have him march in here, as if he owned the place, with not a word of apology for his adultery – and with a woman old enough to be his mother!

'According to their lights. I did not tell them who I was.' He stretched out his hand, and after a brief hesitation she placed the razor in it; it was the first time they had touched. 'I shall also need a sarong.'

'Your clothes are here,' she said.

'Ah! I would have supposed Lee would have thrown them overboard.'

'He told us how you had been taken.'

'Did he now.'

'He told us about the princess, and you,' she snapped.

'Did he tell you how she died?'

'No. Ali told me that. When he returned from seeing Bodaw Wing.'

'Ah!' Michael said again.

'I am sorry about what happened to her, Michael,' Alicia said. 'But really! I'm not sure she didn't deserve it.'

Michael got out of the bath and stepped towards her. Taken unawares as he scattered water, she failed to react in time, and he caught her wrist. 'If you ever say anything like that again,' he said in a low voice, 'I will break your neck. Understand me.'

Alicia gasped with both pain and fear, and he threw her away from him. She rolled across the bed and nearly fell off the other side.

'Now, where are these clothes?' he demanded.

Alicia sat up, eyes blazing. 'Do you think you can just walk in here and take over my life again? You, with your harem, pretending to be dead, you . . .' her voice died as he looked at her.

'I will do whatever I please,' he said. 'It is a rule I intend to keep. Now, I am going to get dressed, and then eat, while you prepare yourself and the children, and then we are leaving here.'

'Leaving here? For Hong Kong?'

'No,' he said. 'Not for Hong Kong. We are going to do something I should have done long ago.' He listened to the sound of hooves, galloping up the drive, and went to the window to look down. 'But first,' he said. 'I am going to kill your brother.'

9

The Cauldron of God

'You . . .' Alicia ran to the window beside Michael. Ali was accompanied not only by his father, but by several Chinese, led by Teng Tang. And they were armed.

'My clothes!' Michael snapped.

She pointed at the chest.

'Lock that door.' He began to dress.

Alicia hesitated, then did as he had told her. She could hear the excited hubbub from downstairs. 'They will not let you get away.'

'Then you will have to help me.'

'To kill my own brother? You must be mad. Promise me that you will not harm him.'

Michael pulled on his boots. 'He attempted to have me murdered. He did have the princess murdered. And he is responsible for the death of Ho Chu. I intend to avenge them.'

'You cannot mean those things.'

'They happen to be true.'

Alicia bit her lip in indecision, and there came a banging on the door. 'Are you in there, Harrington?' Ali called. 'You had best come out. I have a warrant for your arrest. And if you have harmed my sister . . .'

Alicia glanced at Michael in a panic, then drew the bolt and threw open the door. 'He has not harmed me. Ali, he says . . .'

Ali pointed with his sword. 'Seize him.'

The Chinese men came into the room.

'Ali!' Alicia shouted. 'Will you please listen to me.'

'When that scoundrel is locked up.'

The Chinese looked at Michael; some of them had sailed with him.

Michael buttoned his shirt and stood up, apparently undisturbed by their presence. 'You want to think well what you do,' he told Teng Tang. 'That man is responsible for the death of Teng Lee's widow. Of your sister-in-law, Teng Tang.'

Teng Tang frowned at him.

'That is a lie,' Ali snapped.

'Has any Teng ship ever been attacked before?' Michael demanded. 'Are you not aware that Ali has been supplying Bodaw Wing with guns and powder for years, and pocketing the profits?'

'How can this be?' Teng Tang asked in bewilderment.

'Lies!' Ali shouted.

'Why do you not ask Lee Tung? Or Wong Sung? Or any of their crews?' Michael told Tang. 'Ali and Bodaw Wing are friends. Bodaw Wing does what Ali tells him to do. And Ali told him to have the princess and myself murdered. I escaped, the princess was not so fortunate.'

Teng Tang looked at Ali again.

'Liar!' Ali shrieked, and lunged with his sword. Michael sidestepped the thrust and swung his fist; it caught Ali on the side of the head and tumbled him against the wall. He dropped the sword, and Michael snatched it up.

'No,' Alicia screamed. 'No!'

Already half committed, Michael checked himself. The man deserved to die, a hundred times over. But *he* was not a murderer. And perhaps Ali had been unaware that Jalina was on the ship.

'Then fetch your children and your maid,' he said. 'And have the phaeton brought to the front.' He kept the sword point close to Ali's throat as his brother-in-law stared at him.

'Where will you take us?' Alicia asked.

'Away from here,' Michael said. 'Do as I say, or your brother dies.'

Alicia hesitated, then ran from the room.

'You'll hang,' Ali snarled. 'By God, you'll hang.'

'Entirely my sentiments regarding you,' Michael told him. 'When I can prove my case. Teng Tang, keep this

228

madman here. I swear the next time I see him I'll run him through.'

Teng Tang looked more bewildered than ever, and quite incapable of deciding what should be done. Michael took advantage of his uncertainty, backed to the door, whipped the key from the lock, stepped through, and locked it behind him. Alicia stood on the landing with little Ralph in her arms; Joanna clung to Melinda.

'Downstairs!' he snapped.

Elizabeth Hammond stood in the hall; her husband was seated in the drawing room, apparently overcome by the excitement. 'You have no right,' she said. 'You are kidnapping my daughter.'

'I am reclaiming my wife,' Michael said. 'Step aside.'

'You . . .'

'Please, Mama,' Alicia said. She was not at all sure what she was doing, could only take refuge in the thought that he might hurt someone if she did not go along with him. Besides, if anything he had claimed was true . . .

The door was open. She ushered Melinda and the children through. The phaeton for which she had called waited, with Mansur standing beside it, also totally confused.

Alicia checked. 'We have no clothes.'

'You'll stand it.' Michael followed her on to the porch, tucking Ali's sword through the waistband of his trousers, listening to the banging and the sound of splintering wood from upstairs.

'You are a monster!' Elizabeth Hammond shouted at him.

Michael ignored her, went down the steps. 'We have no need of you, Mansur,' he said, and took the reins himself.

Alicia sat beside him. 'They will send behind you,' she said.

He flicked the reins, and the equipage moved down the drive.

'Do you suppose you can run for ever?' she asked. 'Or shelter behind me, for ever?'

He glanced at her, and she flushed. Then frowned as she saw the direction he was taking. 'What are you doing?'

'There is someone else must accompany us,' he said, and turned into the drive of the princess's house. 'Step down,' he commanded as he braked. Alicia hesitated, then obeyed. 'You stay here,' Michael told Melinda. 'And behave yourself. Remember that your mistress is with me.'

Did he really intend to harm her? Alicia wondered. Of course he did not. What she had to decide was her attitude to him. Of course he was behaving in a wildly romantic manner, like the desperado he was, and she loved to see him act this way . . . but he had still not apologized for or attempted to explain his adultery.

And now . . .

The door was opened, and Jalina's servants, wearing mourning white, were peering at the intruders. With them was a four-year-old boy, brown skinned and with sensitive features.

'Janus,' Michael said. 'You are to come with us.'

The boy stared at him, eyes enormous.

'How can you take him?' asked the oldest of the women. 'Where can you take him? The princess left him in our care.'

'I will take him to his mother,' Michael told her. 'It was the princess's last wish.' He held out his hand. 'Come, boy.'

'To Mother?' the boy asked.

'That's right.'

Janus ran forward, and Michael scooped him from the floor. 'You can hold him, if you like, Alicia.'

'I think he is disgusting. I think you are disgusting.' She was determined to stay angry until he apologized . 'And if you think you are carrying me off to see one of your mistresses then you are mistaken.'

'Shut up,' he said, 'and take your seat.'

Her head jerked. No one had ever spoken to her like that before.

'Quickly!' he snapped.

Alicia obeyed. Perhaps he was drunk, she thought, as she scrambled on to the driving seat in an undignified swirl of skirts. The little boy was set beside her, and Michael sat on the other side. He flicked the reins, and the phaeton moved off.

'There!' Alicia pointed back at the Hammond house, uncertain whether to be pleased or sorry at the sight of Ali running down the front steps, followed more slowly by the Chinese.

'He'll have to get more help,' Michael said, and drove down the hill to the harbour.

Alicia decided against being too angry. 'Michael,' she said. 'I am sure it would be best for you to return home and discuss the whole business with Papa and Mama and Ali. And myself. I simply cannot believe the accusations you levelled against him. I am sure you have made a mistake. I also feel you owe me a considerable explanation of your actions during the past few months. I am sure I wish to forgive you, but not if you persist in this mad course.'

'Shut up,' he said again.

Alicia's mouth snapped shut in anger. She wanted to shout at him, but was acutely aware of the little brown face staring up at her. Besides, Michael was in such a mood she had no idea how he might react.

And they were already at the dock, drawing curious stares as they clattered along the quay to where the *China Star* was making ready to cast off. 'Haste, Wong Sung,' Michael snapped. 'We will soon have the military after us.'

Alicia stared at the Chinese captain as she was ushered up the gangway. 'You knew of this?' she demanded.

'Captain Harrington is my friend. He came to me the moment he returned to Singapore, Mistress,' Wong explained. 'And I am sworn to avenge the princess.'

'You mean . . .' Alicia's head swung to look at Michael, who was handing Melinda and the children on board.

'I have been in Singapore for three days,' he explained. 'Now get below.'

'I will not be spoken to like a servant,' she shouted, stamping her foot.

Michael looked at her, then suddenly ducked and drove his shoulder into her stomach. She gave a gasp and felt herself being lifted from the deck, across his shoulder. In front of all the crew. She thumped her fists into his back and attempted to kick him, but he held her across the thighs and carried her into the cabin, where he threw her on the nearest bunk. She landed with arms and legs and skirts flying, and was again winded. Michael turned to Melinda, who had followed her mistress, still clutching the children. 'Be sure she stays here,' he told the maid. 'Or I will take my belt to her. Remember that.'

He went on deck, and Alicia listened to the stamping of feet, the thrumming of sheets and halliards. She sat up. 'He has gone mad!' she snapped at Melinda.

'Is a fact he does be angry,' Melinda agreed.

Alicia glared at her. No doubt the wretched woman, who had been on the end of her anger often enough, had enjoyed seeing her manhandled and humiliated. Well . . . she found herself looking at the Indian boy. 'Oh . . . go away!' she shouted.

Hooves, on the quay. She scrambled off the bunk and ran to the stern window, to look back at the shore. There were soldiers there, shouting and gesticulating. Ali was with them. But they were too late; there was a fresh breeze blowing, and the junk was clear of the docks. Now she was gathering speed and racing for the Dragon's Teeth.

Michael himself conned the junk through the reefs, Wong Sung at his side. There had been a great hubbub on the quayside, and there was considerable interest in their departure being evidenced by the other vessels in the pool, amongst which were several warships. But it would take several hours for the necessary orders to be given, and long before then they would be out of sight.

He looked at Wong Sung. 'You have burned your boats,' he said.

'I could not sail for Hammond and Teng again, if Ali

232

truly murdered the Princess, Michael,' Wong said. 'It was a decision I should have taken earlier.'

Michael nodded. 'I sailed for them, worked for them, too long, as well. But it is a hard course I have plotted for us.'

'You must tell me what it is.'

'Yes,' Michael said. 'You have my word that any man who does not wish to follow me will be set ashore in Hong Kong. Ali will undoubtedly follow us there, and your people can claim they were driven to it by you and me.'

'Those who wish to do so,' Wong said. 'So, is the course for Hong Kong?'

'Not immediately,' Michael said. 'There is that duty you and I first have to perform. Did you lay on those extra supplies I asked for?'

'Of course,' Wong said. 'But . . . it will still be a risky venture.'

'It is what the princess would have wanted,' Michael said. 'I will not fail her again. Your course is for Sarawak.'

For if he had spared Ali for the sake of Alicia, he had no intention of sparing Bodaw Wing.

'Go and see who you can find,' Alicia commanded Melinda.

'But Mistress, he will beat me,' Melinda complained.

'The children must be fed,' Alicia said severely. They had been at sea over an hour, and Ralph was both hungry and thirsty. So, she thought, was the half-caste boy, although his feelings did not really interest her. Joanna was clearly too afraid to feel anything more than that. And herself? Well, of course she was not afraid. How could she be afraid of a man to whom she had been married for six years, even if he had apparently taken leave of his senses? But she was certainly not going on deck to be humiliated again in front of the Chinese crew. 'Hurry up,' she snapped.

Melinda hesitated, then cautiously opened the door, to jump backwards with a squawk of alarm as Michael entered. 'The mistress . . .' she gasped.

233

Alicia stood up. 'The children need something to drink. And eat,' she said.

Michael nodded, snapped his fingers. Two of the Chinese cooks came in with food, water and tea, which they placed on the table; the junk was plunging slightly as she ran downwind but hardly rolling, and in any event the fiddles kept the bowls from sliding off.

Melinda hastily arranged the two smaller children before the meal.

'You'll attend to Janus as well,' Michael commanded.

Melinda hesitated, looking at Alicia.

'Oh, do as he says,' Alicia said. 'I would like to have a word with you, in private, if you please, Michael.'

'In there,' he said.

She glanced at the door to what she knew was one of the luxurious sleeping cabins – indeed, it was the same one in which they had honeymooned. 'I think, on deck. If you promise to behave yourself.'

'In there,' he repeated.

She wanted to stamp her foot in rage, but could not risk another physical confrontation in front of the children, especially the Hindu boy. She opened the door and went into the cabin. Michael followed her, with a bottle of wine and two glasses, closed the door behind him.

Alicia sat on the starboard bunk, facing him, trying to keep her face composed, to ignore the pounding of her heart and the heat she could feel in her cheeks. 'You are behaving quite abominably,' she said.

Michael poured two glasses of wine, and held one out. 'Take it,' he commanded when she hesitated. She obeyed, and he drank deeply, then refilled his glass and sat on the other bunk, leaning against the bulkhead.

'As I was saying,' Alicia said. 'You are behaving quite abominably. I can only suppose that you have either been drinking or are suffering from a touch of the sun. Perhaps both. Well, I will acknowledge that you seem to have had a difficult time. And it is because of that I have agreed to come away with you, bringing the children, despite your disgusting behaviour. But I will not, I will *not*, be treated like a servant. I demand a proper respect. And I wish to be told exactly what you are doing, where we are going. If you think . . .' she checked, because he had finished his second glass of wine and refilled his goblet a third time. Now he was placing the glass on the table and standing up.

'Finish your drink,' he suggested.

Alicia obeyed before she had time to consider a refusal. Michael took the glass from her fingers and placed it on the table beside his. 'We are going,' he said, 'to settle accounts with Bodaw Wing, once and for all.'

'In a single junk?' Alicia was aghast. 'And with children on board? Now I know you are demented.'

'They are my children,' he pointed out. 'Janus is my foster child, as of this minute. They live and die with me, not without me. As do you, because you are my wife. In any event, we will not be in a single junk; James Brooke is waiting for my return to assist me. That ship I happened to hail took me to Kuching, and it was Brooke who restored me to life. He too has a score to settle with Bodaw Wing. As for afterwards, if Melinda wishes to be set ashore in Hong Kong, which is our destination after Palawan, then she will be.'

'Set ashore? Hong Kong? Michael . . .'

'Because you and I, and the children, are then going on to China.'

'China?' Her voice had risen into a shout.

'You once told me you wished to visit China. Well, you are going to have your chance.'

'China?' she screamed. 'You are insane. What are you going to do in China?'

'Something worthwhile with my life. More worthwhile than selling opium to people too weak-minded to resist it.'

'China,' she said, more quietly, but more desperately as the true implication of what he had said began to sink in. 'Michael, please. You will be an outlaw. The children . . .'

'Will be outlaws too, until Hung gains his victory. So will you, my sweet Alicia.'

'Michael . . .'

'Now, you can tell me why I should not take the skin from your ass for deserting me and running off with that reptile of a brother of yours.'

'You . . .'

He finished the wine, took off his shirt.

'Don't you dare,' she said. 'You have behaved abominably. You owe me . . .'

He placed his hands on her shoulders and pushed her back against the bulkhead. She panted, but was powerless before his strength. 'I owe you nothing,' he said, staring into her eyes. 'I was the truest husband I have ever heard of, until you decided to believe I wasn't. To this day I have never bedded Malama. I cannot imagine why. Now you may as well know that I have a Chinese wife.'

'You . . .' again she strained.

'She is what in England would be know as common-law. But she is the mother of my son. My eldest son. I lived with her for two years. Oh, long before I proposed to you, my dear. I am returning to her. As I am now going to Malama. So you will not lack for company.'

'My God!' Alicia gasped. 'You can stand there and say such things to me? A wife? A son? The Hindu? If you think I am going to . . .'

'You are,' he said.

'I refuse. I absolutely refuse.'

He released her. 'You'll get used to the idea. Now undress.'

'Are you out of your mind? You *are* out of your mind.'

'If you don't undress,' he explained. 'I will probably tear your clothes. And you should remember that those are the only clothes you possess.'

She stared at him. 'You intend to rape me.'

'I intend to co-habit with you as my wife.'

She pressed herself against the bulkhead, knees drawn up. 'You wouldn't dare.'

He kicked off his boots, dropped his trousers.

Alicia rose to her knees. 'Michael . . .'

He stood in front of her. 'Very well.' He reached for her bodice.

'No!' She twisted away from him. 'I will do it. Just . . . leave me alone.'

He sat on the other bunk and waited as she undressed. Perhaps, in Jalina's arms, and then existing on the memory of that fragile beauty, he had forgotten the true beauty of his wife, that flawlessly white body, those strong legs, those large breasts, only enhanced by motherhood and her thirty years. When she was finished she stood by the port, half turned away from him. 'Come here,' he said.

She was breathing heavily, but she knew she was lost, turned and crossed the cabin. He held her arm and made her sit on his knee. 'You once set out to make me forget Malama,' he told her, kissing her nipple. 'Now make me forget Jalina.'

In two days they were in Kuching Harbour, and Alicia was being introduced to Rajah Brooke, as he called himself, a vigorous forty-six-year-old with piercing eyes. 'Your husband spoke of you,' he said. 'I am pleased to make your acquaintance. You must be proud to be married to such a man.'

Alicia bit her lip. Proud, she thought. How could any woman not be proud to be married to Michael Harrington? But how could she show that without being humiliated all over again?

'No warships, I see,' Brooke was saying to Michael.

'No. But I still intend to smoke that devil out.'

'Then I shall accompany you. But perhaps your wife and the children would stay here. It will be a dangerous business.'

'Less so than you think,' Michael told him. 'I have worked out how to deal with Bodaw Wing. And my wife and children will stay with me, if you don't mind; there can be no doubt that her brother will send here to look

237

for her. Now, James, if you would like to assemble your twelve best men, I will demonstrate our tactics.'

He had already chosen the most reliable of Wong Sung's crew, and these, together with Brooke's people, he brought together in the waist of the *China Star*. 'The pirates are formidable,' he told them, 'because of their speed and their numbers. And because the aim of every ship they attack has always been merely to repulse them or escape them. They do not make the mistake of attacking warships. So, normally, unless they can be sunk by gunfire at a distance, which is difficult because of their speed, once they come alongside they cannot be stopped, by conventional methods, because they always outnumber the crew of any merchantman. Our aim must be to combat these two advantages. And our objective is neither to repel nor to escape. It is to destroy.' He signalled Wong Sung, who had the hatches rolled back. 'There . . .' he pointed to the four huge tubs of animal fat. 'Is weapon number one. We will coat our topsides and bulwarks with this fat. The pirates come on board by grappling and then climbing up the sides of their victim. They will not find that easy to do when those are too slippery for a hand or foot hold. That will be victory number one. Victory number two will be their destruction.' This time he introduced the extra barrels of gunpowder Wong had taken on board, and at another signal Wong passed him up two of the grenades he had already made. 'This is simply a wine bottle, as you can see. This one is filled with powder. That one is filled with oil. And you will see that the stopper is merely twisted paper. The slow matches will be burning on deck when the pirates attack. We will wait until they are alongside, and then each man of us will light the touch paper, and immediately drop the grenade into the boat beneath us. The explosions and the resulting fire will destroy the proas, but will not be sufficient to harm the junk's teak sides.' He looked over their faces. 'It goes without saying that there can be no hesitation in using these things, and any man who drops one will probably blow himself to pieces. That is why Rajah Brooke

238

and I have chosen you. You will be our grenadiers, and between us we will settle with Bodaw Wing once and for all.'

The Chinese sailors gave a roar of approbation. There was hardly one who did not hate the pirates – if only for being Malays.

'By heaven, but your scheme is brilliant,' Brooke exclaimed. 'And simple. Like all good schemes.'

Michael stared at him. 'I meant what I said, James. I am on a mission of extermination. I intend to sink their ships, burn their village, and destroy their crops, regardless of whether women and children are killed as well as men. They are all cast in the same mould. I have seen them at work.' He gave a grim smile. 'I have *felt* them at work. I do not mean to leave those vipers any prospect of recommencing their activities.'

Brooke nodded. 'I agree with you. Now let us put to sea.'

Alicia had watched the demonstration with sombre eyes, the children clustered round her. She no longer made any objection to the presence of Janus; her personality had been, even if temporarily, overwhelmed by this grim, vengeful figure into which her husband had turned. Even his lovemaking was inspired by an angry rather than a loving passion. 'You must have loved the princess very much,' she remarked as he came aft.

'I never had the time, to love her,' Michael said. 'But she was the most loveable woman I have known.'

'And when she is avenged, will you be able to smile again?'

Michael looked at her. 'Ask me when that moment is here.'

The picked men spent the two days approaching Palawan, with the mountains of Sarawak clinging to the southern horizon, making the grenades, until Michael felt they had enough to destroy many times the number of proas Bodaw Wing could command. The rest of the crews were lowered over the side on cradles with buckets of the grease to coat the topsides. This was actually left until Palawan was in sight, as the fat would of course melt after being exposed to the heat for too long.

By then the two ships had assumed their selected positions, Brooke's schooner lowering her sails so as to be left behind. Much the faster ship, certainly to windward, she would resume her course after four hours, leaving the *China Star* apparently alone as she approached the pirate island. Nor did Michael fly the flag of Teng on this occasion, but instead the Red Ensign alone, and under shortened sail and into a north-westerly breeze the junk made poor speed, wallowing through the slight swell as though heavily laden. Michael had no doubt they had been seen from the headland, and sure enough, with his glass he made out two proas, as usual close inshore where they were less likely to be observed. He had no doubt the third would soon appear.

'Let me see,' Alicia asked, and he gave her the glass. She stared at them, and shivered. He had told her exactly what had happened to the princess, but the concept of such a thing happening to her was impossible for her to imagine. And yet, if his plan miscarried, the grenades did not explode, or did not stop the pirates . . . she gave him back the glass, her face pale.

'Now go below,' he said. 'The doors will be locked, and you will be safe until after the victory.' The cabin windows had already had boards nailed across them to prevent anyone breaking in below deck.

Alicia hesitated. 'I will wish you God speed, for all our sakes.'

'I doubt God will wish to be involved in what is about to happen,' Michael said. 'But there is nothing for you to be afraid of.'

He himself locked them in, kissing his two children, holding Janus close for a moment. It was the first spark of real humanity he had revealed since his return to Singapore, and Alicia felt tears spring to her eyes. Undoubtedly his experiences, perhaps ever since the appearance of Malama in Hong Kong, had driven wedges of iron into

240

his soul. Perhaps, when this task was completed, he would again be the man she remembered, and with whom she had fallen so desperately in love. Because she could not love this other man? Oh, indeed she could. But this man she was afraid of, as well.

Every order given, the grenadiers standing by, Michael continued to study the approaching headland and the waiting proas. Even from the west the creek and the village were invisible behind the curving natural breakwater; how Bodaw Wing must have felt himself totally secure when he had first found so splendid a natural hideaway.

'They are coming,' Wong Sung said quietly.

'And there is the third,' Michael said. As was the usual pirate practice, Bodaw Wing had waited until they were abeam of the headland, so as to catch them between two attacks. 'You'll hold your course,' he reminded the captain.

Wong nodded. He had himself taken the wheel, and his hands were tight on the spokes.

Even the normal chatter of the crew was quiet now as the men waited for the battle to commence; as instructed, the grenadiers were crouching below the bulwarks to conceal themselves. Michael levelled his glass astern, and could just make out the topsails of Brooke's schooner. The pirates would not have seen it yet, except possibly from the shore. But they would still assume there was sufficient time to deal with the junk first, and then seize the schooner afterwards.

He went down the ladder to join his grenadiers, who were stripped to the waist, heads bound up in bandannas, eager for action. He himself, in addition to his sword, wore one of the new Colt revolving pistols, given him by Brooke, which possessed six chambers and at close quarters was a deadly weapon. 'Open fire,' he now told the gunners.

The three cannon in the starboard broadside exploded, and plumes of water shot upwards from the sea. But as usual the fast moving proas, now rowing at full speed, were nearly impossible to hit. However, Michael had the guns fired again and again, as any terrified shipmaster would have done, while at the same time men heaved on the halliards to send more wooden-slatted sail aloft in an apparently vain attempt to outsail their enemies. For the proas were very close, and they could clearly see the sarong-clad Malays, sweat gleaming on their arms as the sunlight gleamed on their weapons. Michael could not immediately make out Bodaw Wing, but where the chieftain was did not interest him at the moment; every man he could see was equally guilty.

'Cease firing,' he commanded the gunners; the proas were within a hundred yards and the cannon could not be depressed sufficiently. The boat astern was coming up very rapidly as well. 'Stand by,' he told the men crouching beneath the bulwarks. The Malays were shouting now, bloodcurdling shrieks intended to terrify their presumably already frightened victims, and now the proas came thudding alongside, grapples flying through the air to lodge on the bulwarks and crunch into the wood. 'Now!' Michael snapped, and lit his touchpaper.

His men rose as one, also with flaming grenades, six on each side. Michael tossed his, which contained oil, into the centre of the starboard proa, as the pirates began swarming out of her, their hands grasping the ropes attached to the grappling irons, but their feet slipping to cause them to fall back with shouts of dismay. The glass shattered and the flaming oil ran fore and aft, to be joined by a powder grenade, which exploded on impact. The others followed, both oil and powder, and the entire interior of the proa was turned into an inferno. Men screamed as they were burned or mutilated by the powder blasts, while the rest of the junk's crew lined the bulwarks and began firing muskets into the heaving mass below them. The Malays had no time to work out what was happening to defeat them. Several still tried to climb the impossibly slippery topsides, and one or two even reached the gunwales, to be met by slashing cutlasses and swinging muskets. The rest screamed their agony, and Michael, having had his men toss a second barrage of grenades into their midst, turned his attention to the port side, where Wong had left the helm to take command, and the second proa had been reduced to a burning coffin. Then he ran aft to see what had become of the third pirate ship.

The crew of this had observed the disaster which had overtaken their compatriots, and had backed off in terror. Michael decided they could be ignored for the moment, and now the schooner was coming up very fast, heeling over as she beat into the wind. The crews of the proas alongside were trying desperately to free themselves of this tartar they had caught, but now Wong had his men hurl grapples of their own, to hold the two craft alongside, while shots and grenades were rained down on them, and the gunners even enthusiastically dropped their cannonballs. Both boats were now sinking, and those pirates still capable of movement were leaping over the side. Michael levelled his revolver and shot one man through the head, hit another in the shoulder. Blood began to spread and black fins to appear. The warm green water became a place of horror.

'All right, Wong,' Michael said. 'Cast them off.'

The proas, already almost submerged, although the oil continued to burn even as the water rushed in, were let go.

'Now bring her about,' Michael commanded.

The sheets were adjusted and the junk came round, carving her way through the dead and dying men in the water. The crew of the remaining proa realized that they were going to be attacked, and at the same time noticed the schooner, now only a few miles off. They put about to make the island, but, downwind, the junk could sail as fast as they could paddle, and Michael took his place in the bows with a rifled musket and one or two other good marksmen, and began picking men off. The two vessels raced at the headland, where a large number of people were gathered to watch the disaster which had overtaken their menfolk, and at the schooner which was steadily moving inshore, and was now closest to the headland. The crew of the proa realized they were going to be cut off, and turned, away from the schooner, to make the beach. But the manoeuvre allowed the junk to come closer, and Wong put the helm up to allow his guns to bear. The shot plunged into the water to either side of the pirate ship, and she turned back again. Michael could now make out the figure of Bodaw Wing in the stern, shouting orders, but there was no necessity for him to do likewise. Wong had the light of battle in his eyes and, still downwind, the junk was immensely easy to steer. Now he altered course, within fifty feet of the proa. The pirates screamed their terror, and then came about in an effort to get past their enemy. Wong saw their intention, and wrenched on the wheel. The two vessels turned into each other with a sickening crunch, and the proa immediately began to sink. The pirates tried to climb up the junk's topsides, but met the same fate as those earlier, slipping and sliding back into the water, while grenades were rained down on them. Bodaw Wing stood in the stern, waving his sword and shrieking at the top of his voice. Michael discovered that his revolver was empty, but a bag of cartridges hung at his waist. He reloaded, and then, ignoring the pandemonium around him, took careful aim, and fired, again and again. The first bullet missed. The second struck Bodaw Wing on the shoulder, and half turned him round as he dropped his sword. The third struck him in the chest, and blood gushed to join his scream. The fourth hit him in the belly and he dropped to his knees. Michael's fifth shot blew half his head away, and as he fell to the now water-covered deck, Michael put the last bullet into his back. 'Sleep easy, little princess,' he said, as the hammer clicked on an empty chamber.

Brooke waited for Michael to pilot him and Wong into the creek, and the work of slaughter went on. Only a few men had remained in the village, and these were soon put to flight by the ship's cannon, taking with them those of their women and children who survived the bombardment. Their wails could be heard long after they had disappeared and Michael had led his men ashore systematically to destroy the village. Every building, including the palace and the mosque, was burned, and the fire allowed to rage out of control so that it took in the surrounding forest and even reduced the rice paddy to a charred ruin. When the two ships stood back out to sea, the smoke still billowed from behind the headland, while they waited for the final act which would destroy the pirate base forever. For Michael had buried one of the unused barrels of gunpowder in a carefully chosen spot near the inner end of the cliff, and set a time fuse. Now the entire afternoon rumbled as the earth collapsed, tons of rubble pouring into the creek effectively to block the entrance.

'That will never be used again,' Brooke said with some satisfaction.

'And they will remember this day,' Wong said, equally pleased.

Janus clapped his hands. 'Now we go to Mother,' he said.

'Aye,' Michael said, and ruffled his hair, while looking across him at Alicia.

'Are you content, now?' she asked.

'In that I have accomplished one of the things to which I am pledged, yes,' he said.

'But you will not relent, as regards the others.'

'No.'

She gazed at him for several seconds, then went below to join her children.

Was he sorry for her? Or was he still as angry as he pretended? He could not be sure. He could not be sure how guilty she was, how guilty he wanted her to be. However inadvertently, she had caused a great deal of the calamity which had overtaken their lives, by her inability to trust him. And she was Ali's sister. And at the same time his wife; in that regard he was not prepared to feel the least guilty about Jalina, except in so far as he had been unable to save her life. He knew he still loved Alicia, though he could no longer respect her or even accept her as his equal, just as he intended to demonstrate to her that her assumed superiority over women like Malama or Wu Yei was a figment of her imagination. That would be to expose her most cruelly both to privation and humiliation, and perhaps that was unjust of him. But for that too, he felt no remorse in his present mood. She had selected him to marry with a total insouciance. She had made that bed, apparently assuming she could leave it whenever she chose or the going got rough. Well, now she would have to take that rough with the smooth, until he decided she had suffered enough.

Yet he knew too that her behaviour had played an important part in crystallizing the understanding he had gained when with Hung, of how he had been wasting his life, and for that he was grateful. It had also brought him those unforgettable hours with the princess, even if it had also been responsible for her death. He smiled grimly. It had also, nearly, brought him control of Hammond and Teng. Neither Alicia nor her brother would ever know how near they had come to that catastrophe, with all that would have been entailed. With that power he could have offered Hung more than merely six cannon and a few volunteers. But fate had decreed it otherwise. He would still play his part to the best of his ability.

'If you ever need a home,' Brooke said as they shook hands, 'you will find it here with me.'

Michael smiled. 'A day's sail from Singapore, where there is a warrant out for my arrest? Several, by now, I should think. I have not only stolen Ali Hammond's sister, I have stolen one of his ships, and I have invaded Spanish territory. I am as much a pirate as ever Bodaw Wing was.'

'I would not let them take you. Nor, I think, would they wish to, when they hear what you have just accomplished. To run away from them . . .' he shook his head. 'Being a pirate is no life, especially with a family in tow.'

'It's not my intention either to run or act the pirate more than I have to,' Michael promised him. 'I go to

246

undertake a new life. One for which perhaps I was always intended.'

'Then I will wish you every good fortune. And Michael . . .' he hesitated. 'I know only a little of what lies between Mrs Harrington and yourself. But I will say this: she is as spirited as she is beautiful. If you break that spirit, you will only ever have half of her.'

'As you say, James, you only know a little of what lies between us. But I thank you for your advice. As I am in any case eternally in your debt for your help. Now I must be on my way before the monsoon breaks. Or the Navy comes looking for me.'

They shook hands again, and Brooke turned his schooner to the west. The *China Star* made north, her crew ebulliently elated with their victory over their oldest foes. Most of them were prepared to follow Michael to the ends of the earth if need be. The next day he assembled them to tell them what he and Wong intended, and again offered to set any of them who wished ashore in Hong Kong. Only half a dozen elected not to return to the mainland from whence their families had fled a generation in the past, and resume the fight against the Manchu. Michael decided against putting into Victoria, just in case a fast sloop had already got there from Singapore, and instead gave them one of the boats when within a few miles of Hong Kong Island.

To Alicia's consternation, Melinda asked to accompany them. 'I ain't able to go live with no Chinese, Mistress,' she said.

'But . . . you can't desert me now,' Alicia cried. 'What about the children? And . . .' she glanced at Janus.

'You will find somebody else, Mistress.'

Alicia looked at Michael. 'You can't let her go, Michael. I must have a maid, and the children must have a nanny. Make her stay, Michael.'

'I said I would take no one who did not volunteer,' Michael reminded her.

'Except me,' she said bitterly.

'You volunteered to share my life,' he pointed out.

247

'Which you are now doing. Melinda never did that. Over the side with you, Melinda.'

'Oh!' Alicia shouted, and hurried below to weep in the privacy of her cabin.

Then the junk stood on, to the north.

Alicia returned on deck to watch her erstwhile home receding into the distance, and sighed, and then looked at the empty coastline ahead of them, and shuddered. 'Have you no pity?' she asked. 'So to expose your children to danger and deprivation?'

'If I survive, so will they,' he promised her. 'And so will you. We are going to *do* something with our lives.'

'I hate you,' she snapped. 'I cannot believe I ever voluntarily tied myself to you.'

'But you did,' he reminded her, and went to join Wong and study the coast through their glasses. He soon identified the bay he sought, but as he wanted both daylight and a high tide it was next morning before he stood into it, conning the junk through the rocks and shallows which encumbered the approach. As they approached, although they could see no houses, they could make out men watching them from the shore, obviously mystified as to their intentions, but Wong continued to steer straight for the beach as Michael had instructed him. The wind was light and onshore, and the junk moved smoothly through the calm water, which slowly turned from blue to a steadily paling green. Everyone was on deck, the Chinese seamen chattering amongst themselves, and all armed, as Michael had no idea what reception they would get when they went ashore. Alicia and the children were aft with him, staring in open-mouthed consternation at the approaching beach.

'You mean to strand her,' Alicia gasped.

'Aye,' Michael said. 'Now sit down on the deck and hold the children.'

Alicia hesitated, then obeyed, hugging Joanna and Ralph, while Janus sat beside them. The water was now almost white, and a moment later there came the jar as the bottom encountered the sand. The junk was travelling

248

faster than Michael had supposed, and the impact snapped off the foremast and sent it over the side in a welter of canvas and cordage. But the main held, and the ship continued to drive on to the sand, her timbers giving off a terrible grinding sound. It was the very top of the tide.

Michael allowed the junk to drive on for another half an hour, until the carpenter reported that she was making water from opened seams forward. Then he commanded the sails to be lowered, and breakfast to be served. Meanwhile the tide steadily fell, and by mid-morning the wrecked ship was all but high and dry. He was first over the side to test the situation, discovered that he stood in two feet of water. Wong joined him, along with a dozen armed men, and they went on to the beach and waited. Soon enough some of the fishermen came down to him.

'Do you worship God?' Michael asked.

The men exchanged glances.

'I too, am a God Worshipper,' Michael told them. 'I and my men have come to join with Hung Hsiu-ch'uan in his fight against the Manchu. I would have you tell him we are here.'

'It is many days to the home of Hung Hsiu-ch'uan,' one of the men said.

'But you have horses. If you will not go yourself, hire me one of your horses, that I may send a messenger. Be sure that Hung will be pleased with the man who tells him of my arrival with the guns. He expects it. And be sure, too, that his wrath will fall upon the man who fails in this task. He, and his family, will suffer.'

The men certainly understood that. 'We will send to Hung Hsiu-ch'uan,' the spokesman said. 'But you will be destroyed when the bannermen come this way.'

'Does that happen often?' Wong asked.

'Often enough.'

'Then we have the more reason for making haste. Send your messenger immediately, and then have your people assist mine in unloading the ship.'

Michael's natural air of command, his claimed friendship with Hung, acted as a spur. A horseman was dispatched for the interior immediately, and the rest of the little fishing community, men, women and boys, arrived to assist in unloading the junk. Alicia and the children were lowered over the side and carried ashore by the crew; Michael himself carried Alicia. Then it was the turn of the guns, but there was no time to move them that morning, as while it was essential to have them ashore at low tide, it was also necessary to prepare some means of getting them up the sand without their wheels sinking irretrievably. Michael had every sail stripped off and spread to make a wood and canvas roadway; it did not quite reach the firm ground, but of course could be taken up behind each cannon as it was moved, and relaid at the front. Meanwhile work at other unloading went on apace, even when the tide came in – for the smaller equipment, the powder and shot, they could use the remaining boat. They hardly stopped to eat or drink as they worked through the day. By evening the tide was falling again, but it was dark before the water was low enough to risk the cannon. Then they were lowered by the halliards from the two remaining masts, although not without difficulty and danger, as both ropes and timbers groaned beneath the unaccustomed weight.

Only three of the guns could be taken off that night, and then once again it was necessary to wait, and watch, both the weather, and the shore for any signs of the Manchu cavalry. But fortune was with them, and next morning the last of the guns was pulled and pushed over the sinking canvas on to the solid earth, and thence to the grotto which Michael had chosen for their concealment, and where they were hidden beneath a pyramid of stones and rocks so as to be invisible to all but the most careful inspection.

The Manchu came that very afternoon. Michael was alerted by Ling Su, the headman of the fishing village, and together with him and Wong Sung he crept through the grass on top of a hummock overlooking the bay, from which he saw the group of armed horsemen, some twenty strong, their yellow banners streaming in the breeze as they trotted along the sand, pausing to stare at the stricken junk. Then they hurried forward with excited cries, but the tide was now again in, and they were reluctant to drive their horses into the deep water. But they noticed the scuffed beach, and one also pointed at the empty gunports on the ship. They understood that the wreck had been stripped, and stared at the dunes and hummocks which masked the land.

'Do they know of your village?' Michael whispered.

'Indeed they do,' Ling Su replied. 'As they collect taxes from us. But they will not come to us with only twenty men. They will return tomorrow.'

'And then?'

'They will ask us about the ship, and its crew, and its contents, and we will tell them that we know nothing of these things.'

'Will they accept that?'

Ling Su gave a grim smile. 'No, Mr Harrington, they will not accept that. They will seize some of us and beat us to force the truth from us. They may even execute some of us. And they will rape our women. It is their usual practice. But we will not tell them.'

Not for the first time Michael was astounded at the way these people could so calmly face an unacceptable situation. 'I cannot permit this,' he said. 'How many men will return tomorrow, do you suppose?'

Ling Su shrugged. 'Enough to be sure that we do not resist them. We are forty-seven men of good health. They will bring at least seventy-five soldiers.'

'You are now seventy-two men of good health,' Michael said.

Ling Su looked at him.

'My crew numbers twenty-five,' Michael explained. 'What is more, they are experienced fighting men, and they are well armed.'

'You mean you wish us to fight the Manchu?' Ling Su was astounded.

'Is that not what Hung Hsiu-ch'uan is dedicated to doing?'

'Hung Hsiu-ch'uan is the right hand of God,' Ling Su explained.

'Well,' Michael remarked. 'I am Hung Hsiu-ch'uan's right hand. We have a chain-of-command situation.'

He doubted Ling either understood or appreciated his humour. 'If we fight, and win,' he said, 'they will send many more soldiers against us. They will send an army.'

'We will fight, and win,' Michael said. 'And then we will go and join Hung. All of us.'

'We are simple fishermen,' Ling-Su protested.

'I will make you into soldiers,' Michael promised him. 'Now, mount a good lookout, and let us prepare ourselves.'

He put one of his own sailors with the two fishermen Ling dispatched to watch the beach to the south; he did not yet trust the mental toughness of the fisher-folk. And indeed he was aware that he was entirely disrupting their lives, as he had disrupted so many lives this last year. But having determined on a course of action he was not going to allow any backsliding; he could not move the guns until Hung brought the necessary transport, and to have them falling into the hands of the Manchu would be to negate everything that he had so far accomplished.

He had food and clothing carried to the hut where Alicia and the children had been taken, all of them crammed into a single room, and accompanied it. 'Has your friend arrived?' Alicia asked.

'No. It will take a while yet. Here, I have brought you a change of clothing.'

Alicia looked with distaste at the baggy trousers and loose smock, the flat hat, the soft boots, and wrinkled her nose. 'They aren't clean.'

'Well, washday in a village like this is only about once a year. But they will be warm, and somewhat more practical than your gown. Which, incidentally, doesn't look too clean either.'

She looked down at her distinctly soiled dress, then glared at him. 'The situation amuses you.'

'I think we had better learn to laugh at it whenever we can,' Michael agreed. 'We are going to be offered far too many opportunities for weeping, I can assure you.'

'And you brought us to this.'

'Why, so I did. We are going to occupy our lives to some purpose for a change. But the first rule of the new life we are going to live is to make the best of each moment, and never to waste time in idle recrimination. Are you not comfortable here?'

Alicia looked around her. As there were no chairs in the hut she sat on the floor. As there was no cutlery and she had not mastered the use of the food sticks, she had been forced to eat with her fingers – as had the children with great glee. As there was no mirror she had not been able to attend to her toilette, and auburn hair lay in a great untidy mass on her neck, while her cheeks were smudged with dirt. 'Are you joking again?' she asked. 'Oh . . .' she gave a most unladylike wriggle.

'Where does it itch?' Michael inquired.

She gave him another glare. 'That happens to be my business.'

'I'm afraid lice is the business of all of us.'

'Lice?' she shouted.

'I suspect that is what is ailing you. I also imagine it is in your pubes. If you do not find and destroy it, or them, you will be very uncomfortable and perhaps even unwell. Let me do it for you.'

She gathered her skirt tightly about her knees. 'You dare!'

'My darling Alicia, I am your husband. I have been your husband for some years. Don't you think it is a little late to act the prude?'

She continued to glare at him for several seconds, then her shoulders sagged; the discomfort was obviously intense, and it was impossible for her to scratch without in any event lifting her skirts. 'Then send the children away,' she muttered.

'Take the others outside, Janus,' Michael said. 'And remember, you are responsible for them.'

'Yes, Uncle Michael,' Janus agreed, and ushered the two smaller children through the door.

'I suppose he could be trained as some kind of replacement for Melinda,' Alicia said.

'He is going to be trained to be what he is, their older brother,' Michael told her, pushing her on to her back and himself raising her skirts and removing her drawers.

'Oh, you . . .'

'Got one.' He snapped it between his fingernails. 'Full of your blood. And there's another. I imagine there are hundreds in the furbellows on your petticoats. You really would be better off without them.'

'And are you going to pretend there are no lice in those Chinese clothes?'

'I am sure there are. But they are easier to spot and remove.'

'I . . .' she gave a strangled scream, and sat up, as the door opened without a knock, to reveal Ling Su.

The headman gave her no more than a glance. 'Mr Harrington,' he said. 'The bannermen are coming.'

10

The Angels of Destruction

Hung Hsiu-ch'uan himself led the regiment of horsemen and draught mules across country to discover if it was true about the guns. Feng Yun-shan was sceptical. 'And if he is there,' he remarked, 'what will you do about the woman? You will have to kill the Englishman.'

Feng really was an irritating man, Hung thought. First of all he lectures me for not having a woman, then when I take one he prophesies nothing but trouble. 'I am the Right Hand of God,' he said. 'Michael knows this, and knows too that what I want, I must have. Besides, if I kill him, who will know how to fire the guns?'

But he left Feng behind, in command, and took with him Yang Hsiu-ch'ing. Yang was a young man who had risen from the ranks of the God Worshippers by sheer military ability. His strategic eye was unlike anything Hung had ever known before; he could see at a glance the weakness in any plan, or in any enemy position, and he could also see the way to correct it. He was the man, Hung knew, for whom he had been waiting, to lead his hordes to certain success even when opposed to the full might of the Manchu – but even Yang was first interested in obtaining a battery of cannon.

Three hundred strong, the regiment rode straight across country north of Canton and arrived above the fishing village in only a week, to gaze down at the junk, beginning to break up now as there had been some wind, but still a symbol of a power Hung had not yet considered mastering.

'I see no cannon, Great Hung,' Yang complained.

'They are there, as the ship is there,' Hung said. His heart swelled. Michael had not, after all, failed him. Then what of the woman? But Michael had another woman, Wu Yei, who was also the father of his son. And besides, Hung Hsiu-ch'uan was the Right Hand of God.

Their approach had obviously been sighted from the village, because people came into the streets to greet them, Michael conspicuous by his height. 'Michael!' Hung dismounted to embrace him.

'Hung! It is good to see you.'

'I would have you meet my army commander, General Yang.'

Yang bowed, and then shook hands.

'As I would have you meet my shipmaster, and the man who will command your artillery,' Michael said. 'Captain Wong Sung.'

'You will command my artillery, Michael,' Hung said. 'With Wong as your second-in-command.'

Yang, who had been frowning, now greeted Wong in turn. 'The guns,' he said. 'Where are the guns?'

'We will show you, great gentlemen,' Ling Su said. 'And we will also show you where we have buried your enemies.'

Hung frowned at him. 'There has been a battle?'

'The bannermen came,' Ling said proudly. 'And we met them and destroyed them. But a few escaped.'

Hung looked at Michael.

'It was necessary, to save the guns,' Michael explained.

'But this is great news.' Hung embraced him again. 'And it was your doing. I congratulate you.'

'The bannermen will return,' Yang remarked. 'With reinforcements.'

'I agree with you,' Michael said. 'That is why the sooner we leave here with the guns the better.'

'Take me to them,' Yang commanded Ling. 'And then prepare your people to move out.'

'I congratulate you again,' Hung said. 'But your ship is wrecked. How will your people leave again?'

'They are not going to leave again,' Michael told him. 'Like me, they have abandoned Hong Kong, to join you in your fight for China.'

'But that is splendid news,' Hung said, thoughtfully.

'How is Malama?' Michael asked as they walked towards the hut he had made his home, while the villagers stared at the great man of whom they had only ever heard, but to whom their battle with the bannermen had irretrievably tied them.

'Well,' Hung said carefully. 'She is well.'

'I am looking forward to seeing her again,' Michael said.

'Even if you cannot take her away,' Hung said, more carefully yet.

'I still think I can make her happy. I have brought her son to her.'

Hung stopped walking. 'Her son? Your son?'

Michael shook his head. 'No. She was married. Did you not know of this? She came to you because she had killed her husband.'

'Killed her husband. And a mother,' Hung said. 'No, I did not know of these things. She has told me nothing of them.'

'I doubt she has yet picked up enough Chinese to do so,' Michael suggested.

'Yes,' Hung said. 'I would see this child.'

'Of course.' Michael opened the door of the hut. Alicia stood there, with the three children in front of her. Janus had been so unfailingly helpful over the past week that she had almost come to accept him, just as she had finally accepted the Chinese smock and loose trousers – after Michael had escorted her to the beach to bathe, herself and the children, and also to rinse the clothes, again and again. Now her pale-complexioned face and arms, and her head of gloriously undressed auburn hair, stood out from the blue of her garb like a beacon. Hung stared at her in amazement.

'My wife,' Michael said. 'This is the boy.'

Hung ignored Janus to stare at Alicia. 'Does she speak Chinese?' he asked.

'Only a word or two. But she will learn.'

'She is very beautiful,' Hung said.

257

'Yes,' Michael said.

'And she is your wife. But what of Malama?'

'She has never been my wife,' Michael told him. 'She was, is, my ward.'

'Ah,' Hung said, and patted Janus on the head, while he still gazed at a totally embarrassed Alicia. He was aware of a great sense of relief. He was not going to have to quarrel with Michael after all. He had not wanted to do so, because the man was a friend – and more than that, he had to be regarded as a symbol of good fortune, as well as commander of the guns. Had they quarrelled, he might have had to do as Feng had suggested, and have him beheaded. Now he could live . . . at least until he had trained some Chinese gunners. Besides . . . until this moment he had not realized there could be so much beauty in the world. He held out his hand, and after a glance at Michael, Alicia allowed him to take her fingers. 'Your wife is very beautiful,' Hung said again.

The horses plodded their way to the west. Yang had thrown out a screen both ahead and behind them, and to either side, and in the midst the mules strained at the cannon, surrounded by the other soldiers, and by the fishermen and their wives and children, carrying their pitiful bundles as they embarked on this new life; there were not sufficient horses for them all, and in any event they were required to heave and push whenever one of the cannon wheels got bogged down in a rut or pothole – the roads were in any event little more than tracks, and now it had started to rain . . . the monsoon was all but upon them. But there were horses enough for Hung and his immediate entourage, which included the four Harringtons and Janus; the Indian boy rode alone, while Ralph sat in front of his mother, and Joanna in front of her father. Neither child had yet become entirely reconciled to him, as a father, but they could understand that he was their protector in this strange environment in which they found themselves, and however uncomfortable the steady rain made them, they were better off than trudging through the mud.

'So these are the men who are going to conquer China,' Alicia remarked.

Michael wished Alicia could manage a little more acceptance of her situation. 'Yes, they are,' he agreed.

Alicia gazed through the drizzle at Hung, riding in front with his general. 'I do not like your friend. I do not like his eyes.'

'They are strange eyes,' Michael agreed. 'Magnetic.'

'When they look at me, they . . .' she glanced at him. 'They seem to undress me.'

'Well, he regards you as very beautiful. He has told me so.'

She shuddered. 'And you have placed us entirely in his power.'

Michael frowned at her, then laughed. 'You entirely mistake the character of the man. He is not interested in women. His entire life is bound up in politics. Besides, he is my friend. Therefore he is your friend as well.'

'I hope you are right,' Alicia said, hugging Ralph against her.

She was at least not grumbling any more, Michael thought with some relief. About being here. And he had no doubt that once the life became familiar to her, and they managed to escape this unceasing rain, and when she was able to appreciate the vast undertaking Hung was about, the reverence in which he was held by his people, she might even understand his own motives in returning to China. And therefore him.

His anger with her had long faded. He had not slept with her since the assault on Palawan. There had hardly been the time, and besides, he was not by nature a rapist, even of his wife. He had humiliated her, and by merely bringing her here he had punished her sufficiently for her desertion of him. Now he wanted her back as his wife.

And his other two wives? For there was nothing now to restrain him from either resuming his relations with Wu Yei or beginning a relationship with Malama. Wu Yei

259

Alicia would in any event have to accept. Malama . . . that would probably be the crowning indignity. He was not sure he wanted to do that to her any more. And yet he could not help but look on Malama as some kind of alter ego of the Princess Jalina, and as such he owed her as much happiness as he could provide – quite apart from the love she would give in return.

And yet he loved Alicia. Once again he had three balls in the air, quite unsure which one he truly wanted to catch. But even more than Wu Yei, Alicia was the mother of his children.

Horsemen splashed out of the rain mist, agitated and pointing behind them. 'There are bannermen,' they said. 'Not five miles away. They know of our march.'

'How many?' Yang demanded.

'Many hundreds. And accompanied by Green Flags.'

'The Viceroy has called out an army,' Hung muttered. 'What must we do?'

'Only the cannon matter, Great Hung,' Yang said. 'And yourself, of course. The rest must stay here to hold them off. You will continue with the guns and a small force.'

'Those who remain will be killed,' Hung said.

Yang inclined his head. 'In time.'

'Then you must come with me. I cannot lose you.'

Yang inclined his head again.

'And the white woman,' Hung said. 'With her children. And the Hindu boy.'

'And the Englishman?'

Hung hesitated. But he had not yet resolved that question in his mind. 'Him also.'

Yang halted the column and gave the necessary orders. His soldiers obeyed him without question, dismounted, and began throwing up defences. Michael rode up to where Hung watched them. 'You cannot mean to abandon these people?'

'I have no choice. The guns must be saved.'

'I promised them they would be taken to safety with your army.'

'If they came to me, Michael,' Hung said, 'it would be

to fight with me, and die for our cause. All my people must be prepared to do that. It is unfortunate that their time has come sooner than they may have expected. It does not alter the situation.'

'Then I will stay with them.'

'You will obey my orders, Michael. What, would you abandon your wife and children? Besides, I need you, and Captain Wong, to command the guns.'

'At least take the women and children.'

'They are an encumbrance,' Hung said. 'We have no horses for them, and they would slow us too much. Now prepare to move on. The bannermen are only a few miles behind us.'

Michael hesitated, then walked his horse back down the line to where the fishermen were helping the Hakka soldiers to block the road. 'I am sorry, Ling,' he said to the headman. 'It goes against the grain. But the guns must be saved.'

'You have taught us how to fight, Mr Harrington,' Ling said. 'We are proud to serve our master, the Great Hung.'

Michael clasped his hand, then rode back to Alicia. Who, if she could not yet understand any appreciable Chinese, could yet understand what was happening, as the women and children were gathered behind the defenders and the small band of the elite prepared to move on. 'I suppose every commander has to make intolerable decisions on occasion,' Michael said. 'But truly, it goes against my instincts to abandon these faithful people.'

'The Right Hand of God,' Alicia remarked. 'You had best pray, Michael Harrington, that your friend is not truly the right hand of the Devil.'

When it was certain that the guns were beyond the reach of the bannermen, Hung and Yang summoned Michael and his family and rode on ahead. Wong remained with the cannon for the last stage of the journey. They rode into Kung-Si, where the advanced camp of the God Worshippers was, to be greeted with acclamation as the news spread. Feng Yun-shan shook Michael's hand. 'I did not

261

expect you to accomplish so much,' he said. 'I congratulate you.' He looked at Alicia. 'You have a handsome wife,' he remarked. 'Has Hung told you of his?'

'Why, no,' Michael said, and looked at Hung. 'You old son-of-a-gun.'

Hung was clearly displeased at being addressed so casually. 'It was the decision of my father,' he said. 'That I should take the Hindu as my woman. But she is not my wife. The Right Hand of God cannot be wed to any single woman.'

'What did you say?' Michael asked.

'That the Hindu is fulfilling her duty to our master,' Feng said carefully.

Michael stared at him, then at Yang, then at Hung, and realized that these men had anticipated this moment. 'Willingly, Hung?' he asked softly.

'Of course,' Hung said. 'And I am pleased that you have brought her son to her.'

'Am I allowed to see her?' Michael asked.

'The woman of the Right Hand of God is not for prying eyes,' Feng said severely.

'I am almost a father to her,' Michael protested.

'Then you have fulfilled a father's duty in delivering her to the Highest,' Yang told him.

Michael hesitated, still looking at Hung.

'I will inform Malama that you have arrived, safely, with your wife and family,' Hung said. 'She will be pleased to know that. But your other wife, and your son, are also waiting for you. Now come, boy.' He held out his hand, and Janus shrank away from it.

A million thoughts rushed through Michael's brain, even as he felt he had been kicked in the stomach. He could not believe that Malama had gone to Hung, that she would have gone to any man apart from himself, willingly. On the other hand, he had refused her often enough. And Hung was the master here. She could well have settled for that.

But Hung had broken his solemn word to him. The one thing of which Michael had been certain was that

Malama would be safe in the care of a man who was at once his friend and had never shown the slightest interest in women. To learn that she had been once again sacrificed to male lust was horrifying. And yet . . . had she? And had Hung actually betrayed him? He had agreed to take the girl into his protection; well, he had certainly done that. Michael realized that he was making excuses, that he did not really want to quarrel with Hung. Because he could recognize the man's greatness? That was a worthy thought. But there were others less worthy. Such as the fact that he and Alicia and the children were now entirely in Hung's power: he had placed them there. Or worse, that this again represented a settlement of the Malama problem, a settlement he desperately needed if he were ever to be reconciled with Alicia; Wu Yei had been his woman long before he had married, and Hung Cho was his eldest son – Malama was the one who was peculiarly unacceptable to Alicia.

He stroked Janus' head. 'Mr Hung will take you to your mother, Janus,' Michael told him. 'You must go with him.'

'Mother!' Janus cried, and ran forward.

'He is an affectionate child,' Hung said, and followed the boy into the house.

'Your house is over there,' Feng said. 'Where Wu Yei awaits you.'

Alicia had been increasingly pensive as their journey had continued. Michael suspected, and hoped, that she was indeed at last coming to understand something of the immensity of the adventure on which he had embarked; certainly she had been astonished at the immensity of China. She had been born and lived all her life on an island; if she had been aware of the proximity of the mainland of Malaya to Singapore, she had equally been aware that it was possible to sail from say Malacca, on the west coast of the peninsula, round Singapore to Mersing, exactly opposite it on the east coast, in a few days. To travel due west on land for nearly a month, to leave one village behind and come to another with unfailing regularity, to top one mountain pass and always look across a plain at another, was totally outside her experience. Yet had she continued to earn his respect and even his admiration by the manner in which she had endeavoured to cope with her situation, at least once she had accepted that there was no escaping it. No longer did she complain. No longer did she shudder with distaste when it was unavoidable to perform her necessaries in public, or sleep on the earth. No longer did she hesitate at the concept of doing all her own cooking or stare in disbelief as those once beautifully manicured hands turned brown and rough, even as her pale flesh became reddened and blistered from the sun and the wind. No longer did she hug her children fearfully; they, indeed, led by Janus, had actively enjoyed the long, often wet, always exhausting journey. And as she could converse with no one else except Wong Sung and Hung himself, she and Michael had again almost become friends, even if it was quite impossible for them to live as man and wife for the time being. No doubt, he thought, to her great relief.

Yet that period of enforced celibacy was now coming to an end, if only temporarily; Michael knew that Hung intended to withdraw all of his people to his real stronghold, the land of the Hakka, his own kinsmen, and there, hopefully, prepare the revolution. What sort of a revolution? If Hung's behaviour over Malama had been disconcerting, Alicia's words, spoken in angry contempt, he knew, yet haunted him. He had seen Hung and his followers at work in the old days, and been appalled at their contempt for human life. But that had been a prevalent Chinese attitude, and the lives involved had been the Manchus and the landlords and their supporters. Hung had always been conservative of his own followers. Had that been merely because he had then had so few? Now he could spare lives, so long as he could ride off into the sunset. With his cannon. Military necessity. Of course it had been, and Michael knew that he was the one showing weakness. Alicia did not understand about these things.

Perhaps she was beginning to understand that as well, now.

As she now had to understand about even more important matters, to her. Wu Yei was waiting for them in the doorway of the house to which they had been directed. 'Master,' she said, placing her hands together and bowing her head.

'Wu Yei!' He embraced her, and then Hung Cho.

Alicia and the children waited, until Michael took her hand and led her forward. 'This is my other woman,' he explained, in Chinese.

Wu Yei bowed. 'It will be my business to make her welcome, Master,' she said.

Michael looked at Alicia, whose face was expressionless. 'Do I serve her, or she me?' she asked quietly, her anger carefully suppressed.

As Michael recognized. He smiled at her. 'You each serve me,' he told her. 'And are friends.'

Hung stood in the doorway of the inner room in his house, and regarded Malama. As she always did on his entry, she bowed low, her hands together before her forehead. He could never be sure whether or not she was pleased to see him. She had been afraid when he had first gone to her, but it had not seemed in her nature to resist. And as a receptacle for his long-suppressed sexuality, she had been all he had ever dreamed of. That he had not used his power to seduce the comeliest of the women, maiden or matron, amongst his followers, who would willingly have submitted, had always amazed him, but never so much as in retrospect.

Obviously it had been his father's will, not to allow him to become embroiled in harem politics. Just as it had been his father's goodness to send him this delightful, isolated creature, who knew so much about the art of love, who submitted without demur, who showed no sign of resentment or shame, or contempt, for the aberrations which were his weakness. Yet he could not help but look upon her with fresh eyes, today. She had killed a man. Her

265

own husband. The most dreadful of crimes, when seen from a husband's point of view. How to understand his father's meaning? Not for the first time he felt himself floundering in a morass of uncertainty.

She was a woman apart. A woman now to be discarded, executed, for her crime? However she had satisfied him, and would continue to do so? Or a woman to be cherished, because of her strength, which so few other women possessed? He did not know. Right this minute, having been away from her side for a month, he did not wish to know. Besides, having the power of life and death, over this woman as he did over Michael – and *his* woman – and over virtually everyone who followed him, made him ever more aware of his omnipotence, more certain of his true stature as the Right Hand of God. Time enough to consider Malama's just deserts when he had finished considering Malama.

'The guns are here,' he said, in English.

'I am pleased, Great Hung.' She replied as he had taught her to. But anxiously.

'They were brought by your master, Michael Harrington.'

Malama drew a long breath. 'I am overjoyed, Great Hung.'

'He has come to join us, and fight with us.'

Malama sighed.

'And has brought his wife with him,' Hung said.

Malama raised her head.

'So it would be best for you not to see him, or to think of him,' Hung went on. 'He is pleased that you are well, and that you are now my woman. This relieves him greatly.'

Malama bowed her head again.

But Hung was not a leader of men, and women, for nothing. He knew how to mix bad news and good, with just the right timing. 'He has also brought your son to you.'

Malama's head came up again, and Hung smiled, and

stepped aside. 'Your mother awaits you, boy,' he said through the doorway.

Janus ran inside, then stopped, and bowed.

'Janus.' Malama was on her knees, arms outstretched. 'Oh, Janus.'

He went to her and was held close. Tears streamed down her cheeks, and through them she looked at Hung. 'Am I not permitted to thank Mr Harrington for this, at least?'

'It is neither necessary nor appropriate,' Hung told her. 'As it was I told him to bring the boy.'

Malama's eyes were enormous. 'You knew of him?'

Hung stared at her. 'Am I not the Right Hand of God?' he demanded. 'Do I not know all things? All things,' he repeated.

Malama swallowed, unwilling to believe what he claimed – or its implications for her.

Hung smiled, and crossed the room to rest his hand upon her head. 'Your forgiveness for any crime you may have committed is my prerogative,' he said gently. 'And my pleasure. Now send the boy away, and come to me. I would have a son for myself.'

'We have fifty thousand men, ready to march,' Yang Hsiu-ch'ing declared. 'And ten times that number waiting to join us when we are successful. We have the cannon to make the Manchu tremble and batter down their walls. The rains have ceased, the roads will soon be dry. And we have retreated long enough. It is time to advance, to victory. There is nothing now to stop us, Great Hung, but your word.'

He sat down, and Hung Hsiu-ch'uan stood in turn, to look over the faces which stared back at him. With the ending of the monsoon he had withdrawn his people into Kwangsi, to his home town of Chen-t'ien, in the land of the Hakkas. Here his brothers had been left to spread his fame these past months and years, to spread the word of his triumphs, and encourage more and more people to believe in the one god, and his prophet, Hung Hsiu-ch'uan. He had enjoyed being at home again, no longer the younger brother, the failed civil servant, the derisive prophet of an unknown god, but a leader of his people in the greatest crusade of all, against the Manchu. He had basked in that glory while Yang had trained his men and Michael Harrington had practised his gunners. Now his brothers sat in front of him, together with his generals, and Michael and Wong Sung, the men from across the sea. All waiting for the word from him, to unleash themselves on the Manchu, and every Chinese who refused to acknowledge their supremacy.

It disturbed him that these were all fighting men, or thought of themselves as fighting men, even his own family. They were the instruments his father had sent him to use, and use them he would, but they also had to be made aware of the purpose which lay before them, the great awakening of China, to assume her rightful place amongst the nations of the world, an awakening which would encompass a throwing off of the shameful treaties negotiated by the British and the French and the Germans and the Russians, which would in fact make those nations perform the kowtow, to him, where they arrogantly refused so to respect the Ch'ing Emperor.

But he knew that these great ends could not be accomplished by generals alone. He needed the entire nation to be stirred from its apathy, and brought to a state of heavenly grace. To do that it might be necessary to be hard, even cruel, even illogical, but he would not shirk from that. The idea entranced him. He had seen enough of the Manchu to understand that true greatness lay at the end of a whip.

'I will give the word,' he said. 'But we must be clear what we do. We go forth to destroy the Manchu and every man of Han who supports their evil and tyrannous regime. Our hearts must be hard on this, my brothers. We shall show our enemies no pity.' He paused to look over their faces. 'But victory is not enough. It is what we do with the victory that counts. We shall set up our Kingdom of Heavenly Peace, our Tai-p'ing T'ien-kao, and rule according to the dictates of my father. But even that is not enough. We must raise our people, our followers and those we shall rule, to a new moral awareness. To this end I now decree an end to the smoking of opium. Anyone found buying or selling opium, or with opium in his possession or under its influence, will be executed immediately. This must be understood. I outlaw gambling, and decree death for anyone found indulging in that bestial pastime. I outlaw adultery, and indeed sexual contamination of any kind; our men and women shall couple for the sole purpose of reproduction, and any lewdness will be punished by death.'

Once again he paused, and smiled at the consternation on the faces in front of him. 'This law does not apply to me, or to you, my faithful generals. We are the elite of my kingdom. Our morals do not require uplifting, and our creature comforts need to be cared for. It is the rank and file, the hoi polloi, who wallow in filth and must be raised. And to do this I also decree an end to the difference between the sexes. Our women shall be the equal of our men. We shall let them fight alongside us, and share our glory as well as our risks. Except of course those chosen handmaidens whose purpose is simply to better our lives. To this end I further decree that the practice of footbinding will be abolished; all Chinese women must be able to walk like any man. I also decree all personal wealth to be abolished. Every God Worshipper will receive from the common granary, the common fund, all the requirements of himself and his family.' Again he smiled at them. 'Our needs are of course greater than those of the common herd. These decrees of mine will become laws for my people as of this moment. Then we shall await the new year. And then we will march.'

No one seemed disturbed by the utter hypocrisy they had just heard.

'On Canton,' Feng said eagerly.

'Not on Canton,' Hung said. 'General Yang will explain.'

Yang stood up, his eyes gleaming. 'To attack Canton

269

would be to reveal ourselves, our strength, too soon, and might bring us into conflict with the foreign devils.' His gaze rested for a moment on Michael. 'At this time we are a rebellion in the mountains, of no account to the Ch'ing. When we become of matter to them, we must already be too strong to be challenged. We shall march to the north and east. Our goal will be the Yangtse Kiang, and Nanking, the ancient capital of Han. When we have seized the Yangste Kiang, we will have cut China in two. Then Canton will fall to us like a ripe plum, whenever we are ready to pluck it, and the whole of South China will be ours. Then we will be able to deal with the foreigners as equals, and then we will prepare our march on Peking and the Ch'ing.' He grinned at them. 'If they have not already fled.'

'In the new year,' Hung repeated. 'Then we shall march.'

'You are going off to fight, and perhaps be killed, and leaving us here?' Alicia asked. She spoke Chinese, as in the months she had lived amongst the God-Worshippers she had readily learned the language.

'It is the way of men,' Wu Yei observed.

The two women had become fast friends, to Alicia's total amazement. If her earliest reaction to Michael's absurd decision to abandon everything he had accomplished in life and take off in the support of some obscure revolutionary simply, so far as she could determine, because the fellow had once saved his life – and worse, involved her and the children in his crazy plan – had been tempered by her admiration of his prowess as a man and an acknowledgement that he might have some reason for seeking so much revenge for her behaviour, that had rapidly become submerged in her resentment at the sheer discomfort, the filth and the primitiveness of the existence into which she had been forced. Yet she had determined never to give him the pleasure of jeering at her, had attempted to accept every misfortune in a spirit of stoicism which might have been envied by the princess herself. Her only fear had been for the children, and to her relief – and secret delight – they had taken to their new lives like ducks to water. Her own humiliation she had anticipated, and again, been resolved to meet with total composure; he would not have troubled to bring her did he not love her beneath his anger – thus he would soon grow tired of humiliating her and wish to love her only. Once that stage was reached, she could begin to re-establish her position, and perhaps her superiority.

Thus Wu Yei was someone to be accepted, treated with contempt, and eventually established as a servant. To Alicia's dismay, however, this had not been easy to do. With Michael busy so much of the time practising his men at the guns, or conferring with Hung, she had had no one to turn to except the woman with whom she shared her husband, and had discovered to her amazement that Wu Yei was not only an utterly charming young woman without an ounce of malice or jealousy in her entire body, but that she was anxious to teach her new friend every-thing she knew.

Even certain aspects of the art of love which were essen-tially Chinese. This had been the strangest thing of all. Alicia had been reluctant to resume marital relations with Michael, as much from the continual presence of the chil-dren in the one room in which they lived as from observing him sharing a cot with Wu Yei. This had distressed Wu Yei as much as it had angered Michael, and it had been the Chinese girl who had done more than Michael – who had been inclined to let matters take their course – to overcome Alicia's repugnance for the situation in which she found herself. Alicia had been appalled when, in Michael's absence, she had been approached by the Chinese woman, wishing to undress her and look at her, to indicate by gestures how she could make herself more acceptable to her master! She had supposed she was about to undergo some fresh humiliation, and being the bigger and stronger, had been about to defend herself when she had realized that Wu Yei was genuinely anxious only for her to share Michael with herself. Then there had been

271

the fear that Michael would know of it, that Wu Yei would tell him. But she had not, however much she had showed pleasure when Alicia had at last submitted to him. The sharing of this first secret had instantly produced mental intimacy, and instead of rivals they had become friends. Their friendship had grown until they had become almost sisters, while Alicia treated Hung Cho almost as her own son, or at least her nephew. Michael could now feel assured that he was leaving them both in good hands, even if he could marvel at the very fact that Alicia Hammond could exist in a single room with five other people and but a single change of clothing – and become the intimate friend of a Chinese prostitute. If he had wanted these things to befall her, to punish her for her desertion of him, he had never expected them to happen in this form.

And now it was important. Because now the great adventure was about to begin. And where it would end, no man could say.

But for Alicia it was another catastrophic turn of fate. If she had submitted to his masculine authority, she had never lost sight of her own goals, had determined that she would never become as mentally subservient as Wu Yei. To have him march away from them both, perhaps for months . . . 'What of Hung's decree, that we are all equal?' she demanded.

Michael could not resist a smile. 'All except the chosen few, whose duty it is to serve their masters.'

'Ha! I suppose Malama is accompanying the army.'

'No, she is not. She is remaining here with you, until the victory is completed and you will be sent for to join us in Nanking. I would in fact be grateful if you tried to see her, in Hung's absence, and make sure that everything is well with her. There is no need to fret. You will be joining us in a few months, as soon as we take Nanking and have established ourselves.'

'And if you do not send for me you will be dead,' Alicia said, as she lay in his arms that night while the snow clouded down to blanket the town. She had no more time

272

for barriers and mental attitudes. He could indeed be about to be killed.

'I am to command the artillery,' he said. 'Artillery commanders seldom get killed.'

But Alicia had read her history. 'As long as the armies they serve are winning. When the army runs away, artillerymen are the most vulnerable.'

'I do not think this army will run away,' Michael told her. 'I think it will advance until it drops, and I think it will win a great many battles. It possesses a quite remarkable general, who will take advantage of every opportunity that is presented to him.'

'Then your faith in Hung is restored,' she murmured, speaking English.

Michael sighed. 'My faith in Yang grows every day, even if he clearly has no use for me. So I say we will gain the victory. My faith in Hung . . . you have listened to his decrees.'

'Very like those of the early Christians. Except that perhaps they practised their precepts themselves.'

'Yes. I do not quarrel with his precepts, or even with his hypocrisy.' He held her close. 'I am glad to be able to take advantage of it. But I fear for what he is doing. His aim is clearly to create an entire nation of self-denying fanatics, whose sole gratification in life will be in carrying out his orders to destroy their enemies. I wonder how he will control them when there are no more enemies to be destroyed.'

'Then he will start to destroy his friends,' Alicia said.

He looked down at her in the darkness. 'Do you perceive no good in him at all? Perhaps that is because you have not seen just how evil the Manchus can be.'

'Perhaps it is because I am unable to accept degrees of evil. The word to me is absolute.'

'And no doubt includes me.'

She appeared to consider. 'Surprisingly, no, Michael. You are a man of strong passions, and even stronger attachments. I can understand your feeling that you were wasting your life in Hong Kong, or anywhere, working for my father and marketing opium. As I know that I was wrong to condemn you without trial, as it were, I can even understand your behaviour towards me, even if I can never forgive it. Especially as it encompasses the children. But I would describe you as misguided rather than evil.'

'Quite a homily.' He smiled into her hair. 'But no doubt a just assessment. Very well, Alicia. I cannot reverse the situation at this moment. But I will give you my word that when we return from this campaign, victorious, with all South China ruled by Hung, I will see that you are returned to Hong Kong, and thence back to your family, if you so wish.'

She caught her breath; she had not expected that. 'But you will not accompany me.'

'I cannot promise to do so. I have committed myself to the cause of the Tai-p'ing T'ien-kao until all of China has been freed of the Manchu. Anyway, would you really want me to?'

She was silent for a few minutes, then said, by way of a reply, 'In any event, your return is an if, not a when.'

'It will be when,' he promised her.

When, he thought. The army, some fifty thousand strong, moved north the moment the mountain passes were open. They marched out of their fertile valley and into the awesome plateaux and peaks of the Nan Ling, reminding Michael of a horde of locusts, for they ate up everything in their path. More because of this than because of the appeal of Hung's exhortations, which were delivered to every community they encountered, they attracted a vast number of recruits – it was either march with the army or remain to starve. Few of the recruits were in any way soldiers or even military material, but they helped to give an impression of enormous strength.

Not that they met with any immediate opposition from the Manchu. Undoubtedly the Viceroy in Canton was aware that there had been an upheaval in Kwangsi, and no doubt even that a large body of the Hakkas and their associates had moved to the north, into the mountains.

He was just happy to see them go; perhaps they would die there. And that certainly appeared a possibility as their progress became slower and slower, and the distances in front of them seemed to grow longer and longer. Even Michael, who having sailed along the coast and up some of the rivers had some idea of the immensity of this country, was aghast at the never-ending hills and valleys which unfolded before them. Hung, who had not attempted to study the land he intended to conquer, was more angry than aghast. 'Did you know of this?' he demanded of Yang.

'It is on the map, Great Hung,' Yang told him. He was growing increasingly insolent towards his master, as their roles subtly changed and he became the more important of the two.

'Then why did we not assault Canton?' Hung asked. 'It would have made more sense.'

'Our strategy must be unchanged, Great Hung,' Yang insisted. 'It is the only one which guarantees us success.'

Hung snorted and went off to find his latest concubine; however vigorously his rules on celibacy were enforced, he took for himself the comeliest girl in every village they overran.

Few of his generals followed his example; they did not have the time, and Michael at least was content to remember what he had left behind and would be returning to. To set Alicia free? That was a promise he wanted to keep; he now knew that he had wronged her far more than she him.

But memory became a torment when winter overtook them again still hundreds of miles from their goal. They spent the cold months in the valley of the Xiang Jiang, where at least they did not freeze to death, but there was no possibility of their being able to get through the mountain passes in front of them until a thaw, and by the time the snows began to melt they were starving to death in their hundreds.

'You are destroying my people,' Hung complained.

'Those who survive will be the stronger for it,' Yang retorted.

Hung was not mollified, and was aghast to be informed, when at last it was possible for the army to move on, that the passes to the north were blocked by a large Manchu force. 'We are trapped,' he moaned. 'We will die like rats.'

'We could not expect to march all the way to Nanking without opposition, Great Hung,' Yang said contemptuously. 'The Viceroy in Canton might have been happy to let us leave his territory; the Viceroy in Hankow obviously does not want us in his.'

'What are we going to do?' Hung wailed.

'We will fight our way through.'

'And if we fail?'

'If we fail, we die, Great Hung. It is the eventual fate of us all, in any event. I will lead the assault. You will follow with the main force, and the women.'

'You will need the guns,' Michael suggested.

Yang shook his head. 'They will be ineffective in a mountain pass, and they are too valuable to lose. You will remain here with your cannon, Mr Harrington. If we fail to clear the pass, we will have them to fall back upon. If we do clear the pass, you will harness up your guns and follow with all possible speed, together with Great Hung.'

'But you expect to clear the pass,' Michael suggested.

Yang smiled. 'I intend to clear the pass, Mr Harrington.'

He was as good as his word. Michael saw nothing of the fighting, as he and Wong Sung remained with the guns while the elite of the Tai-p'ing army marched out behind their general. Yang might be a born strategist, but he either knew nothing of or cared nothing for tactics. His plan was to let loose the fanatical courage of his men in a frontal assault on the bannermen, who were truly more accustomed to bullying a subservient people than to facing the dangers of a battle. And so it proved, as the Manchus broke and fled before the fury of his assault, and word was sent back to tell Hung that at least one of the passes was open. Hung and Feng and Michael went forward, to survey the piled bodies, the wheeling vultures, inhale the ghastly stench of the battlefield. The Tai-p'ing horde resumed its march, now convinced of its invincibility. Even Hung regained his confidence.

But Yang was too good a leader not to understand that morale was an uncertain quality, and that he would do well to capitalize on the army's present mood after the privations of the winter. Thus he now changed the direction of their march, and again made north instead of north-east, seeking the shortest possible route to the Yangtse, at the point where it was joined by the Han Kuang to become the mighty river which debouched at Shanghai. The Yangtse was the principal waterway – and thus trading route – inside China, and on its banks several sizeable cities had grown up. The greatest of these were of course Shanghai and Nanking, but upriver from Nanking was the provincial capital of Hankow, a huge walled city situated on the north bank and facing the smaller town of Wu Chau. These objectives could be reached by the summer, Yang was certain, and would provide the Tai-p'ing army with a solid base for the operation against Nanking, which would now have to wait until the following year.

Three years, Michael thought. It was already more than eighteen months since he had last seen his family.

Yet no one now doubted that they were going to gain the victory, and as they descended from the mountains to Lake Tungking in the boiling July heat, Hung was at his most ebullient.

On the eastern shore of the lake lay the city of Yochau, which indeed stretched as far as a bend of the upper Yangtse itself, walled and garrisoned by a Manchu army. 'Now, General Harrington, now Captain Wong,' Yang said, as they sat their horses and gazed at the purple walls in the distance, thrown into sharp relief by the shimmering waters of the lake. 'Let us see how effective are your cannon.'

Michael was quite nervous as the mules pulled the six

guns into position; it was some two years since they had been fired against the pirates, although he had been solicitous in making sure they had been kept greased, and the powder dry – but the iron cannon balls were a mass of rust. He also expected some counter-action from the garrison, but there was none. The peasant farmers living outside the city had been faced with the usual choice: join the Tai-p'ing or die. Those who could had fled to the walls. Their landlords had been given no such options. They were dragged before Hung, with their women and children, and in front of him were decapitated while his followers laughed and jeered, and the blood mingled with the flowing black hair, and Michael felt his belly roll and told himself that these had to be guilty people and deserving of this horrible end to their prosperous lives, and that their destruction was necessary to the accomplishment of Hung's purpose. To consider anything else would have been to admit that he had made the most ghastly mistake of his life.

The area in front of the city was therefore devoid of humanity or – the Tai-p'ing army having camped there for some days – of cattle either, as the battery was ridden forward and emplaced, opposite the main gate of the city. The walls were now lined with soldiers, their banners flying over the towers, and they kept up a tremendous din at the sight of the cannon being prepared only six hundred yards away. But, after Yang's victory of the previous spring, they were disinclined to try their luck in the open. They had cannon of their own and occasionally fired, but the shooting was wild and there could be no doubt that they were at once impressed and horrified by the huge mass of Tai-p'ing warriors who formed a dark cloud behind their artillery. Yang had his men well in hand, and their silence was as impressive as their numbers.

When the guns were ready, Michael gave the signal, and Yang sent his herald forward. Riding the best of the horses they had captured from the farms, the herald, one of the biggest and most richly dressed of the Tai-p'ing, carrying the yellow banner with the sun and dragon insignia of his master, rode to beneath the south gate, and delivered his ultimatum: surrender the city immediately to the might of the Heavenly King, when only the guilty would be punished, or oppose him, when they would all be destroyed. Michael knew what the ultimatum was, even if he couldn't hear the words being spoken; he had not expected the Manchu commander to surrender – as he could certainly expect to be named amongst the guilty – but even so he was shocked when, after booing and catcalling while the herald was speaking, there was a sudden volley of musketry, and the man fell from his horse, riddled with bullets.

Yang had ridden forward beside the guns. His face never changed expression, save that his eyes gleamed more than usual. 'They have chosen death,' he said. 'We shall grant them their wish. Knock down that gate, Mr Harrington.'

Michael gave the orders and the guns commenced firing. Smoke surrounded them and billowed into the still air, and the garrison began replying in earnest. The shooting on both sides was wide at first, but Michael's seamen were the first to find the range, and soon their balls were hammering on the gate, which quickly began to sag on its hinges. Now shot after shot was poured into the prospective breach, while the Manchu continued to shout their defiance, until with a mighty crash one of the huge panels collapsed.

Without even waiting for Michael to give the order to cease firing, Yang gave the command to charge. The mass of the Tai-p'ing rushed forward, those who had firearms discharging them at random, the others waving their swords. It was the most unmilitary display Michael had ever seen, and he had no doubt that a single one of Wellington's Peninsular regiments would have stopped the advance and turned it into a rout, but the bannermen were not that well led or disciplined. They swarmed to the gate to meet their enemies head on, and were hurled back. For a few minutes the battle raged in the gateway itself, while Michael and Wong looked on, their part completed, then the Tai-p'ing burst into the streets by the sheer force of numbers. Even at a distance Michael could hear the screams and shouts, the bloodcurdling shrieks which told him of rape and murder. He watched smoke rising, and the Manchu banners being torn down, to be replaced by the flag of Hung.

Who had come to stand beside him. 'It is time for us to enter,' he decided. He rode forward, Feng at his elbow, Michael and Wong behind him with the soldiers of his bodyguard. Yang waited in the gate to welcome him, also surrounded by a bodyguard; there were still pockets of Manchu resistance to be eliminated.

They rode through smoke-filled, reeking streets, littered with mutilated bodies, listened to the dreadful sounds continuing to emanate from the shattered houses to either side. It was far worse than the battle in the pass outside Fu-chuang, far worse, indeed, than anything Michael had ever envisaged. But Hung was clearly delighted, as were his men.

'You have gained a great victory, General Yang,' Feng said.

Yang bowed over his horse's head. 'I am honoured, Feng Yun-shan,' he said.

'The victory was the work of my father,' Hung declared, and entered the city, while Yang fell into place behind him, his face expressionless at his denigration. The entourage proceeded to the central square and the governor's mansion, and here they were confronted by the governor, already bound, together with his wives and daughters.

'You are irresistible, Great Hung,' the governor said. 'I yield to you my city.'

'My father has given me your city, wretch,' Hung replied, and looked at the women, who were exceedingly pretty. He pointed. 'That one,' he said, 'will live until morning. Take her to my bedchamber.'

The girl gasped, and her mother spoke in Manchu. The governor stared at Hung. 'And you call yourself the Right

Hand of God?' he demanded. 'You are filthier than the men you lead.'

Hung glared at him, then stamped his foot in rage. 'Tear out his tongue. Tear it out.'

Yang snapped his fingers, and men hurried forward to grasp the governor's arms while others forced open his mouth and held his jaws apart. His wife and daughters fell to their knees to beg for mercy, all except the one marked out by Hung, who remained standing, staring at the man who was destroying her family. The governor made a horrible sound as he was mutilated, and when released, fell to the floor, blood pouring from his mouth, while the severed tongue was placed on the table; to Michael's horror it still seemed to move.

'Now cut off their heads, so that he can see,' Hung declared.

The governor's wife was dragged forward and made to lean over the table, staring at her husband's tongue while she was stripped of her tunic and her head held rigid by her hair, and the sword flashed through the air.

Michael turned away and went outside; his stomach could take no more. Had he, then, made a ghastly mistake? It seemed impossible to doubt that, any longer. And what could he do about it, save commit Alicia and the children, and Wu Yei and Hung Cho, and perhaps even Malama and Janus, to the catastrophe which would overtake him were he to oppose Hung in any way. But to continue to be a party to such brutality, an accomplice in such mass slaughter – for if the governor was about to die in peculiarly unpleasant circumstances, tens of thousands of his followers were also being murdered at this very minute – was impossible.

He heard a movement, and turned, to face Feng. The Chinese looked serious. 'He has a taste for blood, this master of ours,' he said.

'I had supposed you approved of it.'

'I have no choice, in his company. And neither do you, Mr Harrington. That is not to say that we must accept it as the basis of our new kingdom.'

Michael stared at him, not quite sure what he was being told.

'Our master is essential to our eventual triumph,' Feng went on. 'Not only because he is our master, but because this victory, coming on top of the other, will truly increase his stature and make people believe he is the Right Hand of God. Thus we must aid him in every way to accomplish the triumph he seeks, at whatever cost to our honour or our morals. Once that triumph is completed, however, the reason for shedding blood will have ended, and he must be made to understand this. Hung has great qualities. His abilities and his leadership and the respect the people have for him will be invaluable when we come to rebuild our land. We must hope and pray that he achieves sense and humanity by the time of our final victory.'

'And if he does not?' Michael asked bluntly.

Feng gave a slight bow. 'Then it may be necessary to adjust the situation.'

'To do that, we will need the aid of Yang. He has the army at his call.'

'Yang is an ambitious man,' Feng said quietly. 'As you say, he has the army at his call, and is aware of this. I think he sees himself as Hung's successor – and at a moment of his choosing. We could never trust him to assist us, except as a means to our destruction. But he is not the only man of the army the soldiers respect, and indeed, revere. After today, your stock is high, Mr Harrington. You commanded the guns which made our victory possible, and to these simple soldiers guns are in themselves mystic creatures, to be worshipped and feared rather than understood. It will be necessary for you to knock down many gates and walls before we take Nanking. And each event will enhance your standing with the army.'

Michael grinned at him. 'And you don't suppose I might have ambitions of my own?'

Feng bowed again. 'I have no doubt of it, Mr Harrington. But hardly here in China. You are not Chinese, and

282

can therefore never be anything more than a power behind the throne.'

'On which you see yourself.'

Feng's expression did not change. 'I am prepared to serve where God calls me, Mr Harrington. But all this is mere speculation, until Nanking is ours. That is our first priority.'

Until Nanking is ours, Michael thought, his spirits suddenly restored.

The advance continued apace, and Hankow duly fell before the onset of winter. Although Yang intended to use this as the springboard for his assault on Nanking, and was determined to adhere to his original plan, he immediately thrust out advanced prongs, before which the cities of Wusu and Kiukiang quickly surrendered. It seemed that the Tai-p'ing were invincible. 'Victory will crown your arms in the spring, Great Hung,' Yang promised. 'When I hand you the keys of Nanking.'

'In the spring,' Hung said. 'Nanking.' His gaze swept over his officers. 'In the spring.' He looked at Feng Yun-shan.

And that winter Feng Yun-shan died.

PART THREE

The Kingdom of Heavenly Peace

11

The Intruders into Heaven

Had Feng been murdered? Poisoned, perhaps at the orders of Hung? Or of Yang? Or had he simply succumbed to one of the many epidemics, ranging from the common cold to typhoid fever, which swept through the now enormous Tai-p'ing army from time to time? It was impossible for Michael to be sure, because both Hung and Yang treated him with as much respect as ever. Of course neither of them could know of the conversation he had had with Feng on the day Yochau had fallen – but neither did he know the identities of the other men with whom Feng must have discussed the situation – and one of whom could well have betrayed him.

In any event, the conspiracy, if there had been a conspiracy, was now a dead letter; Michael could only hope to accompany Hung and Yang to their ultimate triumph, and then, having fulfilled his part of the bargain, ask to be allowed to leave. With Alicia and Joanna and Ralph, of course. And Wu Yei and Hung Cho? He certainly could not abandon them for a second time.

Then what of Malama? Here again, he could only hope and pray that Hung might have tired of her dusky beauty by then.

Nanking fell, as promised by Yang, in the spring of 1853. The entire Yangtse was in the hands of the Tai-p'ing, save only for the river mouth and the city of Shanghai. Yang was, however, still against antagonizing the British by proceeding down the river – he seemed to have a very healthy respect for the power of the lion – and instead was for pressing on immediately north of the river for the Hwang Ho, and then the Peiho and Peking, while his men were invincible.

Hung was quite prepared to allow his principal general to continue on his victorious way, but he declined any longer to accompany him. In fact, he was not merely tired of the rigours of unceasing campaigning, and become anxious to enjoy some of the perquisites of his new position as ruler of virtually half of the greatest country in the world; he was also now revealing a grasp of the realities of power which was considerably greater than Yang's and which Michael found most reassuring. 'We have achieved the most remarkable victories in the history of mankind, thanks to the will of my father,' he told his officers. 'There will be others. But now we must organize our achievements before we press on to new fields. We have gained thousands, millions of recruits to our armies, but to feed them we are stripping the country bare of everything that sustains life. Where would be our ultimate victory if when we hang the Ch'ing in front of his altar we look over our shoulders at a barren desert, a starving nation? We cannot allow this to happen. Therefore I decree that we now commence to implement our land programme, and return those people who are farmers to the land, under our protection. We will make Nanking the capital of our Kingdom of Heavenly Peace, at least for the time being. You, General Yang, will take Peking, and bring me the Ch'ing Emperor, and all his brood, in chains, but I decree that Nanking will henceforth be the centre of the Chinese empire.'

'Your words are those of great wisdom,' Yang said, with a sardonic smile. And Michael recalled Feng's words to him on that fateful evening; were Yang indeed to return from Peking with the Emperor in his baggage train, he might decide that the moment was right to assume Hung's prerogatives. Or he might not return at all, but merely, from the Celestial Throne in the Forbidden City, decree the destruction of his erstwhile master.

If such apprehensions crossed Hung's mind, he gave no indication of it. 'They are the thoughts of my father,' he said. 'You will provide me with a list of the officers you will require.'

'General Harrington, certainly, to command the artillery,' Hung said. For the Tai-p'ing army now did command an artillery, some sixty guns, mostly captured Manchu pieces, old and unreliable, but capable of a great deal of noise.

'It is the will of my father that General Harrington should remain in Nanking,' Hung said quietly. 'You will take Colonel Wong Sung as your artillery commander.'

Yang frowned. 'I need my best officers, to defeat the Manchu on their own ground.'

Michael raised his eyebrows; Yang had never praised him before.

'You will defeat them, because my father wills it so,' Hung told him. 'With the aid of Colonel Wong. General Wei Ch'ang-hui will remain to command the garrison of this city, and General Harrington will remain to command the guns.'

The decision to allow him to cease fighting at least for a while was a welcome one for Michael, even if he could not determine whether Hung disliked the idea of Yang and himself going off campaigning together – and therefore conspiring together, perhaps – or whether he genuinely trusted his Irish general more than any of his Chinese aides, and wished him in support at his side. But he was even more relieved at the suggestion that Hung, having achieved his primary goal, was at last prepared to reveal qualities of true statesmanship – most necessary as the epidemics which were decimating the Tai-p'ing and completely destroying those who did not join them were mainly caused by malnutrition. Even if it could not truly be called Christian statesmanship – there was no diminution of the horrors that Hung perpetrated on those of his enemies that fell into his hands. More than ever Michael felt he could no longer support such a man, while he had by now all but convinced himself that it would be safe for him to return to his own people – who could tell what had happened in Hong Kong or Singapore in so long a time? Thus, as soon as Yang and his army had crossed

the river and commenced their northward march, he
sought a private interview, or rather, he supposed, audience was the word Hung would have preferred. 'I can
only congratulate you, and your father, Great Hung,' he
said. 'Both for your mighty victories and for your understanding of the requirements of empire.'

'My father advises me in all things,' Hung said. 'As he
dictates all things. Did he not send you to me?'

A cue? Or a warning? Michael plunged onwards. 'And
I, and Wong Sung, and our cannon, have performed our
duty to you, Great Hung. And to the Tai-p'ing.'

'I am pleased with your accomplishments, Michael.
And so is my father.'

'But now that you no longer require me to command
the guns, Great Hung, I have no further reason for being
here. Great Hung, I have served you faithfully and well
for three years. I can serve you no longer. I am a sailor,
not a farmer, or a politician. I long to return to sea, to
my profession. I seek your permission to go back to
Kwangsi, to my wives and children, and depart with them
for Hong Kong.'

'If you return to Hong Kong,' Hung said mildly, 'you
will be arrested, if what you have told me is true.'

'I have been away too long,' Michael said. 'They will
have forgotten about me by now.'

Hung smiled. 'You mean you have been away from
your wives for too long. I have observed that you have
not sought comfort at the hands of any of our captured
handmaidens. This was unwise of you, Michael. As Con-
fucius himself wrote, a man not only needs the relief of
sexual companionship, but it is his duty to posterity.'

'Yet you forbid it for your people,' Michael said.

'I would have their morals improve, certainly. I am
doing so. But procreation is also their duty. Enjoyment
of the act can be reserved for people like ourselves, who
will appreciate it. In any event, your celibacy will soon
be ended. I have sent for our womenfolk to join us, here
in Nanking, where they may live in a style more becoming
them than is possible in Kwangsi.'

'Here?' Michael asked in alarm, for apart from the rigours of the journey, the city was rife with disease. 'Is that not to risk their lives?'

'Our lives are at risk every time we breathe, Michael. It is the will of my father who lives, and who dies. It is no concern of ours. As for leaving me, how can you say your task is completed? If I am to rule China, I need far greater armies than those I now command. It will be your task to train those armies in the use of artillery. Besides, I promised you once that you would ride at my side when I enter the Tien Mien, and put a noose around the neck of the Ch'ing Emperor. When Yang has finally defeated the Manchu, that is what we will do, together. Three years? What is three years? We are talking about our destiny.'

Three years, Alicia thought. What is three years? She and Michael had been separated for three years before. But then she had been a girl, and she had never known the comfort of his arms. Now, three years was an eternity. Yet an oddly happy eternity – although she would never have confessed it to Michael. If she had been desperate for him to come seeking her in Singapore, she had certainly not anticipated that his return would mean her abduction to a life of unimaginable hardship and privation – which would also involve her children. She had meant what she had said when she told him she would never forgive him for that. At least, then.

Equally had she not anticipated having to share her life, in every detail, with her husband's Chinese mistress and his bastard son.

Yet, once she had come to terms with the lack of hygiene, with removing ticks and lice from her body and those of the children as a daily routine, to eating food which in Singapore and Hong Kong she would have rejected as absurd much less edible, to having only a single change of clothing, which she had to wash herself, and most important of all, once she had realized that it was possible not only to survive, but to remain healthy in these conditions, she had almost found herself enjoying her new life.

She knew this was at least partly because she was Elizabeth Blaine's daughter. Mama had never spoken of her experiences in the hands of the Malay pirates when she had been even younger than Alicia, but it must have been very like hers in Kwangsi. And although Alicia did not dare imagine what her constant exposure to wind or sun was doing to that complexion of which she had been so proud, and was indeed thankful that she had no mirror to find out, she could remember that Mama had survived her ordeal to remain a very real beauty.

She could also reflect that she was better off than Mama in that she had never become the plaything of any man save her husband. This had its drawbacks, of course. If Mama had had to submit to Bodaw Minh, she also could have felt no anger or jealousy when the pirate turned his attention to one of the other women in his harem. The first time Alicia had lain in her cot and listened to Wu Yei gurgling with pleasure as Michael had entered her she had thought she would die. Yet Wu Yei was now her closest friend. Her only friend. The most precious friend in all the world.

For Wu Yei had taught her how to survive. In all the straightforward things, of course, such as how to use her food sticks, and how to use the coarse bone needles which were all the sewing utensils the Hakkas possessed, how to clean her teeth with a twig broken from a tree, and how to make the various sauces which helped to tenderize and sweeten the toughest and most rancid of goat meat. Wu Yei had also taught her how to keep the children healthy, and Wu Yei had taught her, and them, to speak Chinese.

Wu Yei had also taught her that her greatest happiness, as well as her eternal duty, was to make her husband happy. And this was not only to be achieved by faithfulness, which Alicia was prepared to accept, or by total subservience, which she was not, in the beginning at any rate – it was also to be achieved by being everything he

292

might want in bed. Alicia had always supposed she had been that, simply by making her magnificent body available and by being an enthusiastic partner. Wu Yei had reminded her that it was essential to resume her enthusiasm, but had also taught her that a woman's role should be active as well as passive; only in the act of love, indeed, did the Chinese girl seek total equality with her partner.

Her teaching was itself insidiously gratifying. There was nothing either lascivious or prurient about it. But there was sheer enjoyment when she stroked herself, or encouraged Alicia to follow her example. And Alicia, who once would have shrunk away in outraged horror from even the idea of touching her private parts before a Chinese, also found herself enjoying their now total intimacy, the more so in that there seemed nothing unnatural in it – Wu Yei's concern was simply to make herself, and her companion wife, the more desirable to their mutual master, whenever he should send for either of them. In Alicia's upturned world, the upturning of her inbred sexual mores seemed no more than natural. And had indeed become necessary in their long separation from their master. Three years!

Three years in which the children had ceased to be children. Joanna was eight years old, Ralph seven. Young enough in English eyes, perhaps, but the only eyes that ever looked on them were Chinese, and they were quite old enough to be taught both the martial and domestic arts, and to work in the fields. Alicia was appalled at the idea, but Hung Cho was already a labourer – he was thirteen – and readily took his half siblings under his wing. Besides, they enjoyed the life so. They were presumably unable to remember any other. And their outdoor work was making them strong and keeping them healthy, even if their complexions were an unnatural brown and their manners hardly acceptable for a Singapore dining room. Alicia could not imagine what Mama and Papa would make of them now. This was the only thought that could nowadays bring tears to her eyes. Mama and Papa would undoubtedly suppose them dead.

And what of Malama? Alicia had actually endeavoured to carry out Michael's instructions and speak with the Indian girl, but it had been impossible as she remained very carefully guarded and secluded. No doubt, like Michael, Hung Hsiu-ch'uan had not expected to be away more than a couple of months, and had thus made no provision for a longer absence. Presumably Malama was allowed to exercise herself and was well taken care of, but she was definitely not allowed to mix with the other women of the town, even those who belonged to the other army commanders. Her son, Janus, however, was seen from time to time, escorted by soldiers of the garrison, although he was not sent into the fields. He was somewhat younger than Joanna, but was a bright and articulate boy, as Alicia remembered. She had no opportunities to speak with him either, but observed that he wore an habitually sad look, as if he understood that his mother was to all intents and purposes imprisoned.

Alicia did not know whether or not to be sorry for her. For all her acceptance of her situation, she would have been less than human had she not blamed Malama for the entire position in which they found themselves. Michael had told her how Potts had beaten his wife and threatened his child, but Alicia could reflect that there were many such marriages in Singapore, and even more, if Mama was to be believed, in England – which did not necessarily end in murder. Malama's criminal act had plunged all their worlds into turmoil, and if she was now suffering a long overdue incarceration it was really nothing more than she deserved.

But they were all really in prison, until the men sent for them, or returned to them – the understanding that neither of those things had to happen, supposing Michael might be killed, was nearly unbearable for her, as it would mean her sentence would be for life. With her children. What made their waiting the more difficult was a complete lack of information, over long periods of time, as to what was happening, or who was alive and who dead. It took three months for news of the victory at Fuang-hu to drift back to Kwangsi, and two months more for them to learn of the fall of Hankow. It was midsummer when they heard that Nanking had fallen. Three years, she thought. In which Michael had miraculously survived. Three years in which she had not lain in his arms. Why, she would be like a bride again.

It was autumn, and raining, before the messenger arrived to command the ladies of the court to be sent to Nanking.

Immense excitement. Litters were prepared, and horses for the male children. Alicia and Wu Yei and Joanna travelled together, and now for the first time Alicia caught a glimpse of Malama, being assisted into her litter, which was at once ornate – having been requisitioned from a provincial governor – and private, thanks to the heavy curtains which concealed the interior. Malama was very finely dressed, as befitted the head concubine of the Right Hand of God, and there were jewels in her headdress, but her face was sad and it seemed to Alicia that she was thinner than before.

But they were all thinner by the time they reached Nanking, which took them until the following summer. Once again Alicia was astounded by the sheer size of this country, the immensity of the mountains, the stark grandeur of the landscape. Equally was she aghast at the trail of destruction they seemed to be following. There were days on end when the only living creatures to be seen were hideous bald-headed vultures, circling over some long-dead carrion, peering inquisitively at the caravan as if knowing they too would soon have to lie down and die. This seemed a definite possibility on more than one occasion, for although they had left Kwangsi well provided with food, and with their own herd of goats, these very rapidly died or were slaughtered, or stolen by bands of starving men who came down from the hills.

Then it was a matter of bullying food out of the various towns and villages they encountered. The ladies had been provided with a strong escort, and so terrified were the hill folk of the very name of Hung Hsiu-ch'uan or his famous generals, Yang Hsiu-ch'ing or Michael Harrington, that there was no risk of physical opposition, but there was much protestation and complaint and downright begging, all of which had to be overcome by the determination of the caravan commander, Ho Wan. He was certainly capable of browbeating anyone, but there were times when there was simply nothing to be obtained from people who were themselves clearly starving.

As these circumstances continued, the caravan insensibly lost some of its discipline and seemed to close in on itself. It was indeed possible to suppose that they were taking a long march across a previously unknown planet. Segregation became impossible, except in sexes – the soldiers were well aware of the decrees of Hung, and had no desire to lose their heads, even if they were escorting some of the comeliest women they had ever seen. It was while the women huddled in their communal tent during one of the many storms which beset them that Alicia managed to sit next to Malama, whose fine clothes had become sadly tarnished.

'Our masters lead us a hard life,' she remarked in English, surprised to realize this was the first time she had ever spoken to the girl.

Malama turned her head, equally surprised. 'Yes,' she replied.

Alicia had expected something different, just as she had also somehow expected to be addressed as 'Mistress', and had to remind herself that of course Malama, as Hung's woman, was actually now her superior. 'Are you looking forward to regaining the Great Hung?' she asked.

'He is my master,' Malama said simply. 'Are you not pleased to be returning to Michael Harrington?'

'Oh, yes,' Alicia said. 'Very much.'

'You are a fortunate woman.'

'And you are not? Many women would wish to be the woman of Hung Hsiu-ch'uan.'

'It is not my Karma to be fortunate,' Malama said.

'Because you love Michael, and not Hung?'

296

Malama's head turned. 'You wish to harm me,' she remarked.

Alicia flushed. 'I do not. That is why I am speaking English. No one will ever know what you tell me. Not even Michael. I will give you my word.'

Malama considered, as if wondering what Alicia's word might be worth. But the opportunity to talk was too rare to be rejected. 'It is not possible,' she said. 'To love Hung Hsiu-ch'uan.'

Alicia frowned, again surprised by her choice of words. 'Not possible?'

'Yes.'

Clearly she was not going to say more than that. 'But it is possible to love Michael.'

'I have always supposed so.' Another quick glance. 'Have you not found that?'

'Yes,' Alicia said. 'Have not you?'

'From afar,' Malama said. 'Why do you ask me these things? Have you not already asked Michael, and been answered?'

'Yes,' Alicia said.

'And do you not believe your husband?'

'I know a man can desire more than a single woman.'

'Then he has Wu Yei. It would please me to be desired by Michael, Mrs Harrington. It was always my hope that it would happen. But it has never been so. I think perhaps he feels for me as a daughter. And now . . . now it is too late.'

'Too late?' Alicia asked.

'When one has been . . . loved, by the Great Hung,' Malama said, 'it is not possible to be desired by another. Or to wish it.'

Her face was inexpressibly sad, and Alicia remembered that Malama had found it necessary to kill her first husband.

Once the river was reached they could take to the waiting sampans and the journey became both quicker and more comfortable. Ho Wan now reimposed a proper discipline on his charges, and Malama was again segregated, but in the weeks before that happened Alicia had often sought out the Indian girl, and talked with her. Malama's earlier suspicions, her perhaps justifiable fear that Alicia was her enemy, had dwindled. In her loneliness she desperately sought companionship, and of course dared not risk confiding in any of the Chinese women, who might relate her unhappiness to Hung. She did not confide any sexual secrets to Alicia either, however much the Englishwoman hinted her curiosity. But she did enjoy talking about her girlhood in the delta of the Ganges, and about the Princess Jalina, whom she clearly worshipped, and of whose fate she had no concept. She was horrified when Alicia told her that the princess was dead, and how she had died. Alicia also looked for a reaction when she told how Jalina had been Michael's mistress, but Malama merely gave a sad smile. 'She was then blessed,' she said. 'But, I think, so was Michael.'

A point of view, Alicia supposed, *she* should have taken as her own a long time ago.

Food was more plentiful on the river, and as they no longer had the daily backbreaking journeying, they began to fill out again. 'We will be fat as pigs by the time we reach Nanking,' Alicia told Wu Yei.

Who merely giggled. 'Then our master will like us the better for it,' she said.

If he likes us at all, Alicia thought, suddenly wildly nervous. Four years! In that time he could have bedded half the women in China, she supposed, and perhaps found many that were at once younger and better groomed than herself. She was thirty four, a hopeless age to be going to a man virtually as a bride. Desperately she used her fingers to comb her hair, longer now than ever before in her life, and without a trace of artificial curls remaining, hanging in thick red waves down her back. Then she joined the other women in peering at the walls of Nanking rising out of the river mist.

They were greeted by a guard of honour, and escorted, in closed litters, to their various houses. Nanking was the biggest city Alicia had ever seen; she had never been to either Canton or Calcutta, but Wu Yei told her Nanking was even bigger than Canton, and Michael had told her how great a city that was.

Yet peering through the curtains she was horrified at the destruction which was everywhere evident; whole streets had been pulled down or were in the process of being destroyed by work gangs which consisted equally of men and women. True enough, other buildings were rising from the rubble, but these were invariably palaces. Such ordinary folk as she saw seemed to be living in small makeshift huts, or in the open. Dogs barked and snarled, mules brayed and relieved themselves, children played and wailed, and their parents stared apathetically at the litters of the great, while overall there hung the stench of decay.

This was sufficiently disturbing but, continuing to peep through the drapes of her litter, Alicia was horrified to observe several Europeans, whom she suspected to be Englishmen, gathered on a street corner haggling with a vendor over the purchase of a tame monkey. Hastily she sank back out of sight. She had no desire to come face to face with any European in her present condition.

Not even Michael? Because that moment was coming ever closer. They left the busy part of the city behind and passed through a guarded inner gateway into an entirely different world, where the streets were wider and far more clean, where there had been little destruction, and where the houses wore the aspect of palaces. Here she gathered were the quarters of Hung Hsiu-ch'uan and his principal officers. The various litters now separated, as the women were sent to their respective masters. Malama's arm emerged from the drapes of her litter for a moment, in a gesture of farewell, and was then withdrawn, leaving Alicia to wonder if she would ever see her again.

Her litter and that of Wu Yei were taken down a side street, the children following behind, and arrived before a comparatively modest house, where bowing servants awaited them. The five of them stood in the centre of a wide porch and looked around in bewilderment. Nothing more completely removed from the devastation prevalent in the outer city, or from the primitive conditions that had obtained in Kwangsi, could have been imagined. Here was all rich drapes and cloth of gold, and gold and silver cutlery and crockery. 'Our master has become a wealthy man,' Wu Yei said wonderingly.

'Our master sits beside the Right Hand of God,' the major-domo pointed out. 'I am Li Yuan. I am my master's servant. I will show you to your apartments.'

They followed him through wide hallways and beyond a lacquered screen to rooms overlooking an inner courtyard, where there was a fountain and colourful flowerbeds. 'Here you will live, ladies,' Li Yuan said.

'Is our master not at home?' Alicia asked.

'Who can say?' Li Yuan replied, clearly disapproving of her curiosity.

Wu Yei squeezed her arm when she would have persisted, and shook her head. Li Yuan then departed. 'You must act your role, Alicia,' the Chinese woman said. 'Now that our master has arrived at greatness, he is indeed master of all our destinies within this house. We must not anticipate his pleasure – or incur his displeasure.'

'I assure you that Michael will never become an oriental despot, at least as regards me,' Alicia insisted, and then caught her breath as the door opened again, and there he was.

He wore a tunic and trousers of green silk, with a green silk hat and leather boots. A red sash was round his waist, but he was unarmed. Somehow he looked bigger and stronger than Alicia remembered, and even more confident – but there was also a remoteness in his eyes which made her feel more than ever that she was in the presence of a stranger.

The children stared at him with wide eyes as he first of all lifted Joanna from the ground for an embrace, then little Ralph, before shaking hands with Hung Cho. Wu Yei and Alicia stood side by side, waiting for him to notice them, and to Alicia's chagrin he embraced Wu Yei first. 'I feared for your lives,' he said. 'Was not the journey a difficult one?'

'A long one, Master,' Wu Yei replied. 'We were concerned to keep you waiting.'

'But now you are here.' He embraced her again, then turned to Alicia, who found that she had been holding her breath. He stood in front of her, taking her in, then put out his hand to remove her hat, stroking her hair as he did so. 'And were you also concerned to keep me waiting?' he asked in English.

'Should I not be, as you are my master?' she replied, and bit her lip as he frowned; she had not intended to be so tart.

'It has been a long four years,' he remarked in Chinese. 'Hung Cho, you will take your brother and sister into the garden, and play with them. I would speak with your mothers.'

'Of course, my father,' Hung Cho said.

The children filed outside, and Michael went to the door. 'Come and inspect your home,' he told Wu Yei and Alicia.

They followed him on a guided tour of the palace, which was even larger than they had supposed, an endless succession of rooms and hallways, down to the kitchen from which nostril-tingling smells were arising, and where they were greeted by bowing servants.

'Truly must you be Hung Hsiu-ch'uan's right hand, My Lord,' Wu Yei remarked.

'One of them,' Michael agreed.

'You will have to tell us our duties,' Alicia ventured.

Michael stopped in front of a pair of double doors. 'Here in Nanking, you have no duties save pleasing me, Alicia.'

She gave a mock bow. 'Then you must indicate, My Lord, which of us must first undertake her duty.'

Again she was holding her breath, praying that her brusqueness, entirely the result of her nerves, had not truly angered him. Yet his reply took her entirely by surprise. 'After four years, Alicia? I doubt I am capable of making the choice. I think I would like you to please me together.'

Almost she refused; such a concept was too utterly unchristian. But then, for all of Hung Hsiu-ch'uan's convictions, this was not a Christian world. And for all her reservations, to share Michael with Wu Yei in an immediate sense was but a projection of the intimacy they had already established – at least on this first occasion after so long, she was the ultimate receiver. Yet she felt disappointed, with herself, for where Wu Yei had smiled and whispered and nibbled with total abandon, Alicia had seriously concentrated on being everything he might wish – and felt she had failed.

Then why, she wondered, had she tried? Her dislike of subservience was ingrained, and not to be overcome. She could never be just Michael's plaything; she was a human being in her own right. In a world which did not admit of such things, except for the favoured few. And for those not favoured, existence was only possible in the shadow of their master.

This was brought home to her far more strongly in Nanking than ever in Kwangsi. In the south, before the inauguration of the Kingdom of Heavenly Peace, there had been a certain rough camaraderie, an awareness that they were all together in a great enterprise which could well result in their deaths. If Hung had been the apex of their social pyramid, he had yet been a man, approachable, capable of smiling and even joking, of exchanging points of view. In Nanking he was the Viceroy of God. The wives saw him quite often, as he indulged in a succession of state occasions, entertaining delegations from the provinces, graciously receiving messengers from his generals when they arrived to announce another victory – for the subjugation of the north was continuing, and soon Yang sent word that he was besieging Tientsin, the port of Peking. When that fell, the capital would be at his mercy.

Nearer at hand, Hung was now in contact with the British, who had established themselves in Shanghai, and who he encouraged to ascend the river and trade with Nanking – it had been some of the earliest to take the risk whom Alicia had seen on her first day in the city. It was, for the moment at least, an amicable relationship – the British, always anxious to find new trading outlets, letting it be known that so long as the Tai-p'ing did not interfere with them, they would not interfere in Chinese internal matters. Women were not of course entertained on these occasions, but Hung liked them to attend, and stand in a group to watch the ceremonies and their men-folk eat, and afterwards he would walk amongst them, almost as if he were inspecting them, a disturbing event for her because he always gave her a very long stare, and on occasion touched her hair.

'He terrifies me,' she confessed to Michael – for however omnipresent was Wu Yei, they could of course speak English whenever she wanted privacy. And once back in his company she had quite overcome her fear of him, or her feeling of strangeness with him. Whatever wealth and power he had achieved, he remained her desperado, and also, she felt, her honest man, who hated his position.

'He is a terrifying figure,' Michael agreed.

'And yet you work for him, remain with him.'

He ruffled her hair. 'I have no choice, my dear girl. He has made that plain enough.'

'You mean we are prisoners.'

'In a manner of speaking. Until we have completed the conquest of China.'

'Which could take years.'

'A few, certainly. It is what I set out to do.'

'To give your life to a megalomaniac.'

He sighed. 'I will confess that I rated him higher than he is, as a man. But perhaps he is a product of his time – and more, of his people. I still think he is a better bargain for China than the Manchu.'

'He seems to have destroyed most of his people,' Alicia

pointed out. 'You did not see the desert through which we passed.'

'I helped to make it into a desert,' he reminded her.

'And when I see these poor people being marched off to execution, or wearing those horrible great wooden collars they call cangues on their shoulders, or being bastinadoed . . .' she shuddered.

'That is the Chinese way of life. And we are in the middle of a revolution. I believe Paris was no place to be, in the 1790s. Only sixty odd years ago, you know. And out of that came a much better France.'

Her turn to sigh; he would not be swayed from his purpose. 'The thought of anything like that happening to Joanna or Ralph, or of Hung getting his hands on them . . . or me . . .' she gave another shudder.

He squeezed her against him. 'I can promise you that it won't. And if I thought for a moment that it might, or could, then I would leave him no matter what he said. But I have not forgotten my promise to you. I am working on ways and means of getting you and the children down to Shanghai. From there you can obtain a passage to Hong Kong, and thence Singapore.'

'But you will not come.'

'No.'

She considered this for a while, then said, 'If you can get the children and me out, surely you could also escape.'

'I have nothing to escape for, Alicia.'

She frowned at him. 'You cannot believe they would still wish to arrest you? I will not let them. Papa will listen to me.'

Michael sighed. 'I did not know how to tell you this before, Alicia, but your father is dead.'

'Papa? But . . .'

'And your mother. I learned this from the factors who came up the river. Ali is now in sole control of Hammond and Teng. Teng Tang does what he is told, and so does your brother Pieter, who is now factor in Hong Kong. Until I heard that I did dream of returning to Singapore, or at least Hong Kong. Now . . . there is still most definitely a warrant out for my arrest.'

Alicia stared out of the window and wondered why she did not weep. Because it had been too long? Or because she had experienced too much for tears ever again to be a solace. Mama and Papa . . . and they would have gone to their graves thinking her and their grandchildren dead. Perhaps it had been that supposition, which had brought them down.

And Ali . . . she gazed at Michael.

'Do you suppose you would have any influence with Ali?' he asked.

'No,' she said. 'No. Then . . . there is nothing for me to return for either, is there, Michael?'

He was of course delighted at her decision, even if he worried about her choice, and with more reason when in 1856 the army came flooding back from the north. For the first time the Tai-p'ing had been defeated by the Manchu – outside the walls of Tientsin.

Hung stared at his only slightly crestfallen general in utter disbelief. 'You have been defeated?' he asked. 'You?' he shouted. 'Have been defeated? Have you lost your senses? Or have you . . .' he pointed, 'broken the word of my father?'

'Rather must we ask ourselves if there was ever any word from your father,' Yang retorted. 'His only value was as a rallying cry to the peasants, who understand nothing. And perhaps as an inspiration for yourself, Great Hung. But it was you cost me that battle outside Tientsin. You would not let Harrington command the guns. We lost the battle because the guns were badly served.'

'I cannot believe that of Wong Sung,' Michael protested.

'Wong Sung died of fever, two months ago,' Yang said. 'No doubt another inspired message from the heavenly father. But I receive messages of my own, from above. Why, the old man with the golden beard appeared to me but a few days ago, and told me that a man who kicks his concubines should be whipped and degraded.' He stared at Hung.

Who had continued staring at him. Now he suddenly sprang to his feet, face contorted with rage. 'Blasphemer,' he shouted. 'Foul thing from the pit of hell. Take off his head. General Wei, take off his head. Now.'

Wei Ch'ang-hui hesitated but a moment; only Yang stood between him and command of the armies. 'Guards,' he snapped.

Taken by surprise, Yang had no time even to draw his sword before his arms were seized and he was forced to his knees. 'You cannot kill me,' he shouted. 'I am commander of the army. My men will avenge me.'

'Your men know only that you led them to defeat,' Wei said contemptuously, and grasped Yang's hair, while signalling one of his men.

'You cannot . . .' Yang was still screaming the words when the sword blade crashed through his neck, and Wei threw the reeking head across the floor to come to rest at Hung's feet.

'Blasphemer,' Hung growled. 'Now my kingdom will rest easier.'

Amazingly, he meant what he said, although Michael did not immediately appreciate it. Utterly shocked by what had happened, Michael seriously contemplated escaping as soon as possible, no matter what he might find in the outside world, only to discover that his every move was watched, and his house virtually become a prison; when he met with the English factors from Shanghai, which was often enough to discuss matters of trade, it was always with an English-speaking Chinese present.

There was no way he could dare risk accusing Hung of imprisoning him, but he tried another approach to the matter. 'Where is our conquest of Peking now, Great Hung?' he asked.

'It is the will of my father,' Hung said. 'That we should rest here, and consolidate our kingdom. When he is ready to resume our advance, he will give me the signal.'

'Resting here, I am accomplishing nothing,' Michael protested.

'You are accomplishing great things, by being at my side, Michael,' Hung told him. 'Have we not been brothers in arms now, for nearly twenty years? I have made you famous. The English merchants who come up the river speak of you with awe. And I will make you more famous yet. When my father gives me the sign to march once more, I will place you at the head of my armies, and you will bring me the ultimate victory. We will yet march in triumph through the Tien Mien to humble the Ch'ing. It will not be long, now.'

Only another lifetime, Michael thought bitterly. And yet he could not help but be attracted to the concept. Once he had been amazed at the idea that an Irish adventurer could rise to be the head of the greatest trading concern in the East. That had proved only an idle dream. Now he could again let himself contemplate his triumph as head of the army which would reunite China beneath its rightful rulers. There would be immortality. Even if accomplished by an effusion of blood? But had not Bonaparte shed an effusion of blood, and yet gone down to history as a great man?

Besides, the bloodletting seemed to be slackening. Perhaps only from necessity. If Hung had early realized that he had to feed his people, it was now necessary for him to realize that they were still starving, because the fanatical Tai-p'ing whom he placed in charge of grain production knew nothing of it. Thus he had to empty his prisons of those survivors of the landlord class still awaiting execution, who did know when to sow and when to reap, and how to care for the soil. Food production immediately improved, and the Kingdom of Heavenly Peace at last began to take on a viable outlook. Hung himself seemed to mellow, and it was even possible for Michael to be happy, on occasion, at home in his palace as he played with his rapidly growing children, and enjoyed the company of his wives. Of Malama he could no longer afford to think. She was buried away in the confines of Hung's

307

now extensive harem, and although he knew she was alive, for Hung often reassured him of that, she might have been dead as far as the world was concerned.

And happiness was a fleeting business where Hung was concerned. From time to time his anger continued to explode, and another unfortunate head would roll across the floor, spouting blood. Or his lust would overcome his dignity, and he would send for some girl he had seen on the street, and have her prepared for his bed. While more and more he seemed to be attracted to Alicia, would now interrupt an important meeting to go amongst the women to speak with her. Michael could only thank God that the one law which Hung had never broken, which he regarded as sacred, was the decree against adultery. But Alicia's situation were he to sicken and die would be horrendous, nor could he truly contemplate Joanna and Ralph becoming adults in such a society. So again his thoughts turned seriously to escape, and again and again he thought he had devised a way to smuggle them out of the city, and every time he came up against an insurmountable obstacle. He had not yet found the answer when, in the autumn of 1859, ten years after he had first joined the Tai-p'ing, and six after the capture of Nanking, he was summoned to Hung's palace to meet, not a British factor, but a British envoy.

'Humphrey Lane, at your service, Mr Harrington. I have heard a great deal about you.' Lane was a somewhat portly man, wearing the insignia of a captain in the Royal Navy, and aglitter with gold braid on his blue frock coat and cocked hat, with gold-hilted sword, spotless white breeches and stockings, highly polished leather shoes; the Chinese were regarding him with some awe.

'None of it to my credit, I would say,' Michael replied.

'Well, sir, there are charges of piracy and such things against you, to be sure, but that is a long time ago. I am empowered to indicate that all these annoyances would be dropped were you now to cooperate with Her Majesty's Government.'

'Me?' Michael was amazed, but his heart was beginning to pound.

'You, sir. No doubt you have heard of the *Arrow* incident?'

Michael shook his head.

'Well, sir, you will recall that following the lesson we taught these arrogant fellows seventeen years ago, they conceded our requests for full trading rights with their country, and granted us the use of certain treaty ports.'

'I remember.'

'Well, sir, Canton is one of these ports, as you are no doubt aware.'

'Yes. That is why His Highness Hung Hsiu-ch'uan has not yet assaulted it.'

'Good sense, sir. Good sense. But then, he seems to be a sensible chap. Which is more than can be said for our common enemy, the Manchu. They have been growing more and more arrogant and difficult to live with, and the upshot has been that three years ago their Viceroy in Canton seized the ship *Arrow*, flying the Union Jack, and imprisoned her crew.'

'My God!' Michael exclaimed. 'No news of that has reached here. It reminds me of what happened in 1839.'

'Exactly.'

'But you say this happened three years ago? And you are only now taking action?'

'We took action then, sir, and once again seized the Bogue forts, as we did in your day. But the Ch'ing climbed down immediately, and agreed to a treaty which included an indemnity and further extended the treaty ports. That was thought to be satisfactory, but then the dishonest fellows abrogated the treaty, and forbade us to use any of the ports. Well, sir, Her Britannic Majesty could not accept such treatment from dishonest heathens.'

'Oh, quite,' Michael agreed. 'Besides, it would mean an end to the opium trade.'

Lane seemed unaware that any sarcasm was intended. 'Exactly so. Well, sir, it was immediately determined to teach these scallawags a lesson, and so last June one of

309

our squadrons bombarded the Taku forts at the mouth of the Peiho River, and then landed troops to destroy the places. Unfortunately, sir, things did not go well. The resistance proved far stronger than anticipated, and frankly, we got a bloody nose. In fact, had it not been for the aid of an American squadron in those waters, we might have suffered a disaster.'

Michael frowned. 'You mean the Americans are helping us in this?'

'No, sir. Their attitude is strictly neutral. But when their commanding officer saw our people being shot down in their boats as they tried to evacuate, he ordered his ships to provide covering fire.'

'Good Lord! How did he justify that?'

Lane gave him an old-fashioned look. 'I believe Commander Tattnall used the words "Blood is thicker than water", sir.'

Which was an original way of looking at things, Michael supposed. But it indicated that the Manchu were certainly determined to fight for North China; perhaps Yang had not been such a failure after all.

'Well, sir,' Lane went on. 'You will agree that it is therefore more than ever necessary to teach these scoundrels a lesson. We are going to avenge our dead, sir, at the very gates of Peking. I am happy to say that the French have associated themselves with us in this determination.'

'I can appreciate your attitude,' Michael agreed, deciding not to remind the good captain that the Manchu were only defending themselves. 'But I do not see how I can be of any assistance to you.'

'Well, sir, you can, in more ways than one. It is our purpose to exert the maximum pressure on the Ch'ing to make amends, but not to spill blood wantonly. Nor do we have the men really to demonstrate to the Manchus the true strength of Britain. Thus my commanding officer, Admiral Sir Michael Seymour, wishes to negotiate, at the muzzle of a gun, perhaps, but still, negotiate in order to show these people that they simply must behave in a civilized way. Learning that you were serving with the

Tai-p'ing, he has sent me to make the following propositions to you, acceptance of which, as I have said, will mean that all charges against you will be dropped. The first proposition is that you encourage your general, Hung Hsiu-ch'uan, to resume his warlike activities, so as to remind the Ch'ing that they have serious internal problems to deal with . . .'

'And you do not suppose that will cause additional bloodshed?' Michael asked.

'Well, sir, it will be Chinese steel shedding Chinese blood, and that can hardly be our concern. Nor can we be blamed in the Commons for it.'

'I am bound to say that that smacks of hypocrisy, Mr Lane,' Michael said.

'Which is but another word for politics,' Lane replied, without embarrassment.

'You mentioned two services I could perform for you.'

'Ah, well, the other may be even greater, if you've the stomach for it. It is our intention to send an embassy to Peking, and have it out with the Emperor face to face. We have already informed the gentleman that unless this request is granted we shall take extreme measures to force his hand. Now sir, it is the opinion of our appointed ambassador, Mr Parkes, that you, with your unrivalled knowledge of both the country and the people, and the language, would be an invaluable addition to our negotiating team, as it were.'

'Hm,' Michael muttered thoughtfully – his brain was doing handsprings.

'As you will no doubt know,' Lane went on, 'part of our problem in dealing with these people has arisen from a lack of understanding of the nuances which can be contained in their speeches as well as their minds. A Chinese diplomat can appear to be saying something perfectly straightforward, and can then turn out to have meant something entirely different.'

'Yes,' Michael agreed.

'It is Mr Parkes' opinion that to have you at the negotiating table would be very nearly as useful as possessing a Chinese of our own, if you follow me.'

'I am very flattered, I'm sure,' Michael remarked drily.

'Well, sir, will you accept our invitation?'

Michael's brain was in a whirl. Would he ever be given a similar opportunity? He could leave Nanking, legitimately, because he was sure he could convince Hung that in going to Peking he could further the Tai-p'ing cause. And he would be pardoned by the British, and able to resume his life and career. Because once he was away from Nanking, with Alicia and Wu Yei and the children . . . abandoning Malama for ever. But had he not already abandoned Malama for ever?

'Well, sir?' Lane pressed.

'I will have to discuss the matter with His Highness,' Michael told him. 'You will have your answer tomorrow.'

Hung was certainly anxious to learn what the English officer had had to say, as was Wei Ch'ang-hui. The three of them sat down in private while Michael related the conversation.

'It is useless to attempt to negotiate with the Ch'ing,' Wei said derisively. 'If the British do not yet know that, they are fools. But if they wish to go to war with them, then they may be of use to us.'

Hung nodded. 'It is a wise course, to let two enemies destroy each other.'

Michael began to feel desperate. 'Yet do I think I can serve you, Great Hung, by joining this embassy.'

'How?' Wei demanded.

'In two ways. Firstly, I will be taken into Peking, and indeed into the Forbidden City itself, as part of the embassy. This will give me an unequalled opportunity to study the place, the garrison, the dispositions we will have to overcome when we march on the city. For is that not still our ultimate goal?'

Wei stroked his moustaches thoughtfully.

'And secondly, once I am there, I can declare myself

312

to be an ambassador for you, Great Hung. I will be able to present your demands . . .'

'Our only demand of Hsien Feng is that he hang himself and commands his family to do the same,' Wei said.

'Well, then, your ultimatum. The Emperor pretends to ignore us, supposing that in time we will go away. If I appear as your ambassador, Great Hung, beside the British envoy, he will have to accept that we are a power in the land, and may become more than that.'

It was Hung's turn to stroke his moustache.

'A waste of time,' Wei growled.

'I think not,' Hung said at last. 'There is much in what you say, Michael. I think it could well be of service to my father were you to undertake this mission. If you can obtain an audience with the Emperor, and perhaps persuade him to a meeting with me . . .' he stroked his moustache.

'Do you seriously suppose Hsien Feng would ever agree to meet with you, Great Hung?' Wei asked. 'He regards you as a bandit.'

'Perhaps, but I am a bandit who rules half China, more absolutely than he rules the remainder.' Hung was in one of his quiet, introspective moods when it was still possible to discern the greatness that might have been his. 'I think you should put this point to him, Michael. You have my blessing on your enterprise.'

'I will make my preparations immediately, Great Hung,' Michael said, trying to conceal his elation.

'You will need an entourage,' Hung remarked mildly. 'As my ambassador.'

'A small one, Great Hung. My wives, my children, and four servants. That is all.'

Hung stroked his moustache. 'You may take Wu Yei. She is your senior wife. Your children and your junior wife will remain in Nanking.'

Michael's head came up in dismay.

'If you feel the need of further creature comforts, take a handmaiden as well,' Hung said. 'I give you permission to choose one from the girls of the city.'

'My comfort comes from my wives,' Michael said desperately.

'They are both old,' Hung said. 'You need a younger woman. I will select her for you myself. But your junior wife remains in Nanking.'

'With respect, Great Hung . . .'

'Or I might come to suspect that you mean to desert me, Michael,' Hung pointed out, still speaking mildly but fixing him with that magnetic stare.

Michael swallowed.

'You may rest assured that your wife and children will be waiting for you when you return to me, flushed with the success of your mission,' Hung told him. 'When you have made the Manchu tremble at the power of my name. You have my personal assurance on that point.'

Michael inhaled . . . but he had tossed and lost. He must now try to make the best of it. 'And when I have done that, Great Hung, will I be allowed to return to my own people? Now that I am able to do so?'

Hung nodded. 'Yes, Michael. I think, when you return from this mission, that I will grant you permission to return to your own people.' Hung smiled. 'I will give you my personal assurance on that point also.'

He had hardly expected such ready acquiescence. He would succeed after all. 'Then Great Hung, may I remind you again that my wives, and my children, are placed in your protection.'

'I have said that their protection will be my pleasure and my duty, Michael,' Hung agreed. 'Until you return.'

'You can't,' Alicia cried, aghast. 'You cannot leave me and go off with Wu Yei. Please, Michael. You cannot.'

'I have decided not to take Wu Yei either,' Michael reassured her. 'This is a mission which must be accomplished as quickly as possible. I had intended to take you all out, but as I cannot . . . the sooner I am back the better.'

'And if you do not return?'

'How can I not return, Alicia? I am going as part of an

314

official British embassy. I will be safer there than anywhere else in the world. And when I return, we have
Hung's word that we will be allowed to leave. We can go
back to Singapore, Hong Kong, anywhere you choose.
Don't you see, I'll be free of all the charges levelled against
me. Not even Ali will be able to harm me. Don't you
want to go home, my darling?'

'Of course I do.' Although she did not sound at all
certain. 'But . . . Hung's word. I do not trust him.'

'Well, I promise you that you can. He has given me his
solemn assurance.' He wished he could feel as reassuring
as he made himself sound. But again he had no choice;
Hung would never let him abandon the embassy now, and
besides, this was their only hope of escape.

'You left Malama in his safekeeping, once,' Alicia
reminded him. 'And look what happened.'

'Malama was unattached. You are my wife. Hung has
issued laws against adultery. And they are the only laws
he regards as also applying to himself.'

'I was not thinking of me, Michael.'

He followed her gaze out of the window to where Joanna
was arranging flowers on the inner porch. He had not
known Alicia at fifteen, but if he had, he had no doubt
that here he was looking at her. For a moment he doubted.
But he could not afford to doubt. Or that beautiful girl
would be forced to live in Nanking for the rest of her life.

'She is only a child,' he said.

'A very beautiful child.'

'Nonetheless, Hung has never indulged in children,
either. But wouldn't you say, as Joanna is certainly growing up, that is all the more reason for us to leave here,
just as soon as we can?' He held her close. 'Hung has
given me his solemn word. We must trust in that.'

12

The Victims of the Gods

The overall commander of the British force assembled in
Hong Kong was Lieutenant General Sir James Hope
Grant, who had some eleven thousand British soldiers
with him, including such famous regiments as the Royal
Scots, The Queen's, The East Surreys and the King's
Royal Rifles, as well as a large contingent of Indian sepoys.
In view of the fact that the entire British Empire was still
seething with the shock waves generated by the mutiny
of elements of the Indian Army only a couple of years
previously, these were regarded with some suspicion by
both officers and British enlisted ranks, but they were in
the main Sikhs from the Punjab region and were quiet,
well-behaved, very efficient and intensely loyal soldiers,
proud of their red jackets, and distinguished from their
British counterparts only by their complexions and their
turbans. Also present was a French contingent of seven
thousand under Lieutenant General Cousin-Montauban.
The troops themselves made a colourful display on the
shore, with their flags and bugle calls, but in even greater
evidence was the armada assembled to transport them;
the straits and the harbour of Victoria were alike crammed
with men-of-war and transports, quite a few of them steam
powered, the first time Michael had ever seen such vessels.

'Depend upon it, Mr Harrington,' the British general
said, 'we do not intend to make any mistakes this time, I
can promise you that. Now get yourself some proper clothes, for God's sake.'

Michael could not resist going ashore to see the changes
which had taken place in the last ten years, and was
amazed at the growth of the colony, which had now quite
spilled over on to the mainland. The warehouse of Ham-

mond and Teng looked as prosperous as ever, and so did the house on the hill; however, he decided against investigating either too closely, or making his presence known to the present factor. Time enough for that when he was finally ready to resume his former life.

A step he was in a hurry to take; for all the confidence he had shown Alicia he was desperately anxious when he considered what might be happening in Nanking, and of course his full pardon did not come into effect until he had played his part in the coming embassy. He had forgotten how slowly and ponderously military expeditions moved towards their goals. Although he reached Victoria in February 1860, the final preparations were not completed until May, and it was the last week of July before the fleet appeared in the Gulf of Chihli, having sailed and steamed majestically up the coast, between the huge island of Formosa and the mainland, past Shanghai and the mouth of the Yangtse Kiang – off which they anchored to remind both the Viceroy, and any Tai-p'ing who might be in the vicinity, of the military might of Great Britain and France.

Here Michael, uncomfortable in the stiff collar and clinging trousers he had not worn for so long, was summoned to the general's cabin to interview a young man who had been sent out to the fleet as a prisoner, an American named Frederick Ward who, it turned out, was like himself a merchant navy officer, if considerably younger, being only thirty-two.

'This fellow,' General Grant explained, 'has been causing all manner of trouble, by trying to recruit an army amongst the Chinese in Shanghai, with the intention of leading them against the Tai-p'ing. Now we, and, I may say, the Americans themselves, are determined to keep out of any internal Chinese squabbles, and we simply cannot have this sort of thing going on. I wonder if, Harrington, you could persuade him that your Tai-p'ing friends have no intention of assaulting Shanghai?'

Before Michael could think of a reply, Ward's sharp

317

features glowed with indignation. 'Say, you're not that guy Harrington who fights for Hung?' he cried.

'I'm afraid I am.'

'And they've arrested *me*! Great balls of fire. General, this guy is a self-confessed mass murderer.'

'Are you really?' General Grant inquired with considerable interest.

'You ask him how many millions of people have died since the Tai-p'ing took over South China,' Ward suggested.

'There have been epidemics, and a good deal of starvation,' Michael conceded.

'And how many people has your friend Hung had decapitated? Let me tell you, General, I sailed up the Yangtse, and what I saw sickened me.'

'It has, on occasion, sickened me,' Michael said.

'So you admit it, huh. Then you are one hell of a scoundrel. You want to do something about this character, General. I'm trying to protect people against the likes of him.'

'I'm afraid Mr Harrington, having belonged to the Tai-p'ing movement since before any official government policy towards it was formulated . . .'

'Actually, before it became the Tai-p'ing movement,' Michael interrupted.

'Quite. Well, he is beyond my jurisdiction, Mr Ward, and is in any event contributing valuable services towards my present campaign. The conduct of Westerners in and about Shanghai is, however, in my jurisdiction, and I simply cannot permit hotheads like yourself to cause trouble.'

Ward looked so woebegone that Michael felt he had to go to his rescue, in so far as he could. 'Ahem,' he remarked.

The general turned his head.

'I'm afraid that Wei Ch'ang-hui, who is the Tai-p'ing commanding general, has every intention of attacking and taking Shanghai, whenever that can be done without having to fight the British.'

'What did I say?' Ward cried triumphantly.

'That day is hardly likely to arise,' Grant pointed out.

'But it can hardly do any harm to reorganize a defence force amongst the Chinese themselves,' Ward argued.

'Hm,' the general commented. 'I will have to consider the matter, Mr Ward. In the meantime, you will remain with the fleet, if you please. Thank you, gentlemen.'

Michael followed Ward outside, to where a marine corporal waited. 'British justice,' Ward remarked. 'But say, Harrington, it was real good of you to chip in at the end. When this Hung takes on Shanghai, won't you be firing his guns for him?'

'Hopefully not.'

'But you still reckon he's a good thing.'

'I still reckon he has to be better than the Manchu.'

'It's a point of view.' Ward held out his hand. 'Thanks, anyway.'

Michael shook the proffered fingers. 'Wei is no man to lose a battle to, Ward.'

The American nodded. 'I'll remember that.'

But Michael did not think it was going to deter him.

Next day the fleet resumed its journey north until it arrived off the mouth of the Peiho, where the same Taku forts as had proved so much trouble in the past continued to glower at them.

During the voyage Michael had made the acquaintance of Harry Smith Parkes, who was going to lead the British negotiating team when the Chinese had been 'brought to their senses', as the soldiers would have it. Parkes had been acquainted with China almost as long as Michael himself, although like Ward he was some thirteen years the younger – he smilingly reminded Michael that they had actually met, in 1843, when, although only a boy of fourteen, he had been a secretary to Sir Henry Pottinger, as he had already lived in China for some time with his sisters and his brother-in-law, a missionary, and spoke the language fluently. Since reaching manhood he had served as assistant consul in several of the treaty ports, had been in Canton when the *Arrow* had been seized, and indeed had been the principal British voice for immediate retribution. Michael could not remember him as a boy, but there was no doubt that he had grown to manhood as an intensely self-confident empire builder, who wore the fashionable long side whiskers, and whose eyes, set around a prominent, inquiring nose, gleamed with an almost fanatical contempt for all things not British.

He had, as Captain Lane had said, specifically requested the assistance of Michael in negotiating the conclusive treaty that Great Britain was determined to force out of China, and explained why with perfect candour. 'This is our last chance to settle our position here in the East, finally and conclusively, Harrington,' he said. 'We can never apply the force necessary to conquer this country; India was eaten up bit by bit, as it were, thanks to the internecine quarrels of the Indians themselves, and also to the temper of the people back home. It is all very well to say that the Mughal Empire was in as decrepit a state in 1750 as the Manchu is today, but our people do not any longer seem to have the stomach for empire. I can tell you in confidence that the party of peace at any price, even with the heathen, is more powerful than ever in the House of Commons, and although the country as a whole has supported Lord Palmerston's views at the last election, that the British flag must be upheld and respected wherever it flies, he must have it much in mind to avoid at all costs another Crimea, eh?'

'Oh, quite,' Michael agreed. 'There is also the small point that China actually belongs to the Chinese, rather than either the Manchu or the British. Or,' he added, 'the French or the Germans or the Americans.'

Parkes frowned at him for a moment, and then smiled. 'A small point, as you say, my dear fellow. But I trust you will concede that India is better governed under the British than it ever was under its own people.'

Michael remembered the teeming cesspool of Calcutta, and the palaces on the hill above, but decided against quarrelling with this totally dedicated man, however wrong he might consider the dedication – at least until after their mission was concluded. 'I will concede that the British have raised the art of government to a fine one,' he said.

Once again Parkes' ready smile had to come to the relief of his frown. 'I had forgotten you have an Irishman's way of looking at the world. However, to revert to what I was saying, what we obtain now, with the support of this fine army and navy, must be absolutely binding upon the Ch'ing, and we must make sure of that, or the lives of our missionaries and merchants here in China will not be worth a damn. If you knew some of the physical crimes I have seen and heard perpetrated . . .'

'And felt?' Michael suggested.

'My dear fellow, forgive me. I had forgotten you were imprisoned by that scoundrel Lin. Well, as I was saying, we must make sure such a crime can never happen again. And frankly, our comrades, I know from experience, are far too easily taken in by a smooth-talking Chinese politician, especially when his words are translated by an even more smooth-talking interpreter. When Lord Elgin was negotiating the Treaty of Tientsin, two years ago, I had the devil of a time trying to persuade my colleagues, who were also regarded as my superiors, to pay attention to the fine points and, indeed, argue them out. Well, I think I may say I have been proved right by events. This time I shall head the negotiating team, and with you at my side, able to support my interpretation of what is being contended, I think we may hope to reach a successful conclusion.'

'I'll say amen to that,' Michael agreed.

'Do you suppose your family is safe in Nanking, in your absence?'

'I don't have too much choice other than to suppose that, Mr Parkes, as they are there.'

Parkes studied him for several seconds. Then he said, 'Tell me about the Tai-p'ing. Do you suppose they can really drive out the Manchu and rule China?'

Which Michael was beginning to suspect might be the real reason he was here at all.

'I think they have every chance of doing so,' he said. 'Especially if you fellows continue to nibble away at the Manchu.'

'I assume you know this fellow Hung Hsiu-ch'uan personally?'

'I think you could call him my oldest friend,' Michael said.

'Is that so. How remarkable. The future emperor of China, perhaps. If he is indeed your friend, I am surprised you wish to desert him.'

'Desert is hardly the word,' Michael protested. 'I have served Hung faithfully and well for ten years. I am prepared to continue doing so for much longer than that, until he reaches his goal, but it is time for my European family to resume a more normal way of life. My son and daughter need proper schooling. My wife a chance to revisit her home and enjoy some of the blessings of western civilization, supposing there are any . . . Hung runs, shall I say, rather a tight ship.'

'Yes,' Parkes said thoughtfully. And then smiled. 'Well, we must certainly get your family out of his clutches.'

'I think I may be able to manage that for myself,' Michael said.

'Nonetheless, as they are British, we must make sure of it. Even if we have to knock down one of your friend Hung Hsiu-ch'uan's walls.'

'I think you will find Hung something of a tougher nut to crack than the Ch'ing,' Michael suggested.

Parkes smiled again. 'Cracking tough nuts is my speciality, Mr Harrington. I shall look forward to it.'

Michael did not doubt his determination to try, and could not help but look forward himself to a confrontation between the two most arrogant men he had ever met – although he had a suspicion that Parkes had better make sure to have a British fleet at his back when he entered upon that meeting. He wondered which side *he* would be on – but if Parkes did intend to undertake a campaign against Hung to free Alicia and the children as part of his principle of upholding the British flag, there could only be one side for him – that of the Tai-p'ing, to prevent their execution. His only hope of saving their lives was to succeed in this mission and get them out of Nanking before the British really turned their ferocious gaze upon the Kingdom of Heavenly Peace. And to do that, presumably, he must back Parkes to the hilt for the time being, however much he might dislike the man and what he stood for.

The campaign commenced next morning, when, no acknowledgement of their presence having come from the Chinese, the troops were put ashore. Two more weeks were occupied in establishing camps and logistical arrangements, again without any word from the Chinese, not even an inquiry as to the meaning of this invasion of their country, and then, on 21 August, the forts were assaulted, by the combined armies from the landward side, while the fleet bombarded from the sea, much as the Bogue forts at the mouth of the Pearl River had been taken in 1841. As in the previous year, there was an American squadron looking on, and Ward was also on deck to oversee the proceedings, but this time there were no mistakes. Perhaps the resistance was less vigorous than the previous year, but in any event the forts were flying the Tricolour and the Union Jack by nightfall.

The armies then moved up the river as far as the city of Tientsin, the port of Peking, a sizeable place which to Michael's interest was situated at the northern end of the Grand Canal, cut some two thousand years before by the first of the emperors to link the Yangtse and the Peiho, a perfectly prodigious piece of engineering covering very nearly a thousand miles which made the work being carried out at Suez by Ferdinand de Lesseps seem like a bucket and spade affair. Tientsin readily surrendered and there a general headquarters was established while preparations were made for the march on the capital. Michael

323

had of course taken no part in the fighting, having this far been merely an observer from the ships, but he could not help but remark, not for the first time, how spineless the Manchu resistance was, and that of the Chinese when led by Manchu officers. 'Can you really hope to create a force capable of withstanding Wei's hordes?' he asked Ward.

'Sure, if you Limeys will let me. Any man will fight, providing he is sufficiently well trained.'

'And inspired, surely,' Michael argued. 'The Tai-p'ing are genuine fanatics.'

'Whereas my people merely wish to defend their homes,' Ward agreed.

'And their wealth. History is against you. Think of the way the Arabs overran the world in the seventh and eighth centuries.'

Ward grinned. 'They were checked at Constantinople. And in France, by discipline and determination. We shall have to see, Mr Harrington.' Again the two men shook hands. 'I'll wish you joy with your mission.'

For the fleet was being left behind, as the armies commenced their march up the Peiho, the British on the right bank, the French on the left – a somewhat dangerous arrangement, it seemed to Michael, as there was no way the two forces, separated by the swift-running stream, could come to each other's assistance in the event of a crisis. It was a slow business, across country composed for the most part of low, rolling hills, heavily cultivated and with an appearance of great prosperity. The peasants turned out to stare at the British red jackets and the French blue, but made no effort to interfere with their march, and readily sold their produce to the hungry and thirsty soldiers. Of Manchu bannermen they saw nothing until some forty miles from the town of Tung Chow, when firing was heard from the advance guard, and reinforcements were hastily hurried forward. Michael would have liked to accompany them, but Parkes forbade it. 'We are here to handle the negotiations, Mr Harrington,' he said. 'Not the fighting.'

Whatever forces had opposed them were rapidly brushed aside, and the armies encamped for the night; the river had now narrowed considerably, and communication between French and British had greatly improved.

Next morning horsemen were seen approaching under a flag of truce, and soon Parkes and Michael, as well as Mr Harry Brougham Lock, who had arrived as representative of the British government – thus superseding Parkes, who had been chosen by the military from amongst Englishmen on the spot – were summoned to General Grant's tent, where they found four Chinese officials waiting, together with an interpreter. 'These fellows would like to parley,' Grant explained. 'They say that one of the imperial princes is at present in Tung Chow, and wishes to discuss our invasion. What do you think of that?'

'That is what we came for,' Lock replied. 'If we can settle this business without further bloodshed, the Commons will be well pleased.'

'I meant, can we trust these fellows?' Grant said. 'Mr Parkes?'

'I think we must, Sir James. We will have to negotiate with them at some time.'

Grant looked at Michael.

Who shrugged. 'I agree with Mr Parkes.'

Grant nodded. 'Very well. However, we will do the thing properly. I will inform General Cousin-Montauban of the situation so that he may send some of his own people along, and I will arrange a strong escort for you.'

'With respect, sir,' Parkes said. 'I think it would be best if the delegation were to be kept small, and if there were to be no red or blue jackets included.'

'Are you sure? My dear fellow, my personal feeling is that these people only understand naked force.'

'Then we must teach them to understand moral force as well,' Parkes insisted.

As the acknowledged China expert, he got his way. Michael, who had only ever negotiated with the Manchu at the point of a gun, also had to accept that Parkes knew best; he was in any event in favour of anything which would bring the campaign to a speedy end, and himself into contact with the Ch'ing ministers; one of the Emperor's brothers would certainly be satisfactory.

The party eventually consisted of twenty-four, Lock and a French officer wearing a civilian coat, Parkes and Michael, as chief interpreters, two French and two British secretaries, and seventeen Indian dragoons commanded by an English subaltern. They rode out of the British encampment at dawn – it was the middle of September – under a white flag, and covered the forty-odd miles to Tung Chow by nightfall. On their way they were accompanied, at a distance, by a body of bannermen, but there was no contact between the two forces.

A hotel had been prepared for them, and they dined in considerable luxury. 'I must say, I had not expected this,' Lock remarked, as the pretty waitress delicately picked the roast duckling clean, before spreading her sauce and wrapping the meat in the most tasty small pancakes. 'These people are pretty civilized.'

'They have been for some time,' Michael pointed out, which earned him an old-fashioned look; Lock did not apparently consider his presence as necessary at all.

'Even if they have some pretty uncivilized habits,' Parkes put in.

'Any people who can make crêpes as good as these are civilized,' said the French representative, Captain Lemarche. He raised his glass of plum wine. 'I drink to the success of our mission.'

Michael drank to that, readily enough, but he had the strangest sensation as he retired for the night. They were in the middle of men whom he knew to be utterly ruthless, and so pragmatic as to be treacherous – words given and safe conducts granted would mean nothing should an immediate advantage be considered possible by breaking either. And when he recalled his experience in Canton . . . more than twenty years ago. What an eventful twenty years they had turned out to be, thanks to Hung Hsiu-ch'uan. But here in North China there was no Hung to come to his rescue.

And without himself, what would happen to Alicia and the children? Perhaps, he thought, he had needed this break from them to discover just how much he valued them, how eager he was to have them back in civilization, no matter what the cost to himself personally.

Despite his apprehensions he slept soundly, and next morning the allied delegation met with the Manchu, in the courtyard of the hotel. Their hosts were smiling and unctuous, thrusting their hands into the sleeves of their silk jackets and bowing ceremoniously whenever they spoke. Their leader, who arrived after the delegates had waited for something more than an hour, in a palanquin carried by six men and draped with imperial yellow silk, was introduced as Prince Ch'un, younger brother of the Emperor, a sleepy-looking man who waved them to their seats and then closed his eyes.

'My master, our masters, wish to know what justification you have for invading our country,' said the man seated beside him.

Parkes translated for the benefit of Lock and Captain Lemarche, then answered, 'The justification of the treaty signed by you with Lord Elgin in 1858, and which you have now broken.'

'That was not a good treaty,' the Manchu spokesman remarked.

'Nevertheless, it was signed by you,' Parkes reminded him. 'But we are here to negotiate a new treaty.'

'Ah.' The Manchu brightened. 'Perhaps these terms will be more acceptable.'

'I wouldn't count on it,' Parkes muttered in English, and then proceeded to outline them. Michael studied the Manchu faces as Parkes listed the usual indemnity – far greater than before – the demand of the British government for an increase in the number of treaty ports – including several up the Yangtse, even as far as Hankow, which was either to ignore the existence of the Tai-p'ing altogether or a threat to negotiate direct with the God Worshippers if the Manchu refused to do so – the punishment of various offending commissioners and viceroys,

327

the cession in perpetuity of the territory of Kowloon, on the mainland opposite Hong Kong, the free movement of British and French nationals within China, and of course, the ultimate requirement, the establishment of British and French embassies within Peking itself.

The Manchu faces grew longer and longer as the list was enumerated, although Prince Ch'un did not appear to react at all, and could well have been fast asleep. He was not, however, for when Parkes had finished speaking and the Manchu spokesman was gazing at him in dismay, unable to reply, the Prince at last opened his eyes. 'These are many and varied requests,' he remarked. 'They will have to be studied. My brother the Emperor will inform you of his decision when this has been done. Until then, it is my brother's assumption that the invasion of your army into his territories will cease.'

'Providing that the Emperor's reply is not delayed,' Parkes told him. 'Our armies will remain in their present positions for a space of thirty days. On the thirty-first day from today our advance will be resumed.'

The Prince gazed at him. 'Thirty days,' he said, reflectively. 'Thirty days.'

He signalled his guard, who assisted him to his feet and into his palanquin, which was then carried out of the courtyard. The rest of his entourage remained while jasmine tea was served. 'I think that went off very well,' Lock said optimistically.

'That we shall have to wait and discover,' Parkes said. 'You don't look entirely happy, Mr Harrington.'

'I was wondering what would be the reaction of Lord Palmerston were a Chinese delegation to arrive in London demanding the cession of the Isle of Wight, an indemnity, and the right of free trade, with their own laws, in the ports of, shall we say, Plymouth, Portsmouth, Southampton, Dover, Harwich, Liverpool, and of course, London itself.'

Lock stared at him. 'That would depend, would it not, Mr Harrington, on whether the Chinese had recently defeated the British Army and the Royal Navy.' Then he turned his back on him and began speaking with Parkes and Lemarche.

Michael shrugged; it was really impossible to feel any affinity for a man who could only see one side of a question. Although had he not been like that himself, once? Besides, he had his own purpose to achieve here. He found himself standing next to one of the Manchu. 'My name is Michael Harrington,' he said. 'Perhaps you have heard of me.'

The Manchu frowned at him, obviously having done so. 'You are a member of this delegation.'

'Indeed. But I also represent my master, Hung Hsiu-ch'uan, the Right Hand of God.'

'You admit this?'

'I am proud of it. Should I not be? My master's arms have proved invincible throughout South China. That he was defeated outside Tientsin some years ago was due to the incompetence of his general, Yang Hsiu-ch'ing, who has since been executed. Now his armies have been reconstituted, and he awaits only my word to march on Peking itself. Will your bannermen or your Green Flags, be able to prevent this? My master disposes of a million men.'

The Manchu stroked his moustache. 'Why are you telling me this?'

'My master has no wish to turn China into a desert. He believes a course honourable to both the Emperor and himself can be found. He seeks a meeting with an imperial representative to discover this course.'

'Like dogs, when the dragon is ill,' the Manchu remarked, 'your master and his people seek to attach themselves to the coat tails of the British. But this dragon is not so ill, Englishman.'

'Irishman, if you don't mind,' Michael pointed out. 'I agree with you, my friend, but I would have you consider this: was not the dragon the symbol of Chinese might centuries before Nurhachi led the Manchu across the Great Wall? Consider this, and repeat my words to Prince Ch'un. The Emperor's private word to me is all that is necessary. And remember, too, that Hung Hsiu-ch'uan's army lies virtually at the gate of Shanghai.'

The Allied delegation left the next morning for the journey back to the encampment, in high spirits. 'Depend upon it,' Lock remarked. 'These fellows have no desire to hear British guns battering at the walls of Peking.'

As usual they were accompanied, at a distance, by a body of horsemen, who today were Green Flags, Michael noted – and also seemed larger in number than the bannermen of two days earlier. 'I think the sooner we regain the army the better,' he muttered to Parkes, having moved up to ride alongside the delegation's leader.

Parkes glanced at the distant horsemen. 'They look peaceable enough to me.'

'Maybe, but they are irregulars.'

'Is that important?'

'It could be. Were anything to happen, the Ch'ing could either take advantage of it, or disown the action and punish the offenders, depending on which circumstances might appear more favourable to them.'

'Oh, come now. They will hardly restart the war, having asked for the truce, until our ultimatum has at least been considered by the Emperor.'

'I think Prince Ch'un had plenipotentiary powers,' Michael told him. 'And whatever decision we are going to receive has already been made.'

'Well, we shall have to wait and find out. I am certainly not going to start fleeing from a bunch of bandits.'

Michael sighed. For all his lifetime in China, Parkes still could not grasp the fact that the Chinese also believed in naked force – when they were in a position to apply it. He was very tempted to ride like the devil himself, but that would be seen as an abandonment of his companions, and besides, he still hoped to hear from the Emperor, Hsien Feng, regarding a meeting with Hung.

So they proceeded on their way, at hardly more than a walk, and stopped for lunch as usual. To Michael's dismay not even a picquet was mounted, the Indian troopers being allowed to eat their curry and chappatis in a group some distance away from the white men.

'Those are curious fellows,' remarked Captain Lemarche, pointing at the Green Flags, who had moved perceptibly closer.

'They are interested in our habits,' Lock explained.

Michael studied the Manchu soldiers, who were now forming ranks. 'They are interested in us,' he snapped. 'I beg of you gentlemen, mount and ride.'

He leapt to his own feet, his meal only half eaten. Parkes also reached his feet, while the others looked around in surprise. But it was too late. At a signal the Green Flags had moved forward to block the roadway, while others had formed up behind. There was only the river on their right, and open country on their left – but there would be other horsemen waiting out there.

'Lieutenant Brown,' Michael snapped. 'Form your men into a perimeter and open fire the moment those fellows move. Gentlemen, we must ford the river and attempt to make our escape that way.'

'Here, I say,' Lock protested. 'Captain Lemarche is the ranking officer present. You are not even a soldier at all, Harrington.'

'For God's sake,' Michael shouted . . . but the Green Flags were already charging. The troopers, not yet alerted by their officer, had no time to form any kind of rank before they were surrounded. Michael drew his revolver and fired once, bringing down his man, but then he was struck by a horse and bowled over, and the afternoon became a kaleidoscope of horror, painfully reminiscent of that terrible day on the banks of the Pearl River, as they were kicked and beaten by their captors, tied by their wrists to horses' saddles, and dragged, stumbling and gasping, back to Tung Chow. Dimly he heard Lock protesting, but soon there was no breath for that, as the clouds of dust from the horses' hooves clogged their nostrils.

In Tung Chow there was the usual turnout of hooting, jeering, stick-wielding people, men and women. Here they were at least given a drink of water, but no rest, before their captors moved on again. If Michael had been looking forward to his first glimpse of the high purple walls of Peking, by the time they got there, in the middle of the night, he was past caring as his body jerked and bumped over the cobbles. The Manchu, he reflected with one of his few coherent thoughts, was like the leopard: he never changed his spots.

Full consciousness returned in another of the hideous underground cells looking on to an execution ground. Here they were again given water and fed, and then abandoned, twenty-four men packed almost shoulder to shoulder in a space intended for half that number.

'My word,' Lock gasped. 'The scoundrels. The utter scoundrels. When General Grant hears about this . . .'

'Is he going to hear about it?' Lemarche asked. He had cut his face and bled heavily; the blood had now dried but he was clearly weak, and he was going to be scarred for life. 'What is your opinion, Mr Parkes?'

'That the general can hardly fail to understand what has happened to us when we do not return. Besides, I imagine the Manchus will proffer some kind of ransom demand. As to whether General Grant will feel empowered to agree to it . . .' he shrugged.

'In which case we could be here a very long time,' Lock pointed out.

'I'm afraid that is possible. So . . . Harrington, how long were you imprisoned by the Manchu in Canton?'

'Several months.'

'Several months?' echoed Lieutenant Brown in consternation.

'And what did you do about it, sir?' Lock demanded.

'Not a lot. Because there was not a lot we could do. I seem to remember we prayed quite a bit.'

'And survived,' Parkes reminded him.

'Thanks to some outside help.'

'Well, we know that we also have outside help. Gentlemen, we must meet our situation like true-born Englishmen. And Frenchmen, of course,' he added hastily.

He did not mention true-born Indians, Michael thought, gazing at the troopers, who were clearly quite mystified by the mess their officers had got them in through lack of orders. But perhaps Parkes assumed, as they served the raj, that they counted as true-born Englishmen.

They had only been in the cell a few hours when the door was thrown open and an official peered at them – backed by a file of soldiers. 'Parkes,' he said. 'Parkes.'

Parkes hesitated, then got up.

'By God!' Lock exclaimed. 'Can they mean to execute you?'

'I must hope not,' Parkes said, and went through the door. There could be no doubting the fellow's courage, Michael thought.

Parkes was gone for some two hours, and then was almost thrown back into the cell. They crowded round him anxiously. 'My dear fellow,' Lock said. 'What have they done to you?'

Michael held the last of the water to Parkes' lips, and after a moment or two he was able to sit up. And even smile. 'Nothing irreparable,' he said. 'A few kicks. A few needles . . .' he looked down at his swollen hands, and shuddered.

'The swine,' Lock said. 'My God, they are swine.'

'They are worse than that,' Lemarche pointed out.

'What actually did they want?' Michael asked.

'They wanted me to sign, on behalf of us all, a document to the effect that the treaty agreed with Lord Elgin is invalid, and to indicate that the British and French governments agree to a new treaty between them and China.'

'Somewhat in their favour,' Michael suggested.

'Certainly not in ours.' Parkes looked from face to face. 'This we must remember. We must refuse to treat with them, except on the terms delineated by our governments. No matter what pressures are brought to bear. No matter what.' Again he looked from face to face.

'Of course,' Lock agreed. 'They will get nothing out of me.'

An hour later the door of the cell opened again. 'Parkes,' said the gaoler. 'Are you ready to return to an audience with Prince Ch'un?'

'I will return,' Parkes said, 'when the Prince has given orders for all of my companions to be released, and when he has indicated that he is willing to agree to the terms put forward by my colleagues and myself.'

The Manchu gazed at him for several seconds, then he grinned, looked them all over, one by one, and pointed at the lieutenant. 'That one.'

Brown gave a strangled exclamation as the guards forced their way into the cell and grasped his arms. In the crowded and confined area it might have been possible to overwhelm them, but the courtyard had suddenly filled with guards as well, and there were more in the corridor. And neither Parkes nor Lock gave any signal for revolt, although Brown called for help as he was taken away. 'For God's sake!' he shouted. 'For God's sake!'

'Act the man, sir,' Lock shouted back. 'Act the man.'

The subaltern was taken into the courtyard and there stripped, while the others looked on. 'My God!' Lock muttered. 'They're not going to castrate the poor boy?'

'Not yet,' Parkes told him. 'They are going to bastinado him. I wouldn't say that is an easier fate.'

Once again Michael's memory took him back to Canton in 1839, or indeed, to some of Hung's summary courts of justice since – but the victims he had then seen had all been either Chinese or Manchu, not only foreign to him in every way, but steeped in stoic fatalism. Brown was a white-skinned Englishman, with an Englishman's belief in hope. And he was very young. He was screaming in terror even before he was stretched naked in the dust and the first blows began to fall. Then his cries took on an almost animal-like quality of pain and humiliation.

His comrades watched in furious horror as the beating went on. Soon there was blood dribbling from his buttocks, and flying into the air with every stroke of the canes. And the strokes went on and on. The white body writhed and heaved, and piteous sounds issued from the boy's mouth. Until suddenly it lay still.

'They've murdered him,' Lock whispered in disbelief.

Water was thrown on Brown's head, and after a moment or two he stirred again. Immediately the beating recommenced. 'No,' he screamed. 'No.'

The secretaries, also young men, could look no longer, and collapsed in the bottom of the cell. It was not until Brown had received some four hundred strokes, and had fainted at least four times, that he was thrown back into the cell, without his clothes. Michael took off his shirt to bind over the lacerated flesh while the others stared in horror. 'I wonder,' Michael remarked, 'which of us is going to be next.'

His own mind was a turmoil. No response had been made to his overture, and he could not help but wonder if the knowledge that a secret emissary from Hung Hsiuch'uan was in the Allied party had at least partly influenced Prince Ch'un's decision to risk the wrath of General Grant by imprisoning them. In which case Michael himself was responsible for Brown's shocking treatment. But he had to reflect that if that were so, then why had he not immediately been tortured or executed?

The gaoler returned next morning, and when Parkes again refused to agree to scrap the treaty and sign a new one, one of the secretaries was given the bastinado, another horrifying display of pain and brutality; by then Brown was running a high fever and was clearly very weak; the secretary was no better when he was tossed back into their midst.

'By God, Parkes, but how long can this go on?' Lock demanded.

'We cannot betray our country's interests,' Parkes insisted. 'No matter if they execute us one by one.'

They looked at each other. They knew he was right, and they also could no doubt remember making some such statement themselves, theoretically, in the cool comfort of an officers' mess in Calcutta or Singapore or Hong Kong;

here in the broiling heat of a Peking cell, with two of their number bleeding and moaning on the ground at their feet, it was less easy to be heroic.

That afternoon another of the secretaries was flogged insensible, and Michael became aware of a mounting sense of hysteria in the cell. He did not feel so calm himself.

It was dusk when the door opened again and the gaoler looked in. 'Harrington,' he said. 'Harrington.'

'God speed you,' Parkes muttered as Michael went to the door and was seized by the arms and pulled outside. He braced himself for the coming ordeal, desperate not to shriek and beg like the younger men, wondering what the blows actually felt like – and discovered to his surprise that he was being marched past the gateway into the courtyard and into an outer guardroom of the prison. Here his wrists were bound behind his back, and a hood was dropped over his head, so voluminous that it fell past his shoulders, thus not only preventing him from seeing where he was being taken, but also making it impossible for any watcher to identify him.

He braced himself for some unexpected form of torture, and instead found himself being guided to a horse, and assisted to mount. The hands were rough, but no attempt was made to hurt him. He settled himself, and felt someone take his reins. Then the horse moved forward.

Presumably by now it was dark, and for a while the hooves struck cobbles. Then there was a challenge, answered with one word by his guards – they were speaking Manchu, and he could not understand what was being said. Now their speed increased, and the cobbles were left behind. So were the odours of the city, the barking of the dogs, and the explosions of the firecrackers with which the Chinese celebrated every event. Instead there was a cool breeze in his face.

Michael found it difficult to estimate how long they rode at a brisk trot, but at last the pace slowed, and then they stopped altogether. There came another challenge, and another reply. A gate creaked, and the horse moved forward again, its hooves once again striking cobbles. So, they had left Peking, and ridden across country for some distance, before coming to another . . . town? There could be no other town this close to the city – not as he recalled his map.

The horse stopped, and he was made to dismount. Men were talking around him, and then he was led from the courtyard and up some steps into what felt and sounded like a marble floor. Here the hood was taken from his head, and he blinked in the glare of the hundreds of candles which illuminated the huge chamber in which he stood. A chamber decorated with the richest drapes and carpets, the most exquisitely carved furniture, he had ever seen – the prevailing motif, that of the dragon, and the colour, yellow, told him that he was in an imperial palace.

There were half a dozen soldiers, presumably his escort, standing about him, while their commanding officer was speaking with two men, richly dressed but obsequious in manner, from whose high-pitched, somewhat harsh voices and hairless faces Michael recognized them to be eunuchs. The discussion completed, the eunuchs came forward to peer at him, wrinkling their noses in disgust at his naked torso and the stench of the cell. Then they beckoned him to follow them.

He glanced at the captain of his escort, who nodded. 'Go with these creatures, Harrington,' he said in Chinese.

Michael's heart had begun to pound quite hard as he had realized that he was being conducted to a private interview with someone who had to be interested in what Hung Hsiu-ch'uan had to say; now it slowed as he understood he was being given into the power of these 'creatures' as the captain had called them. But, with his wrists still bound behind his back, there was nothing for it. He followed them up to the head of the huge chamber, and there through a narrow doorway into a corridor, which opened into a much smaller reception room, in which the drapes concealing the walls and the carpeting were as rich as before, and there was but a single chair. The eunuchs motioned him to stand before the chair, and then one of them stepped behind the curtain on the further side of the room, leaving Michael with the other; he stood against the drapes with his arms folded, one hand resting on the hilt of his sword, gazing at his charge. Michael did not doubt he could strangle the fellow were his hands free, sword or no sword. But they were not free – and in any event, it could serve no purpose; he had little chance of escaping the palace, and every reason for being here.

So he waited, for perhaps half an hour, before the curtains parted again and several people entered. Four of them were eunuchs, but the other three were richly dressed and hirsute men, two of whom were armed. The third, unarmed, man sat in the single chair, gazing at Michael.

Michael gazed back, feeling very much as when he had first met Hung Hsiu-ch'uan. But in this case it was the whole demeanour, rather than the eyes alone, which suggested a total superiority to all other men. He was not tall, and indeed his boots hardly reached the floor when he was seated. He was also quite bald, and by no means old. His moustache was worn short and did no more than curve around his lips. The lips themselves were flat, the nose large and straight, the eyes cold. He sat with one hand on the arm of his chair, the other on his left knee, and Michael observed that the nails were worn long. His clothes were absolutely simple, a green silk tunic which stretched to his ankles, but fell away to reveal an imperial yellow robe beneath. There was no jewellery. But Michael knew he was in the presence of power, and bowed, as best he was able with his hands behind his back. 'Your Majesty,' he ventured as he straightened.

One of the eunuchs stepped forward and struck him across the face; his head jerked, and he tasted blood, and understood that he should not speak until addressed.

The man in the chair continued to regard him for several moments. Then he said, in Chinese, 'You claim to represent the bandit, Hung Hsiu-ch'uan. Yet you were with the party of foreign devils.'

He paused, and Michael looked at the eunuch.

'You may answer,' said the man in the chair.

'I could think of no other way to gain an audience, Your Majesty,' Michael said.

'You will address me as Your Highness,' the man said. 'I am I Hsin, Prince Kung. My brother is the Emperor.'

Michael bowed; it seemed the safest way of acknowledging the statement.

'You come to me,' Prince Kung said again, 'both as a foreign devil and as an emissary from a bandit. Tell me why I should not strike off your head.'

Michael inhaled sharply. 'Because, Your Highness, to execute me as a foreign devil, or indeed to execute any of my companions, will lead the British and the French to make war upon you. They will destroy your city.'

The two armed men moved their feet angrily, but Prince Kung motioned them to be patient.

'And to execute me as the representative of Hung Hsiu-ch'uan will not stop him from waging war upon you. Your Highness, only an ostrich buries his head in the sand. The wise man looks his problems in the face. Your Highness, it is a fact that Hung Hsiu-ch'uan controls virtually all China south of the Yangtse Kiang. It is a fact that he commands upwards of a million men. It is a fact that your bannermen have thus far proved incapable of standing against the Tai-p'ing except on one occasion, and then, as I have said, our general was incompetent. Is it not wise to appreciate these things?'

Prince Kung stared at him, while the room was silent, and yet, suddenly filled with an extra presence. The drapes along the inner wall moved as if there was a breeze, but the room was windowless, and the air became filled with a subtle scent. Michael felt the hair on his neck standing on end, and he could see that the other men in the room were similarly affected by the unseen presence.

Prince Kung rose and left the room without a further word. His two aides-de-camp went with him, accompanied by their eunuchs; only the original two remained, and they looked distinctly apprehensive.

Michael shared their feelings as he gazed at the trem-

bling drapes. He had no idea what to expect, was taken
utterly by surprise when they parted again to allow four
women to enter the room. Three of them took their places
behind the chair, while the eunuchs bowed. He decided
to do likewise, as the fourth woman seated herself in the
chair. Michael held his bow for a moment longer, afraid
actually to look at her, and she said, quietly, although
her voice had a touch of harshness about it, 'You may
straighten, Harrington. You may look upon me.'

Michael did so, and was even more surprised. For the
woman in the chair was hardly more than a girl, certainly
only in her middle twenties. She was by no means beautiful, for she had somewhat crowded features, and it was
impossible to determine her figure beneath the voluminous
robe she wore, but she exuded beauty, in her carriage, in
her clothes, for her outer robes consisted of a tunic in
imperial yellow, decorated with red dragons surrounding
the sun to which the emperors sacrificed, worn over a
skirt in which lines of white, blue, red and yellow formed
a huge vee pattern, while her headdress, also in yellow
and red, formed two huge wings above her ears; her hair
was mostly concealed beneath this outsize nurse's cap,
leaving her neck exposed, but the fringe visible above her
high forehead was jet black, and above all in her eyes,
huge and dark and luminous. And cold as ice, although
there could be no doubt that she was pleased by his
obvious admiration. 'You will tell me about this bandit,
Hung Hsiu-ch'uan,' she said. 'Remember that when you
speak to me, you are addressing His Celestial Majesty
himself. For I alone have his ear. I am the Principal
Concubine, Yi. My name is Tzu-hsi.'

13

The Kingdom of Heavenly Peace

Michael realized that he was obtaining a glimpse into the true power structure of the Manchu court. For the Emperor not to appear in person, but require his affairs to be handled by his brothers, was a perfectly natural oriental procedure – but for those brothers to yield in deference and, it seemed, authority, to a young woman who was only a principal concubine, was startling – and revealing.

Certainly she seemed arrogantly confident of her position. Yet she was only a girl. He wondered if she could be frightened. 'My master, Hung Hsiu-ch'uan, is a great and formidable man, Your Highness,' he said. 'He is great because he has vision, and power, and he is formidable because he commands the hearts and minds of the Chinese. He has sent me to tell you these things, Your Highness, that the Emperor may know of them.'

'Why?' Tzu-hsi asked.

The abrupt question surprised him. But there was no help for it. He drew another long breath. 'He means to restore China to the rule of the men of Han,' he said. 'He demands the withdrawal of the Manchu back to their homeland of Jehol. He will not trouble you there, Your Highness.'

Tzu-hsi stared at him, and the stare became a glare. Then she shouted a command in Manchu. Before Michael knew what was happening, he was kneeling before her, a eunuch's fingers twisted in his hair, while the other had drawn his sword. The ladies of the court clapped their hands in delight.

Michael tensed himself for the last blow he would ever feel, but that curious voice was speaking again, and he was dragged back to his feet and marched from her presence. She had exercised a woman's prerogative and changed her mind, which did not mean he was about to escape punishment. Instead of being taken back to the great reception hall he found himself hurried down some stairs into a small courtyard; here there were several more eunuchs who promptly stripped him of his clothing and stretched him on the earth, his wrists untied then held above his head as his ankles were similarly pinned. He was to be bastinadoed after all.

Now it was again necessary to tense himself, but to no avail. He hardly felt the first few blows, but then the pain began to build and become an agony, and he had to clench his teeth tightly to stop himself from crying out. Yet again, however, just when he found his resolution sagging, the blows ceased, and he was dragged back to his feet. He could hardly stand, and his body was coated with dust which had clung to his sweat and where he had unwittingly relieved himself – and once more he faced Tzu-hsi, standing with her ladies on a small balcony above him. The ladies were again delighted with him, clapping their hands and pointing and giggling behind their fans, but their mistress was solemn, her anger apparently having fled, her features and eyes quiet, and striking, as she stared at him for some minutes, taking in every aspect of his body.

'When we speak again,' she told him at last, 'perhaps you will have learned civility.'

He still did not know what to expect, especially with a woman so changeable. Nor could he be certain of his own feelings; furious outrage at the beating he had suffered at her command was oddly mingled with the sinister attractiveness she exuded. And the next few days were extremely pleasant, at least compared with the cell he had left. He was imprisoned alone, and the new cell had a cot bed. He was given good food to eat and as much water as he wished. He was left in peace while the pain in his buttocks gradually eased, and he was inspected every day by one of the eunuchs. When the torn flesh had healed he was actually taken out and allowed to bathe, and then given clean Chinese clothes to wear.

He could not help but wonder how his companions were faring – it was extremely doubtful that they were doing as well. And the only way he could help them was by gaining another interview with either Prince Kung or Tzu-hsi. This he constantly importuned the eunuchs who attended him to achieve, sure that they understood Chinese, but they preferred not to understand him. He had just about lost track of the days when he was commanded to bathe again, and shave, and having done that, was escorted through one of the subterranean passages in the building – which he had ascertained was the Summer Palace situated some miles away from Peking – and emerged into a sunken garden, where there was quite a crowd: the usual eunuchs, the usual ladies, a horde of yapping little dogs with curiously Chinese-like faces, all gathered round Tzu-hsi, who was the only one seated, in front of an easel on which she was painting – in water colours with some skill – a gardenia being held by one of her ladies. Michael was marched forward to stand beside the lady, and thus directly in front of Tzu-hsi, facing the rest of the entourage. However his anger at her still seethed in his mind, he knew he was once again under her spell.

She did not appear immediately to notice him, and kept on making bold strokes with her brush, then she said, 'As you have cleaned yourself and dressed yourself, Harrington, have you also learned civility?'

'I am your most humble servant, Your Highness,' Michael replied. 'But I have always understood that the greatest of all incivilities is to lie.'

Her head turned, sharply, and she glared at him. He tensed himself for another explosion of rage, but this time her anger appeared to subside very quickly. 'Your soldiers are marching upon Peking,' she said. 'They have defeated my army. My soldiers are weaklings.' Her voice was loaded with contempt. 'What can be done about this, Harrington?'

'You must release the delegation, Your Highness. Immediately.'

Tzu-hsi added another stroke to her flower. 'They too are weaklings,' she remarked. 'Some have died.'

Brown, Michael supposed. And the young secretary. And who else?

'The foreign devils will wish an indemnity,' Tzu-hsi said. 'Always an indemnity. They wish to take all the silver in China.'

'An indemnity would be better than having them burn Peking, Your Highness.' Another shaft of pure venom was directed at him, but now he knew she was afraid. 'And those who are yet living must be released.'

'And you?' she asked. 'You are not truly a member of the delegation. There is no reason for me to release you, Harrington.' She seemed to like saying his name.

Michael bowed. 'My fate is to serve my master until the day of my death, Your Highness.' He could be as unctuous as any mandarin.

Another glare. 'And what will you say when I bring your "master" here in an iron cage, and take away his manhood, and place his head upon a stake?'

Michael bowed again; he also knew she was susceptible to flattery. 'When you have done that, Your Highness, why, you will command my allegiance, because you will have proved yourself the greater of the two.'

She stared at him, then threw down her brush and got to her feet, speaking in Manchu. He expected some other physical onslaught, but she merely left the garden, followed by her people and dogs. He was returned to his cell, unharmed.

And remained there, for certainly more than another week, still well cared for. The principal concubine was clearly undecided as to his fate. Just as she was clearly the only one who *could* decide his fate. His mind became clouded with unthinkable thoughts, in which the memory of another princess played its part, but also, as the man in him could not help but still resent the flogging she had inflicted, an imagined sequence of events which would have Hung entering this palace in triumph, and the principal concubine stretched at his feet in suppliance.

Another bath meant another audience, and another surprise. For this took place in Tzu-hsi's boudoir, it seemed, and the eunuch left him at the door, although he remained in the doorway, with drawn sword.

Tzu-hsi sat in an armchair, and her hair was loosed as she wore no headdress. It was the longest hair Michael had ever seen, longer even than Jalina's. With her was a single lady, who on this occasion gave him a slight bow as he entered. My God, he thought . . . but dare she risk it? Then must she indeed be all-powerful.

'Be seated,' Tzu-hsi commanded, and he perched himself on the one other chair in the room. The door beyond stood open, and he could see a huge bed. His heart began to pound. It was not merely that he had been chaste now for several months, or that the luxurious scents and furnishings with which he was surrounded were affecting his senses; it was not even the undoubted sensuality of the principal concubine herself. It was the thought that he might be at the very heart of Manchu power, from each beat of which went the directives to all the viceroys and commissioners throughout the far-flung empire. And be about to enter that heart itself? What would Hung say to that?

'I have released the foreign devils,' Tzu-hsi said. 'Those of them that survived.'

'Did many die, Highness?'

'Too many. Only the man Parkes, and the man Lock, and some of the dark soldiers, were sent back.'

Michael sighed. 'It will be a heavy indemnity.'

'I await news of it. But it is done. Now I would speak of the bandit Hung. Tell me again, and tell me the truth. Is he as formidable as you say?'

'He is more formidable than the British and the French, Your Highness,' Michael said. He was sure he was telling the truth.

'Then he must be crushed. Once the foreign devils have left my soil, my armies will defeat him, and bring him to Peking in an iron cage.'

'Your armies, Your Highness?' Michael could not resist the question.

Her eyes flashed at him, then she smiled. 'Cannot a woman command armies, Harrington? There have been famous empresses in history. Perhaps it is not my fate ever to be an empress. But the Emperor is sickly, and his brothers . . .' she allowed her clenched fist to open, violently, to express her contempt.

'Yet, should the Emperor die,' Michael ventured.

'I will be as nothing,' Tzu-hsi acknowledged. 'Unless . . . I have a son. Did you know of this, Harrington? A son who is yet a babe. That is why I am the principal concubine. My son will rule. While yet a babe.'

'It is a dangerous role you pursue, Your Highness.'

Tzu-hsi gave a brittle laugh. 'And when you learn that I have been taken from my bed in the night, and strangled with a silken cord, will you smile, or weep, Harrington?'

'I will weep, Your Highness,' Michael said, not at all sure he was lying.

Tzu-hsi gazed at him. 'Then you must help to make sure that it does not happen. You have brought the bandit Hung great good fortune, Harrington. You may do the same for me. You will remain here, as my prisoner. I can offer you no more than that, at the moment. However, should my circumstances change, then I will make you my adviser in matters pertaining to the Tai-p'ing, and to the foreign devils.'

Michael bit his lip. Things were getting out of hand.

'You do not wish to do this? As I rise to greatness, so will you.'

There was no way he could refuse her, or tell her about Alicia or Wu Yei, and live. She had a good deal of the dragon in her soul. 'You do me an honour above my station, Your Highness,' he said.

'I was but the daughter of a humble Manchu banner-man,' Tzu-hsi said, 'who was noticed for her beauty, and

346

chosen for the bed of my lord. And see where circumstances have conspired to place me. Who knows where they may place you, Harrington? Now, I would speak with you further, in private.' She turned her head to address her lady, who frowned and appeared to demur, while Michael's heart began to pound again. But he was not to discover just what the principal concubine had in mind, for suddenly there was a good deal of commotion outside, and a moment later several armed men appeared in the doorway, looking very agitated.

Tzu-hsi snapped at them, but they stood their ground, and her anger dissolved into fear. She stood up and gave orders to her lady, who had been joined by several others. Then she looked at Michael. 'The foreign devils still come,' she said. 'They are at the gates of Peking.'

'Allow me to intercede for you,' he offered.

'You wish me to surrender to the foreign devils? That can never be. The Emperor is preparing to leave for Jehol. I must go with him.' She hesitated, considering him, then gave an order. Immediately several of the eunuchs surrounded him.

'And I must die?' Michael asked, his earlier ebullience fading into despair.

Tzu-hsi's face softened. 'No,' she said. 'I would not have you die. But you cannot accompany me to Jehol. I do not yet command that much power. You will remain here, and await the foreign devils. They will scarcely harm you.'

She had made another of her lightning changes of mind, and it occurred to Michael that the main reason for the utter inability of the Ch'ing government to cope with any crisis might not be, as was generally supposed, the ineptitude of the Emperor, but the caprices of the young woman who was so obviously in the process of usurping his power. In that case the country was indeed Hung's for the taking, and necessarily so, if it was to remain a coherent whole and not fly apart into a million splinters.

If he was ever going to be allowed to regain Hung and tell him that vital piece of information.

But at least her fear of being taken by the foreign devils had not driven her to command his death. He was returned to his cell and abandoned there, some food and water being left with him. However, he did not have long to wait.

The Summer Palace fell silent as the last of the servants departed behind their fleeing masters and mistresses, for perhaps a couple of hours, then Michael heard other sounds, the clanking of arms and the jingling of harnesses, and shouts of command, in French. 'Hello!' he shouted. 'Hello!'

It seemed no one heard him. For the shouts were changing from those of men expecting battle to men discovering an abandoned treasure trove. There was laughter and boasting, and the sounds of destruction from above him. He had to wait another few hours before at last there were booted feet in the corridor outside his cell, and the door was thrust in. 'Mon Dieu!' said the officer who peered at him. And then launched into French so quickly that Michael, who in any event knew little of the language, could not understand.

'Harrington,' he said. 'I am Michael Harrington.'

The officer peered at him some more, then beckoned him from the cell and took him up the stone stairs. They emerged into an antechamber, and into the midst of total chaos. Baggy-red-breeched poilus ran to and fro, waving their spoils, from priceless drapes to gold lamps and ornaments. There had obviously been a total breakdown of discipline, as the French conscripts had been confronted with more wealth than any of them had seen before in their lives. Michael was happy to be taken into the courtyard where there was a group of officers, regarding the destruction of the Ch'ing wealth with gloomy, and somewhat envious, admiration.

One of these spoke English. 'Michael Harrington! They said you were dead, taken away to be executed.'

'Well, I survived. I'd be grateful if you could lend me a horse and direct me to General Grant's headquarters.'

'I think General Grant will soon be here,' the officer said.

Michael now became aware that from the direction of Peking there was the rumble of artillery and the rattle of musketry; the city was indeed being taken by assault. He was given food and wine by his French rescuers, who told him that Captain Lemarche was amongst those who had been murdered by the Manchu, and then left him to sleep. When he awoke at dawn some semblance of discipline had been restored, and the regiment was preparing to march off, on the arrival of General Grant and his staff.

'Harrington?' Grant was equally astonished. 'We were told you had got the chop.'

'No, sir.'

Grant stared at him. 'Just about everyone else did. Except for Parkes and Lock. And they are both in hospital.'

'Yes, sir.'

'But you are alive. And well. And wearing Chinese clothes.' Clearly he found something sinister about the business.

'Yes, sir. Prince Kung, who it seems is something of a rival to his brother, Prince Ch'un, wished to interview me privately.' He had decided to keep Tzu-hsi out of it.

'I see. Did you compromise our terms?'

'No, sir. The Prince was more interested in learning about the Tai-p'ing. He knew my name, you see..'

'Ha! Well, a dozen good fellows have been murdered by these monsters. These princes will have to answer for that. I was told this is their home in the summer. Where are they now?'

'They have fled, Sir James. For their homeland of Jehol.'

'By God, the cowards.' Grant put his hands on his hips and stared at the palace. 'Their summer home, eh? We'll make sure they don't come back.' He beckoned his adjutant. 'Where is Captain Gordon?'

'Here, sir.' The captain, wearing the red tunic and dark blue breeches with the heavy red stripe of the Royal Engineers, stepped forward and saluted. He was a tall, slim young man, twenty-eight years old, with bright, alert features and a small military moustache.

'Burn this place, Gordon.'

The captain gulped as he looked at the centuries-old palace, the magnificent carvings on the walls, the priceless windows; however looted by the French, it remained an outstanding work of Manchu art. 'Burn it, sir?'

'Burn it to the ground. We don't want to leave a stone of it standing.'

'Yes, sir.' Captain Gordon saluted again and hurried off.

Michael was aghast. 'You can't be serious, Sir James.'

'It will make these scoundrels realize they cannot murder Englishmen with impunity.'

'But . . .' it seemed such an act of schoolboy vengeance. 'To destroy such a beautiful building . . . it has already been desecrated by the French.'

'Yes,' Grant said. 'Our people were left to do the fighting, while they did the looting. Damned frogs. But we'll do the burning, by God. Now come along, you'll want to see Parkes. I know he'll want to see you.'

Michael looked across to where Gordon was commanding his men to prepare their combustibles. The young captain met his gaze, and shrugged.

Parkes was cold. He seemed to feel that Michael had somehow acted dishonourably in allowing himself to be separated from the rest of the party, and worse, in surviving, apparently little the worse for wear. That he and Lock had also been separated from the rest of the party, and had also survived, did not appear relevant – they had been threatened with execution and had been half starved. 'I am sure we are grateful for all you must have contributed to our cause, Harrington,' he said. 'And I will make sure it goes into my report. But now I imagine you are in a hurry to regain Shanghai. Good day to you.'

He did not offer to shake hands, and Michael went out

of the field hospital, and gazed at the clouds of smoke rising into the air a few miles away. Tzu-hsi's boudoir would have been consumed by now. He wondered if the painting of the gardenia had still been there, or if she had taken it with her. He wondered if she would ever return to continue her intrigues.

And he wondered if these men, who stood around him and pointed at the smoke and laughed, really understood what they were about. He thought Gordon had.

Ward, released at least in part because of Michael's earlier intercession, accompanied him back to Shanghai. 'I don't think they understand what they are about,' the American remarked. 'Very few of us do. Governments, in our society, are supposed to be elected by intelligent people, but when a man comes to think about politics and voting he ceases to be intelligent, and is just a puppet, manipulated by the guy who can appeal to his basest instincts. Wealth, power, or just plain greed, they hide them under words like national pride, prestige, honour . . . it turns your stomach. I don't reckon there is a single family in Britain would go without a meal if you guys pulled right out of China and let these people get on with their lives. But in the name of national honour you kill, and maim, and burn, and destroy priceless works of art. Oh, don't get me wrong, we're just as bad. There's an election going on at home right this minute, and there's talk that Senator Lincoln will win it. He's standing on an anti-slavery platform. How do you feel about that?'

'He'd get my vote,' Michael said.

'Sure he would. He'd get mine, too. But then, you see, I'm from Salem, Massachusetts, not from Charleston, South Carolina. The folks down there, and in most of the southern States, are pro-slavery, and so anti-Lincoln that there's talk if he's elected they'll secede from the Union. There's democracy, eh?'

'So what will happen?' Michael asked.

'Search me. All I know is that the nation which has the potential to be the greatest in the world is going to fall

351

apart. Sure makes a nonsense of everything our ancestors died for.'

'You going home now?'

'No, sir. I don't have a ship, anyway. But it seems your people have had a change of heart. Apparently Hung Hsiu-ch'uan has been making warlike moves towards Shanghai recently. I guess he heard how the Manchu were preparing to take your army on, and felt that now was the time to buck the British and get away with it. So they've told me to go back and raise my army, if I can.'

'God damn,' Michael said.

'Because you're going back to Hung?'

'Yes.'

'You know, I'd be really happy if you were to join me.'

'Sorry. I can't.'

'Your family is in Nanking. I can understand that you have to go back and get them out. But you said you were quitting.'

'Maybe I am.'

Ward frowned at him. 'But you won't fight for the Manchu?'

'I'm more than ever convinced that Hung and the Tai-p'ing are the sole hope for the future of China. The Manchu are in a mess. If Hung were to strike north now he could bring the whole rotten edifice down.'

'And take another twenty million lives.'

'They're liable to die anyway. Ward, the Manchu are rotten, from core to skin. You have got to realize that.'

Ward grinned. 'It's a point of view. I happen to feel the same way about your Mr Hung.'

'That's because you've never met him.'

'I mean to, one day. Along the barrel of a gun. You ever met any of the Manchu?'

Michael hesitated. Yes, he thought. The most formidable little girl I have ever encountered. But successful empires aren't ruled by little girls who change their minds every few minutes and fall in and out of love as often as that too. That knowledge was his secret. 'Yes,' he said.

'A couple of the princes. Not one of them has Hung's drive or determination.'

'But they're there. Hung isn't.'

Michael sighed. 'You won't stop him, you know.'

'A disciplined few against a mob? I guess we'll just have to wait and see.'

They gazed at each other, and Michael was reminded of the young Yang Hsiu-ch'ing, so totally confident. He was reminded, too, of his own thoughts as he had first seen the Tai-p'ing horde unloosed at Fu-chang, that a regiment of Wellington's Peninsular veterans would have shattered them in minutes. But Ward did not have veterans, or Englishmen. He was seeking to create something which had never existed in China.

'It's just possible that I may be at the other end of that gun too,' he said.

'I would sure hate that,' Ward agreed.

But neither would, or perhaps could, change their point of view. Michael supposed their situation was very akin to that obtaining in the United States at that very moment, according to Ward himself, where men who presumably could meet and be friends on almost every count, differed inexorably on the one that mattered. It was easy for him to consider Ward absolutely deluded, to feel certain that if he could see the singleminded fanaticism Hung was capable of inspiring, or the inept indecision of the principal concubine – much less both – he would have to realize his mistake. But then, Ward no doubt considered that Michael himself was blinded by fanaticism. Certainly he meant to tell Hung just how little risk would attend a march on Peking, especially with the Ch'ing royal family hiding in Jehol. One more campaign could well unite the entire country, north and south, behind the Tai-p'ing. And enact that imagined scene, of Tzu-hsi, bound and helpless, before the warlord? He was not sure whether he wanted that to happen or not.

Because he was unsure of so many things. It was almost like 1849 all over again. He had promised to send Alicia and the children back to Singapore to resume their lives as English gentlefolk. He had intended to accompany them. But to what was he going? Ali reigned supreme in the Hammond world, and to that world, at least as represented by the men who had burned the Summer Palace, Michael Harrington was something of a traitor. He could expect no support from anyone. Not even Alicia? For ten years he had not been sure about that, where once, briefly, he had basked in its heady expectancy.

But if he let her go, this time, and remained with the Tai-p'ing, he knew he would never see her again. Or the children.

Although there had been several clashes between the Manchu bannermen and the Tai-p'ing in the towns and villages upriver from Shanghai, the lower Yangtse was a peaceful place, due in part to the presence of a British man-of-war, although the Navy had instructions not to interfere in any internal Chinese squabbles, as the Tai-p'ing revolt was apparently considered in London, unless actually fired upon. Trade upriver was however only attempted by the bolder spirits, and it took Michael several weeks to find a place on a sampan prepared to go west, and even then the captain would only take him as far as Chinkiang, situated at the southern end of the Grand Canal, and which was in Tai-p'ing hands. The watch on the city gate seemed amazed to discover that the white man wearing Chinese clothing who stepped ashore was Michael Harrington, and word was immediately sent to the garrison commander, to whose house Michael was taken in haste. 'I must have transport to Nanking, immediately,' Michael told him. 'I have important information to give the Great Hung.'

'Of course, Mr Harrington, of course,' the general agreed. 'Horses will be made ready for you; they will serve your purpose more quickly than the river. But you must be exhausted. It is necessary for you to sleep, and eat, and rest.'

Michael supposed he was right; he was exhausted. He

slept soundly, and next morning a horse was waiting for him, together with an escort of five men under a captain, a man named Lo Tang, whom he knew well as they had campaigned together. 'It is good to have you back, Mr Harrington,' Lo Tang said as they rode out of the city gate. 'The Great Hung will be pleased that you are returned safe and sound.'

They followed the riverbank, where there was a good track. 'And is all well in Nanking?' Michael asked.

'All is well, Mr Harrington. The army prepares to march on Shanghai.'

Just in time, Michael thought. If he could direct them away from a clash with the British, or with Frederick Ward for that matter, and head them north, persuade Hung and Wei that a dash on Peking would gain them the ultimate triumph they sought, then the end of the war might be in sight. 'And my family?' he asked.

'I am sure you will find out how they are soon enough, Mr Harrington,' Lo Tang said. But his voice had subtly changed. Michael turned his head and frowned, and the captain drew rein; they had entered a woody copse, and were out of sight of the traffic on the river; west of Chinki-ang this was all Tai-p'ing controlled. 'I have a message from the Great Hung for you, Mr Harrington.'

The rest of the escort had also reined their horses.

'Concerning my family? Then why the devil didn't you give it to me earlier?'

'I do not know if it concerns your family, Mr Harrington,' Lo Tang said carefully. 'Although I would suppose it does. And it was My Lord Hung's command that the message be given to you at this place.' He felt in his saddlebag, and brought out a length of silken rope. 'It is My Lord Hung's command that you use this cord, Mr Harrington.' He indicated the branches of the trees. 'Here is material enough.'

Michael stared at him in utter consternation. That Hung was capable of quite irrational rages he had known for years, since the death of Yang. But something quite as coldblooded as this was impossible . . . and when he

355

had so much to offer. He licked his lips. 'There must be a mistake,' he said.

'I was given the instruction by My Lord Hung himself,' Lo Tang said.

'Well, I still say he has made a mistake. I will not use the cord. I will return with you to Nanking and see Hung myself.'

'Mr Harrington,' Lo Tang said gravely. 'I am instructed by My Lord Hung that if you do not use the cord of your own free will, my men and I are to remove your head and your genitals and bring them to him. That will be a distasteful task for me to have to carry out where an old comrade in arms is concerned, and it will be painful and humiliating for you. As well as damnable. How may a man enter heaven with his body in three parts?'

'Then tell me the truth about my family.'

Lo Tang shrugged. 'It is my understanding that My Lord Hung has commanded their execution also. Except for your daughter, who the Great Hung would take to his bed.'

Michael gazed at him while his stomach filled with lead and he heard the rasp of swords being drawn from behind him. So why not take the cord and hang himself, like an honourable Chinese? What did he have to live for, if Alicia and Wu Yei and Ralph and Hung Cho had already been murdered, and Joanna was about to be prostituted? Only revenge. The lead in his belly seemed to be turning molten. Alicia had feared this would happen. She had never trusted Hung, had never been able to perceive his greatness. Because, Michael realized, there had never been any greatness to perceive. He had allowed himself to be deluded, out of gratitude in the beginning, perhaps, and then, as he now had to admit, out of a stubborn refusal to admit he could have been so wrong. So, live, until he had squeezed the last breath from the betrayer's lungs. And on the way to that goal, destroy every Tai-p'ing on whom he could lay his hands.

He had not felt such a surge of demoniac energy since he had leapt from the cliff in Palawan.

Lo Tang was extending the cord again. He had not drawn his own weapon, because Michael was apparently unarmed; Lo Tang had not troubled to ascertain whether or not his victim carried the deadly revolver . . . in fact, the Chinese had never properly grasped the worth of the six-chambered weapon – whose butt pressed against Michael's stomach where it nestled under his blouse.

He stretched out his left hand for the cord, and thrust his right under the blouse. Lo Tang reached forward, and then realized what was happening. He jerked backwards, drawing his sword as he did so, and Michael shot him through the chest. In the same movement he was wheeling his horse to face the drawn swords behind him. They shouted and rode at him, and he fired as rapidly as he could, without taking proper aim. Only three men fell, and one of the survivors brought Michael's horse to the ground with a thrust. Michael stepped out of the stirrups and turned to fire again, but the hammer fell on an empty chamber, and the two men were now riding at him, swinging their swords.

He hurled himself behind a tree, stumbled and heard a blade biting into the wood above his head. He was helpless against them without a weapon, and he had none. But when he scrambled past the next tree he suddenly found himself on the riverbank, gazing at the swirling current. It was a long twelve years since he had had to swim for his life, and in the interim he had not really swum at all, seriously. But it was his only hope. As the horses surged nearer he threw up his arms and dived.

The doors of the inner apartments of the Nanking palace crashed open. 'It is the Great Hung,' announced the major-domo in a mixture of fear and awe.

Alicia had been sitting at her needlework, Wu Yei and Joanna beside her; it was their principal relaxation, and Wu Yei, anxious to become westernized in all things in order to please Michael, had proved as apt a pupil as she had once been a teacher. In the courtyard behind them, Ralph and Hung Cho practised their swordplay. Ralph

357

was sixteen now, a big strong boy who looked like his father, and who worshipped his older brother. Her family, Alicia thought, feeling like a matriarch. Gathered around her, at the moment of crisis – which she had known for two years, or perhaps for many years before that, since Hung had looked upon her in the fisherman's hut – would one day arise.

Having been aware for so long of the shadow beneath which she lived, she was more in control of herself than she had feared would be the case, as she rose to her feet. Yet the fear was there, lurking at the edges of her subconscious, threatening to overwhelm her. Perhaps it had been there even when Michael had been in Nanking. Michael might be bigger, stronger, and, she believed, bolder and tougher than Hung or any of his followers, yet was he but one man, and he had this peculiar ability to see in Hung something over and above mere humanity – hardly a fault as it was an emotion shared by several million people. Of course the idea that Hung would ever dare attempt to take Joanna into his harem was impossible, at least as long as Michael lived – whatever his lusts, he had been careful never to indulge them on the families of his principal officers. Yet the mere fact that he lusted . . . because he did, every time he saw either of them.

And the lust had grown with Michael's departure. He had made a point of calling at the Harrington house, at least once a week, to bring her up to date with the news, so far as he was aware of it. Thus she had been told of the great British armament sailing up the coast from Hong Kong, undoubtedly with Michael aboard, and later, of the clash between the British and French and the Manchu. Hung had been pleased about that, and had almost made up his mind to follow Wei Ch'ang-hui's advice, and take advantage of the mutual embroilment of his two enemies to seize Shanghai. Yet had his caution prevailed. Then there had been a hiatus in the news, and Hung had ceased to call. Alicia had been beside herself with worry. But now . . . she faced Hung as he strode into the private chamber, his ever-present guards at a respectful distance behind him.

His gaze roamed over the three women, and then looked through the open doors at the young men, who had ceased their fencing to bow at his entrance. He went to the doors first. 'That is good,' he said. 'Would that all of my soldiers practised as assiduously. But it is not good to have drawn swords in the presence of the Right Hand of God. Lay them down.'

Hung Cho obeyed immediately. Ralph glanced at his mother and received a quick nod before obeying.

'Now come here,' Hung commanded.

This time both the boys obeyed immediately.

'Stand over there,' Hung commanded, pointing to the wall.

Once again they obeyed, shoulder to shoulder, sweating, muscular arms touching; if Ralph was already the taller, Hung Cho was the heavier-set.

Alicia watched the guards stand beside them, and felt her stomach muscles tighten.

Hung faced her. 'I have sad news, Alicia,' he said.

Alicia inhaled, and heard a low moan from Wu Yei; she also had feared, although the women had deliberately not discussed their fears.

'Michael is dead,' Hung announced.

They stared at him. The statement had been so bald.

'I wish it were otherwise,' Hung went on. 'He returned from the British, to Shanghai, and took a sampan to Chenkiang. There my governor welcomed him, and gave him horses, and an escort to Nanking. But they were beset by bandits. I will have their heads, you may be sure of that.'

'And Michael was killed, Great Hung?' Wu Yei asked in a low voice.

'Alas, yes, together with four of my people. The survivors arrived not an hour ago. They say that Michael fought like a devil, as we know he would, but that he was cut down and fell into the river, and that they saw him drown.'

Joanna gave a gasp, and her knees gave way; no one moved as she sank into a chair. 'She is but a child,' Hung remarked kindly.

'Is it possible to speak with these men, the survivors of the escort?' Wu Yei asked.

Hung frowned at her. 'What is the point of that? Michael is dead. There is an end to the matter.'

Alicia could see blood rushing into Wu Yei's face, and made herself speak, to avoid a crisis, where she wanted only to lie down and weep. 'Was Michael's body regained, Great Hung?'

'Alas, no,' Hung told her.

Alicia bowed her head. 'Then am I a widow, as is Wu Yei. As our children are orphans. We are useless mouths for you to feed, Great Hung. We have neither talent nor strength to offer you, in Michael's death. I beg you to provide us with a sampan that we may descend the river.'

'To surrender to the Manchu?' Hung was amazed.

'To surrender to the British, Great Hung. They are my people. They will welcome us, and restore us to my family. That is the only course open to us.'

'Come here,' Hung said.

Alicia hesitated, then went to him.

He took her hand. 'Do you suppose I do not know my duty, Alicia?' he asked. 'Michael was my friend, my comrade. We have ridden shoulder to shoulder, at least mentally, for twenty-two years. I have no older follower.'

Because you have killed them all, Alicia thought. Oh, my God, because you have killed them all.

'So do you think, now that Michael is dead, that I am going to cast you out?' Hung asked. 'Send you back to the foreign devils, a supplicant? You are my care for the rest of your life, Alicia. You and your children.' He glanced at Ralph, briefly, and then allowed his gaze to linger on Joanna, who was remembering her manners and pushing herself back to her feet. 'It is my determination,' Hung said, 'to take you into my household, and treat you as my own. It is the least I can do, as Michael died for me, in my service.'

Alicia stared at him, what he was saying only just sinking in.

Wu Yei reacted more promptly. 'Liar!' she screamed. 'Liar! You want them for yourself. You have had Michael murdered. Liar!'

Hung stared at her in consternation, totally taken aback by the outburst.

'Murderer!' Wu Yei screamed, and ran into the yard.

'Arrest that woman!' Hung snapped, and four of his guards moved forward.

Wu Yei had reached the discarded swords and picked one up. This she now whirled above her head, at the same time calling on her son to avenge his father. Hung Cho hesitated, then ran forward, to be checked by a sword presented at his throat. Ralph also made to move and Alicia recovered her senses. 'No,' she screamed. 'Ralph!'

He hesitated in turn, and had his arms seized by the guards. Wu Yei had already been disarmed by the men who had easily avoided her attempts to wield the sword. Now she panted, plump body straining against her enemies.

'Hang her,' Hung said. 'Hang her, for daring to attempt the murder of the Right Hand of God.'

'No,' Alicia begged. 'No, Hung, please.'

He ignored the disrespect of her address, looked at her.

'Spare her life,' Alicia begged. 'And . . .' she bit her lip. But she had nothing to offer, where he was about to take.

Yet was he apparently pleased, and mollified. 'If I spare her life, you will come willingly into my household? With your children?'

Alicia drew a long breath. 'I will, Great Hung.' Oh, Joanna, she thought. My poor dear girl. But it was the only way she knew of saving any of their lives, and she could not doubt it was the decision Michael would have taken, had he lived. Had he lived, she thought. This was the third time she had been informed of his death – and on the first two occasions he had come back to her, each time different, stronger and more purposeful. Oh, pray to God that he could do so a third time, to avenge what was going to happen to his daughter. But that had to be a dream.

'You will remain here, Wu Yei,' Hung said. 'With your son, until your temper improves. You, Alicia, take your children to my palace. I will send for your things. There is a litter waiting.'

Alicia bowed and beckoned Joanna and Ralph to accompany her. Ralph just had the time to pull on his blouse as they were hurried out of the house and down the steps to the waiting litter – and another escort of Hung's personal bodyguard. This was the third house she had called her own from which she had also been dragged, Alicia thought.

The drapes fell shut, and the journey through the streets began. 'Is Father really dead, Mother?' Joanna asked.

Alicia didn't know what to say to that. To allow the girl to hope . . . 'We must believe that he is.'

'Then what made Aunt Wu so angry?' Ralph wanted to know. 'She was dreadfully rude to the Great Hung.'

'Yes,' Alicia said. 'I suppose she was.'

'I think he is being awfully kind,' Joanna said. 'Taking us into his own home.'

'Yes,' Alicia said. The journey had been a short one, and they were already entering the courtyard of the Palace of God. The litter was set on the cobbles, the drapes were drawn, and Alicia stepped down into the midst of bowing guards and officers. They are treating me like a queen, she thought. Well, am I not the mother of the Great Hung's latest queen? If only there was some way she could inform Joanna of what was about to happen to her . . . without immediately driving the girl into hysterics.

They were taken in a side entrance, through corridors she had not seen before; her visits to the Palace of God had been only on state occasions. When they reached a cross corridor they were met by other officers. 'The boy will come with us,' one said.

'Where?' Alicia snapped.

The officer bowed. 'Is he not a man, great lady? He belongs with men.'

Alicia sighed, but again there was nothing she could do. 'Will I see him again?'

'Of course, great lady. Whenever the Great Hung wills it.'

'I can take care of myself, Mother,' Ralph said.

Alicia embraced him, and watched him being led away. One by one, she thought. The family with whom she had been so content. One by one.

The officers were waiting, and they were led on to a silk-draped doorway where they were greeted by several eunuchs; Hung had assumed entirely the trappings of empire, as interpreted by previous Chinese rulers. These bowed in turn. 'Great ladies, you will come with us.'

Now they were leaving the world of men and entering that of women, and sexuality. Here there were subtle scents and sounds, pleasant and unpleasant, whiffs of exotic perfume followed by traces of body odour, giggles of laughter mingling with the sound of weeping. The hall in which they stood was empty, but for the eunuchs, and empty of furniture too, save for a single carved chair, from where, no doubt, Hung reviewed his harem when the mood took him, Alicia supposed. She and Joanna followed three of the eunuchs the length of the hall, their slippered feet whispering on the marble floor. At the far end another silk drape with a dragon design was pulled aside, and they were ushered into a small antechamber, off which radiated several corridors. They were led down the centre of these, until they arrived at a closed door, upon which the leading eunuch knocked. Instantly it was opened, by another of the harem guards, but this one more richly dressed than the others.

'The Lady Alicia, and the Lady Joanna,' their escort said.

This new eunuch bowed. 'You are expected, great ladies. Will you not enter?'

Alicia realized that her throat was dry and her stomach light, where Joanna was clearly fascinated by her novel surroundings. They went into another antechamber, and then through a curtained doorway into a much larger room, where Alicia paused in dismay. Here were several other women, most of them young and even attractive, but from their dress clearly servants, as well as another half dozen eunuchs; they had been sitting, and reading or sewing, but now they hastily rose to their feet and bowed, while Alicia looked past them, at Malama.

It was now seven years since she had seen Malama, but the seven years need never have been, from the point of view of the Indian girl. Because she was still a girl, Alicia thought enviously; she was still only thirty-five years old. But for those seven years she had lived as the chief consort of the Right Hand of God, and she had assimilated her position. She had been seated on a kind of throne, watching her servants at work. Now she too rose, although she did not bow. Her body, as slender as Alicia remembered it, was encased from neck to ankles in a tight-fitting imperial yellow silk tunic dress, which also descended to her wrists. The nails on the two smallest fingers of each hand had been allowed to grow to a length of several inches, to indicate that she exerted herself to eat and sign her name, and nothing else. Her midnight hair was gathered in a vast chignon, and through it was thrust a huge pearl and ivory pin. Her beautiful face was composed, and had lost the sadness Alicia could remember; if it had not yet become arrogant, it certainly possessed the calm certainty of power. How high had a casteless Hindu peasant from the mudflats of the Ganges risen, she thought.

Malama extended her hand. 'Alicia,' she said, her voice as soft as ever.

Alicia didn't know whether she was required to bow or not, so she advanced as well, her own hands outstretched.

Malama embraced her, as a great lady might embrace a supplicant. 'I have heard the news,' she said. 'Hung has told me. I have wept.'

Alicia realized that she had not, yet. She had not had the time. 'Is the news true, Malama?'

'You should call me Highness,' Malama said, quietly and with no suggestion of reproach. While her eyes gazed into Alicia's, perhaps conveying a warning. 'How can the news not be true? It was told to me by Hung himself. And this is your daughter? Come here, child.'

Joanna went forward wonderingly.

'You were indeed a child when last we met,' Malama said. 'But you do not recall that meeting.'

Joanna shook her head.

'And now you are a woman. A beautiful woman.'

'For whom Hung has certain plans,' Alicia said, reminding herself to add, 'Highness. Do you know of this also?'

'Are you not flattered?' Malama asked. 'There is no higher role.' Once again she held Alicia's gaze, and Alicia suddenly understood: clearly the head eunuch, who was close by, spoke English.

'It is too sudden,' she said. 'Too soon after her father's death. And she is not prepared.'

'She will be prepared,' Malama said. 'And it will free her mind of grief, perhaps.'

Joanna looked from one to the other of the women in bewilderment.

'You will accompany Wo Tu,' Malama said. 'Our lord is an impatient man, and he will soon return.'

The eunuch bowed, and indicated another curtained doorway, at the rear of the room.

Joanna looked at her mother, who looked at Malama. 'Oh, you will accompany her,' Malama said. 'I will, also.'

Alicia didn't know whether that would provide a measure of protection or not; Malama had clearly assumed the duties of chief procuress for her master. Once again she was aware of a feeling of utter helplessness as she followed Joanna and Wo Tu through the doorway to find herself on the marble surround of a large bathing pool. Here there were two other eunuchs, and two maids – as well as another of the throne-like chairs, on which Malama seated herself.

'Great ladies will disrobe,' Wo Tu commanded.

'Both of us?' Alicia demanded.

'But of course. Great ladies will bathe.'

'It is customary,' Malama said.

Alicia hesitated, but was undressing in front of a Hindu who also happened to be the chief consort of the Right Hand of God any different to undressing in front of Wu Yei? 'Do as he says,' she told Joanna.

Joanna obeyed. She had been brought up to less modesty than her mother. Malama gazed at her. 'She is very beautiful indeed,' she remarked. 'Hung will be well pleased.'

But now she was looking at Alicia. At least not with contempt, Alicia thought with some pride. If she had put on weight, with her height she was merely more voluptuous than ever, and her complexion had largely recovered its glowing whiteness during the years of luxury and protection. She sank into the water and was horrified to discover that the eunuchs and the maids were joining them; the girls stripped, but to her enormous relief the eunuchs retained a loin cloth. But that they intended to soap them could not be doubted.

She looked at Malama. 'Is this necessary?' she asked.

Malama inclined her head. 'It is necessary,' she said.

Alicia looked at Joanna instead, but the girl seemed more intrigued than alarmed, as the soft hands slid over her shoulders and breasts, and down her flanks to her legs and between – no doubt she was experiencing certain sensations for the first time in her life, Alicia thought: sex was not a subject she had ever discussed with her daughter . . . she had dreamed of being able to do so in proper surroundings when they returned to Singapore.

But now the hands and fingers were assaulting her in turn, their owners smiling at her. There could be no doubt that the girls enjoyed their work. And the eunuchs? She found herself staring at Malama. Who understood her thoughts. 'They yet have instincts,' she said. 'The ladies of the harem find them most stimulating, on occasion.'

Alicia opened her mouth, and then closed it again; there could be no doubt that the ladies of the harem included Malama herself. How far, she thought. Here was a level of sophisticated amorality to which she had never aspired, nor ever could, she knew.

They were soaped, and rinsed, and soaped again, and then taken from the water and wrapped in enormous, sweet-scented towels, to be gently patted dry by the maids. This operation was not yet complete when the doors to the outer room were opened by bowing eunuchs, and Hung Hsiu-ch'uan entered.

Instantly the girls abandoned their tasks and fell to the floor in a kowtow, naked bottoms thrust into the air as they touched the marble with their foreheads, hair clouding about them. The eunuchs followed their example. Alicia hastily grabbed her towel back to conceal herself, and Joanna did the same; they both remained standing. Malama had also risen, and bowed deeply to her lord and master.

Hung ignored the servants as he came into the room, and the door was closed behind him. 'Truly,' he said, 'has my father been good to me.' He stepped past Alicia to look at Joanna, who was trembling very slightly; nothing like this had ever happened to her before, and even in her innocence she could tell that she was about to become a victim of this man's lust. Alicia watched tears fill the girl's eyes, and her lower lip quivered.

'She is very young, Great Hung,' she said.

'Beauty is ageless,' Hung said. 'Show yourself, girl.'

Joanna looked at her mother, and Alicia sighed, and nodded. The towel was let slip. Joanna, Alicia thought, is even more lovely than I, at her age.

'Beauty,' Hung said again. He stretched out his hand to touch her breast, and Joanna shivered. 'And unaware. Now yourself, Alicia.'

'Me, Great Hung?'

367

'Is not the daughter but a reflection of the mother?'

Alicia drew a long breath, while memories drifted through her mind, of the way he had looked at her when first he had seen her, more than ten years before. He had waited a long time for this moment. Could he really have had Michael killed to achieve it?

She let the towel slip, and Hung gazed at her. 'Yes,' he said at last. 'Beauty. Do you not think so, Malama?'

'Beauty,' Malama agreed, and went to yet another inner door, which she opened. 'Great ladies?' Her tone was slightly mocking.

Uncertain what was to happen next, Alicia hesitated, looked down at the towel around her ankles, then stepped out of it and went through the doorway. If she had expected some kind of a dressing room she immediately realized her mistake; this was a bedroom. She turned, sharply, and was cannoned into by Joanna, immediately behind her. She held the girl's arm and pushed her into the room, then faced Hung, who stood in the doorway. 'Are you a fiend?'

Hung raised his eyebrows. 'Will the girl not be nervous, as she is a virgin?' He frowned. 'She *is* a virgin?'

'Of course she is. But . . .'

'She will learn from you.' He came into the room, ran his fingers into Alicia's hair and down her back to stroke her buttocks, then clasped them. 'Perhaps even I will learn from you, Alicia. Do not fear. Malama will be here to protect you.'

Alicia turned her head to watch Malama closing the door. And then release her yellow tunic. 'My God,' she said, 'you are a monster.'

Hung smiled at her, and removed his own tunic. 'Of desire, fair Alicia. Of desire. I have waited too many years for this moment.'

14

The Ever Victorious Army

Frederick Ward gazed at the bedraggled figure standing before him in the doorway of the hut which was his headquarters, flanked by two of his soldiers. 'Great balls of fire,' he remarked. 'You look done in.'

'I am done in,' Michael told him. 'I spent damn near twenty-four hours in the river, and then another three days crawling along the bank trying to avoid the Tai-p'ing before I came across your patrol.'

'Have you eaten?'

Michael nodded. 'They gave me some rice.'

'Chiang Ting, prepare a meal for Mr Harrington. And fetch some brandy right away. But what the hell happened?'

'Seems like you were right and I was wrong.' Michael slumped into the canvas chair before Ward's desk and told his story, gratefully accepting both the brandy and the cheroot offered him by the Chinese servant.

Ward also lit a cheroot and listened in silence. 'Hung sure seems to dispense with those he no longer wants,' he remarked. 'But why you? I thought you had quite a reputation as an artillerist.'

'I'm the best he has,' Michael agreed. 'But he had a reason, all right. My daughter.'

'God Almighty! The Right Hand of God?'

'He has more concubines than he can count.'

'So what are you going to do?'

Michael looked at him. 'There is not a lot I can do, Ward. I have to face the fact that I have devoted the better part of my life to supporting a lecherous, bloodthirsty thug who is guilty of the murder of both my wives, both my sons, and has raped my daughter. That makes me feel a million miles tall.'

'Yeah,' Ward said.

'So why the hell I didn't just let them kill me, or drown myself in the river, I don't know. Or maybe I do. I want him, dead. That's all I want from life, now.'

'And when you've done that, you will have saved China from the horrors of Tai-p'ing rule.'

'And perpetuated the Manchu,' Michael said despondently.

'Their laws are at least not the arbitrary moods of one person.'

Michael scratched his head. 'Do you really believe that? Anyway, if they stopped Hung once, they're not likely to do so again, after the pasting they got from the British and the French. They've all fled to Jehol.'

Ward grinned. 'Don't you believe it. The Ch'ing are back in Peking, ruling. And ready to take the fight to Hung.' He tapped one of the papers on his desk. 'A lot has happened in the past few weeks. Seems that the Emperor just couldn't stand up to the humiliation of being licked and driven from his capital. He just turned his face to the wall and died.'

Michael stared at him in consternation. 'Then who is the emperor now?'

'Some little kid, hardly a couple of months old. So there is a regency, headed by the boy's mother. I don't reckon she's very important; my information is that she's just a girl who was the late Emperor's favourite concubine. The man to watch is the dead king's brother, Prince Kung. He's a go-getter. This arrived only just after you left. I am now a brigadier general in the Chinese army. It's signed by Prince Kung himself.'

'Prince Kung,' Michael muttered.

'Say, you know the guy?'

'I met him, in Peking,' Michael said, and suddenly gave a bitter laugh.

'Share it,' Ward suggested.

Prince Kung, Michael thought. The man to watch,

because the principal regent was just a young girl of no account. Ward had no idea of the truth . . . but if Tzu-hsi was prepared to commission Ward and carry the fight to the Tai-p'ing, it could only be because of what he had told her. Tzu-hsi, back in power! In fact, as regent for her infant son, Tzu-hsi, really in power for the first time.

Ward had been studying him. 'With my new authority, I can make appointments, Michael. How would you like the rank of colonel, and command of my artillery?'

Then I'd be working for Tzu-hsi, Michael thought. From one totally irresponsible, bloodthirsty megalo-maniac to . . . another? But was there any other way to avenge the wrong Hung had done him?

He looked across the desk. 'Just tell me one thing, Frederick,' he said. 'You genuinely mean to carry this war to the Tai-p'ing? To lick them?'

'That's the idea. My instructions are to knock them out of Nanking for a start.'

Michael held out his hand. 'You have got yourself a colonel of artillery.'

Supposing it was possible to beat the Tai-p'ing with Chinese troops. Michael's heart sank when, having eaten his first square meal in nearly a week and slept like one dead for twelve hours, he accompanied Ward on an inspection of the encampment of his little army, which was situated just outside the walls of Shanghai. Because little was the operative word: he doubted there were two thousand men present.

'Wei Ch'ang-hui commands well over a hundred thousand men, in and around Nanking,' he told Ward.

'You ever read any history?'

'Some.'

'Well, Alexander the Great licked the Persians at odds of sometimes fifty to one. He did it by discipline and by knowing what he was doing, and by personal leadership. Don't tell me that the general in command doesn't charge at the head of his troops, nowadays. Clausewitz would have a fit and Napoleon would turn in his grave. But you know something? Napoleon earned his reputation, and the love of his men, by leading from the front when he was a young man: remember the bridge of Lodi? And you know something else, warfare in China is still medieval. I can beat your friends Wei and Hung, Michael. I know I can. Just bear with me.'

His enthusiasm was infectious and consuming. So was his energy. He cared nothing how an end was attained, so long as it was attained. He begged and bullied the Viceroy in Shanghai, went down on his knees to the British commanders in the squadron lying in the mouth of the Yangtse . . . and accumulated uniforms for his men; blue jackets and white breeches, with gaiters and boots and kepis. No Chinese army had ever been so equipped, and when they paraded, huge crowds turned out to watch them – and then to volunteer.

But Ward was not interested in numbers. 'There'd be no point in opposing Wei's rabble with a rabble of our own,' he said. He was interested in quality, and he would take no men he could not adequately arm. Here again he worked wonders, and equipped his men with modern rifled muskets and, even more important, with bayonets, a weapon of which the Chinese only knew it could be deadly in the hands of British or French soldiers.

Once armed, he set to work to train his men, knowing full well that time was not on his side; although Michael had not revealed to him the hand of Tzu-hsi behind his appointment, he understood that his employers were totally fickle, and might change their minds about supporting him at any moment. But he would not take the field, he explained to the Viceroy, who daily rode out to inspect the troops, with half-trained levies.

Actually, the business took less time than Michael had feared. Quite a large number of the recruits had trained with Ward the previous year, before the British had put a temporary stop to his activities, and therefore already possessed the rudiments of parade ground drill, the beginnings of esprit de corps, in which every man knew he could rely upon the man at his shoulder, because they had all been trained to do the same thing at the same time in response to the same situation. Basic drill completed, Ward concentrated on battle tactics, on forming square and re-forming column with precision and in the minimum of time, and on delivering a bayonet charge after a volley at close range had disorganized the enemy. The Chinese began to worship the bayonet, and their shouts as they pierced the straw-filled sacks which represented their enemies were bloodcurdling.

'They think they are invincible,' Michael remarked.

Ward winked. 'Well, that is the first requirement of a good soldier.'

Michael indicated the newspapers which had just arrived, telling of the outbreak of the Civil War in the United States, and of the initial defeats suffered by the Union troops. 'Wouldn't you rather be there?'

Ward's mouth twisted. 'I'm a merchant sailor, not a West Pointer. They wouldn't even give me a gun back home, save as a buck private. Here's where I'll carve my niche in history.'

'Is that important to you?' Michael asked.

'Sure it is. Isn't it to you?'

Michael had never really thought about it. Presumably, as Hung Hsiu-ch'uan's artillery commander he already had a niche in history, if the history of the Tai-p'ing was ever written. And now he had the opportunity to gain another, for Ward had also wheedled two batteries out of the Manchu, and had Michael exercising the twelve guns and his volunteer gunners from dawn until dusk. 'You know my tactics,' he would say. 'Deploy, disrupt, destroy. Except in the most favourable circumstances, the disruption has to come from you, Mike. You are the lynchpin of the whole operation.'

His amazing mind ranged over every aspect of warfare, however, and he was already looking ahead to the capture of walled towns. 'We need a qualified military engineer,' he said. 'I don't think those field guns of yours are going to make too much difference to walls.'

'I don't think there's such a Chinese animal,' Michael said. 'Do you know who you need? Charles Gordon.'

'Friend of yours?'

'Acquaintance. He's fought against the Manchu. But I think he has the good of China at heart, and he's a capable engineer, from everything I've heard.'

'So we'll have Gordon. If he'll volunteer.'

Michael remembered the way the tall young captain had shrugged with distaste when ordered to burn the Summer Palace. 'I've an idea he might.'

Once more Ward applied to the British naval commander, for the secondment of the Engineer officer.

Gordon had not yet arrived, however, when the army had its first taste of war. Although the Tai-p'ing had occupied Chenkiang and were probing up the Grand Canal – mainly in search of food supplies, Michael surmised – they had not yet made a concerted effort to continue down the Yangtse, although from time to time they indulged in large-scale raids, like the bandits they basically were, again in search of food. Word was now brought in that one of these considerable Tai-p'ing forces was probing down the right bank of the river towards Shanghai. 'I suppose Wei feels confident that unless he assaults the city itself, he won't have to take on the British,' Michael remarked.

'But he will have to take on Brigadier-General F. T. Ward's brigade,' Ward said with a grin. 'Those whom the gods would destroy they first make mad. Mike, old son, I think we have trained long enough.'

The Viceroy did not see it that way. 'You will bring your men inside the city, General Ward,' he said. 'And help my bannermen to defend the walls.'

'No, sir,' Ward said.

'But there is panic in the city. And if Shanghai were to fall . . .'

'The quickest way to have Shanghai fall, Your Excellency, is to man the walls and sit tight. That's how the Tai-p'ing have managed to win so many victories, simply because your people have always stood on the defensive. We are going to lick those guys in the open field.'

'But there are many thousands of them,' the Viceroy wailed.

'That gives us more of a target,' Ward told him.

The city walls were crammed with spectators as the little force marched out of its cantonments, applause being mixed with a good deal of fearful comment. Ward had already sent his very limited force of cavalry – hardly a squadron in strength – out ahead under the most reliable of his Chinese officers, to reconnoitre the country and discover the whereabouts of the enemy. Now he had his men perform a forced march of some twenty miles before allowing them to pitch camp, whereupon he and Michael walked their horses to a low rise which allowed them to overlook an extensive plain, mainly of rice paddies. To their right the river flowed by, to their left the land rose again, while through the paddies there ran a roadway. 'Here would be the place to stop them,' Ward said, having clearly reconnoitred this ground himself on some previous occasion. 'Supposing they come this way. I think they will, using the river as guard and support.'

He was proved right that afternoon, when the cavalry rode into camp, wildly excited. They had actually encountered the Tai-p'ing, and exchanged shots with them, before galloping away for their lives.

'What size force?' Ward asked.

Captain Phang spread his arms. 'It is difficult to say, Your Excellency. But a great many.'

'Estimate.'

'Not less than thirty thousand men, Your Excellency.'

Michael could not suppress a low whistle.

Ward did not look disturbed. 'And coming this way. How far away?'

'They will be here by morning, Your Excellency.'

'That will be ideal,' Ward said. 'Thank you, Captain Phang. You will rest your men and water your horses. But you will be ready to mount again at midnight. Understood?'

'Yes, Your Excellency,' Phang said.

He left the tent, and Ward lit a cheroot. 'Tell me about this fellow Wei. Any good?'

'Brave as a lion.'

'I meant, tactically.'

'Well, he grew up in the school of Yang. Or maybe you, for that matter. Point the sword, and go.'

Ward grinned. 'I hope you give me credit for a little more finesse than that. But he sounds just the sort of man I want to meet. All right, Michael, I would like you to move your guns up to the ridge now. Emplace them just on the reverse slope, where they won't immediately be spotted by the Tai-p'ing. Then stay there with your gunners. We don't really know how soon the enemy will be on us. But while it is still light, place a marker, a mile away down that road, and train your weapons on that. Got it?'

'Yes, sir,' Michael agreed, not in the least abashed to be taking orders from a man thirteen years his junior, because this was one of the most remarkable men he had ever met. He assembled his gunners, and the mules pulled the cannon up the ridge, while he sent one of his men a mile along the road to plant a stake in the ground, and carefully trained the first gun on it. It was dark by the time the last was emplaced, but all were given the same elevation. Ward had by then moved his brigade forward as well, positioning them also on the reverse side of the slope and thus concealed from any enemy advancing from the west; the men had rested all day and were fresh and eager, but he made them sit down and cook their dinners and commanded them to have a sleep. Then he rode over to see how the artillery were getting on. 'Shall I keep the mules handy, in case we have to withdraw in a hurry?' Michael asked.

'No,' Ward told him. 'There will be no withdrawal.'

Sleep was next to impossible with such a prospect, for either Michael or his men. While soon after midnight they became aware of a seething sound in the distance. It could have been a strong wind, but it wasn't. The Chinese gunners gazed at each other in the darkness, and whispered, 'Tai-p'ing.'

Just before dawn Michael had them stand by the guns, for flaring torches could now be seen, lighting up the sky. 'They really are sticking their chins out and saying "hit me," ' Ward commented, having ridden over to make sure the artillery was ready for action. 'I figure they've been marching all night; they may have stopped to eat, but not to sleep. And they're going to come on us just as the sun gets up, and shines straight in their eyes. And they have made absolutely no reconnaissance.'

Michael observed that his friend had discarded both sword and revolver, and was unarmed save for a cane. 'I'm glad to see you have opted for generalship rather than heroics,' he remarked.

Ward merely grinned. 'Swords are such infernally heavy things, and frankly, Mike, I have no idea how to use one. Or fire a pistol. I'd be more dangerous to my own men than the enemy. Besides . . .' he winked. 'Charles XII of Sweden never carried more than a cane, and he only lost one battle in his life. Now await my orders.'

He lived in a dream world, of past famous generals and heroes. But, Michael thought, as he had said of his men, was not that the best, perhaps the only, way to become a hero oneself? And he was also a painstaking tactician, the true mark of the genius.

Ward called Captain Phang forward and told him to send out six of his best horsemen, along the road until they were a quarter of a mile beyond the mile marker on which Michael's guns were trained. The moment the Tai-p'ing came close enough to be recognized, they were to return to the ridge with all speed.

The horsemen rode off, and the darkness began to fade; the torches came closer. Mainly they were on the road, but they spilled over into the fields to either side. Michael was aware of a great dryness in his throat, and he could not eat any breakfast. He had sat like this, with his guns, *behind* those men, often enough; he knew the fate of those of their enemies not killed outright. As for being dragged before Hung . . . who perhaps did not even know he was still alive . . . and who might have Joanna cowering at his side, having watched her mother and brother executed – a fate he had forced upon them, unwittingly perhaps, but nonetheless forced. He had followed a star, and found it out to be a comet, a ball of flaming hatred. Then he must hate himself, and destroy, with all the venom Hung had ever displayed.

Shots drifted towards them on the morning breeze, and a few moments later a horseman urged his mount up the slope, followed by the others of the patrol. 'They have reached the mile marker, Your Excellency,' they told Ward.

Ward looked over his shoulder. The sky to the east was lightening with every minute, but the sun had not yet risen. 'Open fire, Colonel Harrington,' he commanded. 'We need to check them for a little while.'

Michael gave the command, and the cannon roared and bucked as the batteries fired in unison. The noise in front of them grew, but the flaming torches were no longer advancing. 'Load,' he snapped.

The gunners had been well trained, and worked with smooth precision. Another salvo was dispatched into the darkness, and again there was a good deal of confusion in the enemy ranks – but now the torches were advancing again. And now, behind the tiny Manchu army, there rose the sun, into an almost cloudless sky. The gunners stood up to peer down at the suddenly illuminated plain, and to catch their breaths. Before them, and hardly more than half a mile distant, was the huge cloud of the Tai-p'ing. Michael thought that thirty thousand might be a conservative estimate. And they had advanced a considerable way since the first cannon shots; he could tell this by the scattered red and blue mounds on the roadway behind them. But they were not about to be stopped now; they presented a seemingly solid mass of swords and pikes, while those who had muskets were discharging them into the air as fast as they could load, and all the while they kept up an enormous high-pitched roar.

'Now Michael,' Ward said. 'I want you to concentrate your fire on the centre of that mob. Three more salvoes will do the trick. Then cease firing.' He grinned. 'If anything goes wrong with my plans, you will be in command. But in any event, keep the horsemen with you, and charge when you deem the moment right. I will be unable to give you any more orders.'

Because after all he meant to advance with his men – still armed only with a cane!

The Tai-p'ing had stopped again, and their generals – the only mounted men in their army – had ridden forward to ascertain where the defiant firing was coming from. Michael could recognize none of them, even through his field glasses, but he had no doubt Wei was with them. Then the cannon exploded again, and the grapeshot tore into the huddled mass in front of him. The Tai-p'ing involuntarily separated, breaking to either side, into the paddy fields, while the officers waved their swords to drive them back to the advance.

'Load,' Michael shouted, his voice hoarse, and looked to his right to see the blue and white ranks of Ward's brigade marching over the hill. The Tai-p'ing gazed at the tiny force in astonishment, then uttered another roar of contempt and moved forward. As they came together, Michael fired again, and once more their ranks were disrupted. While the brigade was now advancing rapidly down the hill, muskets still sloped, with every barrel topped by an eighteen-inch-long steel bayonet, gleaming in the sun.

'Fire!' Michael bellowed for the third time; Ward's calculations had been exact, and in another few seconds his men would be too close for the artillery to avoid hitting their own people.

For a third time the Tai-p'ing wavered as the shot tore into their ranks, but they had the courage of fanaticism, the confidence of invincibility, and came on again, while the scattered wings, having already advanced beyond the rest, now began to close on the small force marching on their centre. From the hilltop it looked as if Wei was the

379

one fighting the classic battle, using the tactics of Marathon or Cannae, with his wings overlapping and now about to envelop the enemy. It did not seem possible for Ward to escape, or a single one of his men. The general had dismounted before leaving the hillside, and had walked at the head of his troops. Now he could be seen in their centre as they formed square with perfect discipline, front rank kneeling, rear rank standing. Michael could not hear the orders, but as the Tai-p'ing clouded around, the brigade rippled fire, and again, and again; their muskets might only have a single shot each, but by discharging their pieces in alternate ranks they made it appear as if their fire was continuous. The Tai-p'ing recoiled from the deadly wall of lead; those who got through it died on the even more deadly wall of steel within.

The battle raged for perhaps ten minutes, then the Tai-p'ing began to retreat, leaving hundreds of their number on the ground. But Ward, as he had declared, had come there to destroy, not defend. Once again carrying out their manoeuvres with perfect unison, the square turned into a phalanx of bristling bayonets, and while the Tai-p'ing soldiers were still trying to catch their breaths, moved, like Alexander the Great's Immortals at Arbela, in a straight line for the enemy generals.

The result was startling. The generals saw the massed bayonets cutting through all who would oppose them, while Ward's flankers continued to fire on those of the enemy who remained to either side, and turned and fled. Their men followed them. 'Now, Captain Phang, now's your chance,' Michael shouted, and himself leapt into the saddle and drew his sword, leading the two hundred horsemen in a mad dash down the hillside, into the midst of the fleeing Tai-p'ing, cutting and slashing. The huge force which had been opposed to them became a disorganized mob of fleeing unarmed peasants, for most of them had thrown away their weapons. The horsemen continued their charge until they reached the brigade, which had halted, again formed square, and was firing into the retreating enemy. Now the cease fire was sounded, and Michael dismounted. 'Frederick,' he said. 'That was the most brilliant thing I have ever seen.'

Ward, who still carried only his cane, and looked totally unruffled, embraced him. 'That was only the first, Mike. Only the first.'

'The Ever Victorious Army,' Gordon said, his eyes gleaming. 'That's what they are calling you, you know, Colonel.'

Michael grinned. 'Well, we've met the enemy about six times, and we haven't lost yet. What do you think of our commander?'

'That he's a genius,' Gordon said readily. 'The sort of chap who makes a nonsense of staff colleges and military theories.'

'Not entirely,' Michael told him. 'He's read his Clausewitz. Now tell me what you think about fighting for the Manchu?'

Gordon smiled. 'It's a living. It was no pleasure, burning that palace, Colonel. I'm a soldier. I do what I am commanded to do. You should have asked, what do the Manchu think about employing me.'

'Oh, I can answer that one,' Michael said. 'The Ch'ing just want to see the Tai-p'ing beaten. They'd employ anyone.'

In fact the determination of the Ch'ing government – inspired by Tzu-hsi, Michael had no doubt at all, for the news coming out of Peking indicated more and more that she was now the true power behind the throne – to take advantage of the amazing victories gained by Ward's tiny force, always against overwhelming odds, and destroy the Tai-p'ing once and for all became more and more evident. For Ward, however often he might defeat the hordes Wei Ch'ang-hui threw against him, yet lacked the strength to attempt an advance up the river; if his tactics were aggressive, his strategy was forced to remain defensive. But now the ablest generals the Ch'ing possessed, men like Tseng Kuo-fan and Li Hung-chang, were sent to Shanghai, Tseng as Viceroy. Li had raised his own army in the west to combat the Tai-p'ing efforts to advance in that direction, with some success; now he was ordered to bring it to the east and engage in the assault upon Nanking. His force numbered forty thousand men, and if it was not quite in the state of discipline achieved by Ward, was yet the most formidable fighting army in China.

The accretions of strength should naturally have reduced the importance of Ward and his devoted band, but they did not. Ward had the aura of invincibility about him, as well as a personal invulnerability, for however often he led his men into battle – and he was always at their head, armed only with his cane – he never suffered even a wound. Nor did he seem concerned at the way his orginal total authority had been whittled away, happily saluted both Li and Tseng, and agreed with their strategical proposals. 'We all have only one goal,' he said. 'Nanking and that fellow Hung Hsiu-ch'uan. It'll need all of us to get him.'

And more. For the British now began to realize that it would be useful for them to have their presence on the Yangtse underlined, as it were; Nanking and Hankow had both been listed as new trading ports granted to them by the Treaty of Peking. True they had an engineer captain serving under Ward, but they could hardly count Michael, nor was the fact that they had helped both to arm, and equip, the Ever Victorious Army well known. Now British observers and liaison officers appeared with the armies, and Michael was utterly taken aback one morning, as he shaved outside his tent before yet another advance, to find himself gazing at Jeremy Cooper.

Jeremy was a year or two older than himself, and had spent his entire life in the army – he had served right through the Indian Mutiny a few years earlier – but had yet, Michael could not help being pleased to note, only reached the rank of colonel, although he looked very smart in his red jacket, blue trousers and white solar topee. 'Michael!' he said.

Michael shook hands. 'What brings you here?'

'You, mainly.'

'Me?'

'Well, yes. And perhaps a desire to find out some things. There are all manner of rumours about you, you know.'

'I didn't, actually. My dear fellow, come and sit down.' Michael summoned his servants to unfold two canvas camp chairs and prepare breakfast. 'What sort of rumours?'

'Well, is it true that Alicia is dead?'

'I'm afraid it is.'

'And the children?'

'To all intents and purposes,' Michael said grimly.

'Good God. I say, I am most terribly sorry, old man. So that's why you fight against the Tai-p'ing now.' He sighed. 'Margaret is dead too.'

'I didn't know. I'm sorry. But presumably Ali still rules the roost in Singapore.'

'Yes,' Jeremy said thoughtfully. 'Have you never thought of going back?'

'When Alicia was alive. But even then, I didn't suppose I would be very welcome.'

'Hm. Pieter is still alive, you know. He's the Hong Kong managing director.'

'Managing director?'

'Well, Hammond and Teng have grown far beyond the factor stage. You should see their offices in Calcutta. Wouldn't you like to?'

Michael's servant had brought coffee, and now he sipped his as he studied his erstwhile brother-in-law. Jeremy definitely had something on his mind. 'Why should I wish to see the offices in Calcutta?' Michael asked quietly.

Jeremy also drank coffee, or rather, gulped at his cup and had to wait until his throat ceased burning. Then he said, 'Because it's yours, old man.'

Michael put down his cup slowly. 'I have somewhat lost my sense of humour,' he remarked.

'But it's true, old man. Virtually. Pieter Hammond confessed it to me. It's been on his conscience ever since he found out. He only did so when old Clive died and he became the second man in the firm; Teng Tang has also gone to his ancestors.'

Michael scratched his head. 'Are you trying to tell me that Clive Hammond left Alicia part of the firm?'

'Oh, good Lord no. Ali had him rewrite his will so that all his shares in the company went to Ali, with just fixed incomes to the other three children. I imagine there's a tidy balance in Alicia's name in the bank in Singapore, although I suppose Ali will take it back now she's dead. But that's hardly relevant. The fact is that Clive Hammond only held forty-eight per cent of the company.'

Michael felt curiously breathless. 'The other fifty-two belonged to Teng Lee.'

'Exactly.'

'And therefore to his widow, the Princess Jalina,' Michael said slowly.

'Who left them to you in her will,' Jeremy said.

For a moment he couldn't think. Would you like to control the company? Jalina had asked. Because I can give it to you? Because she already had. If only she had told him that.

'You mean you didn't know?' Jeremy asked.

'No,' Michael said.

'But . . . you were lovers?'

'Yes,' Michael said. 'Do you know when that will was dated?'

'Oh, some time in 1848. Well before the great bust-up, anyway.'

Well before the great bust-up, Michael thought. She had made the will in his favour before she had even gone to his bed. Because she had always intended to do that? Or because she had always feared the entire company belonging to Ali, or to someone Ali could bully and control, and had chosen him, Michael, instead of, for instance, Jeremy himself. If only he had known that. If only he had waited to find out. Alicia had wanted him to do that, and he had refused. And taken her off to her death. His fingers curled into fists.

'Ali of course found out right away,' Jeremy went on.

'But then you were considered to have been murdered by the pirates. When you reappeared and, well, carried Alicia off into the wilds of China, no one knew whether you were going to live or die. According to Pieter, Ali wanted you declared dead and the will declared void, but the Calcutta lawyer would not have that, insisted he wait seven years as required by law. Well, by the end of that time everyone was hearing about the Irishman commanding the Tai-p'ing artillery.'

'So what did Ali do then?' Michael asked.

'Well . . . nothing. I mean, there was nothing he could do. Save, I imagine, keep praying that you would stop a bullet. But of course, in your absence to vote against him, he has remained chairman of the company.'

'Yes,' Michael said. 'You say Pieter Hammond told you all of this. Did he tell you, knowing that I was still alive?'

'Indeed. In fact, he told me knowing that you had rejoined the British forces. He found out just after you had left Hong Kong for Peking; he had no idea you were ever in Hong Kong at all. I believe he wrote to you then, but before the letter could have reached you, you had apparently rejoined the Tai-p'ing. It wasn't until early this year that we discovered you were actually fighting with this Yankee fellow Ward, and then I volunteered to come and find you. I must say, old man, you do change sides somewhat.'

Michael ignored the comment. 'But Pieter felt I should know about it.'

'Well, I don't really think he gets on very well with his half-brother.'

'And you felt I should know about it, too.'

'Well . . . I suppose you could say the same for me. What are you going to do about it?'

'What would you like me to do about it?' Michael asked.

'Well . . . go back to Singapore and take over, I suppose. I mean, the company is doing very well, but some of Ali's methods are not quite out of Debrett, if you follow me.'

'Yes,' Michael said. 'I'd be a liar if I didn't admit that

I owe Ali a great deal, and I would just love to come back and sort him out. But there is someone I need to sort out even more.'

Jeremy frowned. 'This fellow Hung?'

'He murdered my wife. Both my wives. And both my sons.'

'But . . . he's in Nanking.'

'That is where the army is headed.'

'Yes, but I say, old man, not even Ward expects to take Nanking before next year. You could be killed, at any time.'

'True. I tell you what I'll do. I will make a will of my own, here and now, leaving my share of the Hammond and Teng company to you and Pieter, jointly. If I am killed, you can do what you think best. If I survive . . . you might just find me turning up in Singapore, one day.' Because, what else would he have to do with his life?

As if it mattered. To become master of Hammond and Teng, to rule that vast empire, he needed a consort, to be proud of him, and for him to love. All the four women he had ever loved were dead – he could not possibly hope that Malama could have survived Hung's megalomania. Far better to remain in China. Fighting for Tzu-hsi and the Manchu? He could not yet reconcile himself to the whims of fate.

And still the advance continued. 'Tomorrow, we take our first city,' Ward said on 19 August 1862. They had sat in front of Tzeki for over a week, while Gordon had dug his mines, and the assault was now ready to commence. 'I give you a victory.' Ward raised his glass as he looked over his officers. And smiled. 'It will be our twelfth successive victory. A round dozen. We shall have to double that.'

They drank their toast with utter conviction. No one doubted Ward any more; they were all veterans of his unending success. Nor could they doubt that his first encounter with stone walls would end any differently to his encounters with walls of men. There was no indication that the Tai-p'ing were even aware that their walls had been mined, and next morning the operation began as usual, with Michael beginning a general bombardment; he now commanded six batteries. Jeremy was with him as the balls thudded into the defences, and through their binoculars chips of masonry could be seen flying, and chips of men, too. 'And you have now done this eleven times,' he remarked.

Michael gave a grim smile. 'Much more often than that, old boy. I spent several years doing this for the other side.'

Jeremy scratched his head and looked to the right, where the blue jackets of Ward's brigade were assembled – he had refused to increase the size of his army, only ever replacing casualties, and thus making it more and more of an elite corps – and then to the left, where the much greater mass of Li Hung-chang's force was gathered. Then the boom of the cannon, and the replies from the town, were drowned in the deeper explosion of the mine. One of the towers on the outer city wall seemed to rise in the air, and then dissolve, carrying its defenders with it. The rest stopped firing in dismay, but Michael kept up his cannonading, while Ward raised his cane and the blue-jackets moved forward in their usual compact mass.

'Cease fire.' The order went along the batteries as the brigade charged at the breach. On the left Li's men also moved forward, equipped with scaling ladders; they would make their assault on the unbreached wall the moment Ward's men gained a position inside the city itself.

The attack went like clockwork, because Ward's attacks, always so meticulously prepared and calculated, always went like clockwork. Nothing was ever left to chance, and within an hour the dragon flag of the Manchu was being hoisted over the captured city. Gordon had ridden across from the mouth of the mine shaft to watch with Michael and Jeremy, and now he raised his hat. 'The dozen our general wanted,' he said. And then frowned, as he saw a horseman spurring towards them.

It was Captain Phang himself, as much a veteran of victory now as any of them. 'Colonel Harrington,' he gasped. 'Captain Gordon . . .' There were tears streaming down his face.

Because in battle, there was always one thing which had to be left to chance. By the time Michael and Gordon gained the city and had made their way through the dead and the dying, Ward was already far gone. 'A stray bullet,' he said, his breath coming in great pants, frothy with blood. 'A stray bullet. Of all the luck.'

'We'll get you back to Shanghai,' Michael said.

Ward looked at the Chinese surgeon, whose face was a picture of misery. 'These guys don't know how to lie, Mike. I'm done. God damn it, done. I wanted to see that flag flying over Nanking.'

'It will fly over Nanking,' Michael said, feeling the fingers on his arm slowly losing strength. 'I will hoist it personally.'

'When you've settled with Hung,' Ward muttered. His head fell back, and then lifted again. 'Say, Mike, will I get into the history books?'

'You're there already,' Michael told him.

'That'll please Dad,' Ward said, and closed his eyes.

Michael discovered that, like Phang, he was weeping.

'It is obviously the wish,' Viceroy Tseng said, 'of our masters in Peking that General Ward's brigade be kept in being at least until we have gained the final victory over the Tai-p'ing. It is also the wish of Prince Kung that the brigade commander should be a Westerner.' His lip curled slightly, as if he personally did not understand the necessity for this.

'Of course,' Charles Gordon said. 'Colonel Harrington will take command.'

Tseng gave a little cough. 'No,' he said. 'You will take command, General Gordon.'

'Me?' Gordon raised his eyebrows.

'It is the express wish of Prince Kung.'

'Colonel Harrington is not only my senior in the army, Your Excellency, he is also a far more experienced soldier than I,' Gordon argued.

'It is a debatable point,' Tseng said. 'You fought in the Crimea. That was a great war. You are a professional soldier. Colonel Harrington has always been an amateur.'

'What you really mean is that Colonel Harrington once served with the Tai-p'ing,' Gordon said. 'And your masters in Peking don't like the thought of that. Well, I can tell you, Your Excellency, that it will have to be Colonel Harrington or nobody, because I will not accept the commission.'

'I think you should, Charles,' Michael said.

Their heads turned. He had hitherto been silent throughout the argument, but it was his opinion which mattered. He did not really wish to command the army; he was well aware that he had none of Ward's military genius, or military knowledge. Gordon certainly possessed the latter, if not the former. He was also a charismatic character – in that war, and fighting, were the sole reasons for his existence. Michael knew they were not his. He would fight this war to its conclusion, but for only one reason, to avenge the murders of Alicia and Wu Yei. That alone left his judgement too coloured by personal animosity to make him a capable leader of men. Nor could he really bring himself to look beyond the conclusion of that vengeful quest.

Yet he could not help wondering whose decision lay behind his exclusion. Common sense told him that it was indeed because he had once served with the Tai-p'ing, and even more, had been on his way back to them when he had been forced to change sides. But he also knew that Tzu-hsi did not rule through common sense, only through her own instincts and desires. So, had she excluded him because she mistrusted him? Or because she felt he might grow too powerful were he to become General of the Ever Victorious Army? Or simply to preserve his life, she supposed?

He wondered if he would ever know the answer.

But the answer to the problem at hand was his to give. 'I should be proud to serve under you, General Gordon,' he said.

Charles Gordon had his own ideas on how the war should be fought. Unlike Ward, who was a supreme tactician, Gordon was more interested in the strategic aspects of the situation. He could point to the fact that Ward had indeed defeated the Tai-p'ing on twelve consecutive occasions, but so enormous were the Tai-p'ing forces that they still lay within thirty miles of Shanghai, and Tzeki was in fact the first city of any size that had been recaptured for the Ch'ing. 'The way to victory,' he told Tseng and Li, 'lies less in defeating the Tai-p'ing in the field, for they are like the sand on a beach, which when washed away by the sea merely re-forms itself somewhere else. It is to take away their means of existence.'

Tseng nodded. 'This is sensible. We will starve them into submission.'

'And many millions will die,' Li observed.

'It was their decision to fight this war, General Li,' Gordon reminded him. 'If we do not end it soon, many millions will die in any event.'

The Tai-p'ing were confounded by the change of emphasis, for suddenly Ward's brigade, as it was still known, avoided battle with them, and instead slipped up the river to the southern end of the Grand Canal. The Tai-p'ing had retained their grasp on this, and were using the country around as a vast granary, while the canal itself provided them with a waterway for transporting their supplies. This waterway Gordon now cut, by building forts opposite Chenkiang, where the canal debouched into the river. Meanwhile Li was applying frontal pressure, and now at last the Tai-p'ing began to fall back, as their bellies rumbled with hunger.

The work was slow, and unglamorous; there were few battles any more. It was also on occasion intensely distressing, as, hungry, the Tai-p'ing reverted to type and took what they wanted where they could find it, including human beings. Evacuated villages too often were found to contain women, children and old men in the last stages of starvation, and of course disease was more rampant than ever.

'It is no way to wage a war,' Gordon agreed. 'But it is the only way we can wage this one, if we are not to be fighting here at the turn of the century.'

'My fear is that there will still be someone fighting here at the turn of the century,' Michael said. 'Even if we win this particular war.'

'Well, no doubt we are fortunate in being unable to see the future.'

That his tactics were proving successful, however, could not be argued, especially when, early in the summer of 1863, an entire Tai-p'ing division surrendered, the first time this had happened. Michael sat on his horse with Gordon and Li and Tseng and watched the wretched men being rounded up and pushed into a vast mass by the triumphant Manchu soldiery.

'The beginning of the end,' Tseng said triumphantly.

'Yes,' Gordon said thoughtfully. 'And the beginning of a huge headache for us, Your Excellency. We can hardly feed our own men.'

'Of course. We are certainly not going to feed those scum.'

Gordon's head turned sharply. 'They are prisoners of war.'

'They are surrendered rebels, General. Guilty of every crime known to mankind. As well as treason to their rightful masters.'

'Nonetheless, they surrendered in good faith,' Gordon insisted.

'Their faith is no business of yours, General Gordon. It is a business for myself. And my decision has been taken. Those men will not be fed.'

'They will resume fighting when they discover that,' Michael told him.

Tseng smiled. 'That would be simplest, I agree, Colonel

Harrington. As they no longer have any arms, they will die quicker.'

Michael looked at cannon being placed on the slopes overlooking the valley.

'Oh, indeed,' Tseng said. 'None will escape.'

'That will be plain, simple murder,' Gordon snapped.

'Execution, Mr Gordon. That is the common fate of traitors and rebels.'

'I will not be a party to it, Your Excellency. Those men surrendered to me.'

'I am your superior officer, General Gordon.'

'Not if you persist in this decision. I will resign my command.'

Tseng gazed at him for a moment, and then bowed his head. 'That must be your decision, General.'

'I rather suspect he was angling for that,' Michael told Gordon when they regained the encampment.

'Meaning that as I have not attracted the glamorous publicity of Ward, I am dispensable.'

'In a sense. Ward was necessary to the Ch'ing, for the creation and maintenance of morale. He never showed them how to win the war, but then, it is a Chinese characteristic never to win wars, but to let them drag on until they just dwindle away. In those circumstances, the maintenance of morale is very important. You have come along and showed them how this war can actually be won, and without fighting too many battles. Well, having learned that, it is obviously in the Ch'ing interests to have the victory gained by their own officers rather than a foreign devil.'

'I have no doubt you're right,' Gordon agreed. 'Well, they're welcome to the glory. I will not change my mind. It is very difficult to decide which is the worse, the Taip'ing or the Manchu.'

'I've had that difficulty myself,' Michael said.

'So, what are you going to do.'

Michael sighed. 'Stay with the army.'

Gordon frowned at him. 'You condone the massacre Tseng is preparing?'

'I hate the idea of it as much as you do. But it is going to take place whether you or I remain here or not. And this army is the only hope I have of returning to Nanking, and finding my daughter, if she is still alive.'

'Or avenging her if she is dead. I understand your situation, Michael, just as I understand that perhaps, having lived with these people longer than I, you have more stomach for their excesses.' He held out his hand. 'I doubt we shall meet again, so I will wish you good fortune with the brigade; you should have had the command from the beginning.'

Michael was indeed confirmed as Brigidier-General and took over the blue-jackets – there was no one else – but it was Tseng's decision, no doubt on orders from Peking, to end their independent role, and they were included in the army as a whole. Which satisifed Michael well enough; Jeremy had by now returned to regular duty in Hong Kong, but Michael had an English adjutant, an enthusiastic young man named Peter Lucas, while Phang had been promoted to Colonel. The brigade, he felt, was more efficient than ever, and more than ever the instrument of his vengeance. Because now the end was in sight, as they moved slowly up the river from Chenkiang, the Tai-p'ing everywhere collapsing before them. Those who surrendered were summarily executed, and there must have been thousands of them. Even more non-combatants were visibly starving to death on every side, but the army remained supplied, and in the early summer of 1864 they saw the walls of Nanking in the distance.

'A formidable place,' remarked Viceroy Tseng after studying it through his binoculars.

'And they have become used to our mining,' Michael agreed. 'We must just batter at the walls and see if we can create a breach.'

'We will emplace the artillery, certainly, General Harrington,' Tseng said. 'But we will save our strength for the time being. We will let them starve a little, first?'

For he had thrown part of his force above the city, and Nanking was entirely surrounded. It was impossible to consider what conditions might be inside the walls; certainly they were manned day and night by Tai-p'ing warriors, apparently as fanatic as ever, keeping up a constant chant and a beating of drums, while the sun and dragon flags coiled and fluttered in the breeze above their heads. But there could be no doubt that they were short of food. Hung as well, and his concubines? Michael doubted that, at the moment. But even they would starve eventually, unless they surrendered. And then? It was not something he cared to think about. He did not know if Joanna still lived, and he did not know if, when rescued, she would still want to live. But then, he did not know if *he* would wish to remain alive, when he had rescued her.

He returned to the brigade, and his tent, slept fitfully as the night was close and the mosquitoes were active, and was awakened before dawn by his servant, Lu Chi. 'Forgive me, Master,' the man said. 'But our patrols have taken a prisoner from the river, who has asked to be brought before you, and nobody else.'

Michael frowned as he pulled on his trousers. 'A prisoner? From Nanking?'

'I believe so, Master.'

Michael felt a surge of excitement. Perhaps this was the first crack in the wall of determined resistance. He hurried out of the tent to where the two sentries waited in the darkness, a small, even darker figure between them. Michael's heart missed a beat, for even in the gloom he knew it was Malama.

15

The Kingdom of Lonely Death

The girl bowed, trembling. 'Highness,' she whispered. 'Highness. The Great Hung comes.'

Alicia sat up, pulling hair from her eyes, and listening to the coughing from the hallway. Hung coughed incessantly nowadays, but that had become a blessing. Alicia supposed it had begun as a nervous tickle in the throat, as he had seen his great plans squandered – but then it had developed into a true ailment, lent strength by malnutrition and worry . . . there was not sufficient good food in Nanking even to feed the Great Hung. Thus he had not been to her apartment for several days. Days in which she, and Joanna, had been able to sleep in each other's arms, and dream, and pray.

She sometimes found it difficult to credit that it was now all but three years since Hung had told her of the death of Michael, and commanded her to his bed. With Joanna. And Malama. Then, if her heart had been sick with the understanding that the only man she had ever loved was dead, her mind and stomach had been equally sickened by the requirements of her new master. Hung had spent too many years in sexual excesses to have retained any of the vigour of his youth. Now he required three women, coupling with him and with each other around him, to bring him even partially to erection, and penetration of anything narrower than a human mouth was more often than not beyond him.

They had submitted, she and Joanna, for the same reason that Malama must have submitted, time and again for so many years: Hung held the lives of Ralph and Janus in the palms of his hand. They had submitted then, and they had submitted on all the occasions to come, for three years, while sickened again by the knowledge of the murder of Wu Yei and Hung Cho – apparently within minutes of their arrest – and as his requirements had grown ever more obscene as his body grew weaker. The weakness had not affected his mind. His desires were only an aspect of his turbulent personality, his sudden rages. These were as difficult to survive as his love, and many did not, especially when the Ever Victorious Army had begun to defeat his generals. More and more heads had rolled across the floor before his throne, amongst them that of his last truly able commander, Wei Ch'ang-hui. By then both Ralph and Janus had been officers in the Tai-p'ing army, and every day Alicia had waited with bated breath to learn of her son's death. When, this very spring of 1864, he had been brought home, grievously wounded, but still capable of survival, she had wept for joy – he would not sit a saddle for some months, and who could tell what might have happened by then?

For her decision to survive, so that Ralph might survive, had been rewarded with the most stupendous news. Michael Harrington was not, after all, dead. He had survived his encounter with the 'bandits', and taken service with the famous General Ward. That Hung had intended his murder had been obvious, not only because of his rage when he had been told of Michael's survival, but because Michael, having escaped with his life, had opted to fight for the Manchu instead of returning to Nanking. So, it might appear that he had sacrificed his family to his vengeance. But Alicia knew better. His only hope of regaining them was to bring down Hung, and he was a man capable of making the hardest decisions.

Thus they had another duty, to survive until Michael and Ward got here. But even knowing that, she had been unable to resist taunting her tormentor. 'You have committed adultery,' she told him. 'You should take your own head.'

Almost had she gone too far. He had lost his temper, called his guards, had her stretched naked on the floor and bastinadoed for over an hour in his anger. Even as she had wept and twisted her body and fainted from the pain she had prayed he would not vent his rage on Joanna as well, and he had not, while remarkably he had neither executed *her* nor imprisoned her, but had had her thrown back into her own bed, bleeding and moaning, to be cared for by Malama. Later he had come and stood over her. 'Harrington is dead,' he said. 'It matters not whether he still contrives to breathe. He has joined the ranks of my enemies, and therefore he is dead, as will they all die.' Then he had commanded her to make love to him, even in her condition. Almost had she been tempted to bite it off and die in a blaze of glory. But . . . Michael was alive. And Michael was fighting for Hung's destruction, and her release from hell.

And Michael was coming nearer, every day. Why, a week ago the banners of the imperial army had been planted within sight of the city itself.

She had never had the courage to look beyond the moment of her rescue; it was sufficient that she should be alive when the moment arrived. That she, Alicia Hammond, should be capable of accepting so much, and survive, was a source of wonderment to her. And of pride. When she recalled the self-willed, and indeed selfish girl who had chosen Michael Harrington so deliberately as a husband, she found it difficult to believe they were the same person. Michael had sought to punish her for her desertion of him, by exposing her to an existence she had never known possible. But she had survived that too and, proudly, had won back his love. So now she had much to live for. Too much ever to lose her self-control again.

Or allow Joanna to lose hers. Joanna's composure in her nauseating circumstances had always been as remarkable as her own. Perhaps, Alicia thought, because they had never discussed sexual matters together, and therefore Joanna had not known what to expect – she had certainly been aware that her own parents had conducted a love-hate relationship for a good part of their lives. That all men might want the things Hung wanted had no doubt seemed likely to her, and Alicia had decided against enlightening her. So no doubt she had been utterly debauched, morally; once she had got over the initial shock of having her body turned into a plaything, she had almost certainly enjoyed her experiences more often than not. But for that she might have gone mad, and there had at least been the blessing that Hung had never been able to make her pregnant, even on the rare occasions when he had managed to enter her. Whether Joanna had truly survived, mentally, whether she could ever go to another man and accept love, was something else which would have to wait on their rescue. Alicia conceived that her only duty until then was to ensure the girl's survival as well, and where Hung was concerned that was always at risk. Now Joanna stirred in the bed beside her, and Alicia put her hand on her shoulder warningly.

The girl by the bed had withdrawn into the corner, anxious to be overlooked by their master, and eunuchs were holding the drapes aside to allow Hung to enter, others running ahead of him with lanterns to illuminate the room.

Hung stood above the two women in the bed. 'Where is she?' he demanded.

'We are both here, My Lord,' Alicia answered.

'I seek Malama.'

'Malama, My Lord? Is she not in her own apartments?'

'No, she is not,' Hung said, and paused to cough. 'I would know where she is.'

'I do not know, My Lord,' Alicia said.

He stared at her, and she tensed her muscles. If he were to order another whipping . . . 'You have seen her since the boy died?' he asked.

'No,' Alicia said. 'The boy? Oh, my God!'

'All deaths are the will of my father,' Hung told her. 'Janus fought well, and received a sword cut. He was dead when he was brought back to the city.'

'Oh, my God,' Alicia said again. 'Poor Malama. She . . .'

'She was distressed,' Hung said. 'She does not truly understand the will of my father.'

'And now she has disappeared,' Alicia said thoughtfully.

'You think she has taken her own life?'

Alicia raised her head in surprise. That thought had not occurred to her. Malama had only ever had a single reason for remaining in Hung's power: now that reason no longer existed. And the Manchu army was only a few miles away, with Michael. Malama would know that too. Just as she would know that as Malama, so well known to be the Senior Concubine, she would have no difficulty in persuading guards to let her pass. Oh, lucky, lucky Malama.

Hung had been studying her face, and interpreting her thoughts, correctly. 'You think she has fled to my enemies,' he said quietly. 'Fled to my enemies,' he shouted. 'By the hair on my father's head, I shall have her back. I shall flay her alive and tie her to a dog. I shall have ants eat her womb before her eyes. I shall . . .' he began to cough more violently that Alicia had ever heard him. Perhaps, she thought, he will cough himself to death.

She remained absolutely still, and made Joanna do the same. She had no intention of helping him, and knew that any other movement might be dangerous. She watched him sink to his knees, while his eunuchs and guards also stared at him in terror. It was several minutes before he regained his breath and raised his head. 'Help me,' he whispered.

Two of the eunuchs hurried forward and raised him to his feet. 'Take me to my chamber,' Hung said, his voice stronger. 'And bring me Malama's women. I will begin with them.'

'Release her,' Michael commanded, and the sentries stepped aside. Malama's hands hung at her side, and dripped water, as did the rest of her; she wore only the dhoti of their first meeting, twenty-five years earlier, but then she had been twelve years old; now she was thirty-

399

seven. She was more assured than he remembered her, and the more beautiful for that. If she had suffered, then her suffering had given her a confidence in her own powers of survival which she had lacked as a young woman.

'Brandy,' he told his servant. 'And breakfast. Haste.' He held her hands, drew her into the tent, took the blanket from his cot and gave it to her. She dropped the dhoti and wrapped herself in the blanket, drying the last of the river water. Then she sat on the bed, and a moment later was lying on it. She was exhausted.

'Michael Sahib,' she whispered.

There was so much he wanted to ask her, but she had to rest. 'Sleep,' he said.

'No.' She clasped his hand as he knelt beside her. 'Michael, I . . .' she sighed, and slept.

The servant brought in the brandy and the food, and Michael had him place it on the camp table. He remained sitting beside her for more than an hour, watching water trickling from that midnight hair, the swell of her still-perfect breasts as she breathed, the flare of her nostrils. The last survivor out of all the women who had played their parts in his life, he thought. And the one he had never accepted. Come to him at last. It gave him a curious feeling of regeneration; he could have sat and looked at her for ever.

At last she stirred, and sighed, and opened her eyes. 'Michael . . .' she rose on her elbow in alarm.

'Hush, sweetheart. You are safe now.'

She sighed, and fell back again, but her eyes remained open. 'He killed my son, Michael. He killed Janus.'

He held her hand again, while her nails bit into his palm.

'He was all I had to live for,' Malama said. 'All I had to live for.'

He gave her the brandy to drink, and she sat up again. 'You have everything to live for, Malama. You are safe now, with me. And young enough to have another son.'

She gave him a look which was a mixture of shyness and fear. He could understand that, after so long, and after so many years with Hung. But she, so marvellously resurrected from the grave, and more beautiful than she had ever been, was all *he* could possibly have to live for, now. 'How did you leave the city?' he asked.

'I used the sewer, close by the Palace of God.'

Michael frowned. 'Was it not guarded?'

She shook her head. 'It leads into the river, and is barred where it enters the water, but the bars were sufficiently widely spaced to allow me to squeeze through – I had greased my body. I swam from there. The current carried me, but it was such a long way.' She sighed. 'I came to you for vengeance, Michael Sahib.'

'And you shall have your vengeance,' he promised. 'The city will surely fall. And no Tai-p'ing can expect any mercy from the Manchu.'

She sighed, and finished the brandy. Outside the tent it was daylight.

'So eat your breakfast, and rest easy. I have my duties to attend to, but I will return as soon as I can.'

'Michael . . .' her fingers were again tight on his. 'I could not bring the others.'

'The others?'

She inhaled. 'Alicia, and Joanna, and Ralph.'

He stared at her in consternation. 'Alicia? Alicia is alive?'

'Of course. She is one of Hung's concubines.' She winced as she spoke, and Michael realized that he had been holding her as tightly as she him. He relaxed his fingers.

'And Joanna?'

'Yes.'

'And Ralph?'

'He is lying wounded. But it is said he will recover.'

His family was alive after all, and still waiting for him. 'What of Wu Yei?'

'Hung had her murdered. Together with Hung Cho.'

Michael released her hand, and curled his fingers into fists. Part of his family, at any rate. Alicia! And Malama. He looked at her, and she gazed back.

'Michael, Hung is a sick man. He coughs all the time. Thus he is even more irrational than before. I fear that when your troops storm the city, he will have Alicia executed too.'

'Yes,' Michael said. 'Sick, you say. Does Wei still command his army?'

'Wei was executed for being defeated. Generals are executed almost every day. There is no longer a unified command. No one will take the post, for fear of being executed. Nanking is one huge charnel house.'

'But ready to fall,' Michael said.

'Yes,' she agreed, gazing at him. They were sharing too many unthinkable thoughts, at that moment.

'Eat your breakfast,' he said. 'I will return as soon as I can.'

He went outside, where Lucas was waiting for him. 'Is it true, sir, that a deserter has arrived from the Tai-p'ing?'

'Yes,' Michael said.

'Is the news good?'

'Very,' Michael said. 'I must go and talk with General Li.'

Because the news was very good, from a military point of view. Hung's destructive urge was now ready to destroy himself. Morale in the Tai-p'ing army must be very low, and if Hung was himself ill . . . and Malama had told him something even more important than that.

'They will never be so vulnerable to an all-out assault as now, General,' he told Li.

Li stroked his moustaches. 'Indeed, it would appear so, General Harrington. This is splendid news. Can you trust the one who brought it?'

'Absolutely,' Michael said. 'She is a very old friend.'

Li raised one eyebrow, but made no comment. 'Then we will make our dispositions. You will lead your brigade against the water gate. There can be no doubt that those blue-jackets are greatly feared by the Tai-p'ing. I will take the rest of the army against the south wall. There will of course be a preliminary bombardment, but we will scale the walls if need be. Yes. We will attack at dawn tomorrow.'

'With respect, General Li.'

Li waited.

'It is my opinion that a preliminary bombardment will be useless, and merely inform the enemy of what we are about. I think we may obtain the same result entirely by surprise. To achieve this, I would like permission to lead a forlorn hope, before the main assault.'

'A forlorn hope? Is this necessary?'

'To me, General. I believe that if, with a picked band of volunteers, I can gain entry to the city clandestinely, I can reach the palace of Hung Hsiu-ch'uan, and secure his person.'

'How will you gain this entry?'

'I lived in Nanking for many years. I will enter through the sewers.'

'Will they not be blocked against just such an attempt?'

'Not those that exit into the river.'

'Their inner exits will still be guarded. You will be killed.'

'Not necessarily. Not if we time it so that you launch your attack once I am inside the city. Then we will have reached Hung before he can take command of the defence himself.'

Li frowned at him. 'There is an ulterior motive here. Be frank with me, General Harrington. You seek to be personally avenged on Hung for the wrongs he has done you.'

'That is at least partly true,' Michael agreed.

Li shook his head. 'It is an unmilitary point of view, General. We will all be avenged on Hung when we take the city. And I cannot have you take such a risk. I need you at the head of your brigade.'

'I would also hope to save the lives of my wife and children,' Michael said.

Li frowned at him. 'They are in Hung's power?'

Michael nodded. 'The power of a madman who is about to see his kingdom topple.'

'Yes. I understand. Hm. I should still refuse you. Who will command the brigade?'

'Colonel Phang is fully capable of leading the assault, General.'

'Hm,' Li remarked, and Michael could see how his brain was working; it would mean that the final triumph would be accomplished entirely by Manchu captains, and their Chinese supporters: Peking would have to be pleased about that. And although Li was an honest man, and even something of a friend, yet must he also have it in mind that Peking might be quite pleased were General Harrington to be killed leading a forlorn hope in the final battle. Michael could not help but wonder about that himself. 'I do not think I could refuse any man, even one as important as yourself, General Harrington, the right to see to the safety of his family,' Li said at last. 'Now, let us call in the staff and work out the details of this assault, very carefully.'

It was noon by the time Michael returned to the brigade, where Phang and Lucas were anxiously awaiting him. 'Tomorrow at dawn,' Michael told them. 'The brigade will assault the water gate at zero four one zero hours, that is, ten minutes after the main assault commences on the south gate. You will lead the assault, Colonel Phang, with the brevet rank of Brigadier-General.'

'Me, sir?' Phang was astonished. 'But . . .'

'I will be otherwise engaged,' Michael told him. 'Now I wish you to assemble the men, and tell them I need forty volunteers for a special mission. Make sure every man understands that it is of a highly dangerous nature, and that it is possible none of us will survive.'

'You mean to enter the city,' Lucas said.

'Yes.'

'Can you do this, unobserved?' Phang asked.

'I believe so. I know Nanking very well. Once in the city we will of course have to fight our way to the palace of Hung Hsiu-ch'uan. But, with the advantage of surprise, I believe we can do this. We will make our move at zero two three zero. If the assault takes place as scheduled, we should succeed.'

'It will take place on schedule,' Phang promised.

'Then find me my volunteers. Each man must be an expert swimmer, and I want each man armed with a revolver, spare cartridges, and a bayonet. It will not be possible to swim with a sword. Have the volunteers assembled at zero two zero zero. You understand that no man is actually to know what we are about.'

'Yes, sir,' they said together, and hurried off.

Michael knew they would have no shortage of volunteers; it was a matter of picking the best forty. He lifted the tent flap and went inside. Malama had been lying down, but she sat up as he entered; the blanket was folded across her waist.

'I am sorry I am late,' he said. 'I had a great deal to do.'

'You are going to assault the city?'

He nodded. 'Tomorrow morning.'

'Despite . . .' she hesitated.

'I am going to lead an advance party, through the sewers, and gain Hung's palace before the assault commences.'

'You?' Her face twisted in anxiety.

'It is my family, Malama.'

'You will be killed.'

'Not willingly,' he promised her.

She gazed at him. 'And you will avenge Janus,' she said.

'I will avenge everything, Malama. Including all the ills Hung has committed upon you.' He sighed. 'You have had the most terrible life. And I am responsible for all of it. I feel very guilty about that. More guilty than I can possibly express.'

She took his hand. 'It has not been my Karma to be happy, Michael Sahib, since I left my father. But I am happy now. When I am with you.'

That was all she had ever wanted, and he had never allowed her that satisfaction. And now he was going to

405

leave her again, to rescue Alicia and the children, the only people in the world he loved. And the people who represented his future. Could he but regain them, and with control of Hammond and Teng, there was no limit to that future. He would not be fifty for another year.

But this girl represented, if not his future, so many aspects of his past, for without her, none of this could have ever happened. She was indeed the star who had controlled his destiny for twenty-five years, as she had begun by saving his life, inadvertently. And he loved her, too. He always had. And tomorrow morning he might die, and leave her utterly alone in the world.

Were that to happen, she was far more deserving than Jeremy Cooper or Pieter Hammond. And, he suspected, far more capable of coping with Ali as well, given sufficient backing.

'Listen to me,' he said. 'If I die, everything I possess is yours. I will make a will, tonight, and have it witnessed by Colonel Phang and Captain Lucas. This testament will cancel all my previous wills. Malama, thanks to the generosity of the Princess Jalina, I hold the controlling interest in Hammond and Teng. You will be a millionairess. You can go back to Calcutta and do whatever you please, or back to the delta and give your family all the money you wish. Do you understand this?'

'And if you live, Michael Sahib?'

'I will still have enough to give you anything you wish, Malama. You will never want, never be unhappy again.'

'I will never be happy, Michael Sahib.' She lifted his hand and placed it on her breast. 'I am only happy now. I know you love Alicia. Now you are going to risk your life to save her. Whether you live or die, my happiness ends tonight; money cannot make me happy, unless it can be shared with one I love. Michael, I wish to be happy, once, before we die.'

Once, Michael recalled, he had tried to keep three balls in the air at once. Now there were only two, easy to catch, one with each hand. But in fact, there was only one.

He did not know what Hung had done to this trembling child, because Malama was still that, and could never be more than that; in his arms her aura of confidence and perhaps even power melted away. He did not know whether she was still capable of sexual stimulation, of sexual response. But she was capable of love, as she had loved him with a singleminded devotion for all of her life. And her beauty, the perfection of breast and belly and buttock, the length of leg, the weight of raven hair, had been created for love. For twenty-five years he had neglected this, and for twenty-five years others had abused it. Now, for this fleeting moment, it was his, and she was happy, because she had lain in his arms, and fulfilled a dream.

They ate dinner together, and he introduced her to Lucas. Then they lay again in each other's arms. They might have been suspended in time, because of the many years they had squandered, and the uncertainty of the morrow. Afterwards he slept, briefly, with her head on his arm and her body nestled against his in the narrow camp cot, but awoke to look at his watch at one thirty. Carefully he eased his arm out from beneath her and got out of the bed, reaching for his clothes. He would have dressed outside, when she spoke. 'Is it time?'

'Yes.'

'Michael . . . let me go with you.'

'No,' he said. 'Your presence would distract me.'

'Michael, will you succeed?'

'Yes,' he said.

'Then God go with you, and bring you back.'

'With Alicia,' he said.

It was not a question, but she took it as such, and sighed, and lay down again. 'With Alicia, Michael. Oh, pray God, with Alicia. But Michael . . . kiss me once more before you go.'

Michael surveyed his forty men, assembled in front of the tent. Like himself, they wore only drawers, and a holster and cartridge belt from which were suspended their revolvers and bayonets. He knew them all by sight, and they were in the main the men he had expected to be present.

With them, also stripped, was Captain Lucas.

'You?' Michael demanded.

'Every officer volunteered, sir,' Lucas explained. 'Colonel Phang allowed me to insist.'

Michael did not argue; he knew that Lucas was as good a man as he had in the entire brigade. 'All right,' he said, and looked at his watch again; it was twenty-five minutes past two, and the Manchu camp was beginning to stir. 'Let's go.'

They went down to the river, where Phang had already organized the sampan. Despite the continuous fighting, the river remained what it had always been, the only means of communication between the interior and the coast, and as such was in constant use, while with Nanking in a state of siege, more and more sampans were using the hours of darkness to get past the city, for the Tai-p'ing, unable to obtain food supplies for themselves, were in the habit of firing upon any boats their guns could reach on the water.

Six of the volunteers manned the sweeps, the remaining thirty-four crouched in the empty well, and the craft was pushed from the bank and made its way upstream, slowly against the current. Michael knelt in the bows, studying the city walls as they came abeam. The sewer outfall he wanted was that from the inner city, which was also the upper city. It was therefore necessary to pass the outer walls, and sure enough, even in the darkness, there was a challenge and a shot as the sound of the sweeps crept through the pre-dawn stillness. But the ball was wide, and they continued on their way.

Michael let them go a good four hundred yards above the last tower, before he whispered his commands. His men came out of the hold, and while the sweeps held the sampan as steadily as possible, they slipped over the side and into the water. Michael was last to leave, and the sampan commenced drifting back down. Once again it brought a challenge, and some more shooting from the walls, which suitably distracted their attention from any splashes beneath them. The current carried the men downstream also, but they were making for the shore, and all came safely in, clinging to the narrow mudflats which bordered the water above the city.

Here they paused to catch their breaths, and then Michael led them, slowly and carefully, along the shore-line, beneath the walls now; they could hear the tramp of the sentries above them, and even snatches of conversation, but it was near dawn and the Tai-p'ing were mainly waiting to be relieved.

They smelt the outfall long before they reached it, and Michael made them halt again while every man checked his weapons; the brief immersion in the water should not have interfered with the percussion-cap cartridges. Then he led them forward again, and up to the mouth of the outfall. Here, as Malama had told him, there was an iron grating, and if the bars were wide enough to allow the greased body of a slender woman to pass through them, they were certainly too close together to admit a man. He had anticipated this, however, and it took only a few minutes probing into the old, soft stonework with their bayonets to free the grating and pull it away. The noise sounded very loud to the men crouching around the outfall, but appeared to mean nothing to those on the walls above.

The grating removed, Michael led his men into the interior. If the night outside had been dark, inside the tunnel was stygian, while the stench was so offensive as to be almost poisonous. They made their way up a slope, gentle enough, but also slippery as they were waist deep in slime and water, surrounded by floating effluvia, while rats scurried along the walls, occasionally entering the water with loud splashes. One of the men swore as he was bitten, but if that was the only casualty they suffered they were not going to have much trouble.

It took them very nearly forty-five minutes to crawl up the pipe, and by then it was a quarter to four. The assault would commence at four sharp. But now they were on level ground, and in front of them was a ladder and a manhole. Michael tested the ladder very carefully; he had it much in mind that these tunnels had been dug centuries before, when Nanking had first been the capital city of China. But it held, and he went up it, slowly raising the manhole to look out. He was in the centre of a street he immediately recognized; it was only one removed from Hung's palace. There was a stroke of fortune. But his relief was short lived; as he scrambled clear of the hole there came a challenge. He turned on his knees to see a squad of Tai-p'ing soldiers hurrying towards this strange, odorous apparition who had appeared out of the ground.

Michael drew his revolver and fired. The first man fell but the rest came on. 'Haste,' Michael snapped.

Lucas was second out, firing as he did so, and then the others debouched. Two more of the Tai-p'ing fell, and the rest hastily retreated, but that they would be back with reinforcements could not be doubted. Michael waved his arm and his men followed him on the double, round the next corner and to the gates of the palace of the Right Hand of God, while the city began to awaken, disturbed by the revolver shots. Here they were challenged by the sentries, who died immediately in a hail of bullets; then Michael's men were swarming over the walls and dropping inside the gates to release the bolts, and they were all racing up the paved driveway beyond. More guards appeared on the huge porch of the palace, but as they did so there was an enormous sound from outside the city, a beating of drums and a clashing of cymbals, an explosion of musketry, and the roar of thousands of men hurrying forward to assault the walls.

'We are attacked,' one of the guards screamed, and turned to run inside. 'Great Hung!'

He died as Michael shot him in the back, then hurled his bayonet into the chest of another. Then he was through, making for the private apartments of the war-lord, off which he knew were situated the women's quarters. Eunuchs appeared and one waved a sword at him, but he brought him down as well, listening all the while to the sounds of battle from behind him.

He thrust the silken drapes aside and entered Hung's private reception chamber; Lucas and half a dozen men were at his heels. Here there were more eunuchs, but these fled, shouting their terror. As they left through one door, another opened. Here were more guards, and behind them, Hung Hsiu-ch'uan. 'Surrender!' Michael shouted. 'The city is ours.'

Hung stared at him for a moment, face twisting into a snarl, then the doors were slammed shut and a bolt rasped.

'Break that down,' Michael told his men. Some twenty of them had caught up with him now, and they immediately picked up the heaviest pieces of furniture to hurl against the wood. 'Take command here,' he snapped at Lucas. 'Six of you, come with me.' He charged through the doorway abandoned by the eunuchs, and found himself in the women's quarters, surrounded by screams and fleeing bodies. 'Alicia!' Michael shouted. 'Joanna!'

'Michael!' Alicia shouted back. 'Oh, Michael!'

Then she screamed again, in terror. He looked left and right, unable to determine where her voice had come from, and one of his men pointed. He burst through another doorway, and found himself in an inner court-yard, paused in horror. It was daylight now, and before him a girl was spreadeagled on the ground, wrists and ankles tied to stakes; she had been horribly mutilated, nose, ears, breasts, fingers and toes cut off. She was clearly dead, but only recently, and from the amount of dried blood had been cut to pieces before her living eyes. For a moment Michael nearly fainted, then he realized she was Chinese. One of Malama's serving women, he supposed.

The door on the far side of the courtyard was still open, and through it he heard Alicia scream again. He led his men on, burst into this room, which was one of Hung's private chambers, and faced Hung himself. He had four guards with him, and between them they held both Alicia and Joanna, naked and gasping.

Michael pointed, while his whole being was consumed

with a mixture of relief and anger. 'Surrender, Hung. The city is ours.'

'Surrender,' Hung sneered. 'I am the Right Hand of God. At any moment my father will send down his angels to drive the Manchu into the mountains. And you . . . you will watch your women die, Harrington. Because I know now that you were not sent me by my father, but by the Devil, to encompass my destruction. Cut their throats,' he snapped.

Michael gasped, elation turning to horror, because there was nothing he could do. He had reloaded his revolver, yet could not fire for fear of hitting the women. But at that moment the outer door burst open, and Lucas led the remainder of his men into the room. The guards were distracted, and Michael was upon them, sending the first man to the floor with a blow from his revolver, snatching Alicia from the arms of the other even as he shot the man at close range. Then he turned to see if he could also save Joanna, but Lucas had done that, scattering both her captors with his revolver, and allowing her to faint in his arms.

Still holding Alicia, Michael turned back to face Hung, who had retired against the far wall. 'Listen, Hung,' he said. 'Listen.'

The morning was filled with horrifying noise, screams and shouts, howls and shrieks, but as at least part of it came from terrified women and children, no one could doubt that the Manchu were inside the city.

'Surrender,' he said for a third time.

'I am the Right Hand of God,' Hung said. 'It is not for me to be carried in chains before the Ch'ing. I am immortal. I will live for ever, in the minds and hearts of my people. It matters not whether I am here in person or not. I am the Right Hand of God.' He drew a long dagger from inside his tunic, held it in both hands, and then plunged it into his own stomach. He fell to his knees, while blood poured on to the already reeking floor, but still held the knife in place. 'The Right Hand of God,' he screamed, and fell to the floor.

*

'He died like the vermin he was,' remarked Li Huang-chang. 'Now let us destroy the rest of *these* vermin, before they contaminate us.'

Nanking was submerged beneath the stench of death, as the Manchu soldiery hunted through the streets, killing everyone they could find, man, woman or child. This then was the end of the dream of a China ruled by the Chinese, perhaps for another hundred years, Michael thought. Because the Right Hand of God had turned out to be only a man, after all. And not a very admirable one.

'It is not a task for which I am temperamentally equipped, General Li,' he said. 'Indeed, I have completed my task.'

'There are still many Tai-p'ing followers to the west,' Li pointed out. 'They too will need to be exterminated.'

'With Hung dead, you will not find that a difficult matter,' Michael told him. 'With this victory your Ch'ing masters have regained control of China. I seek your permission to lay down my command and return with my family to my own people.'

Li nodded. 'You have served my masters well.' He smiled. 'Even if it is possible to feel that it was partly due to you that the Tai-p'ing achieved so much.'

'I am aware of it,' Michael said. 'I can take no credit for your victory.'

Li gave another nod. 'It might even be wisest for you to have regained the protection of the British before my masters learn that they no longer have need of you. Take Captain Lucas with you. I may personally congratulate you, General Harrington, and say that it has been a privilege to serve with you, and fight at your side. But then, I am not an emperor.' He held out his hand.

Michael shook it, then stepped back and saluted. 'Mr Harrington, as of this moment, Li. It is a very pleasant feeling.'

A sampan was made ready for them, and into it Michael and Lucas carried Ralph; the wound in the boy's leg was healing well, even if the severed tendons meant he would

413

probably always walk with a limp. Alicia and Joanna and Malama were also placed in the boat, and the crew manned the sweeps, to pull them away from the city of the dead, and the dying, enable them to breathe the fresh air coming up the river.

There had been no time to talk, to explain, anything. But were explanations necessary? Alicia and Malama looked at each other, and embraced, but shared no confidences. Perhaps they had already shared too much. The two women he had always loved more than any other, brought together by the whim of fate and a vicious genius's lust. Their futures, with his, had still to be decided. He was content to wait and let matters take their course.

He did not know if he could say the same for Joanna. The girl looked around her with self-conscious, aware eyes. She did not know what was happening to her, what was going to happen. For three years she had been the plaything of a crazed warlord, had lived herself in a hot-house environment of luxurious but aberrant sexuality. The normal world into which she had again been pitch-forked was abnormal to her; the father she had respected and perhaps feared had become a man – she knew what hung between his legs, and the uses to which he might wish to put it.

Even more sad, she had been taught to deal in superlatives. If she still feared him, Michael thought, because she knew he was now the master of her fate, she had nothing but contempt for the crew of the sampan, or even Lucas, drew her cloak tighter around herself whenever one of them came close. And Lucas had saved her life, and had obviously been much taken by her beauty.

But neither could she be fully rehabilitated until they had regained the sanity of British domination, English manners and clothes, utter security.

He knew he could give her, and her mother and brother, and Malama, these things, if they would accept them. But there too the future was uncertain. If he could lay claim to the control of Hammond and Teng, and all

414

the wealth and power that went with it, he might yet have to destroy Ali Hammond to exert that control. He might feel that Ali deserved anything that was coming to him – he could not be sure of Alicia's response to a confrontation between the two of them.

Again time would be needed to find the answers. But it was only three days down the river to Shanghai. Three days in which he and his family lived in total intimacy on the small sampan, and yet hardly spoke. Each had too much to say, but only in private. It was on the third morning that, as he stood in the bows looking for the first glimpse of the walls of Shanghai in the distance – the city lay up a tributary of the Yangtse itself, the Whangpo, but was yet usually visible from the main river across the flat countryside – that Michael found Alicia beside him.

'Where are we going?' she asked.

He looked down at her. 'Where would you like to go?'

'Anywhere. Away from China.'

'We are certainly about to leave China,' he promised her.

'Well, then . . . tell me where we are going?'

'Hong Kong, in the first instance. And then, Singapore.'

'Singapore? But . . .'

'Don't you want to go home?'

She shivered. 'I don't know. You will have to give me time.' She glanced over her shoulder. 'I think we all need time. Joanna . . .'

'You will all have time.'

They gazed at each other. If she had shown no resentment about the probability that Malama had escaped to his bed, neither had she shown any resentment of the fact that since her rescue he had done no more than touch her hand – but then, he had done no more than touch Malama's hand, either. Malama would wait, patiently, for him to resolve the conflict in his mind, and would accept his decision, he knew. But here again, Alicia was an imponderable. He did not know if, after a five-year separation, she wished to return to him, sexually; he did not

415

know, after three years as Hung's mistress, if she would be able to go to any man, sexually. Here again, he could only wait, and hope.

But yet there were things which needed to be said. 'Alicia, I want you to know that I understand my guilt.'

'Your guilt? You rescued us, Michael.'

'Having been responsible for your catastrophe in the first place. You distrusted Hung on sight.'

'Perhaps I did. But we were already committed.'

'Again my doing. Can you forgive me?'

She smiled. 'We both have certain things to answer for, I think. Only the future should now concern us. All of our futures.' She had not mentioned Malama by name, but she wanted an answer. She looked at him, waiting, and then past him. 'Oh, my God,' she said. 'Oh, my God!'

He turned his head, even as the sampan lost way. Anchored in the river ahead of them was a Manchu war junk, her guns trained on them, her boats already in the water, filled with armed men.

Lucas was at his side in a moment, revolver drawn. 'Put it away, Peter,' Michael said. 'There are too many. Besides, it is me they want.'

To have come so close to escaping, and then failed; even as he was taken on board the junk, the walls of Shanghai came into view.

The women were horrified, and even Malama dissolved in hysterical tears. Still suffering from the shock of their ordeal, they had founded their hopes of the future on their rescuer, the man to whom they had always turned. Now, to have him whisked away . . . to execution?

Michael had time to speak to Lucas, briefly. 'My wife is the sister of Ali Hammond, the Chairman of the firm of Hammond and Teng,' he said. 'Use her name – she will support you – and obtain the necessary credit to get from Hong Kong to Singapore. There they will be safe.'

'My God,' Lucas said. 'But you . . . after all you have done for the Manchu . . .'

'I suspect they remember more what I did for the Taip'ing.' Michael gave a grim smile. 'Perhaps with reason.'

Lucas swallowed. 'Are you not afraid, sir?'

Michael considered. 'Yes,' he said. 'But I think I am more disappointed.'

Once again a glittering future had appeared over the horizon, and once again it had turned out to be a mirage. Every aspect of it, the wealth and the power, the fame, the love of Malama and Alicia, of his children, hopefully, at last, the respect of the community who thought of him only as a desperado, all disappeared . . . beneath the headsman's sword? He could hardly doubt that.

Yet his principal emotion, perhaps fortunately, was one of utter exhaustion. If his life had never been inactive, there had been periods of quiescence when he had lived in Nanking. For the past five years, ever since he had accepted Captain Lane's invitation to join the British delegation to Peking, his brain at least had been constantly straining to achieve a succession of ends. Now it was finished. There were no further ends to be attained. He could only wonder if it was Tzu-hsi herself who had given the order for his arrest, or if he was involved in her own fall from power. No doubt he would soon find out.

He was not ill treated by the captain of the junk, not even chained, although he was confined to his cabin while they sailed through the British squadron at the mouth of the Yangtse. Once clear of the river, however, he was given the run of the ship. Then why did he not end it immediately, and leap over the side, he wondered, and rob them of the pleasure of inflicting any more torments on his body? Only because he had never considered suicide as a practical form of escape. And because he was curious, to the last.

They entered the Peiho and made Tientsin. Again he was confined as they passed through the British squadron in the Gulf of Chihli, and in Tientsin he was transferred, in the dead of night, to a sampan which took him up the river under armed guard. They ascended to Tung Chow, and there mounted horses for the ride into Peking, again at night; now at last his wrists were bound. It was still dark when they entered the Sha-wo-men, the east gate of the Chinese city, and only dogs barked as they made their way through the narrow streets. At least Michael was not blindfolded on this occasion, and could look around him at the huddled houses, inhale the varied odours of the sleeping community.

The heavily guarded Tsien-men gateway allowed them into the Tartar city, and they proceeded up a broad, empty avenue to the Ta'tsing-men, the gate to the Forbidden City itself. Here again there were guards in force, to whom passes had to be shown before they were allowed to enter another broad, straight avenue, and Michael found himself looking at the Imperial Palace.

They dismounted, and he was taken up the great Dragon Staircase, walking to one side so as not to tread on the dragon itself, which was so cleverly painted on the marble that it appeared to move, constantly floating downwards – only His Celestial Majesty was allowed to walk down the centre of the staircase . . . and His Celestial Majesty was a babe in arms.

Inside the palace, in the huge throne room, Michael was handed over to the eunuchs, as he had expected, and taken into a bathing chamber, where he was made both to bathe and shave, and as he had not eaten since the previous evening in Tung Chow, was given food and drink. 'The condemned man's last meal,' he remarked to his attendants, but as usual they did not answer him, while four of their number stood with drawn swords in case he tried to escape them.

Remarkably, when they were finished and he was dressed in clean clothes, they did not rebind his wrists, but merely surrounded him as he was taken through a succession of corridors to an antechamber, where they motioned him to wait, continuing to face him with swords in their hands. He waited here for upwards of an hour, allowing his mind to range over the events of his life, the ups and downs, the disasters and the triumphs – because there had been a few of those. But always he came back

418

to the first time he had waited in an antechamber in a Chinese palace, perhaps the most unforgettable experience of his life. But one which was about to be repeated, because the drapes were trembling, and the room was filled with scent, and Tzu-hsi entered to take her seat.

She was even more richly dressed than the first time he had seen her, and even more arrogantly aware of her position. She gazed at him, and he bowed. He knew better now than to speak before he was addressed.

'I am told the bandit is dead, Harrington,' she said.

'I saw him die, Your Majesty.'

'After having raised him to such strength that he threatened my son's empire,' Tzu-hsi reminded him.

'He was my master. Until he betrayed me.'

'And then you changed sides. Can a man who changes sides ever be trusted?'

'Depending on the reason, Your Majesty. Hung Hsiuch'uan betrayed me, not I him. I was on my way to him with information of great importance to the Tai-p'ing cause, when he sought to have me murdered.'

'What information?'

Michael drew a long breath. But if he was going to die in any event, what did he have to lose? 'I would have told him how weak the Ch'ing were, how divided their counsel, how they had fled to Jehol, and how the road to Peking lay open.'

Tzu-hsi's eyes flashed fire. 'You dare to repeat this to me?'

'I dare to tell you the truth, Your Majesty.'

She continued to glare at him for several moments, but he would not lower his gaze. 'You were also one of the men who burned my Summer Palace,' she said.

'I was not, Your Highness. I disapproved of such an act of wanton destruction. But . . . perhaps it was a just punishment for Prince Ch'un's deceit in arresting our party, which went to him under a safe conduct, and in murdering so many of our people.'

Another glare, and then slowly her expression softened.

'You were always too straightforward, Harrington. A palace can be rebuilt. And now Hung Hsiu-ch'uan is dead. They have sent me his head, pickled in brine. It pleased me to look upon it. You told me once that when I received his head, you would serve me, instead of him.'

'I have served you, for three years, Your Majesty.' His heart was beginning to pound. Could she, after all, not mean to execute him?

'I know of this. You, and Ward, and Gordon, have all served me well. Ward is dead. Gordon has returned to England. I am told they call him Chinese Gordon.' Her lips twisted. 'Only you remain. Would you serve me now, Harrington?'

He was not going to die. He was, after all, going to live, and triumph. His heart swelled. And he could stay here, in the shadow of this magnificent, unstable creature . . . and turn his back for ever on those he loved, and on the life which beckoned him. 'Your Majesty,' he said. 'I would retire from serving others, and serve myself.'

She frowned. 'How may a man not serve his master? Or his mistress?'

'Simply by not having a master. Or a mistress, Your Majesty.'

'But is there not a Queen ruling England, and all Englishmen? I have heard of this queen. Is her name not Victoria? Is she not your mistress?'

'That is so, Your Majesty. But the Queen of England is like a goddess. She rules, but does not seek to interfere in the affairs of men. Those affairs are conducted by her ministers, who are men like myself, and who understand the need for freedom. So long as I obey the laws of the land, they will allow me to pursue my life as I see best.'

Tzu-hsi gazed at him for several minutes, still frowning, and he wondered if he had overstepped the mark. At last she said, 'I thought you could be of service to me, Harrington.' She sighed. 'In many ways. But if you will acknowledge no master, I can see that you would be a disruptive element. And if you always told me the truth,

I should have no choice but to take off your head.' She half turned her own head, and one of her eunuchs hurried from the room. Michael tensed himself, for her final judgement was about to be delivered. The wait was only for a few minutes, then the eunuch returned, accompanied by several others, carrying between them a large tray. This was placed on the ground before Tzu-hsi, and Michael blinked at it in astonishment.

'Despite all, you have done me a great service, Harrington,' Tzu-hsi said. 'I would reward you.'

One of the eunuchs lifted from the tray a riding jacket in imperial yellow silk, with green collar and cuffs.

'I give you this sign of my approval,' Tzu-hsi said. 'It conveys the ultimate privilege, that of being esteemed by the Imperial Ch'ing. And with it . . .' she extended her own hand. 'I give you this ruby button, the badge which pronounces you a mandarin of the first, and highest, rank. No member of my people will fail to pay you everlasting respect while you wear these things. Receive them, Harrington.'

Michael stepped forward, and she placed the ruby in his palm. It was the first time they had touched each other, and she left her hand where it was for a moment. As he was already bowing, he kissed the knuckles. Instantly the hand was withdrawn, and her eyes flashed.

Michael straightened. 'It is the salute I would have bestowed upon Queen Victoria, Your Majesty.'

Tzu-hsi's expression relaxed, and she looked down at her hand. 'Then am I pleased. You may salute me again, Harrington.'

Michael did so.

Tzu-hsi smiled at him. 'Now, leave my presence before I forget that I am the ruler of all China.'

Singapore was busier than he had ever remembered it. But then, so had been Hong Kong. The whole of Pacific Asia was bursting with trade, and prosperity, as Englishman and Frenchman, German and Hollander, Belgian and Russian, and, even while themselves torn by civil war,

American, all competed to sell their marvels to the Chinese. That twenty million people, so it was said, had spent the past ten years in worshipping a false god and then in dying might never have been.

But of all the flags that Michael observed on his journey south, the Union Jack was the most in evidence, and amongst the Union Jacks, the supporting house flag of Hammond and Teng, the dragon and the lion rampant together, was most to be seen – and two of the ships in Hong Kong had been steam powered. He had inherited a trading empire. It only remained to be grasped.

And with it, so many other rewards.

It was now three months since he had seen or heard of his family, three months in which they might well have supposed him dead. He could only remind himself that they had had ample cause to suppose him dead before. He had travelled from Peking as incognito as possible, and if this had been difficult in China, as he had taken passage in an ordinary trading junk he had found it simple enough to accomplish in Hong Kong. Tzu-hsi, in addition to her other gifts, had supplied him with silver, and in Hong Kong he had changed himself from a wealthy mandarin into an English gentleman, all in a week, and all without visiting the offices of Hammond and Teng or the house on the hill. No doubt speculation was rife in the Club as to the identity of Mr Smith, but after fifteen years of constant campaigning his wind-and-sun-scorched face, with its granite etchings at mouth and eyes and chin, and the streaks of grey in the cropped black hair, was not easily recognizable. By the time Pieter Hammond could have worked out who he had to be, and perhaps sent a message to Singapore, Michael had already been at sea, sailing south on a chartered junk.

Perhaps Pieter Hammond would not have sent such a message. But that Michael did not know for sure.

So he could step ashore in Singapore unexpected and unwelcomed, which was how he wanted it. If he still felt strange to be wearing a black top hat, a black gabardine cutaway coat over a fawn waistcoat and trousers, with braided side seams, black boots and a black silk neckcloth, rather than a silk blouse and breeches, it was certain that he appeared entirely part of the scene into which he stepped. For the bustling dockside, where steam-powered cranes swung to and fro and Chinese and Malay stevedores worked shoulder to shoulder, was dominated by the white factors who stood with hands on hips, giving orders, cursing and swearing when anything went awry. None of them was as well dressed as the tall man who stepped from the junk, but none of them gave him a second glance, either; he was one of them, and would no doubt make his business known in the proper quarter.

Michael had hired a servant in Hong Kong, a boy named Kang Lin, and Kang hefted the one suitcase his master possessed while they went in search of a hired phaeton. This accomplished Michael directed it to the offices of Hammond and Teng. He knew a pleasant feeling of anticipation. He had suffered enough from the British establishment, principally in Singapore; now he meant to indulge himself in a little schoolboy amusement of his own, before commencing the serious business of reclaiming his family.

Hammond and Teng had always dominated the Singapore waterfront; it still did, having grown as the city and the warehousing had grown; and there were at least five ships in the harbour flying the house flag, two more of them steamers. The offices now occupied a separate building, four storeys high, between two of the go-downs, and here Michael – having left Kang with the phaeton – encountered, at the reception desk, a bespectacled middle-aged Chinese who peered at him uncertainly.

'I have business with Mr Hammond,' Michael said, in English.

'You have appointment?'

'I'm afraid not.'

'Not possible for to see Mr Hammond without appointment.'

'Ah,' Michael said. 'Well, old fellow, I shall just wander up and surprise him, shall I?'

He went to the stairs and the clerk hurried out from behind the desk. 'You no can go up,' he shouted. 'It is forbidden.'

Michael paused. 'Forbidden by whom?'

'By Mr Hammond.'

'Well, I have just changed the rule. As regards Mr Hammond. If anyone asks to see Mr Harrington, now, *then* you will refuse him, without an appointment. Savvy?'

The clerk gasped, unsure of what to do. No doubt he had heard of Mr Harrington. But he did not know if this gentleman was the missing principal shareholder.

Michael left him to consider the matter and mounted to the first floor, where there was an open room full of Chinese clerks, busily transcribing bills of lading or entering their numbers, contents and ultimate destinations in huge ledgers. As a man they stopped to stare at him.

'I am looking for Mr Hammond,' he explained.

'Upstairs,' one of them said. 'But . . .'

'Thank you,' Michael said, and continued on his way. The next floor contained four English clerks, hardly working as energetically as their Chinese inferiors, who frowned at him severely. 'Upstairs?' he asked pleasantly.

'Upstairs?' One of them leapt to his feet. 'Have you an appointment?'

'I'm afraid not.'

'Then you have no right to be here at all. Your name?'

'I'd rather have yours,' Michael said.

'Why you . . .' the man came forward, and his fellows also rose.

'Your name,' Michael snapped, allowing his voice to rasp.

'Ah . . .' the man checked, staring at him. 'Martin. James Martin.'

'Thank you,' Michael said. 'I will remember it. My name is Michael Harrington. I suggest you remember *that*. Good day to you.'

He mounted the final flight of steps and emerged into a comfortably furnished outer officer. Here a young Chinese man sat at a desk, writing in a book. He raised his head, frowning. 'Who are you?' he asked.

'I am your employer,' Michael told him. 'As of this moment.'

'My . . .' the young man stood up as Michael crossed the room to the inner door. 'You can't open that. You . . .'

Michael had opened it. 'Ali,' he said. 'Your security arrangements leave a great deal to be desired.'

Ali Hammond gaped at him. In the last fifteen years since last they had met, he had allowed himself to put on weight, and was now quite heavy. His clothes were good but like his clerks he had discarded his jacket, and still perspired. But that might have been consternation.

'No one made the slightest effort to stop me as I came upstairs,' Michael told him, taking off his hat and laying it, with his stick, on the table. 'However, that can easily be corrected. I imagine there are many things which will require adjusting. Is there another office?'

Ali seemed to come to his senses. 'They told me you were dead.'

'Yes. But people have been saying that for years, Ali. It was a sport you yourself engaged in, from time to time. Presumably someone, some day, will be proved correct. But not yet.'

'But . . .' Ali swallowed. 'This is great news. Great news. We must have a drink to celebrate.' He hurried to one of the wall cupboards, opened the door to reveal a fully stocked bar. 'Whisky?'

'It's been a long time.' Michael sat down in one of the comfortable armchairs and stretched out his legs.

'Alicia will be quite beside herself.' Ali handed him a glass, took one himself. 'She never would accept that you were dead, of course. He'll come back, she kept saying. He always does. I'm afraid I didn't believe her.'

'Yes,' Michael agreed, sipping. 'How is she?'

'Well . . . what would you expect? I've opened the old house for her, of course, saw to all her expenses.'

'And my children? Ralph?'

'Walks with a limp, but seems in good health otherwise. Rum show that, son fighting against his father.'

'It's been a rum life,' Michael told him. 'What about Joanna?'

'Strange girl, that. Doesn't say much. Looks at you with the oddest expressions. Never smiles. Except when with that fellow Lucas, of course.'

'Peter Lucas? Is he still here?'

'Well, he had to go to Calcutta to sort himself out. I understand his secondment to the Manchu army actually ended with the fall of Nanking. But the blighter has got himself an appointment here in Singapore. Just to be near Joanna, of course. I'm glad you're back to make the decision on that one.'

'Otherwise you would have done so?'

'Well, old man, I am the head of the family . . .'

'Were,' Michael suggested.

Ali opened his mouth as if he would have disputed the point, and then changed his mind.

'Now, tell me, do you know anything about Malama?' Michael said.

'The Hindu? Now there is the oddest thing of all. I would have said she was the cause of just about everything that has happened to Alicia for fifteen years. Quite apart from being a murderess. Yet the two of them seem the closest of friends.'

'Malama is here?' Michael could not believe his ears.

'Alicia has her living up there with her. Can you believe it? Of course, no one knows who she is; she calls herself Panka, and Alicia claims she is a friend she met in China. I am sworn to secrecy.' He paused, to look at Michael. 'But there is talk, I can tell you. The sooner you get her out of there the better.'

'Yes,' Michael said. 'I believe they have a considerable shared experience. Well, I shall go up to the house.'

'There is going to be an enormous celebration. Actually, I was going up there for dinner, tonight . . .' Ali paused.

'Then by all means come anyway,' Michael said. 'As

426

you said, there will be an enormous celebration. I shall come to the office tomorrow morning.'

'Of course, my dear fellow. You'll want to be brought up to date. As I was saying, there is another office on the floor below. Not quite as large as this, of course, but certainly adequate. I'll have it cleaned up, and all the books and ledgers put in there for you to examine, and . . .'

Michael stood up. 'Ali,' he said. 'Have the books put in here. The other office is for you.'

The table groaned beneath the weight of silver, glittered with the crystal reflecting from the glowing chandelier. It was such a table at which Michael had not sat for fifteen years, and in its majesty it seemed to set the seal on his homecoming, on his arrival at that pinnacle to which he had so often aspired in the past, the ascent of which had proved so slippery and uncertain.

Now . . . he looked at Joanna, seated on his right. Joanna was twenty, and had probably lived a fuller life than most women twice her age. With her deep auburn hair and her handsome features and her full figure, perfectly delineated by the décolletage of her green silk gown, she was in fact the most beautiful woman present. And she was smiling. Perhaps with joy at having her father back, but more certainly, he suspected, from the presence of Peter Lucas, seated on her right. There was a stroke of unexpected fortune, that in her misery after her father had again been carried off, she had turned to the only masculine support available, and found it stronger than she had supposed. Michael still did not know what sort of a married life she could possibly enjoy, but that she was willing to contemplate it was sufficient of a relief – and Peter had willingly accepted his suggestion that he resign from the army and join Hammond and Teng.

Further down the table he could smile at Ralph, dressed like himself in black evening wear, a strong and handsome young man for all his limp, and a man as experienced in

427

what the world had to offer as his sister. He too would join the firm and lend his strength to its future success.

Then he could smile at Malama, gorgeous in a gold sari, her face composed, her eyes watchful, her beauty ethereal. She had risked all by remaining here until she could be sure of his death or his survival – not least that of placing herself in Ali's power. But now she would be safe.

And at Alicia, at the far end of the table, no less lovely if in a different manner. The tears of joy were over now. Their life was about to resume its course. Had they yet decided what that course was to be? He had not had the time to find out.

But he knew he wanted to be done with fighting, and bloodshed, and strife. Even fighting with Ali. Whatever had happened was too long ago, and had been expiated by too much death, and suffering. Not by Ali, perhaps, but by himself, and those who had accompanied him through the vale of tears. And Ali appeared to have taken his defeat like a man, accepting his demotion, and was prepared to work in harness for the good of the firm – as he had been prepared to accommodate his sister and not denounce the almost forgotten murderess to the authorities. Perhaps a leopard could, after all, change his spots, which was sufficient cause to forgive him for his crimes. There was real relief, Michael thought, in that the last possible cause of discord between Alicia and himself had been removed. So, perhaps all those deaths and all that hardship had been worth while. He raised his glass, and Ali, seated beside his sister, raised his in turn.

An hour later he left. 'That was a splendid meal, Alicia,' he said as they accompanied him on to the porch to say goodbye. 'And splendid company. Michael, I cannot tell you how good it is to have you back. I'll look forward to seeing you in the office tomorrow. Ten suit you?'

'Eight,' Michael said.

Ali raised his eyebrows, and then smiled. 'Eight it shall be. Well . . .' he turned, and there was a tremendous thwack. 'Jesus Christ!'

'Down!' Michael snapped, throwing Alicia to the floor; he knew the sound of a bullet striking wood better than anyone else, and even as he fell beside his wife there was another thwack, just above his head. While now they heard the crack of the explosions.

'My God!' Ali exclaimed. 'They're shooting at us.'

'At me, I would say,' Michael said. 'Keep out of sight,' he shouted at Malama and the others as they crowded to the door.

'It came from over there,' Ali said. 'And they seem to have stopped. I'd better have a look.'

'Be careful,' Alicia snapped.

Ali grinned. 'I have a revolver.' He ran down the steps, took it from his saddlebag, and hurried across the lawn to the trees of the orchard.

Michael scrambled to his feet and followed.

'Michael!' Alicia called.

'Keep out of sight,' he told her. His brain was spinning. Logic told him it could only be an assassin hired by Ali. Then was his brother-in-law truly the most two-faced bastard who ever drew breath. But how to prove it? Only by being there . . . he reached the trees, and found Ali kneeling above a discarded rifled musket.

'This is the weapon all right,' he said, straightening. 'The fool discarded it.' His voice was loaded with venom.

'Then we'll have him tomorrow,' Michael said. 'This will be easy enough to trace.'

'Yes,' Ali said, thoughtfully, backing away from him. 'So perhaps we should end it now.'

Michael straightened in turn, looked down the barrel of the revolver. 'Are you mad?' he asked. If he had known immediately that his brother-in-law must have hired the assassin, he had also put him down as a man of some sense, who would cut his losses – and perhaps try again.

Ali grinned. 'That musket would be traceable to me. The fool.' He jerked his head. 'We are out of sight of the house. Another shot . . . they will think the assassin hung around after all.'

'They will know it was a revolver.'

'So the murderer carried one as well. As I shall fire several shots after the scoundrel, without unfortunately hitting him, the bullet cannot possibly be traced back to my weapon. And do you know, I am rather pleased to be doing this myself? When I think of the number of times I have ordered your death, always to have the job bungled.'

Michael stared at him, slowly filling his lungs with air. He intended to attack him; it was not in his nature to die without making an effort to live. But Ali was now ten feet away, and Michael knew that he had no hope. So once again, as he reached out to take the crown of victory, it was going to be snatched from his grasp. And this time, by his own carelessness; Alicia had even tried to warn him. His mouth twisted.

'Now,' Ali said, and levelled the gun.

Michael tensed his muscles, and Alicia said, 'No, Ali.'

Neither man had heard her silent approach, as she had stepped out of her gown and reverted to the naked role she had so often played in the past. 'Really, Sis,' Ali commented, 'you are quite indecent.'

'Put down the gun,' Alicia said.

'And be gaoled for life? Now, really, Sis. And you must admit our lives would run a whole lot smoother with this mad Irishman out of the way. I'll find you another husband. I know just the chap. You'll love him. Besides, if you turn me in, I'll see Malama hang. You should remember that. Now . . .' his finger tightened on the trigger, and Alicia raised the pistol she had brought from the house and shot her brother through the head.

Ali spun round and slumped to the ground. Voices shouted and feet crashed through the bushes, and Alicia fell against Michael, the gun dropping from her fingers.

'I was prepared to trust him,' Michael said.

'I was not,' Alicia said. 'I never trusted him.'

'But . . . your own brother?'

She raised her head. 'You are my husband, Michael.'

Malama knelt beside the corpse for a moment, and then straightened. 'Now it is finished,' she said. 'Jalina is avenged. Now I will leave.'

'Leave? You?' Michael and Alicia spoke together.

'Would you really have me stay? You are my friends. My only friends. Your happiness is my concern. My only concern. Once you offered me wealth, Michael.'

'And I still do, Malama.'

'Then I will accept it. And leave your lives, for ever.'

'And go where?' he asked, his mind seething.

Malama smiled, sadly. 'Where I truly belong.'

The man was very old, and nearly blind. He sat outside his hut and listened to the coursing of the river in the distance. He was alone, because all of his daughters had married, or died, or been taken by the tax gatherers. Nowadays it was as much as he could do to gather sufficient rice from the paddy to feed himself, and more often than not he went hungry.

He knew he was soon to die. Partly from age, partly from malnutrition, and partly from lonely despair. His breath was short, he suffered from indigestion, and now from a ringing in the ears. Bells, and strange noises. It was getting worse, and coming nearer. Death was upon him.

Rajinder Lall raised his head to watch the elephant approaching down the track through the forest. It was a huge beast, and richly caparisoned, and there were attendants walking beside it, also richly dressed. It came to a halt before the little hut, and the mahout made it get on to its knees, while the attendants assisted the woman to descend from the howdah. She was the most richly dressed of all, with gold bangles on her arms and legs, clearly visible through the silk sari, rings on her fingers, and even a gold ring through her nose. Was this an incarnation of the Goddess Kali, come to claim him? Rajinder Lall struggled to his feet.

'Do you not remember me?' the woman asked.

'I am ready for death,' Rajinder Lall said. 'I am ready.'

Malama smiled, and embraced him. 'You will not die for many years, my father. And when you do, it will be in great comfort. Come with me. I have a house in Cal-

431

cutta. On the hill,' she added, as she escorted him to the elephant, and the howdah.

d'être en contact avec les autres voyageurs. C'était un bouclier.

Montparnasse. Paule descendit sur le quai et s'engouffra dans un couloir, la meute sur ses talons car elle marchait vite. Direction Porte-de-la-Chapelle.

Lui adressait-on la parole? — dans le métro : « Vous descendez à la prochaine? » ou, dans la rue : « Pardon, madame, l'avenue Anatole-France, s'il vous plaît? » — Paule ne répondait pas. Ses lèvres minces ébauchaient un sourire — c'était d'ailleurs davantage une crispation de la bouche — et elle poursuivait son chemin sans se soucier de l'égaré qui croyait avoir eu affaire à une sourde ou à une étrangère.

Paule préférait passer pour une étrangère.

Le matin même, sortant de chez elle, Paule avait croisé une grosse femme en extase devant les platanes du square Ferdinand-Brunot. Quelques touches de vert, çà et là, annonçaient une renaissance.

— Regardez, madame, c'est le printemps!

Paule n'avait pas bronché et l'autre ne s'en était pas formalisée, l'ayant immédiatement oubliée sous le coup du ravissement. Or, Paule n'aimait pas être ignorée. Méprisée, insultée même, oui; ignorée, non.

Elle n'avait qu'une seule amie. Une amie-ennemie. Gilberte Monestier travaillait à *Châtelet-Retouches;* elle y faisait et défaisait des ourlets, transformait des maxis en minis et des minis en maxis, suivant les caprices de la mode, pour un salaire de misère. Mais que pouvait-elle espérer de mieux à cinquante-cinq ans passés? Gilberte admirait et jalousait son amie. Paule avait été mariée, elle, puis elle avait divorcé... Paule avait perdu un enfant... Paule était femme de chambre dans l'un des plus grands hôtels de la capitale. Une vie romanesque, exaltante... et dont elle prétendait écrire le récit.

— Et votre roman, ça avance? demandait régulièrement Gilberte.

— Petit à petit, répondait Paule, mystérieuse.

Bien entendu, Paule n'écrivait pas; elle en était incapable et elle n'avait rien à raconter. Une existence ratée, point final. Un mariage décevant qui n'avait pas duré un an, une petite fille qui n'avait vécu que vingt-quatre heures et les draps sales du *Crichton* qu'il fallait changer chaque matin. Mais il ne déplaisait nullement à Paule d'être pour Gilberte une créature d'exception, une future femme de lettres.

Tout cela était enfantin, ridicule, mais l'admiration de Gilberte aidait Paule à vivre. Pourquoi s'en serait-elle privée? Et c'était la raison pour laquelle elle lui rendait visite, le dimanche, ou, de préférence, l'invitait dans son petit deux-pièces de la rue des Plantes. Et là, devant une tasse de thé et une assiettée de biscuits, elle multipliait les allusions, les anecdotes relatives aux clients les plus célèbres du *Crichton* et voyait enfin dans les yeux de Gilberte grandir et exister la Paule Jeannet qu'elle aurait voulu être : une femme cynique, brillante, lucide et nullement intimidée par la gloire qui lui était promise.

Triturant de vieux manteaux, de vieilles robes qu'il lui fallait remettre au goût du jour, Gilberte pensait aux aventures sentimentales de son amie. L'un des rares sujets que Paule n'aimait guère évoquer. Cette répugnance poussait d'ailleurs